Peter William Clayden

The Early Life of Samuel Rogers

Peter William Clayden

The Early Life of Samuel Rogers

ISBN/EAN: 9783337056254

Printed in Europe, USA, Canada, Australia, Japan

Cover: Foto ©Raphael Reischuk / pixelio.de

More available books at **www.hansebooks.com**

THE EARLY LIFE

OF

SAMUEL ROGERS

BY

P. W. CLAYDEN

AUTHOR OF

"SAMUEL SHARPE, EGYPTOLOGIST AND TRANSLATOR OF THE BIBLE"

BOSTON

ROBERTS BROTHERS

1888

PREFACE.

THE narrative of Rogers's early life covers a period of forty years, and naturally ends with his settlement in the celebrated house in St. James's Place. Another period of more than fifty years, in which he was one of the chief figures in English society, remains to be dealt with in another volume. I have ample materials for this work in the shape of letters from many of Rogers's eminent contemporaries, but I shall esteem it as a great favor if those who possess letters by Rogers himself will let me have copies of them.

The materials for Rogers's life were placed in my hands by Miss Sharpe of 32 Highbury Place, and Mrs. William Sharpe of 1 Highbury Terrace, the representatives of his nephews and executors, — the late Mr. Samuel Sharpe and the late Mr. William Sharpe; and I am deeply indebted to them for the generous trust they have placed in my discretion. For the use made of letters and diaries I am solely responsible. I wish further to express my cordial thanks to Mrs. Drummond of Fredley and of 18 Hyde Park Gardens, for the valuable and interesting letters of Richard Sharp.

P. W. CLAYDEN.

13 TAVISTOCK SQUARE, LONDON:
November, 1887.

CONTENTS.

CHAPTER X.

CHAPTER XI.

CHAPTER XII.

CHAPTER XIII.

THE EARLY LIFE

OF

SAMUEL ROGERS.

CHAPTER I.

Stoke Newington. — Rogers's Ancestors. — Dr. Price. — Mrs. Rogers. — Her Letters. — Her Character.

In the middle of the eighteenth century the suburban village of Stoke Newington contained a group of friendly households, which embraced many persons afterwards known in the larger world. The pretty village green, then a piece of open grass with a few ancient elms and quaint Elizabethan houses round it, was a centre of political and religious Liberalism. A meeting-house of the English Presbyterian dissent had been built there in 1708, and there the Rev. Charles Morton, the silenced rector of Blissland, in Cornwall, — Defoe's teacher, — had kept his school. In the early part of the eighteenth century, Samuel Harris, an East India merchant, who had married a daughter of Queen Mary's physician, Dr. Coxe, lived in one of the houses on the Green; and in 1731 their only daughter, Mary Harris, — a cousin of William Coxe, the author of the 'History of the House of Austria,' — married Daniel Radford, a warehouseman in Cheapside. Daniel Radford had come to London from Chester with a capital of a thousand pounds, with which he had entered into partnership with Mr. Obadiah

1

Wickes. He was the son of Samuel Radford, a linen-draper at Chester, and of Eleanor his wife, third daughter of the Rev. Philip Henry, one of the most eminent of the clergy who had been ejected on the passing of the Act of Uniformity in 1662. Philip Henry was the son of one of the pages of Charles I. He was born in the palace at Whitehall, had been a playfellow of the Prince of Wales and the Duke of York, had seen the king beheaded, and was in politics a Cavalier. His mother inclined to the teaching of the Presbyterian divines, and the son, after leaving Westminster School, and taking his degree at Oxford, had adhered to the same side in religious matters, and had entered the Church during the Protectorate by Presbyterian ordination. Daniel Radford, his grandson, inherited the serious disposition and the religious principles of his grandfather. Daniel's father and mother, the Chester linen-draper and his wife, had died early, and Daniel was brought up by his maternal uncle, the Rev. Matthew Henry, the author of the celebrated Commentary on the Bible. Daniel Radford's Diary shows the influence of this ancestry and training. He was an introspective person, and religious feeling tinged his life. He puts on record, sometimes day by day, sometimes only year by year, not the day's events nor the year's history, but the serious reflections which the flight of time or the death of friends, or family joys and troubles, suggested to a religious mind. A few events of personal and family interest are noted here and there, but only for the sake of recording some pious resolution, or of writing down some aspiration which had arisen out of them. The Journal begins in March, 1715, with an extract from a devotional book, and ends in June, 1767, less than four months before his death, with the expression of the hope that 'though I shall not die a profitable servant, yet I hope to die a pardoned sinner through Jesus Christ.' In all the two-and-fifty years there is only one reference to a public event, and that is an earthquake,[1] which suggested a religious reflection to his mind.

Daniel Radford was born on the 24th of May, 1691, and died on the 14th of October, 1767, having completed his seventy-sixth year on the 4th of June, to which the change of style had transferred his birthday. He had settled at Newington Green on his marriage in 1731, had lived there all the rest of his life, and there his only child Mary had been born. With Philip Henry for his grand-father, and Matthew Henry, the commentator, for his uncle, it was natural that Daniel Radford should connect himself with the small Presbyterian congregation at the chapel on the Green. The minister was Mr. Hoyle; but a mán destined to European renown, and worthy of it, was living near, and gave occasional help. This was Mr. (afterwards Dr.) Richard Price, who became preacher to the congregation in 1758. Daniel Radford and his daughter — his wife had died in 1738, when Mary was scarcely three years old — were thus brought into contact with one of the most acute and enlightened minds the eighteenth century produced, with the best intellectual and social results to their connections and descendants.

---

[1] This entry in the Diary is as follows : 'In London, on Thursday, 8th February, 1749, betwixt twelve and one o'clock at noon, we were surprised greatly by the shock of an earthquake which was felt in the city and the country round about it. I happened to be shaving then in the counting-house, and I asked the barber what the noise and shaking was. He said he believed somebody had fallen down above-stairs, for indeed it felt as if something heavy was fallen down. I thought it felt as if the house had given way, and so most people indeed did, that were in houses. But, thanks be to God ! it did very little damage anywhere as I heard of, and it was over almost as soon as one felt it. And, alas ! too much so has been the remembrance of the thing itself among us. But shall I not fear always before, and stand in awe of, this great and holy Lord God, who can, whenever He pleases, make the earth shake, with the foundations thereof ?'

Daniel Radford was treasurer to the congregation, and at his death left a hundred pounds towards the augmentation of the salary of the minister.

The little group of people among whom the Radfords lived was Puritan by ancestry and association, in full sympathy with the Whig party in politics, and inclined to latitudinarian opinions on theological questions. In the sixth decade of the century there came into it a young man of altogether different birth and training. In Daniel Radford's Diary there is the record of the deaths of his two partners: Mr. Obadiah Wickes, the father, in 1748, and Mr. John Wickes, the son, in 1750. On the 1st of January, 1753, he writes that he is again in some concern about a new co-partnership into which he has entered with Mr. Rogers. This was Thomas Rogers, a glass manufacturer of Stourbridge, whose only son afterwards removed to London to take part in the business in which his father had thus become a partner. Thomas Rogers lived at a house called 'The Hill,' in the parish of Old Swinford, and his name had been long associated with the manufacturing industry of Stourbridge. The earliest record of the family is that the will of Thomas Rogers the elder, of Amblesant, yeoman, was proved on the 27th of June, 1681, by Anne, his widow and sole executrix. This Thomas Rogers is described as a Welshman, and an eminent dealer in glass, in Holloway End, Stourbridge. He had married the daughter of M. Tyttery of Nantes, in Lorraine, and left two sons, Thomas and James, and a daughter, Sarah. This second Thomas Rogers had a half share in the business, and was apparently the father of Thomas Rogers of 'The Hill,' the partner of Daniel Radford. Thomas Rogers of 'The Hill'—the grandson of the Welshman who had married the Frenchwoman, and the grandfather of Samuel Rogers—was a person of much influence and consideration in the town and county. He had married a daughter of

Richard Knight of Downton; and Richard Payne Knight, the antiquary, and Thomas Andrew Knight, the writer on horticulture, were his nephews. He was a Tory of the old school, and lived on excellent terms with the Tory gentry of the county. In the picturesque and well-kept churchyard of Old Swinford there are still memorials of the Rogers family; and

'You old mansion frowning through the trees,'

of which Samuel Rogers speaks in 'The Pleasures of Memory,' was in all probability the house of Thomas Rogers, his grandfather, which was not far from the church. A few miles off was 'The Leasowes,' where Shenstone lived, and where he died in the year in which Samuel Rogers was born. Close at hand, at Hagley, was George Lyttelton, the friend of Pope, the patron of Thomson, the poet of 'Blenheim' and 'The Progress of Love;' afterwards, author of 'Dialogues of the Dead,' a Tory Chancellor of the Exchequer, and a peer. Farther off, on the other side of Stourbridge, dwelt the Earl of Stamford and Warrington, at Enville; and round about were the houses of many other country gentlemen with most of whom hatred of the Whigs was the chief public passion and virtue. Such was the circle in which, in the second quarter of the eighteenth century, the elder Thomas Rogers lived and Thomas Rogers the younger was brought up.

There is no record of the date at which Thomas Rogers the younger removed to London. He was probably just about of age when he left the Tory atmosphere of the country house in Worcestershire, and plunged into the entirely different moral and social conditions and influences of Stoke Newington. It is evident that he soon won the esteem of his father's partner, for in 1760 he was married to Daniel Radford's only daughter, Mary. The wedding took place at Islington parish

church on the 27th of March, 1760; and on the next
New Year's Day Thomas Rogers joined his father and
father-in-law in the partnership, the latter advancing
him £2,000 to make up his share of the stock-in-trade.
Thomas Rogers yielded quickly and fully to the new
influences around him. As soon as we get any glimpse
of his opinions we find him to be in full sympathy with
the political and religious Liberalism of his wife's family
and friends. He was a good man of business, and pros-
pered in his way. In 1765 he joined George and Thomas
Welch, who were bankers in Cornhill, and the firm there-
after carried on the business under the style of Welch &
Rogers. Meanwhile a family was fast growing up around
him. His eldest son, Daniel, named after his father-in-
law, was born on the 3d of January, 1761; about Christmas in the same year a second son, Thomas, was born;
and a year and a half later, on the 30th of July, 1763,
the third son, who was to outlive every member of the
family, was born, and called Samuel after his mother's
grandfather, Samuel Harris. Other children followed
with nearly equal rapidity: Martha, afterwards Mrs.
John Towgood, in 1765; Mary in 1766; Paul in 1768;
another daughter, who lived but a day, and was never
named, in 1770; Maria (afterwards Mrs. Sutton Sharpe)
in 1771; Sarah (the Miss Rogers who lived to within
a year of Samuel, and was all through her life closely
associated with him) in 1772; Henry (the kind and
thoughtful friend of his nephews and nieces) in 1774;
and Mary Radford in 1776. Of these children three —
Mary, Paul, and Mary Radford — died in infancy, and
Thomas died in 1788, in his twenty-seventh year. Six
saw the nineteenth century: Maria dying in 1806;
Daniel, on whose death Charles Lamb wrote a Sonnet,
in 1829; Henry in 1832, Martha in 1837, while Sarah
lived on till January, 1855, and Samuel till December
in the same year. These two were thus the only long-

lived members of a family, the father and mother of which died comparatively young, and of which only one other member reached the age of threescore and ten.

The charm of Dr. Price's character exerted a considerable influence on Thomas Rogers and his family. Dr. Price lived close by, and a great friendship sprang up between him and the Rogerses. A weekly supping club was established which met at the houses of Dr. Price, Thomas Rogers, and Mr. Burgh in turns. These three, with Mr. Thoresby, the liberal and learned rector of Stoke Newington, were the chief members of the club, and at one of its suppers Dr. Price and Dr. Priestley were afterwards introduced to each other by Dr. Benson. Mr. Burgh was a schoolmaster, who kept a boarding-school at Newington Green, and for a time acted as tutor to Samuel Rogers and his brothers. He was a man of acute mind, who wrote a work entitled 'Political Disquisitions,' but was best known as the author of a book 'On the Dignity of Human Nature.' Dr. Price was as great a favorite with the boys as he was with their parents. They not only listened to his sermons on Sunday afternoons, but enjoyed his sympathy during the week, in their lessons and even in their games. Samuel Rogers spoke of him in after-years with the most sincere affection. He would go in from his study in his dressing-gown to spend the evening with the family, and the children never forgot the impression his conversation made upon them. 'He would talk and read the Bible to us,' said Rogers in after-years, 'till he sent us to bed in a frame of mind as heavenly as his own.' At other times he would take the boys and girls to his house and show them scientific experiments. The Equitable Assurance Society, in recognition of his services in the publication of his 'Treatise on Reversionary Payments,' his 'Northampton Mortality Tables,' and other writings, by which he had laid the scientific foundation of Life Assurance, had presented him with some scientific apparatus, — a telescope, a microscope, and an electrical machine. It is easy to imagine the charm which these instruments, then novel and unusual, had for a group of lively and intelligent children. Dr. Price's delight in the company of children, and his desire to contribute to their amusement and instruction, found in these toys of science an unfailing source of interest and profit to his young friends. But he had 'other and more personal charms. He was a most delightful companion for boys. He seems to have possessed not only a love for children, but much of that boyishness and love of frolic which have often characterized men of genius. In some juvenile recollections of him which Samuel Rogers has left, he tells several amusing stories which illustrate this unexpected side of a great man's nature. He once challenged Mr. Hulton, a commissary in the German war, and commissioner of customs at Boston, a much taller and more robust person than himself, to hop the length of the first field between the meeting-house and Stoke Newington, and won the race. On another occasion he attempted to leap over a honeysuckle bush in the grass-plat in the Rogerses' garden; but, to use Rogers's words, 'he entangled the tree between his legs, and away went the honeysuckle and the doctor together.' The boys said to one another that he had once leaped over the New River; and it was his custom every day at two o'clock to run off for a swim in Peerless Pool. He had frequent falls from his horse, and in Covent Garden was once thrown into a basket of beans. His conscientiousness and benevolence were exemplified in other favorite stories. In a field near his house he once saw some larks struggling in the nets in which they had just been caught. He cut the nets and set them free, but, reflecting on the loss he had thereby caused to some unknown person, returned and deposited some money on the spot. In one of his strolls he suddenly remembered that he had seen a beetle on its back, and he returned through several fields, found it, and set it on its legs. Assailed in a country walk by a footpad, he mildly expostulated with the man and lectured him on the crime of robbery. His absence of mind was another source of continual amusement. It was said that he had gone down to his study to supper an hour after he had eaten the meal. In conversation he turned his wig round on his temples, twisted one leg round the other, and folded his cocked hat into a thousand shapes. But all these things endeared him to the boys as much as his intellectual distinction, his tender religious feelings, and his lively interest in all the questions of the day, attached the elders to him. Rogers describes him as 'slim in person, and rather below the common size, but possessed of great muscular strength and remarkable activity. With strong features, and a very intelligent eye, his countenance was the mirror of his mind; and when lighted up by conversation his features were peculiarly pleasing.' Everybody admired and loved him, and this love and admiration exerted a powerful influence on the family at Newington Green.

Thomas Rogers and his wife were quite worthy of the society of which Dr. Price was the most distinguished member. He was a man of much vigor and decision, and she is described as a tall and handsome woman, with dark hair and eyes and a face of great intelligence. Their children were not very strong. It was the time of *queues* and cocked hats; and Samuel Rogers says that the children wore cocked hats, and he remembered chasing butterflies in the fields with the quaint three-cornered head-covering in his hand. The boys went to day-school at Mr. Burgh's and Mr. Cockburn's; and afterwards, when Mr. Burgh removed to Colebrook Row,

Islington (where Charles Lamb lived at a later day), they
went over to him for lessons. There was plenty of active
outdoor amusement and exercise for the boys, — bathing
in Peerless Pool, riding on the nag, sporting in the pad-
dock behind the house, and rambling over the open fields.
London was two miles away, across the fields and gardens
now covered by De Beauvoir Town. Perhaps the best
account which can be given of the father and mother is
in the self-revelations of their letters, many of which
have happily been preserved. In these letters are the
only remaining records of Samuel Rogers's boyhood ; and
some of them are worth reproducing for the glimpses
they give us of various interesting people, some of whom
are famous and some forgotten, as well as for the picture
they make of the pleasant life a prosperous middle-class
family was living more than a century ago. The earliest
in date are from Mrs. Rogers, and were addressed to her
husband during a summer journey he took with Dr. Price,
in 1772, to visit the doctor's native district in South
Wales, and a short stay Thomas Rogers made at his
father's house on the way home. The letters, from
which some purely business and domestic details have
been omitted, show what kind of woman Rogers's mother
was ; how careful of home concerns, how solicitous for
her household, how open to all the pleasantness of life,
how entirely free from that other-worldliness — as
George Eliot has called it — which is supposed to have
accompanied a Puritan ancestry and training.

Mary Rogers to Thomas Rogers.

'NEWINGTON GREEN, July 4, 1772.

'MY EVER DEAR T. R., — As this method of communi-
cating our thoughts to each other is now the only resource left, it is with great pleasure I sit down to assure
you with sincerity how much I regret your absence, and

to endeavor in some measure to alleviate it by acquainting you with all my proceedings since you left us. But as I know the anxiety that always attends you upon account of every branch of your family, I must first begin by assuring you that we all continue perfectly well. Tommy is got quite well, and is in exceedingly good spirits. The four[1] are at this time particularly happy in exercising Obey's nag about the field, and are very proud in showing their horsemanship. Tommy has been twice to the bath on horseback before Richard,[2] and the horse carries him extremely well. We went to drink tea with Mrs. Wilson[3] after you left us on Tuesday, and had the pleasure to meet Mr. and Mrs. Welch;[4] Mr. Wilson also was at home, and all conduced to make the visit very agreeable. On Wednesday evening we went to town to see Mr. Raper[5] and Miss Raper in Norfolk Street, who both agreed to dine with us at the Green next day; and Mr. Harry Raper being there — and a bachelor at present — offered to be of the party. The coach accordingly fetched them in the morning to dinner upon beans and bacon, a couple of chickens, and a piece of roast beef, and we widows and widowers drank your health and Mrs. Henry Raper's. The two gentlemen and little Harry[6] walked home again about seven o'clock, and Miss Raper stayed with us till last night, — her father and self being to return to Wendover this morning. . . . Yesterday morning Dr. and Mrs. Grant called

[1] The four were Daniel, Thomas, Samuel, and Martha; Maria, the youngest, was only twelve months old.

[2] Sitting before Richard on the horse.

[3] Mother of Thomas and Joseph Wilson of Highbury. Thomas Wilson was the great chapel-builder of the Independents, whose life was written by his son Josiah.

[4] Mr. Welch was Mr. Rogers's partner in the banking-house.

[5] Matthew Raper of Wendover Dean, Bucks, father of the Matthew Raper afterwards vice-president of the Antiquarian Society.

[6] This little Harry was afterwards Admiral Raper.

on us and engaged us and Miss Sally [Raper] to dine
with them on Thursday next. In the afternoon Mrs.
Dunn and family drank tea with us. . . . Mrs. Price
writes to-day to Bridgend, but desires I will likewise
mention that she and Mrs. Barker returned home to-day,
safe and well, about three o'clock, and very little fatigued
with their journey. They desire compliments to you,
and many thanks for the kind call you made them. . . .
Your trunk went this morning from the Saracen's Head.
Richard is gone to have the horse shod, so I can't tell
the name of the wagoner. Adieu, my dearest T. R.
I hope to hear this evening that you are well, which will
always afford the truest pleasure to

'Your ever affectionate and unalterable

'M. R.

'THOMAS ROGERS, Esq.
  'To be left at the Post Office, Swansea, Glamorganshire.'

Mary Rogers to Thomas Rogers.

'NEWINGTON GREEN, Saturday, July 11, 1772.

'MY EVER DEAR T. R., — Many thanks for your very
kind and agreeable letter, which I received on Wednesday last. I assure you I would have endeavored not to
have merited your hint if I had thought you had the
least expectation to have heard from me at Cardiff, as
it is, and always will be, my highest temporal wish to
promote your pleasure in every instance. It gave me
great satisfaction to hear of your health last night from
Mrs. Price, but don't accuse me of recrimination if I say
that a line from your hand would have given your poor
M. R. *a little more self-consequence ;* but I know you mean
always to be kind to me, and therefore I ought not to complain. I called on Saturday evening on Miss Crisp, and
agreed for Patty to go to day-school: £1 1s. entrance
and £2 12s. 6d. per quarter, for which she learns reading

and working, and has five dinners per week. She began on Wednesday, and seems at present very happy with it. The boys left us on Wednesday in pretty good spirits. Tommy continues his bathing as usual. On Thursday we dined at Dr. Grant's, and a most melting day it was. There was no company but an uncle of the doctor's. They wanted us to have gone to Vauxhall in the evening, but we excused ourselves, and agreed to accompany the doctor and Mrs. Grant to Foote's on Monday next to see the Nabob. I came into it, as I thought it would be agreeable to Miss Sally Raper. . . . She talks of leaving us on Wednesday or Thursday next. The doctor says there is no banker in London besides yourself who would have had the courage to have ventured on a journey at this crisis. I suppose you have before this heard of Mrs. Peach's marriage with Mr. Lyttelton. I begin to think that I have got a husband that is possessed of the art of divination. . . .

'We heard the other day that Mr. Gordon's Nursery was in full perfection, and Miss Sally and Miss Mitchell expressing a wish to see it we took a ride there last night, and it perfectly answered our expectations. We laid out ten shillings with them among us, and Mr. Gordon and his son were extremely polite, and made us a present of a most pompous nosegay, which consisted chiefly of his most curious flowers, particularly some charming magnolia flowers, of which tree he has scores in bloom. . . . We all happily continue well, and our little Maria is as lively as a bird, and, in her mother's opinion, daily increases in charms. Master Rickards was baptized yesterday by the name of Samuel, and yesterday Mr. Rickards himself was seized with a fever and speckled sore-throat, and was obliged to sit up in bed while his son was christened. They have had Dr. Grieve, and he is to be blistered to-day, but I believe they don't think him in danger. Adieu, my ever dear and own T. R. May

happiness ever attend you, and may your own M. R.
(if Providence spares her life) grow more deserving of
your love! All join in love and compliments; and I
remain

'Your constantly affectionate

'M. R.

'Thomas Rogers, Esq., jun.
' To be left at the Post Office, Worcester.'

There is a letter from Sámuel Rogers addressed to
his father while he was on the same journey. It is a
child's letter, — he was then approaching the close of his
ninth year, — and it gives a pleasant glimpse of a happy
boyhood.

Samuel Rogers to his Father.

' 19th July, 1772.

'Dear Papa, — I hope you have had a good journey,
and hope my grandpapa and all my aunts are very well,
and my cousin Tommy Bowles. I went to school July
8th, but school began July 6th. I had a very pleasant
ride back again from the Pack Horse at Turnham Green.
My mamma chose to leave off dipping Maria.

' July the 6th I went to Sadler's Wells, and I thought
it was very pretty. Me and Tommy and Dan and Patty
and Hannah and Nurse all went together in the coach.
At last the makerony started out of the floor, with a
long pigtail as big as my wrist, and an artificial nosegay, and came strutting about with his fine cocked hat,
and his hand in his bosom.

'I am your dutiful son,

'Samuel Rogers.

'Thomas Rogers, Esq., jun.
' At " The Hill," near Stourbridge, Worcestershire.'

His mother follows this up with a letter dated from
Newington Green on the 21st July.

Mary Rogers to Thomas Rogers.

'I had the pleasure to receive my dearest T. R.'s kind letter this morning, and am rejoiced to hear he spends his time so joyously, — a proof that he enjoys health, and I hope spirits. Dr. Price returned home on Saturday evening in perfect health, but his complexion has received a very different hue. He preached on Sunday morning, and Mr. Pickbourne in the evening. Mr. and Mrs. Burgh dined and drank tea at Dr. Price's. . . . We went to London yesterday morning, and called in Friday Street. Mrs. Bowles told me she has at times suffered great uneasiness on account of the criticalness of trade, but that Mr. Welch had been extremely kind to them in giving them assistance. Mr. Bowles came upstairs, and seemed in exceeding good spirits, and said, I think, that he wrote to you on Saturday. Bessy goes to school on Thursday, so I asked Mrs. Bowles to dine with us, and offered to send the chariot for her. Mr. Lisle's house is again disposed of to a Mr. Coxe, a refiner in Little Britain. Did you ever hear of him? My expectations are mighty small. Mr. Farmer has resigned Salter's Hall, his health not permitting him to continue it. . . .

'I suppose you will receive poor Sammy's letter tomorrow. You will easily perceive that it was entirely his own. He told me — a little rascal! — that he was determined to tell his papa that I had left off dipping Maria.

'Adieu, my dearest T. R. Be ever assured of my sincerest affection, and continue to love and think of your number five and your own

'M. R.

'Thomas Rogers, jun. Esq.
'At "The Hill," near Stourbridge.'

The letters continue in the same strain. On the 25th of July she tells her husband of Sammy's illness from

the speckled sore-throat, which seems to have been one
of the terrors of the time. She had heard 'a good deal
of city news,' one item of which was that a new bank —
'Sir Richard Glyn's house'— was to open, with 'my
Lord Mayor at its head.' In the next letter she reports
that Sammy's throat is still bad, but that he continues
in charming spirits, and has no fever. 'Dr. and Mrs.
Price spent the evening with us last night, and Dr. Price
was speaking on what very advantageous terms they
were granting annuities on the Douglas and Heron Bank,
— provided the security was good, — upon which he and
Mary Mitchell agreed to go to London this morning to
ask Mr. Welch's opinion of it, and if they should hear
a satisfactory account of it to risk about £200 apiece.'
Dan and Tom had gone to Mr. Burgh's, as Mr. Burgh
was too ill to come to them. On the 29th, the day
before Sammy's birthday, Tommy begins a letter, but
his fluency failing, as his mother says, she completes it,
complaining that the postman had slighted her, and
reporting a visit from Mrs. Cockburn, wife of the schoolmaster, to say that Tommy had fainted at school, but
was better again, and the doctor had advised some bark.
The last of this series of letters is dated on the 1st of
August. She tells her husband of a drive she had taken
to Southgate, to see the Miss Birches, but not finding them
at home she had gone on to Mrs. Jones's, on the Chase,
'where we were received in a very polite and friendly
manner. It is quite a sweet situation, and the walking
about so pleasant that it was nine o'clock by the time we
reached home, rather too late an hour now.' She adds,
'I am afraid my T. R. will think me a racketing female,
but everybody admires the appearance of the horses,
and Richard says he is sure they have not too much
work.' Another item of city information is that 'Mr.
Steed, of Tower Hill, stopped a short time, to the great
astonishment of many, but he now finds that after

everybody is paid he will have an overplus remaining of £10,000.'

This letter was written on the 1st of August, 1772, and on the 1st of September Sarah Rogers was born. She was the ninth child, but, as three had died, the five of whom Mrs. Rogers speaks in one of the above letters formed at that time her whole family. In the succeeding summer Mr. Rogers was away from home during the months of August and September, spending the earlier part of the holiday in a journey to Scotland, and the latter part at his father's house. Scotch tours were then just coming into fashion. Mr. Thomas Pennant made his first tour in Scotland in 1769, and the beautifully illustrated quarto in which he gave the public a lively account of his travels, was published in 1771. It was very widely read, and may be said to have turned the tide of holiday travel northwards. His second tour was made in 1772 ; but the three quarto volumes in which he told the amusing story of his journey were not published till 1775, the year in which Johnson published his 'Journey to the Western Isles.' Thomas Rogers went in August, 1773, over much of the ground covered in Mr. Pennant's first tour, and his wife, sitting at home, traced his course with Pennant's volume in her hand. Her letters, of which a dozen are preserved, are full of domestic, social, and business details, and give further glimpses of the family life at Newington Green. The earliest speak of the ailments of the children, of visitors, one of whom had come unexpectedly to dine because he was sure he should not meet his wife, and of a lawsuit which had been decided in which Mr. Rogers was interested. The fourth letter is as follows : —

2

Mary Rogers to Thomas Rogers.

'NEWINGTON GREEN, August 17.

'MY DEAREST T. R., — It is not in my power to express sufficient thanks for the happiness your last two letters afforded me. To know that you are well always gives me sincere pleasure, but to give me so near together two such strong proofs of your remembrance to your happy M. R. was indeed peculiarly kind; and I can with sincerity say, my dearest T. R., that on receipt of your last letter I felt an affectionate gratitude that no words can express. The children all continue well, and your M. R. is also quite stout, though still but poorly. Mrs. Newman and Misses Sarah and Ruth Raper are come in to dinner, which will oblige me greatly (and much against my will) to shorten my letter. I have had letters from M. M. [Mary Mitchell]. She returns home this week or next, and desires her love to you. Mrs. B. [Bowles] took Patty to London on Sunday. She has got the measles in a very favorable way. Mr. Field attends her.[1]

'Dr. Price is returned from Lord Shelburne's; he entirely cleared up his conduct relating to the India Bill. He entirely disapproved of the measure, but the Duke of Richmond said the Parliament had no right to make such a Bill, in which respect Lord Shelburne differed with him, and said they had a right.

'Mr. Burroughs has accepted of the living. You said I might give Dr. Amory[2] an invitation to come and take a bed sometimes on Saturday night, which I mentioned to him on Sunday, and I don't know whether he will not accept of it next Saturday. We have had violent storms

---

[1] Mr. Field, apothecary of Stoke Newington and Christ's Hospital, father of Henry Field of Christ's Hospital and of the Rev. William Field of Warwick, the biographer of Dr. Parr; grandfather of the late Mr. Edwin Wilkins Field.

[2] Dr. Amory was the morning preacher at Newington Green.

of thunder and lightning, which have in many places done much damage. Mrs. T. Rickards and her little boy are gone to-day to Brighthelmstone with Mr. Mait-land's family. I assure you, my dear T. R., I have been a great housekeeper (I wish I could say a good one). I have scarcely been off the Green since you left me, not above twice or thrice in the coach. Adieu, my ever dear T. R.,

'And always believe me to be
'Your constantly affectionate
'M. R.

'THOMAS ROGERS, Esq.
'Post Office, Inverness.'

The next letters were addressed to Inverary, Dumbarton, and Glasgow; the last containing the news of 'the death of that worthy and great man, Lord Lyttelton,' and of a visit from Mr. Rogers the elder. In another, dated September 4, she says: —

'I had a letter from my sister Mary [her husband's sister at the Hill] on Saturday evening. She says Mr. Rogers is but indifferent, though rather better than he has been. She seems to intimate that it would give him particular pleasure to hear from you. Lord Lyttelton is greatly lamented, as must be imagined. He has long been troubled with a boil, and constant physicking for that, and uneasiness of mind, Dr. Ash thinks, quite broke his constitution. He left his blessing for his son, and desired he might be told that he forgave him. He was speechless for some time; and at last, exerting himself, called Mrs. Lyttelton,[1] gave her his blessing, lamented her situation, and said that in losing him she had lost her only friend. He then called Lord and Lady Valentia,

---

[1] The wife of his worthless son, formerly Mrs. Peach of 'The Leasowes.'

blessed them, and hoped they would continue to live in virtue, as that would give them peace at the last. Mr. Rogers desires that you would give his compliments to Mr. Lascelles, and let him know that he shall be glad of the pleasure of seeing him at the Hill with you.'

On the 23d of September she writes: —

'I had the happiness to receive a very kind letter from you, my ever dear T. R., on Tuesday morning, from Warrington, and was pleased to think that you were drawing so near to your poor deserted wife and her six children, who will all rejoice to receive again their rambling husband and father. You must allow me to be a little saucy by way of variety, though in truth if I was likely to indulge a grave vein, the sentiments I constantly feel would lead me to express my gratitude for your unspeakable kindness to me during your absence, your unwearied attention to your own M. R., and the kind assurances of love and affection that you were constantly favoring her with. My heart sincerely exults in the agreeable reflection, attended with the truest self-congratulation, and determines to increase my assiduity to promote his happiness to whom I am united by the most tender and indissoluble ties; and though above thirteen years have elapsed since that — to me, happy — union took place, I have the daily satisfaction to find that the attachment of my heart is more and more strong, and that the chief of all my temporal wishes centre in him.

'We have this morning been taking an agreeable ride that I have been talking of all the summer: it was to see Mrs. Hanson and Mrs. Berthon, and we found neither of them at home. Mr. Berthon lives on the Forest, just beyond Mr. Bosanquet's. It is a pretty part of the country, and, I think, vastly superior to Clapham Common.

Samuel Derrick, our Uncle Jo's man, is come here to-day; he came to London on Sunday, and returns to-morrow morning. He says all friends are well at Derby. Pray tell Mrs. Bowles that all her young folks dined with us yesterday, and were very well and very merry. We had, also, two of the young ladies from Miss Crisp's, and they were altogether a joyous party. I was much obliged by Mrs. Bowles's letter that I received yesterday, and beg my thanks for it. Mrs. Solly and Mrs. Neal made us a long morning visit yesterday. Mrs. Solly says that they were prevented dining with us early in the summer by the children having the whooping-cough; and that they intended sending to us the week you left home, but were prevented by hearing of your journey. They, however, fully intend it, but must leave it till they come to London.'

These letters sufficiently indicate what manner of woman Mrs. Rogers was. They have been carefully preserved by her descendants, and have kept alive the memory of her virtues as a mother and a wife. She is described as a handsome and accomplished woman, of much vivacity, popular in society, and tenderly beloved by her own household. She was firm and strict in her domestic administration, but so tender and gentle that these were the chief characteristics which afterwards dwelt in the memory of her children. 'I was taught by my mother,' said Rogers to Mr. Dyce, 'to be tenderly kind towards the meanest living thing, and, however people may laugh, I sometimes very carefully put a stray gnat or wasp out of my window.' So do childhood's lessons survive, and a mother's teaching endures. In Mrs. Rogers's diary we get another view of her character, — see what Wordsworth calls 'the very pulse of the machine.' Like her father she was introspective, apt to sit in judgment on herself, fond of putting her good resolutions on record. In these 'sessions of sweet silent thought,' she, like Shakspeare in the sonnet, would 'summon up remembrance of things past,' and in respect, not of outward happiness but of inward character, 'sigh the lack of many a thing' she sought. Into this secrecy there is no need that we should further look. Such a diary is a sacred thing, which only love and reverence should scan. It contains passages from Dr. Price's sermons which show the great influence of his thoughtful genius on her inward life. It was a life nobly planned; and her husband's testimony, when with dimmed eyes he read this record of her pious resolutions, was that it was nobly executed. 'In understanding,' he says, 'she was equalled by few; in humility, good-nature, cheerfulness, benevolence, and tenderness of disposition, a constant desire to please, and in the amiable discharge of every relative and social duty, by none.' She died on the 11th of July, 1776, three weeks after the birth of her eleventh child, who survived her only a couple of months. Samuel Rogers was then within three weeks of the completion of his thirteenth year.

In his poem of 'Human Life' Rogers gives a glimpse of his own boyhood, and shows how vivid was his recollection of his mother's tenderness : —

'He walks, he speaks. In many a broken word
His wants, his wishes, and his griefs are heard,
And ever, ever, to her lap he flies.
When rosy sleep comes on with sweet surprise —
Locked in her arms, his arms across her flung
(That name most dear forever on his tongue),
As with soft accents round her neck he clings,
And, cheek to cheek, her lulling song she sings.
. . . .

But soon a nobler task demands her care;
Apart, she joins his little hands in prayer,
Telling of Him who sees in secret there.

And now the volume on her knee has caught
His wandering eye, — now many a written thought,
Never to die, with many a lisping sweet,
His moving, murmuring lips endeavor to repeat.
Released, he chases the bright butterfly;
Oh, he would follow, — follow through the sky!
Climbs the gaunt mastiff slumbering in his chain,
And chides and buffets, clinging by the mane;
Then runs, and, kneeling by the fountain-side,
Sends his brave ship in triumph down the tide, —
A dangerous voyage; or if now he can,
If now he wears the habit of a man,
Flings off the coat so much his pride and pleasure,
And, like a miser digging for his treasure,
His tiny spade in his own garden plies,
And in green letters sees his name arise.
Where'er he goes, forever in her sight,
She looks and looks, and still with new delight.'

In the notes to the same poem Rogers says: 'We have many friends in life, but we can only have one mother, — "a discovery," says Gray, "which I never made till it was too late." The child is no sooner born than he clings to his mother, nor while she lives is her image absent from him in the hour of his distress. Sir John Moore, when he fell from his horse in the battle of Corunna, faltered out with his dying breath some message to his mother. And who can forget the last words of Conradin when, in his fifteenth year, he was led forth to die at Naples, — "O my mother, how great will be your grief when you hear of it!"'

CHAPTER II.

THE too early death of Rogers's mother did not leave the family without a woman at its head. When Thomas Rogers married he went to live in the house of his father-in-law, and he found there, living as a member of the family, Mary Mitchell, who is spoken of in Mrs. Rogers's letters. She was the daughter of Paul Mitchell, who had married Mary Radford, the sister of Daniel Radford, and she was therefore first cousin to Mrs. Rogers. Daniel Radford had taken his niece, who had been left an orphan, to be the companion of his' only child, and she had lived with her all through her married life, assisting her in bearing the burden of her household cares. Miss Mitchell was a capable and cultivated person, whom the children looked up to as almost a second mother. She lived on with them till the home on Newington Green was broken up, and then with Mr. Henry Rogers at Highbury, where she died. Another of the ladies of the household was Mrs. Worthington, an older and more distant cousin than Mrs. Mitchell. She is the Milly of the family letters, and acted as governess to the children.

The kind of life the family led during Samuel Rogers's boyhood has been sufficiently shown in his mother's letters. In Mr. Hayward's appreciative notice in the

'Edinburgh Review,' written a few months after Rogers's death, there are some speculations on his conduct and character in boyhood, which Mr. Hayward borrowed from a letter written to him by Mrs. Norton, who humorously constructed an imaginary first childhood out of what she had known of Rogers when he was verging towards second childhood. Neither Mrs. Norton nor Mr. Hayward knew anything at all of Rogers's younger days. He was the very contrary of everything they describe in this futile attempt to construct biographical details out of their internal consciousness. He was sensitive, impulsive, imaginative, and emotional, as all lads who inherit the poetical temperament are. He was not strong enough for much athletic exercise, but he took his fair share in the games and adventures of boyhood. 'His life was gentle,' and his was just such a boyhood as thousands of English lads are enjoying now in families of some wealth and much culture, with only the outward differences that the lapse of a hundred and twenty years has made. His father had ideas as to the relation of parent and child which have become old-fashioned now. He was a somewhat strict disciplinarian. His grandson, Samuel Sharpe, describes him as having dressed, according to the fashion of the day, in a brown coat, with great amplitude in the sleeves, and worn a cocked hat, powder, and a *queue*. The powdered hair was, in those days, not inconsistent with Whiggism; a little later, when Fox had set the fashion of leaving his hair of the color nature had given it, the Whigs followed his example, and with them, at least, powder went out of fashion. Thomas Rogers was what would now be described as a Radical, as were all the Whigs of a century ago. Samuel Sharpe tells us that he had voted for the Byngs, father and son, at every Middlesex election, except when he was displeased with the Coalition Ministry. That he was a good man of business his success may be taken to prove. His household was conducted with the regularity which became the chief person in a Dissenting congregation. He read prayers with his family in the morning, and they were regular in their attendance at the Stoke Newington Chapel. In the next pew to them sat Mary Wollstonecraft, then a girl; and the pulpit was filled by Dr. Towers in the morning and by Dr. Price in the afternoon. Thomas Rogers was affectionately regarded by his children, though in those days there was always a certain distance between the head of the house and the other members of the household. His children address him in their letters with the formality now reserved for strangers, and with them all his will was law.

Soon after his mother's death Sam was sent to his last schoolmaster, — the Rev. James Pickbourne of Hackney. Mr. Pickbourne had been librarian to Dr. Williams's library, of which Thomas Rogers was one of the trustees. He had afterwards acted as travelling tutor to some young men, with whom he had made the grand tour. He was the author of a 'Dissertation on the English Verb,' and of another on 'Metrical Pauses.' His school was in Grove Street, Hackney. One of the most lasting friendships of Rogers's life was begun at this school. This was with William Maltby, a near relative of Edward Maltby, who was afterwards Bishop of Durham. Maltby writes to his friend on the 12th of December, 1781, of 'the many joyful hours I have passed in your company under the confinement of scholastic restraint,' and now that school days are over, expresses 'the most sanguine hopes of a pure and lively pleasure from our new correspondence and increasing friendship, the latter of which I flatter myself will neither be dissolved by diversity of opinion nor distance of habitation, but will be as durable as sincere.' Such anticipations are often expressed, but rarely realized. In this instance they were literally fulfilled. The schoolboy friendship proved 'as durable as sincere.' It lasted for more than seventy-two years after this letter was written, and was only dissolved by death. William Maltby went to Cambridge when Samuel Rogers went to business, though, being a Dissenter, he was unable to take his degree. He afterwards practised as a solicitor, and in 1809 was appointed librarian of the London Institution in succession to Porson. He was relieved from duty in 1834, but continued to live in the librarian's house till he died in January, 1854, in his ninetieth year. His schoolboy friend survived him, and erected a tablet in Norwood Cemetery to his memory.

While Samuel Rogers was still at school, Dr. Price suddenly bounded into fame by publishing his great work on the war with the American Colonies. This obscure preacher to a small and decreasing suburban congregation had already become known and esteemed beyond the little circle of those who appreciated his religious teaching and admired his character. He had published in 1758 a 'Treatise on the Foundation of Morals,' and in 1767 a volume of dissertations, among which was one on 'Providence,' and another 'On the Junction of Virtuous Men in a Future State.' These essays attracted the notice of Lord Shelburne, who read them during a period of gloom and depression occasioned by the loss of his wife. Lord Shelburne asked Mrs. Montagu, who had recommended the book, for an introduction to its author, and thereupon called on Dr. Price at Newington Green. The interview was so satisfactory to both that it was soon repeated with important results.

Lord Shelburne felt the charm of Dr. Price's simple and unaffected character; Dr. Price respected and esteemed Lord Shelburne for his serious earnestness, and a friendship was begun which only ended with their lives. This intercourse with Dr. Price led to Lord Shel-

burne's introduction to Dr. Priestley, and to Dr. Price's
acquaintance with Mr. Dunning and Colonel Barré. The
same book which had brought Lord Shelburne to Newington Green soon afterwards brought Lord Lyttelton
thither on a similar errand. His 'Dialogues of the
Dead' had been published in 1760; fourteen years earlier
he had written a work on the 'Conversion of St. Paul,'
and he now went to Dr. Price to talk with one of the
clearest thinkers of the age on the transcendent themes
in which he felt so profound an interest. The acquaintance thus begun between an old neighbor of Thomas
Rogers and his next-door neighbor and minister at Newington Green was cut short by Lord Lyttelton's death
a few years later in 1773. Dr. Price was all this time
becoming known for his philosophical inquiries in another direction. He had written letters to Dr. Franklin,
which had been published in the 'Philosophical Transactions,' 'On the Expectation of Lives,' and 'On the Effect
of the Aberration of Light on the Time of the Transit of
Venus;' and had made a communication to the Royal
Society on the proper method of calculating the values
of contingent reversions. It was said by some of his
friends that the labor of these abstruse calculations
turned his hair suddenly gray. His biographer, Mr.
William Morgan,[1] says that in this latter paper he had
corrected an error into which M. de Moivre had fallen;
but thinking the mistake must be his own, rather than
that of so eminent a mathematician, he 'puzzled himself
so much in the correction of it, that the color of his hair,
which was naturally black, became changed in different
parts of his head into spots of perfect white. All this
must have arisen from his usual diffidence in his own
abilities; for no other cause can be assigned for his
doubts and difficulties in a case which really admitted of

[1] Memoirs of the Life of the Rev. Richard Price, D.D., F.R.S. By
William Morgan, F.R.S.

none.' It was in this same year 1769 that his celebrated 'Treatise on Reversionary Payments' was issued. It was followed up in 1772 by an 'Appeal to the Public on the National Debt.'

These publications had prepared the way for his 'Observations on Civil Liberty and the Justice and Policy of the War with America,' which was issued early in 1776. The outbreak of these fratricidal hostilities in 1774 had deeply stirred the public mind, and one of Samuel Rogers's early recollections was, that on one evening after reading from the Bible at family prayers, his father explained to his children the cause of the rebellion in the colonies, and told them that our own nation was in the wrong and it was not right to wish that the Americans should be conquered. When the news of the battle of Lexington reached England, — a battle begun by nine hundred British soldiers firing three volleys at the little troop of seventy men whom Captain John Parker, grandfather of Theodore Parker, had formed into the first line of the revolution, — Thomas Rogers put on mourning. Being asked if he had lost a friend, he answered that he had lost several friends — in New England. The Recorder of London put on mourning for the same event at the same time, and Granville Sharp gave up his place in the Ordnance office because he did not think it right to ship stores and munitions of war which might be used to put down self-government in the American colonies. To this very strong and widespread feeling Dr. Price's Essay gave powerful literary expression. It was written in the winter of 1775. The battles of Lexington and Bunker Hill had taken place in the preceding summer, and the Declaration of Independence followed on the fourth of July, 1776, about six months after the issue of Dr. Price's pamphlet. The time of its publication was, therefore, most opportune. The public excitement was more intense than anything

this generation has witnessed, and the book was so
eagerly bought that the printers, with the slow machin-
ery of those days, could not keep pace with the demand.
Dr. Price was urged to allow a cheap edition to be
printed, and he at once consented, though by doing so he
sacrificed his pecuniary profits. In a few months nearly
sixty thousand copies, then an almost unparalleled number, had been sold, and Dr. Price's name was in everybody's mouth. The Corporation of London — then, as
in so many parts of its previous history, a really popular
body, representative of the best Liberal feeling of the
time — presented him with the freedom of the city in
a gold box, in 'testimony of their approbation of his
principles and of the high sense they entertained of the
excellence of his observations on the justice and policy
of the war with America.' Fame brought its incon-
veniences together with its pleasures. Anonymous letters were sent threatening his life, and he was obliged
to decline correspondence with Dr. Franklin on the
ground that he had become so marked and obnoxious
that prudence required him to be extremely cautious.
The populace, however, loved and reverenced the coura-
geous advocate of popular rights. As he rode in the
streets of London, on his old white horse, blind in one
eye, clothed, as Rogers remembered him, 'in a great coat
and black spatterdashes,' Rogers says that, like Demos-
thenes, he was often diverted by hearing the carmen and
orange-women say, 'There goes Dr. Price!' 'Make way
for Dr. Price!' The seriousness and gentle mildness of
his character surprised those who only knew him from
his works. When the Duchess of Bedford met him, at
her own request, at Shelburne House, his quiet aspect
and unassuming manners caused her great astonishment.
'I expected to meet a Colossus,' she afterwards said,
'with an eye like Mars, to threaten and command.'
Gibbon is reported to have expressed similar surprise

when he met him in Mr. Cadell's shop. The services he had rendered to freedom were acknowledged in France and the United States, and in most unexpected quarters at home. Congress passed a resolution inviting him to become a citizen of the United States, and to assist them in the regulation of their finances. In later years Turgot corresponded with him, Pitt repeatedly consulted him on great questions of national finance, and a speech of his in proposing the toast of union between England and France was read twice in the National Assembly, the members standing. He was one day at the Bar of the House of Lords, when the Duke of Cumberland came up and told him he had read his ' Essay on Civil Liberty ' till he was blind. 'It is remarkable,' replied Lord Ashburton, who was standing near, 'that your royal highness should have been blinded by a book which has opened the eyes of all mankind.'

It is difficult to over-estimate the influence which this admirable and estimable person exerted over Samuel Rogers and his brothers in the early part of their lives. Dr. Price was no mere controversialist. He was content with the service he had done to freedom, and expressed the desire, after the issue of his second pamphlet, to remain 'an anxious spectator of the present contest with the satisfaction of having endeavored to communicate just ideas of government, and of the nature and value of civil liberty.' He held high and serious views of the responsibilities of his profession as a preacher, and his excursions into politics and finance were only occasional divergences from pastoral work. He had left Stoke Newington in some depression at the smallness of his audience there, and had become morning preacher at Hackney, but remained as afternoon lecturer to his former congregation. Political celebrity, however, brought crowds to hear him at Hackney, and his sermons on the fast days of 1779 and 1781 were published and very widely read. His profound sense of the importance of the pulpit impressed itself very strongly on his young admirer and disciple Samuel Rogers, and led him to desire to adopt it as his profession. He used to tell the story of his father one day calling the boys into his room, and asking them what professions they would choose in life. Samuel replied that he should like to be a preacher. He thought there was nothing on earth so grand. The wish was entirely due to his admiration for Dr. Price and his preaching. It was afterwards over-ruled; but a letter is extant from the Rev. Theophilus Lindsey, the founder of Essex Street Unitarian Chapel, in which he states that he had heard an oration from Mr. Samuel Rogers, who was thinking of entering at Warrington Academy as a student for the ministry.[1] The choice is only now of interest as showing the bent of Samuel Rogers's mind away from business. The weakness of his voice would have disqualified him for any form of public speaking. His father probably saw, moreover, that it was his imagination rather than the imperative call of special faculties and endowments, which had led to his desire to preach; and there was no sign whatever, in any part of his life, that he possessed the peculiar powers which can alone lead to distinction, and to the large usefulness which accompanies it, in the profession of the preacher. Mr. Dyce, in his recollections of Rogers's conversation, — recollections which show on every page that they are chiefly gathered from Rogers's declining days,— reports a freak, which, small as it seems in the record, is interesting as showing that as a boy he was greatly under the influence of a strong imagination. There was a children's ball at his father's house, at which many older people were present. Samuel Rogers,

---

[1] I have not seen the letter, but the Rev. Dr. Sadler, the editor of Crabb Robinson's Diary, clearly remembers reading it, and his accuracy is unquestionable.

then about thirteen, was dancing a minuet with a pretty
little girl, and at the moment when he should have put
on his hat and given both hands to his partner he threw
the hat among the young ladies who were sitting on the
benches, creating much surprise and confusion. 'This
strange feat,' he said to Mr. Dyce, 'was occasioned by
my suddenly recollecting a story of some gallant youth
who had signalized himself in the same way.'

He probably told this story because it showed an un-
regulated and childish form of the desire for distinction
which was an important element of his character as a
young man. There seemed but little chance of his dis-
tinguishing himself when he left school. He was the
third son, and his proper place, in his father's view, was
a stool in 'the shop,' as it was the custom to call the
bank. To the bank, therefore, he went. His eldest
brother, Daniel, had already gone to Cambridge. Daniel
was intended for the bar. His father thought of him as
the member of the family most likely to distinguish himself, and probably anticipated his entering Parliament
and reaching the higher ranks of the profession. But
Daniel never took either to the law or to banking. He
lived and died a country gentleman. Thomas and Samuel were to be the bankers, and they went to business
instead of to the university. The London of those days
was a very different place from the London of the present
generation. Few of the merchants or bankers lived, as
the Rogerses did, away in the suburbs. Some years later,
when Mr. Jones Loyd came to London, he dwelt over his
bank in Lothbury, and there the late Lord Overstone was
born in 1796. On Temple Bar there was a ghastly relic
which testified to the barbarity of the times, for Rogers
remembered seeing one of the heads of the rebels still
exposed upon its pole. It was the London which Dickens
has admirably described in 'Barnaby Rudge;' the London of the Gordon Riots. Rogers recollected the excite-

3

ment and the horrors of the time. He had already gone
to business when the riots occurred; and one of his
most vivid recollections was that of seeing a cartload
of young girls, in colored dresses, passing through the
streets on the way to execution at Tyburn. They had
been condemned to death for taking part in the riots,
though in all probability they had done little more than
look on.

There is no reason to believe that Samuel Rogers
exhibited any strong disinclination to go to business.
The poetical temperament is often intolerant of drudgery;
but he had been too dutifully brought up to allow him
to waste time and strength in protests against conditions
he could not alter. Such sentimental complaints as
Kirke White afterwards indulged against the employment which was generously given him in Mr. Enfield's
office at Nottingham, were not likely to arise from a boy
nurtured in the atmosphere of the Stoke Newington
home. It was a disappointment to Rogers that he was
obliged to take to business when all his tastes and
inclinations led him to literature, but he submitted
without repining. If banking was to be his work,
literature should be his recreation; and if the one was
cheerfully done as daily duty, the other should be joy-
fully sought as a source of never-ending delight. He
never contemplated making literature his profession.
He spoke of it as mere drudgery when it is made the
business of life, but thought that when it is resorted to
only at certain hours it is a charming relaxation. In
these earlier years he was a banker's clerk, obliged to be
at the desk every day from ten in the morning till five
in the afternoon; but he never forgot the delight with
which, after returning home, he turned to the reading
and writing which occupied his evening leisure. In these
days, too, he was not without a lively interest in politics.
One day, in the general election of 1780, Wilkes came

into the bank to canvass Mr. Rogers. He was out, but
Samuel was able to assure the popular candidate for
Middlesex of his father's sympathy; and felt proud at
having shaken hands with him. Wilkes was a man of
good manners, but ugly and with a squint. He was
chamberlain of the city, and Rogers remembered seeing
him going to the Guildhall on foot, in a scarlet coat,
military boots, and a bag-wig, — the hackney coachmen
calling to him, 'A coach, your honor?' but calling in
vain. When Wilkes called to canvass him Thomas
Rogers was probably at Coventry, where he was one of
the Whig candidates. His colleague was Sir Thomas
Halifax, and the Tory candidates were Mr. Edward Roe
Yeo and Mr. John Baker Holroyd, afterwards Lord
Sheffield. The contest was one which attracted great
notice at the time, and the accounts of it which have
been preserved illustrate in a very striking way the
political manners and customs of the age. Daniel
Rogers writes to Samuel: —

'COVENTRY, Sept. 14 [1780].

'DEAR SAMMY, — As I have no doubt you are anxious
to hear of our health, and the particulars of our situation, especially at such a riotous period, I have taken
this earliest opportunity of answering your kind letter
to my father by return of post. Few words are necessary to acquaint you with the state of the election. . . .
Yesterday and to-day the booth has been so encompassed
with a riotous mob that the poll has been adjourned
without proceeding to business. Every equitable proposition to prevent riot and confusion has been rejected
by Mr. Holroyd and Mr. Yeo; but the sheriffs are
determined to persevere in adjourning the poll from day
to day till the freedom of election is restored. At
present our voters are obstructed, beaten, stripped, and
endangered by a hired mob of colliers and others of the

like stamp. The whole affair will doubtless be misrepre-
sented by our opponents in the London papers, but our
friends are convinced we have the majority of voters;
and Mr. Briggs, who has examined the subject, and been
remarkably active, is of the same opinion. . . . With
compliments to Dr. and Mrs. Price,

'I remain your ever affectionate
'D. ROGERS.'

This letter was written on the fifth day after the poll
opened. So great was the rioting that in nine days,
from the 9th to the 18th of September, only eighty-three
persons voted. The sheriffs, determined not to proceed
with the election till peace was restored, closed the poll
on the ninth day, and made no return. The new House
of Commons met on the 31st of October, but there were
no members from Coventry, and the sheriffs were accordingly summoned to the Bar of the House and eventually
committed to prison, and on their release were repri-
manded by the Speaker. In December another election
was held, the same candidates being in the field. Party
feeling still ran as high as ever, and the prolonged polling, which lasted more than a fortnight, gave occasion
for all kinds of disturbance. The election is described
in a letter from his father to Sam.

Thomas Rogers to Samuel Rogers.

'COVENTRY, Saturday evening, 15th December, 1780.

'DEAR SAMMY, — I have received several kind letters
lately from the Green, but, as yours was the last, I have
laid my hand first upon it. I wish I could have the
happiness to make one of your party this evening at the
Green, but, alas! I am still confined to this region of
discord and contention. Coventry seems to be the place
where every unclean bird dwells; for of all the black-

guards in the universe I think the Coventry Blues are the greatest. They still seem confident of success, but I think on Tuesday night they will have found out their mistake. It may possibly end then, but not sooner. Total number polled to-night, 2,317. They have only about forty more to poll, so that on Monday morning we shall soon begin to regain the 150 we first gave them. I have been a good deal indisposed by a cold; but, by attending to it to-day, I am now much relieved, and doubt not by Monday morning to be quite well as usual. I hope to return to my children and family life before this day se'ennight, and to exchange a scene every way hateful for one of peace, happiness, and content. I have sent you one of our new songs, which I hope will please you. I beg my kind love to everybody.

'I remain, in haste, dear Sam,

'Your ever affectionate father,

'THOS. ROGERS.

'Mr. SAM ROGERS,
  'At Messrs. Welch & Comp⁴⁵,
  'Cornhill, London.'

Mr. Rogers's anticipations were realized. The poll was declared on the 28th December: Sir Thomas Halifax, 1,319; Thomas Rogers, 1,318; Edward R. Yeo, 1,298; John Baker Holroyd, 1,295. The Tories petitioned, and a Tory election committee, as was inevitable in those days, unseated the Whigs and gave the seats to their defeated opponents. Thomas Rogers never stood again at any election. Neither the morals nor the manners of elections in those times were congenial to him, and his own strong political convictions were in advance of the age.

There is a further curious illustration of the elections of the reign of George the Third, ninety years before the ballot, in a letter written to Thomas Rogers during the Bristol election in January, 1781.

John Robinson to Thomas Rogers.

'DEAR SIR, — I wrote you from Namptwich [*sic*], and
at the same time enclosed proposals from Harrison and
Houghton's house, to which I suppose you have given
them an answer.   I am now at Bristol, where they have
this day begun a contested election for a member in the
room of the late Mr. Lippintot, deceased.   The candidates
are Mr. Cruger and Mr. Daubeny.   They poll in tallies
of ten each.   They have polled to-day (after squabbling
about three hours before the opening of the poll) six
tallies each, and nine single freeholders, so that they
stand equally, — sixty-nine each.   The Blues are, in their
own opinion, very secure of their election of Mr. Daubeny, but I think, myself, from what I have heard and
seen, that Cruger will run him hard.   He has by much,
to a stranger, the greatest share of popularity ; and if
the gentlemen who manage for him mind what they are
about I am of opinion he will get his election.   They are
extremely riotous, have already pulled down the board
that directed the freemen the road to Daubeny's polling-
place, and knocked down several in the street of Daubeny's party.   I shall be at Coventry in about eight days
from this, where I shall be very glad to receive a letter
from you directed to the King's Head there.   If I can
say or do anything there pray command me.   I shall go
from thence through Birmingham and Stourbridge, where
I shall do myself the pleasure of paying a visit to Miss
Rogers.   Some gentlemen, before the poll began to-day,
taxed Daubeny with attempting to compromise with
another party at the last election.   As you will see by the
enclosed paper, the Dissenters of all denominations are
for Cruger ; and the Quakers — who are numerous here,
and you know are in general a quiet set of people — were
the first who mounted the rostrum to poll.   I can say no

more now, and you must excuse the incorrectness of what I have said, for there is a noise here almost sufficient to crack the drum of a man's ear.

'So must subscribe myself, dear Sir,
'Your very humble servant,
'JOHN ROBINSON.
'BRISTOL, Jan. 30, 1781.'

Mr. Cruger, the Whig candidate, was defeated. He had been Burke's colleague in the Parliament of 1774, and made the celebrated speech in the House of Commons, — 'Mr. Speaker, I say ditto to Mr. Burke; I say ditto to Mr. Burke.'

Thomas Rogers the elder had died a few years before this, and his daughters continued to live at 'The Hill,' where the elder members of the family from Newington Green often visited them. These visits during the life of their grandfather, and afterwards to their aunts, were something more than journeys to the country. They were excursions into another social atmosphere, another political climate, another world. Thomas Rogers was there every summer, and his letters to Sam give a lively picture of the society of the neighborhood. On the 14th of August, 1781, he writes: 'We were last week entirely taken up by Lord and Lady Valentia, who were upon a visit to "The Hill" from Monday to Saturday. This visit has brought on another from this family to Arley, Lord Valentia's house, which takes place to-morrow, and in which I am compelled to take a part. We shall return on Friday. I look upon these engagements as near a fortnight's loss to me. Tom left us on Sunday evening. He intended sleeping that night at Lichfield, and on Monday at Derby. The races were to begin to-day.' On the 6th of September he says: 'We pass our time so uniformly that I have nothing to communicate worth your notice. Among the changes which have taken place in this neighborhood, chance has brought to Mr. Amphlett's house at Clent a Mr. and Mrs. Blair, both Scotch.   They live in one of the polite squares, keep many servants, live in a high style, and are famous for musical parties. Mrs. Blair sings delightfully, and is called "the inimitable Blair."   As they visit a good deal, and Mrs. Blair sings whenever she is asked, and without the least ceremony, they are considered as an acquisition to the county.   But I am afraid they will not stay long, as they are said not to think their house good enough, and occasionally give themselves some consequential airs of that sort which some of their neighbors do not seem to relish.   As Mrs. Blair is a lady of so much tone, I thought I would introduce her to you. . . . We were told last week that the combined fleets were in the Channel, but we disregarded it; the papers to-day confirm it, but nobody seems to think it a circumstance of any moment, and I suppose the same torpid indifference prevails through the country generally.'

The visits to and from the Valentias were repeated in later summers, and Mr. Rogers, in his frequent visits to ' The Hill,' seems to have entered with great zest into the pleasures and amusements of the country life to which he had been accustomed in his early days.   He writes on the 6th of October, 1783: ' Our Assembly is fixed for next Monday, which will give us pleasure on Martha's account, as I hope there will be a smart dance. . . . It is so celebrated a meeting that there are generally four or five hairdressers from Worcester and Birmingham come over to attend the ladies, as the *friseurs* of the town are not found sufficient.'   In October, 1785, he reports the first Assembly of the season at Stourbridge, and adds : ' Four of your aunts and myself were there, and had the pleasure of meeting Captain and Mrs. Cox and many friends.' He notes, moreover, two new features of country life. The first mail-coach had been started at Bristol in 1784, and in 1785 mail-coaches spread rapidly all over the country. 'The extension of the mail-coaches,' says Thomas Rogers, in a letter to Sarah Rogers, on the 18th of October, 1785, 'makes the country towns very gay. We have one comes from Birmingham to Stourbridge, and from hence to Bewdley every day but Monday; and the king's arms on the coach, and the scarlet and gold livery of the coachman, please the populace much.'

Another innovation of the time was the establishment of Sunday Schools. The Rev. Theophilus Lindsey had established such a school at Catterick in 1764, and Miss Hannah Ball at High Wycombe in 1769; but the movement had been made general by the success of the school Mr. Robert Raikes had opened at St. Mary-le-Crypt in Gloucester in 1781. So in this same letter Thomas Rogers reports in 1785: 'Mr. Foley, the rector of the parish, and several gentlemen, are very busy in drawing up a plan for Sunday Schools. Sufficient money is raised, but the school-houses are not yet fixed upon, nor the masters and mistresses appointed. There will be about six for boys, and the same number for girls.' He adds a wish which was realized fifty-five years afterwards by some of his descendants: 'I hope the gentlemen of Islington and the Green will establish some in the neighborhood. I wish one or two could be established at the Green, and the children brought to meeting, as I know no place where there are so many poor people with so little attendance upon public worship.'

The autumn of 1786 finds him again at 'The Hill,' and he writes to Sam, who had just returned from Brighton, of some delightful excursions they had made. 'One to Downton, to Dick Knight's Castle, and over a lofty range of hills in that neighborhood, commanding Herefordshire, Shropshire, and part of Wales.' The other excursion was to Mr. Harley's at Berrington, near Leominster. 'The house not large, but taking in horses' stables, gardens, with the establishment of servants, the whole may be called princely. No park and not much shrubbery, but some hundred acres of ground, beautiful in situation, laid out in great taste, and kept up at a profusion of ·expense.' In this letter he expresses the hope that in Tom's absence Sam will get early to town, and attend as much as possible to Mr. Welch's ease, doing everything he can to relieve him from too much application.

In most of these letters he speaks of Sam's health. In 1781 Sam had gone to Margate, and his father strongly recommends him to take horse exercise, promising to send the brown mare if he cannot get a decent horse by hiring. Sam had said something about dancing, and his father expresses the hope that he will 'be so prudent in the use of it as not, like Penelope, to undo by night the work of the day.' Year after year there are references in the letters to a weakness of the eyes from which Sam was suffering. He seems to have had a very odd experience with respect to them. One of his poems is entitled 'To the Gnat,' and admirably describes in sixteen lines the 'whirring wings' and 'shrill horn' of the mosquito. If it had been written on Staten Island, near New York, or in some other place haunted by the scourge of continental climates, it could not have pictured more graphically the possible horrors of an autumn night; but addressed to our poor English midge, the lines seem exaggerated, and Mr. Sharpe thinks the piece might have been written in order that it might end in mock-heroic style with Dryden's line, —

'They wake in horror and dare sleep no more.'

Yet Rogers always declared that the lines literally described his own experience. In his young days the gnats at Stoke Newington distressed him as the mosquitoes plague an Englishman who without due precautions ventures to sleep with an open window in some parts of the United States. His eyes, he says, were often swollen with the bites of gnats when he woke in the morning. This annoyance was probably due to his weak health. Every year during his clerkship at the bank he took long holidays at Margate or at Brighton; year after year sea-bathing and horse exercise were recommended him by the doctors, and he found benefit from them. His father had to exhort him not to spend too much time in reading, but to lay his favorite books aside and look after his health. In the summer of 1785 he writes to his father: —

'MARGATE, 24 Sept., '85.

'DEAR SIR, — I arrived here last Tuesday night, after a very pleasant journey. The hop-picking had thrown an air of gayety over the country, and women and children were everywhere singing songs and filling their baskets. The weather has been very changeable, and the showers so partial that yesterday when I was riding with Mr. Seawell (who is here, and boards in the same house with me) a very heavy shower fell within twenty yards of us, and we could distinctly see the drops. Margate is rather full, but the height of the season seems to be past. Mr. Seawell and myself propose to take a little trip to Calais next week, and on our return to Dover I shall be met by Mr. Joseph Collier, who will accompany me along the coast to Brighthelmstone. Mr. Wm. Maltby is there for his health, which is very indifferent, and I hope to stay there a week or ten days. The sea has been very calm since I came, and I have bathed every morning. As we shall make easy journeys every day, I mean to bathe at Rye and Eastbourne. Mr. Bearcroft and his family are here, and are extremely civil to me. I walked down to the pier this morning, and counted twenty-four West India merchantmen, which are just visible on the line of the horizon. I have found the sea air have the same effect it used to have, and my appetite is so keen that I am sometimes ashamed of it. I beg my duty to my aunts, and my love to my cousins; and remain, dear Sir,

'Your dutiful and affectionate son,
'SAML. ROGERS.'

He was at this time preparing his first book for the press, but there is not a hint concerning it in any of his letters. There is, however, a letter from his sister Maria, written when she was twelve or thirteen years old, which supplies the material for a slight sketch of Rogers's evenings at home in these early days. Maria speaks of being with him in the study when he is reading and she is writing, and her only pleasure is to look up to him from time to time, wishing to know his thoughts. She speaks in most affectionate terms of his kindness in always doing everything to oblige her, and says she is sure there is not one brother in a hundred who so behaves to his sister. In the Rogers's house the law in the library was that of silence when any one was reading or writing. Samuel could therefore sit and write comparatively undisturbed, and had not to learn, like Maria Edgeworth, to compose amid the prattle of a family. Communication was to be by correspondence, and the letters were put in a place in the library called the 'Post Office.' There Maria placed her letters, and there she found her brother's answers after he had gone to business in the morning. 'In this way a correspondence was carried on between a brother and sister living under the same roof; and Maria says of Samuel's letters: 'If I am grave they make me merry, and if I am merry I still continue so.' As Samuel's eyes were weak, his sisters sometimes read to him; and it is easy to picture the pleasant scene in the study on many an evening in those happy years, --

the girls writing or reading or preparing their lessons, the brothers sitting with them at similar work, and Samuel, the literary brother, studying the poets or himself writing what he hoped might live, or, like a later and less fortunate aspirant for fame, with old bards of honorable name, measuring his soul severely. In this way he became an author.

CHAPTER III.

Early Writings. — 'The Scribbler.' — 'Vintage of Burgundy.' — 'Ode
to Superstition.' — Smaller Poems.

ROGERS did not begin poetical composition very early
in life. He did not lisp in numbers, for he was probably
far beyond boyhood when the numbers came. He had
been kept at school rather longer than Walter Scott, who
was only fourteen when, to use his own words, he 'entered on the dry and barren wilderness of forms and
conveyances' in his father's office. Rogers entered his
father's bank when he was sixteen or seventeen, and he
made his first literary venture before he was eighteen.
He went to business later than Scott, but plunged into
authorship much earlier than his great friend and contemporary. His first printed efforts were not in verse.
They consisted of a brief series of papers published in
successive numbers of the 'Gentleman's Magazine.' Like
most early efforts, these essays are imitations; and as
might be expected, Dr. Johnson is the model. Rogers
never saw Johnson. He records having met old General
Oglethorpe at the sale of Dr. Johnson's library. But
the great autocrat of literature was still exerting his
undisputed sway when Rogers was meditating authorship, and he felt for him not only the reverence which
was then universal, but that which young ambition feels
for old and established fame. One day, in early youth, he
and his friend William Maltby went to call on Johnson
at his house in Bolt Court. 'I had my hand upon the
knocker,' said Rogers, in telling the story, 'when our

courage failed us and we retreated.' Boswell told them many years afterwards that they should have gone boldly in, for the great man would have received them kindly. Johnson died in December, 1784, — more than a year before Rogers printed his first poem, — so that he and his friend could have had no such introduction as the presentation of a book might give them; and it is not likely that, in those early days, his literary friends could give him an introduction to a man who would probably decline to know or recognize them. Nor is there any reason whatever to think that Rogers was sufficiently content with his imitations of Johnson to have ventured to call his attention to them.

These short pieces are only worthy of notice as the earliest productions of a writer who afterwards attained wide celebrity on a different field. It was the custom of the Sylvanus Urban of those days to print in his magazine short series of papers, under titles evidently suggested by the 'Rambler.'

Samuel Rogers gave his papers the title of 'The Scribbler,' and the following is the first number, which appeared in February, 1781: —

THE SCRIBBLER, No. I.

Ut scriptor cyclicus olim. — Hor.

Prompted by the ambition of appearing in print, the Scribbler here obtrudes his compositions on the public. His character may obstruct his success, but it precludes disappointment, for no one can conceive very sanguine expectations of entertainment from the Scribbler.

Though his Essays be not favored with a perusal, though the appellation he has assumed repress curiosity or excite contempt, the satisfaction he will feel at seeing himself in print will amply compensate the mortification of neglect.

If they be favorably received it will indeed be an additional pleasure; if not, he will not be dejected, nor, like Cowley, form

the chimerical design of secluding himself from society and re-
nouncing the chief pleasures of life.

He solicits the contributions of all who are influenced by the
same motives which he has adduced for the publication of his
productions, but declines a correspondence with those who have
the vanity to aspire to literary eminence.

This introduction may be regarded as singular, but the Scribbler disdains the practice of averting the displeasure of the reader
by servile submission, or by affecting that diffidence which he
does not possess.

Had he been a native of Athens, or had he even resided in
Rome in the Augustan age, he would certainly have never conceived the idea of appearing in print, nor have been sensible of
the bliss of publication.

This is a species of luxury of which the Ancients were entirely
ignorant; which even the Despots of Asia had never the felicity
to enjoy. Applause can never be conferred adequate to the
merits of the discoverer of so exquisite a pleasure.

To his memory — to the memory of

FAUSTUS OF MENTZ;

Who by the invention of the art of printing
Has ultimately contributed more to the happiness of Empires
Than all the conquerors and legislators of antiquity,
This Bagatelle
is inscribed by his grateful admirer,
S ***** R *****.

(*To be continued regularly every month.*)

The same strain was continued in the next number,
which began by describing the raptures he felt at seeing
himself in print. The third paper was on 'Eloquence,'
the fourth was on 'the Ancients and Moderns,' and was
reproduced by Mr. Dyce in his Table Talk; the fifth
was a story entitled the 'Pupil of Nature,' supposed to
be translated from the Erse, with the statement that
'Shakspeare had probably seen it when he wrote the

tragedy of Macbeth;' the sixth, 'On the Regions of the
Blest,' a rhapsody, with Cicero's words for a text: 'O
præclarum diem, cum ad illud divinum animarum con-
cilium cœtumque proficiscar, cumque ex hâc turbâ et
colluvione discedam!' The seventh was on the 'Temple
of Fashion,' quoted-below; and the eighth, misnumbered
seven in the magazine, is on 'Virtue.' Mr. Dyce thinks
these papers were 'quite up to the standard of the
periodical writing of the time,' and some of them are
clearly superior to those which were published contem-
poraneously with them. The one which Mr. Dyce quotes
'as a curiosity,' though it shows industry, is by no means
equal in merit to some others of the series. That on
the 'Temple of Fashion,' quoted seventy-five years afterwards by Mr. Hayward in the 'Edinburgh Review' article
on Samuel Rogers, is perhaps the best of the series. It
is written, says the 'Edinburgh' 'with a freedom and
rhythmical flow which are rarely found in essayists of
eighteen.'

THE SCRIBBLER, No. VII.

Sed nihil est magnum somnianti. — CIC.

Reflecting the other evening on the influence of Fashion, I
insensibly fell asleep, and imagined myself suddenly transported
into a magnificent temple, in the centre of which, elevated on a
pedestal, stood a female of very light, capricious air, attended by
numbers of both sexes, who were burning incense on her altar.
But what astonished me most was that the scene experienced a
perpetual change. When she waved her hand the columns of
the temple, which were first of the Ionic, became of the Corin-
thian order, the stucco wall appeared hung with the richest tapestry, the fretted ceiling swelled into a dome, and the marble
pavement assumed a carpet of the brightest tints. These, after
innumerable transformations, were revived, once more to pass
through the same revolutions.

Whether she heightened with a pencil the vermilion of her
cheeks or clothed her limbs with a close or flowing vest; whether

4

she collected her ringlets in a knot or suffered them to hang
negligently on her shoulders; whether she shook the dice, waked
the lyre, or filled the sparkling glass,—she was imitated by her
votaries, who vied with each other in obsequiousness and reverence.   All united in presenting their oblations,—either their
health, their fortunes, or their integrity.   Though numbers inces-
santly disappeared, the assembly, receiving continual supplies,
preserved its grandeur and brilliancy.   At the entrance I observed
Vanity fantastically crowned with flowers and feathers, to whom
the fickle deity committed the initiation of her votaries.   These
having fluttered as gayly as their predecessors, in a few moments
vanished and were succeeded by others.   All who rejected the
solicitations of Vanity were compelled to enter by Ridicule,
whose shafts were universally dreaded.   Even Literature, Science,
and Philosophy were obliged to comply.   Those only escaped
who were concealed beneath the veil of Obscurity.   As I gazed
on this glittering scene, having declined the invitation of Vanity,
Ridicule shot an arrow from her bow which pierced my heart; I
fainted, and in the violence of my agitation awaked.

The publication of these essays in the months from
February to September, 1781, gave their young author
great encouragement.   His nephew, Mr. Samuel Sharpe,
in his sketch of Rogers's Life describes him as looking
forward every month 'to the day of these papers appearing with boyish eagerness.   As the magazine reached him
in the morning it was brought into his bedroom before he
was out of bed, and, month by month, as he cut its wet
pages, and found that the publisher had decided that
his essay was deserving of publication, he was more and
more fixed in his purpose to be an author.'   None of the
later pleasures, even of successful authorship, equal this,
the first and earliest satisfaction that is given to the 'last
infirmity of noble minds.'   It is not fame, but it seems
like the promise of fame.   It gives young energies a
sense of boundless opportunity in which to prove their
quality, and conquer the empire for which they long.
     The imitation of Johnson was a passing phase; and

the writing of essays was soon dropped for more congenial work. In the next year, 1782, we find him already engaged in poetical composition. From the first he had poetry in view, and his love of poetry, even his desire to be a poet, had been known and recognized from comparatively early years. In 1775 Mason published the 'Life and Letters of Gray,' with an edition of his poems; and Samuel Rogers, then twelve years old, read them with delight. Some years later, when he went to business, he walked to town in the morning with Gray's poems in his hand, and could repeat them all. He admired the letters as much as the poems. They had for him, he said, an inexpressible charm. He thought them to be as witty as Walpole's, and to have what he thought Walpole's wanted, — true wisdom. But Gray was not his earliest teacher. In 1771, the year in which Gray died, and when Wordsworth was but twelve months old, the first and best part of Beattie's 'Minstrel' appeared. Rogers was then a boy, and it was probably a year or two later, when on a summer evening he took down the volume from the library shelf and read the story of 'Edwin' with that kindling sympathy which was the stirring within him of his own share in the divine gift of genius. He never forgot that first experience of the poet's spell. It might be described in Wordsworth's lines in his autobiographical poem: —

> 'Twice five years
> Or less I might have seen, when first my mind
> With conscious pleasure opened to the charm
> Of words in tuneful order; found them sweet
> For their own sakes, a passion and a power.'

This seems to have been the dawn of his genius. It woke up the love of song, and sent him to study with enthusiasm the chief poets of the time. He soon turned from Beattie to Goldsmith, and from Goldsmith to Gray.

Goldsmith's 'Traveller' was published in the year after
Rogers was born, and the 'Deserted Village' in 1770;
and these were among the poems on which his youthful
fancy was fed. He soon went back, of course, to older
and even greater masters; but his boyhood's love of
poetry was nourished by the popular poets of the time.
One of the sweetest bits of early praise which reached
his ears was the description of him as 'a child of Goldsmith.' But he was something more. It is needless to
say that a young man of poetical ambition in the second
half of the eighteenth century was a careful student of
Pope and Dryden. Rogers sat at the feet of both these
great men, but his preference was for Dryden. His
father advised him to study Pope's 'Homer,' but, with
all his love and reverence for the poet of the 'Dunciad'
and the 'Essay on Man,' he could never like Pope's
translation of the 'Iliad' and the 'Odyssey.' When
Cowper's version of 'Homer' appeared in 1791 he admired it greatly and read it again and again. The gentle
singer of 'John Gilpin' and the 'Task' was, however, a
contemporary of Rogers, and cannot be numbered among
his early teachers.[1] Those teachers were Gray and Goldsmith, Dryden and Pope; but the influence which the
elders in the brotherhood of genius possess over its
younger sons was exerted in Rogers's case chiefly by
Gray and Goldsmith. Gray inspired him first and Goldsmith afterwards, but he was himself from first to last.
In his imaginative boyhood when, like Beattie's 'Edwin,'
though for reasons of health rather than of feeling, —

> 'Concourse and noise and toil he ever fled,
>   Nor cared to mingle in the clamorous fray,' —

he may have thought himself to be not unlike that hero
of his favorite poem. The excitement with which he

---

[1] 'John Gilpin' was published in the 'Repository' in 1783, and the
'Task' was issued in 1785.

first read the 'Minstrel' was due to the sympathy he
felt with Edwin's dreams. Such revelations of intellectual kinship come to every boy of sensitive nature in
whom the first movements of great faculties take the
shape of ambitious hopes and plans. He does not
merely follow the great examples he admires, but catches
inspiration from them. He does not consciously imitate
them, but hears and obeys the call of innate powers to
go and do likewise. This was Rogers's case. In some
lines written in earlier days, but added to the second
part of his 'Italy,' and dated 1839, when he was seventy-
six years old, he says of himself:[1]—

> 'Nature denied him much,
> But gave him at his birth what most he values,
> A passionate love for music, sculpture, painting,
> For poetry, the language of the gods,

---

[1] In the Common Place Book is the earliest form of these lines, and
they are entitled 'Of Myself — a Fragment.'

> 'My gentle reader, hast thou yet conceived
> A wish to know me? Bear with me awhile,
> And ere my task is ended thou mayst know
> More than thou wouldst. Fortune denied me much,
> Yet gave me, with a smile, what most I value, —
> A passionate love for music, painting, sculpture,
> For poetry, the language of the gods,
> For all or grand or beautiful in nature:
> A setting sun, a lake among the mountains,
> The light of an ingenuous countenance,
> And what transcends them all, a noble action.
> What though my ancestors early or late
> Were not ennobled by the breath of kings,
> Yet in these veins was running at my birth
> The blood of those most eminent of old
> For learning, virtue; those who could renounce
> The things of this world for their conscience' sake,
> And die like blessed martyrs. Health from my cheek
> Fled ere the down was there, and, rain or shine,
> From very childhood was my soul inclined
> To sadness, such as few I hope have known;
> Yet were my waking dreams, when health was mine,
> Not undelightful.'

For all things here or grand or beautiful :
A setting sun, a lake among the mountains,
The light of an ingenuous countenance,
And what transcends them all, a noble action.
        Nature denied him much, but gave him more ;
And ever, ever grateful should he be
Though from his cheek ere yet the down was there
Health fled ; for in his heaviest hours would come
Gleams such as come not now ; nor failed he then
(Then and through life his happiest privilege)
Full oft to wander where the Muses haunt,
Smit with the love of song.'

There was not much opportunity to wander where the
Muses haunt in those early days. Nor was there the
slightest prospect at this time of that dignified leisure in
which his long life was to be spent. If he thought definitely of his future, the shape it took in the dreams of
his ambition was in all probability that which has been
wrongly attributed to him of the 'banker poet.' If this
phrase, now often applied to him, has any meaning, it
describes a man who is actually engaged in the business
of banking at the same time that he is cultivating the
Muse. This is what Rogers did in his early days, — but
in those early days only. He was. then and then only,
in the true sense of the words, a banker poet. It was,
as it were, by accident that he became the chief owner
of the business which was afterwards carried on by his
brother and his nephew on his behalf; and that he, the
third son, was put into the position of the heir. There
can be no stronger evidence of the confidence with which
he inspired his father, who was himself a prudent and
very successful man of business, than that the bank
should have been left in his hands. It is the most con-
clusive proof that could be given of Rogers's devotion to
business and of his capacity for it. But when he began
to write he was not even a partner, and when he pub-

lished his first volume of poems he was only the youngest
member in the banking partnership, with scarcely the
most distant prospect of ever being anything else. The
world has been assured that from the first he laid out
his life with a view to the social distinction he afterwards attained; but such statements have no foundation.
They have been made by persons who have written
about him in complete ignorance of the kind of life he
lived in his younger days. It was a life of steady application to business, of going to and fro between his home
in Stoke Newington and the bank in Freeman's Court;
of immersion for the best part of every working-day in
the dry details of finance. This life of work was varied,
relieved, brightened, and consoled by the love of poetry.
The leisure which business left to him was spent in
literary occupation or in cultivating the society of men
of letters. But Rogers never dreamed of making either
literary or social success his chief pursuit. The opportunity for such successes came afterwards, and awoke
the desire for them; but that opportunity found him
behind a bank counter or in a bank parlor, as the genius
of his country found Burns at the plough.

His first poetical composition has never been published. It took the unexpected form of a comic opera.
The world might never have heard of this production,
of which Rogers himself did not desire much to be said,
but for a Note which, in his 'Table Talk,' Mr. Dyce has
appended to an account given by Rogers of the time
occupied in the composition of his poems. In this Note
Mr. Dyce writes, 'I was with Mr. Rogers when he tore
to pieces and threw into the fire a manuscript operatic
drama — "The Vintage of Burgundy" — which he had
written early in life. He told me that he offered it
to a manager, who said, "I will bring it on the stage
if you are determined to have it acted, but it will certainly be damned." One or two songs which now appear

among his poems formed parts of that drama.' This
statement is only partly true. The manuscripts — for
there were two copies — were indeed torn, but only a portion of each was burned, and the remainder is still preserved. The story of the offer of the opera to a manager,
like many others which Mr. Dyce has reported, was told
by Rogers when his memory was failing. The manager
to whom it was submitted seems, from a letter which has
been preserved, to have been George Colman the elder.
His letter, returning it, is dated from Soho Square, April
8th, without the year, and merely says, ' The little piece,
herewith returned, is, I think, a pretty drama of the sentimental kind, but its success upon the stage must depend
much upon the music. Is not it a translation from the
French?'. This faint praise from the eminent author of
the ' Jealous Wife ' and the ' Clandestine Marriage,' was
probably regarded by Rogers as equivalent to condemnation, and may have convinced him that his chance of
literary success was to be found in a different direction.

The piece was called 'The Vintage of Burgundy — a
Comic Opera in Two Acts.' The larger fragment shows
that the manuscript covered eight-and-twenty pages of
small, clear writing; two of these have been completely
cut away, eighteen are roughly torn down the middle,
and eight are entire. Of the smaller manuscript much
less is left; but it contains a few lines which are obliterated in the other copy. So far as the two can be
compared, the difference between them is considerable.
The description of it as a ' comic opera ' is not borne out
by what remains of it; but it exactly answers to George
Colman's description, ' a pretty drama of the sentimental
kind.' No steps seem to have been taken to get it set
to music, but there is on one of the manuscripts an incomplete cast of the play in which the chief characters
are apportioned to Incledon, Johnson, Blanc, Mrs. B.,
and Mrs. M. The little piece contained at least nineteen

songs, two of which are published among Rogers's poems, — 'The Alps at Daybreak' and 'Dear is my little Native Vale.' Among those which have never seen the light is one of which only part of the first verse remains, the idea of which is expressed in the words of one of the peasants, ''Tis the vintage to-morrow, and if you long for the pure juice of the grape, you may eat a bottle of Burgundy in the way Nature gives it!' The verse may be reconstructed thus : —

'Let the grape's gushing nectar ferment
And sing from the flask as it flows,
But with Nature's [own gift I 'm content],
I 'll quaff the [red juice as it grows].'

There are some dancing songs, sung by a Burgundian peasant girl. One verse can be reconstructed : —

'Each tender youth at every pa[use]
Breathes softly in his partner's [ear]
What most can plead a lover's [cause]
What most she hopes yet d[reads to hear].'

Another of the peasant songs is : —

'At the close of a summer's day,
When all danced over the green,
With my Lubin I stole away
To walk by the hedge unseen ;
And my heart went pit-a-pat.

'"Ah, Annete !" he said with a sigh,
"Could I tell you what I feel !"
And I blushed, though I knew not why,
At the tale he would reveal ;
And my heart went pit-a-pat.

'With such softness he pressed my hand,
Such a kiss enforced his vow,
That I 'd hardly strength to stand,
And I looked — I know not how ;
While my heart went pit-a-pat.

'And when we returned to the green
    So lightly we tripped away,
Such a jig had never been seen
    Since the piper learnt to play;
        For our hearts went pit-a-pat.'

One of the girls employed in the vintage is an Italian
girl, who has run away from a match her father wished
to force upon her, and is followed by the lover she
favors in the guise of an organ-grinder. She sings
the song, 'Dear is my little Native Vale,' and one to
the nightingale.

I.

'Blest chantress of the midnight grove,
    Descend and sing thy serenade;
No parent checks thy little love,
    Or bids thy ruffled plumage fade.

II.

'The moon shines through the dusky trees,
    Her beams among the branches play;
· Let thy wild warblings swell the breeze,
    And softly, sweetly, die away.'

And when her lover finds her, and she will not accept
him without her father's consent, they sing together: —

'*Lucio.*   The opening floweret greets the dawn,
        When genial dews impearl the lawn;
        Up springs the lark with carols clear,
            When day spreads o'er the sky.
Maria.   But when despair has shut the heart
        What joy can any sense impart?
        Then, what is music to the ear
            Or beauty to the eye?'

The piece, of course, ends happily. From the date of
1782, given to the song 'Dear is my little Native Vale,'
it is evident that it was the first of Rogers's completed
productions, and embodied much of his early poetical

effort. He had kept it by him very many years, and had probably re-written and published several of the songs it contained, besides the two already mentioned. He might have said of 'The Vintage of Burgundy,' — as he did of the 'Ode to Superstition,' — that it was written in his teens, and afterwards touched up. This elaborate method was followed in everything he did, — even in the writing of a letter of more than common importance. He wrote nothing in haste, yet he always reconsidered every line at leisure. He said to Mr. Dyce: 'During my whole life I have borne in mind the speech of a woman to Philip of Macedon, — "I appeal from Philip drunk to Philip sober." After writing anything in the excitement of the moment, and being greatly pleased with it, I have always put it by for a time, and then, carefully considering it in every possible light, I have altered it to the best of my judgment.' This rule has the testimony of all antiquity in its favor; but it belongs to antiquity. The custom of the present day is to print at once that which is flung off in the heat of the kindled fancy, and the haste is justified of its children by the gain in strength and fire, though the gain is made at some expense of that grace and polish of which Rogers is one of the latest examples in English literature.

His second poetical composition was the 'Ode to Superstition,' which has been already mentioned. The writing of this poem was one of the chief occupations of his evening leisure in 1784 and 1785. Like 'The Vintage of Burgundy,' it was written and re-written, and was published anonymously in the spring of 1786, with the title, 'An Ode to Superstition, with some other Poems.' It was issued by Mr. Cadell as a thin quarto, at the price of eighteenpence. The other poems were: 'The Alps at Daybreak,' which had been included in the unpublished opera, 'The Vintage of Burgundy;' 'Lines to a Lady on the Death of her Lover,' which were afterwards omitted in the republication of his poems; 'The Sailor,' which is dated 1786 in his collected works; and the pretty song, often set to music and included in collections of poetry, entitled 'A Wish,' and beginning 'Mine be a cot beside the hill.' In describing this first venture many years afterwards, Rogers said, 'I paid down to the publisher thirty pounds, to insure him against being a loser by it. At the end of four years I found he had sold twenty copies.' This was as discouraging a beginning as that which Wordsworth and Coleridge made twelve years later with their joint volume of 'Lyrical Ballads.' Mr. Cottle, the Bristol publisher, paid them thirty guineas each for the copyright, and boldly printed five hundred copies. The first piece in the volume was the 'Ancient Mariner,' yet the sale was so slow that Cottle was glad to dispose of the largest portion of the copies to a London bookseller at a loss, and he gave back to the authors their valueless copyright. Rogers's publisher was at least kept from loss, and Rogers himself was not discouraged by the small sale of the poem. The critics were more appreciative than the public; he was encouraged by them to own himself to be the author of the poem, and was soon recognized as one of the promising writers of the time. He learned too, from the reception of the 'Ode to Superstition,' that it was not in lyrical poetry he was destined to excel.

The first notice of the 'Ode to Superstition' was in the 'Critical Review' for June, 1786. This magazine quoted the first stanza of the Ode, and added only two lines and a half of criticism: 'This exordium — and the other parts of the Ode are not inferior to it — is spirited and harmonious. The lesser poems are elegant and pretty.' A somewhat longer notice appeared in the 'Monthly Review' for July, 1786. 'In these pieces,' said the reviewer, 'we perceive the hand of an able master. The "Ode to Superstition" is written with uncommon boldness of

imagery and strength of diction. The Author has collected some of the most striking historical facts to illustrate the tyranny of the dæmon he addresses, and has
exhibited them with the fire and energy proper to lyric
poetry. The following stanzas are particularly excellent.' The reviewer then quotes the lines:—

III. 1.

'Mona, thy Druid rites awake the dead !
    Rites thy brown oaks would never dare
    Even whisper to the idle air;
Rites that have chained old Ocean on his bed.
    Shivered by thy piercing glance
    Pointless falls the hero's lance.
Thy magic bids the imperial eagle fly,
And blasts the laureate wreath of victory.
Hark, the bard's soul inspires the vocal string !
    At every pause dread Silence hovers o'er,
While murky Night sails round on raven wing,
    Deepening the tempest's howl, the torrent's roar;
Chased by the morn from Snowdon's awful brow
Where late she sat and scowled on the black wave below.

III. 2.

'Lo, steel-clad War his gorgeous standard rears !
    The red-cross squadrons madly rage,
    And mow through infancy and age,
Then kiss the sacred dust and melt in tears.
    Veiling from the eye of day,
    Penance dreams her life away;
In cloistered solitude she sits and sighs,
While from each shrine still small responses rise.
Hear with what heartfelt beat the midnight bell
    Swings its slow summons through the hollow pile;
The weak wan votarist leaves her twilight cell,
    To walk with taper dim the winding aisle;
With choral chantings vainly to aspire
Beyond this nether sphere on Rapture's wing of fire.'

The reviewer adds: 'The picture of night at the end of the first of these stanzas is highly poetical; in the second, the gloom of cloistered solitude is well represented.' 'The Sailor' is described as an elegy 'harmonious and tender,' and the reviewer concludes, — 'the rest of these pieces have the same character of chaste and classical elegance.'

It is probable that a critic of the present day might make a different selection of stanzas for the purpose of showing the chaste and classical elegance of the poem. But these passages met the taste of the time. There may be no conscious imitation in them, but they are evidently suggested and inspired by Gray's 'Bard.' It is needless to say that this criticism gave the young author great satisfaction and encouragement. He afterwards learned that the writer in the 'Monthly Review' was the amiable and accomplished Dr. Enfield, compiler of the 'Speaker,' and author of the 'History of Philosophy.' Dr. Enfield had read the poem aloud to his family. Other criticisms were equally encouraging. His school-friend William Maltby, writing to him soon after the 'Ode' was published, tells Rogers that he has just received a letter from Winchester, with the Poet Laureate's opinion of the 'Ode': 'He thinks it has a great deal of merit indeed, and that the reviewers have not given it more praise than it justly deserves. He wishes much to know the name of the author.' The Laureate at that time was Thomas Warton, whom Rogers never saw, but whose poem 'The Suicide' was one of his favorites. Rogers had made the acquaintance of Mr. and Mrs. Barbauld, who had just established themselves at Hampstead, and a copy of the poem was sent to them through the publisher. Mrs. Barbauld writes on the 4th of September, 1786, expressing the hope that she is not wrong in addressing her thanks for the book to Mr. Rogers. She adds, 'Charmed as she was with the picturesque and

striking beauties of the poems in question, she wished
to have made an earlier acknowledgment of the pleasure
she received, if she had known to whom to make it; and
was delighted when she learned that her thanks were
due to the same gentleman whose conversation had already engaged her esteem. Mr. Barbauld and herself
should be happy to improve an acquaintance which so
many concurring circumstances lead them to value.'
Rogers was then three-and-twenty, and was already becoming known among his contemporaries for those conversational powers for which he was widely celebrated
afterwards.

There are two other short pieces written about this
period which give indications of the true direction of his
muse. The first of these is entitled 'Captivity,' and was
said by Rogers to have been a favorite with Hookham
Frere, who said that it resembled a Greek epigram: —

> ' Caged in old woods, whose reverend echoes wake
> When the hern screams along the distant lake,
> Her little heart oft flutters to be free,
> Oft sighs to turn the unrelenting key.
> In vain! the nurse that rusted relic wears,
> Nor moved by gold — nor to be moved by tears;
> And terraced walls their black reflection throw
> On the green mantled moat that sleeps below.'

The second is dated 1786, and is entitled

Written at Midnight.

> While through the broken pane the tempest sighs,
> And my step falters on the faithless floor,
> Shades of departed joys around me rise,
> With many a face that smiles on me no more;
> With many a voice that thrills of transport gave,
> Now silent as the grass that tufts their grave.

These are early efforts in the direction of his later and more successful style. It may be objected to the stanzas written at midnight, that tempests would not 'sigh' through a broken pane, and that 'falters on the faithless floor' is too alliterative. But the perturbed watcher sees his own agitation reflected in the moaning of the wind, which he thus exaggerates into a tempest; while the silence of the house is equally represented in his mind by the faltering of his step as he treads the floor, the creaking of which betrays his vigil.

THE few years that followed the publication of the 'Ode to Superstition' were the turning-point in Samuel Rogers's history, the period at which all his prospects underwent a change, and life opened out before him with new and boundless opportunities. As the third son he had only the expectation of a share in his father's growing business. He had gone to the bank as a clerk, and in 1784, a few months before he had completed his twenty-first year, he had been taken into partnership. The partnership deeds [1] show that Thomas Rogers the younger and his brother Samuel became members of the firm on the 19th of April, 1784. Mr. Olding, who had been principal clerk for many years, was made a partner in 1771, at a salary, and in June, 1778, his name had been added to that of the firm, and his remuneration fixed at one-sixth of the profits. In 1784, Thomas Rogers, Jr., and Samuel Rogers were introduced on similar terms. The profits were to be divided into sixty-eight parts, of which nineteen were to go to George Welch, nineteen to

[1] The deeds were in possession of the late Mr. Kemp Welch of Woodlands, Parkstone, Dorset, to whom I am indebted for a transcript of their contents.

Thomas Rogers, Sr., and ten each to John Olding, Thomas Rogers, Jr., and Samuel Rogers. The name of the firm was at the same time altered to that of Welch, Rogers, Olding, Rogers, and Rogers, — Samuel Rogers being the youngest partner, and his name the last.

He was already the best known. The publication of the 'Ode,' and the reception it had met with from the reviewers, and especially from persons known or eminent in literature, to whom he had sent it, had already made him the literary member of the household and the firm. He was known to entertain literary ambitions, and his father at least sympathized with them, and did what he could to advance them. There may possibly have been a little feeling among his brothers and sisters, of impatience at his desire for distinction, or at the manner in which it occasionally appeared. This may account for one statement recorded by Mr. Dyce. 'In my youth,' he reports Rogers to have said, 'just as I was beginning to be a little known, I felt much gratified by an invitation to breakfast with Townley, the statue collector, and one night at home I mentioned the invitation. "You have mentioned that before," was the remark,' — in all probability a playful sally of his eldest sister, Martha. He told the story, too, of Sir Thomas Lawrence, who on receiving an unexpected prize from the Society of Arts, went with it into the parlor where his brothers and sisters were sitting, but finding that none of them would take the least notice of it, was so much mortified by their affected indifference that he ran upstairs into his own room and burst into tears. When he narrated this story of Lawrence to Mrs. Siddons, she in her turn exclaimed: 'Alas! after I became celebrated none of my sisters loved me as they did before.' Perhaps this coolness, where it arises, is less the fault of the family than of the individual. Fame is an exacting mistress, and demands an undivided service. Social success can only be pur-

chased at a sacrifice, and the sacrifice sometimes is the
pieties of home. In these early days, however, no such
sacrifice was asked of Samuel Rogers, or was made by
him. He could only have spoken of a temporary misunderstanding, due to his own eagerness; for there are
no signs in the family letters that any but the most
affectionate relations existed between the father and the
children, the brothers and sisters, at Newington Green.

Mr. Thomas Rogers had, at this time, entered into a
new engagement which was very advantageous to his
son Samuel. He had sent his eldest son, Daniel, to Cambridge; but he was fully impressed, as the Unitarians
always were, with the inconvenience of the prevailing
system of subscription to creeds, as a condition of university education. As these barriers shut out their theological students from the national seats of learning, they
endeavored to provide means of academical instruction
for themselves. With this object the Hackney College
was founded, and Thomas Rogers became its chairman.
There are frequent references to this college in his letters. Among the tutors there were the Rev. Gilbert
Wakefield, and afterwards Dr. Kippis, the learned and
accomplished editor of the 'Biographia Britannica.' Dr.
Kippis was in those days a frequent visitor at the house
on Newington Green, and many of Samuel Rogers's early
introductions to literary society came through him. He
had friends among all parties; that hearty Tory, Boswell,
while lamenting that he was a 'Separatist,' speaks of
him as his friend, and in a note to his 'Life of Johnson,'
in which he apologizes for having carelessly joined in a
censure which had been carelessly uttered, bears witness
to 'the manly, candid good temper which marks his character.' Dr. Kippis frequently took Sam Rogers with him
to literary parties; and Rogers himself followed up the
introductions thus given. Dr. Price and Dr. Kippis were
thus, as it were, his literary sponsors. They were both

Fellows of the Royal Society, and had a large acquaintance among scientific men. Dr. Kippis was also a Fellow of the Society of Antiquaries. Samuel Rogers called for Dr. Kippis one evening at Robinson's (the bookseller's), to go with him to a meeting of that society. When Dr. Kippis came down he said, 'Tom Warton is upstairs;' and Rogers always regretted that he had not gone up to see the Laureate. The only letter from Dr. Kippis which has been preserved is dated from Westminster, the 14th November, 1787, and is to inform Rogers that 'Miss Helen Williams desires his company at tea on Monday next. She lives at Mr. Jacques's, the first house in Southampton Row, Bloomsbury, opposite Russell Street.' In 1789 he owed to Dr. Kippis an easy entrance into the best literary society of the Scottish capital.

Miss Helen Maria Williams, to whom Dr. Kippis had introduced him, was at that time living in London with her mother and sisters. She was a year older than Rogers, and had already attained considerable success and reputation as an authoress. At eighteen she had become known as a poetess, and at twenty had published a novel entitled 'Edwin and Eltruda,' written in the sentimental fashion of the time; and two years later she had written a similar tale entitled 'Julie.' Rogers spoke of her in after years as a very fascinating person, though not handsome, and he became at this period of his life very intimate with her. She was a woman of much conversational power, and had the charm of sympathy and the art of bringing people together. She was full of admiration for the French Revolution, and in 1791 the family went to France with the intention of settling at Orleans. They, however, soon removed to Paris, where Rogers afterwards visited her. She was a warm adherent of the Girondist party, and shared their fall and imprisonment, and, but for an oversight, would have been carried with their leaders to the guillotine.

She was liberated after the fall of Robespierre, and became in later years an'admirer of Napoleon. She translated the twenty-nine volumes of Humboldt's 'Personal Narrative' of his Travels into English, and wrote several works on France which were a good deal more read. She continued to live in Paris till her death in 1827. Meanwhile her sister Cecilia had married a Frenchman, — M. Coquerel, — and her son, Athanase Coquerel, became the celebrated Liberal Protestant preacher of the Oratoire, and representative of Paris after the Revolution of 1848. Cecilia's grandson, Athanase Coquerel the younger, was, till his too early death, the genial and gentle, yet high-spirited and vigorous leader of the Liberal section of the French Protestant Church.

Another of Rogers's friends in these early days was Mrs. Barbauld. The Barbaulds had settled at Hampstead in the summer of 1786, where Mr. Barbauld was the minister of a small Presbyterian chapel on Rosslyn Hill. The congregation was one of those which had already become Unitarian in theology. It is now the largest Unitarian congregation in London, and is under the charge of Dr. Sadler, the accomplished editor of Crabb Robinson's 'Diary.' Writing to her brother, Dr. Aikin, Mrs. Barbauld says,[1] 'Hampstead is certainly the pleasantest village about London;' but she adds, 'except Avignon it is the most windy place I was ever in.' She speaks too of 'the long tea-drinking afternoons' which the calls of friends imposed on her, and remarks with pity on the number of young ladies. 'One gentleman in particular,' she says, 'has five tall marriageable daughters, and not a single young man is to be seen in the place.' Rogers had already visited her when she writes to ask him to come again. In the letter conveying the

---

[1] 'Memories of Seventy Years,' p. 63. Edited by Mrs. Herbert Martin.

invitation, which her great-niece, the late Mrs. Le Breton, writer of 'Memories of Seventy Years,' dates in October, 1787, Mrs. Barbauld says:—

'Your visit was so short that we wish to think of anything which may induce you to make us a longer; and as we are to have an Assembly at the Long Room on Monday next, the 22d, which they say will be a pretty good one, I take the liberty to ask whether it will be agreeable to you to be of our party, and in that case we have a bed at your service. I could, I am sure, have my petition supported by a round robin of the young ladies of Hampstead, which would act like a spell and oblige your attendance; but, not being willing to make use of such compulsory methods, I will only say how much pleasure it would give to,

'Sir, your obliged and obedient servant,

'A. Barbauld.'

She adds a postscript to say that their dinner-hour is half after three. This invitation was probably accepted, and Rogers kept the letter all his life. He told Mr. Dyce that he used to go to the Hampstead Assemblies when he was young, that there was much good company there, and that he had sometimes danced four or five minuets in one evening. The acquaintance with Mrs. Barbauld soon became intimate, and the friendship continued unbroken till her death in 1825.

Among the friends whom he made during these visits to Hampstead was Miss Joanna Baillie. Miss Baillie was a year older than Rogers, and died only four years before him, in her ninetieth year. In these early days she was unknown as an authoress, and Mrs. Barbauld says, 'came to Mr. Barbauld's meeting with as innocent a face as if she had not written a line.' Even after the publication of the first volume of her 'Plays of the Passions' in 1799, she kept the secret of her authorship, though the warmest admiration of her writings was expressed in her presence. 'The unsuspected author lay snug,' says Miss Aikin, 'in the asylum of her taciturnity.' Her intercourse with Rogers was constant, and large numbers of her letters have been preserved, but they are of small importance, and are as a rule without a trace of date. Her brother, Dr. Matthew Baillie, the eminent physician, who lived with her, was the successor of Dr. William Hunter in his anatomical professorship.

It was in the year 1788 that the first great change in the prospects of Samuel Rogers took place. His eldest brother, Daniel, was at Cambridge. Daniel Rogers had definitely chosen a career which had left the banking business to his two younger brothers, Thomas and Samuel. He was not adapted for business, and his father did not leave him, in his will, even the estates in Worcestershire and elsewhere which had come to him by inheritance or had been acquired during his life. Sir Egerton Bridges, in his chatty and egotistical autobiography, speaks of Daniel Rogers as one of his fellow-collegians, a very clever man, who had an amazing memory and read much, but he adds, 'I never saw any of his compositions.' Daniel Rogers, in fact, did not become an author. He preferred the life of a country squire. Samuel Sharpe, his nephew, speaks of him as 'a man of delightfully simple mind, a great reader, and throughout life an earnest student of the ancient and Eastern languages.' In the autobiographical sketch I have quoted in his memoir (p. 18) Samuel Sharpe further says of his uncle Daniel: 'He was of delightful guileless simplicity, without a thought that was hidden from you, and was liked by all his acquaintance. His father meant him for the Bar, and had great hopes of his being a distinguished man. But he did not like the law: he preferred classics. He married his cousin, Martha Bowles, and went to live in the coun-

try, much to his father's disappointment. He dwelt first
at Lincoln, where he was intimate with Dr. Paley, but he
afterwards removed to Wassal Grove, near Hagley, where
he had a farm. There I visited him, and spent my time
most delightfully, sometimes rambling in Hagley Park
with his daughters, sometimes walking over the farm
with him and then returning to his study, where he would
pull down book after book to follow a reference or trace
a thought, with an enthusiasm and richness of memory
that was most encouraging to anybody fond of knowledge.
He had at that time been studying Persian.' These tastes
and this disposition in the eldest brother quite sufficiently
account for the abandonment of the bank and all its concerns to the younger brothers.

Thomas Rogers, the second son, was eighteen months
older than Samuel, and appears to have been devoted
to business. He had neither his elder brother's distaste
for it, nor his younger brother's literary ambition. He
would naturally have been his father's successor in the
management of the bank; and his diligence and care
justified the confidence reposed in him. He and Samuel
had become partners at the same time and on the same
terms, and the relations between them were those of
perfect confidence. They dined together every day with
Mr. Olding, who was the resident partner, and lived over
the bank. At holiday seasons they were away from
business by turns; and their father wrote to them with
equal fulness and confidence respecting business and
family matters during his somewhat prolonged absences
from town. There are no references in the family correspondence to any ill-health of Thomas, though such
references are frequent with respect to Samuel ; there
is only the brief record that he died on the 15th of
April, 1788. He was then in his twenty-seventh year.
The last letter from him is dated the 13th of August,
1787, and tells his father of a journey he had just taken

to Ostend and Bruges, and of Sam's setting out for
Launde at the end of that week or the beginning of the
next.   His father replies on the 16th from Derby, and
enters into a good deal of business detail.   Thomas's
death is spoken of by Samuel in the second part of ' The
Pleasures of Memory,' where, after saying that —

> '. . . as the softening hand of Time endears
>   The joys and sorrows of our infant years,' —

so, in a brighter world, —

> '. . . the soul, released from human strife,
>   Smiles at the little cares and ills of life ; '

and after imagining the spirits of the dead descending
to watch the silent slumbers of a friend, he invokes his
brother : —

> ' Oh, thou, with whom my heart was wont to share,
> From Reason's dawn, each pleasure and each care, —
> With whom, alas ! I fondly hoped to know
> The humble walks of happiness below ;
> If thy blest nature now unites above
> An angel's pity with a brother's love,
> Still o'er my life preserve thy mild control,
> Correct my views and elevate my soul ;
> Grant me thy peace and purity of mind,
> Devout yet cheerful, active yet resigned ;
> Grant me, like thee, whose heart knew no disguise,
> Whose blameless wishes never aimed to rise,
> To meet the changes Time and Chance present,
> With modest dignity and calm content.
> When thy last breath, ere Nature sank to rest,
> Thy meek submission to thy God expressed,
> When thy last look, ere thought and feeling fled,
> A mingled gleam of hope and triumph shed,
> What to thy soul its glad assurance gave,
> Its hope in death, its triumph o'er the grave ?
> The sweet remembrance of unblemished youth,
> The still inspiring voice of Innocence and Truth ! '

Nothing can be added to this admirable description of Thomas Rogers's character; and no better account can be given of the relations between the two brothers, or of the death of Thomas.

Henry Rogers, the youngest son, was at this time in his fourteenth year and was receiving his education at the Hackney College. Samuel was consequently left alone with his father in the bank. He had already shown much capacity for business, and the larger responsibility which now fell upon him found him fully prepared by character, training, and experience to meet it. 'He became,' says Mr. Sharpe, 'the friend and adviser upon whom the father relied for help in all matters of business.' At the end of the year in which Thomas died, his father was again out of health, and was advised to take the Bath waters. Sam was now his chief correspondent at home, and the letters which passed from one to the other show the complete confidence which existed between father and son. In one of the letters is an interesting sketch of the company in a boarding-house where Mr. Rogers and his servant Thomas were taking their meals.

'I like my lodging-home exceedingly, and Mrs. Cottle is very kind and obliging to me. There is only one other lodger in the house, — Sir Gervase Clifton, who has the drawing-room floor; I have the dining floor. The worst of it is, Mrs. Cottle has declined keeping a boarding table, but very strongly recommended me to a neighbor three doors from her, and where Thomas and I board. The company is strangely made up indeed, and consists of Sir Gervase, a perfect Nimrod and a very fine specimen of a country knight or squire; M. de Linne, a French gentleman, young, lively, and sensible, who talks English tolerably well, and has been two years amusing himself in England; Mr. Tann, a young German, who speaks all the European languages, is a great traveller, who laughs, talks loud, and is very comical; Major Bennet, in the East India Service, who was very near being taken by Tippoo with General Matthews, but escaped captivity and perhaps death by being left sick in quarters a few days before, — the Major is very good-natured, quiet and civil, but very gouty, and I am afraid not very rich, having no servant with him; a Mr. Law-ley, an old gentleman from Warwickshire, a relative of the county member, one of the most wretched beings I ever saw. He seems perfectly well, but says that such is the state of his nerves that nobody can have any conception of the miserable manner in which he passes his days and nights; he has long been in this way, always complaining but never pitied. The last of our males I shall mention is a very well-behaved young Irishman, who has lately taken orders and serves as our chaplain.'

The account of the women at table is defective, being torn by the seal. Another letter to Sam, dated Tuesday, 6th January, 1789, is worth quoting, as showing what the winter journey from Bath to London was nearly a hundred years ago : —

'The severity of the weather has compelled me to give up all thoughts of riding any part of the way to town, and I have just taken a place in a two-day coach that leaves Bath to-morrow morning at eight o'clock. It stops all night at Newbury, and gets to Piccadilly the next day about four o'clock. You will be so good, there-fore, as to order William to be at the White Horse Cellar, or coffee-house, Piccadilly, at four o'clock on Thursday afternoon with the coach. But as the cold will probably continue to be very intense, he had better put up the horses as near to the White Horse as he can, and be in waiting at the White Horse till the coach comes in.

Before I·took my place I learned that three places were
before taken, so that I hope we shall keep each other
from freezing.'

In the summer of this year Samuel Rogers made a
journey to the north of England and Scotland, of which
he has left some very interesting records in the shape of
letters and diaries. He had just entered his twenty-
seventh year, and among literary people was already
beginning to be known as the author of a volume of
poems, and as a young man of much conversational
power. The journey was made on horseback, with a
servant on a second horse. The route was by way of
Stamford to York, Leeds, and Harrogate, through Settle
and Ingleton to Lancaster, thence by Rydal, Keswick,
and Penrith to Carlisle, thence by Hawick, Selkirk, and
Melrose to Edinburgh; from Edinburgh to Stirling,
thence to Crieff and Inverary, back to Glasgow, and
returning by Dumfries, Carlisle, Appleby, across Yorkshire, and through Mansfield, Nottingham, Leicester, and
Northampton to London. The tour extended from about
Midsummer Day to the end of the first week in August.
Two letters to his sister Sarah will appropriately introduce the Diary, which more fully records his conversations and observations.

'KESWICK, July 8 [1789].

'DEAR SARAH, — I have this moment received Mrs.
Mitchell's kind letter, and desire my best thanks to her
for it. I have also to thank you for yours which I received at Lancaster. I wrote thence to Mrs. W., and
hope she has heard from me before this. On Friday
morning I left Lancaster, and arrived that evening at
Lowwood, a very pleasant lone house on the banks of
Windermere. The next morning I sailed on the water,
and had a few thunder-showers, but enjoyed the day

exceedingly. In the evening saw some waterfalls near
Ambleside, and returned to Lowwood, where the moon
played deliciously on the water. On Sunday I went to
church at Grasmere on my way to Keswick, and afterwards proceeded towards that place, but was soon overtaken by a heavy rain and obliged to shelter in the Vale
of St. John. There I stayed till nine at night, when,
though the rain did not abate, I was obliged to go forward, and had a very unpleasant ride through one of
the most romantic tracts of country in Cumberland.
The next morning proved very fine, and I rode round
the lake of Derwentwater, saw Lodore waterfall, and the
Grange and Straits of Borrowdale. In the evening I
walked in Crow Park, a favorite spot of Gray's. The
next morning proving very clear I was induced to mount
Skiddaw, in company with a young lady from Penrith
(very handsome and very musical), Mr. Ewer, a first
cousin of Mr. Ewer of Clapham, and Dr. Coyte, a physician at Ipswich who has left off practice, a great
botanist and a very agreeable man. We rode on horseback to the summit, from whence we had a very fine view
of Scotland, over Solway Firth, with the Isle of Man.
Many of the lakes and mountains of Cumberland composed the foreground. When we descended, we dined at
a charming house that looks directly up Bassenthwaite
Lake, and returned along one of its sides to Keswick.
We had a very rainy evening. This morning I rode with
the guide up the vales of Buttermere, Lorton, and New-
lands, — places that my father is well acquainted with
most probably, — and in the evening went out on the lake
of Keswick. In returning from my ride about six o'clock
I was wet through; but this was the second time only
that I have been obliged to change everything. I often
change my stockings twice a day; but in general I consider myself as tolerably fortunate in the weather,
though confinement at an inn to a single man is rather

dull. From the rain I derive some advantages. The
waterfalls are improved by it, and it affords me a decent
excuse for calling at the farm-houses and cottages on the
road, where I always find the heartiest welcome, and am
delighted with the simplicity and native politeness of
the inhabitants.   To-morrow I bid adieu to Keswick, and
after spending a day or two at Ulleswater shall proceed
to Carlisle and Edinburgh. Any letter written to me
on or before Wednesday next may be directed to me
at Edinburgh. I hope Henry has recovered his spirits
before this ; indeed I don't doubt it. Pray give my kind
love and duty to my father and [remember me] affectionately to Mrs. M. and Milly. Tell[1] . . . I won't trouble
her to write to me. I will . . . her to read such letters
as I write. [My ex]cuse for them is that they are generally [hurried] over when I am tired and heavy and impatient. Adieu, dear Sarah ; believe me to [remain],

'Your affectionate friend and [brother],

'SAMUEL ROGERS.

'P. S. . I wrote to Patty from Lancaster, and to . . .
from Keswick. I like my servant exceedingly ; he takes
great care of my horses, which are both well. I have
got rid of my cold. I have just read in the papers of the
duel between Colonel Lenox and Mr. Swift. I am sorry
to find the result of it, as Mr. Swift is a very agreeable,
sensible man. You may remember my mentioning that
I drank tea with him last time at Mrs. Williams's house.
With respect to Dr. Kippis, if he has not sent the letters
he promised me, there would, I think, be no impropriety
in just sending to inform him that you were sending to
me at Edinburgh, and to ask him if he has any letter or
commission to convey thither, as I had mentioned my
expectation of something of the kind. Indeed, he told
me that he should at the same time contrive to transact

---

[1] Parts are obliterated by being torn in opening the seal.

some real business with each of the gentlemen he wrote
to. But I would not have it done if thought in the least
improper, though I know Dr. Kippis is the last man in
the world to take the least umbrage at it.

'Miss SARAH ROGERS,
  'Newington Green, Middlesex.'

Another letter gives an account of his visit to Edinburgh : —

'STIRLING, July 21, 1789.

'MY DEAR SARAH, — I received your kind letter on
Friday at Edinburgh, which gave me great pleasure, as
it assured me that you were all well. In consequence of
the letters my father was so kind as to enclose to me my
time passed so pleasantly there that I should have left it
with regret, if the Highlands had not promised me ample
amends. Saturday morning proving rainy, I could not
resist the temptation of staying till Sunday, and I heard
Dr. Robertson in the morning, and Dr. Blair in the
afternoon. They are neither of them orators, but Dr.
Robertson has a serious, unaffected manner which pleased
me very much. Dr. Blair is very pompous in his delivery,
and all the great and fashionable attend at his church.
He gave us a sermon on censoriousness, which I understand is soon to be published, with some others, in a third
volume. I have dined twice at Mr. Adam Smith's, who
is a very friendly, agreeable man, and I should have
dined and supped with him almost every day if I had
accepted all his invitations. He took me to a club, which
is very select, and consists of all the first men in Edinburgh. At his house I met Mr. Mackenzie, author of
"The Man of Feeling," etc., who invited me very politely,
but I had the resolution to refuse. Dr. Robertson called
upon me twice, when I had the ill luck to be out; but I
saw him twice at his own house, and I shall always think
of Edinburgh with gratitude, for the many instances of

attention and civility I met with there; indeed, if I were to judge from my own experience, I should think that the inhabitants (at least the most eminent of them) devoted their whole time to the entertainment of strangers.   Dr. Robertson's deafness affects his spirits very much; but with the assistance of a trumpet he can converse with tolerable ease to himself and other people, and is very entertaining.

'I have been very much struck with the situation of Hopton House and Stirling Castle.   I admire the last even more than Edinburgh Castle, when viewed from a distance.   From hence I shall go on by Inverary to Glasgow, which I shall reach on Saturday, and then leave my horses and proceed directly home, where I hope to arrive on Friday or Saturday following.   I have exceeded my time, and begin to be tired of rambling; but I shall be very sorry if I occasion my father to delay his journey with any inconvenience to himself.   Nothing but his kind assurances to the contrary would have induced me to extend my time as I have done.   I beg my love and duty to him, and desire to be kindly remembered to Mrs. M. and Mrs. W., Martha and Maria; and remain, dear Sarah,

'Your sincere friend and affectionate brother,

'SAMUEL ROGERS.

'P. S.   I am very well, and my horse seems entirely recovered from his lameness.

'Miss SARAH ROGERS,
'Newington Green, Middlesex.'

During his stay at Edinburgh, Rogers kept a .short journal of his visits.   The letters he had taken from Dr. Price, and those which his father had forwarded to him from Dr. Kippis, opened to him the doors of Edinburgh society, — then almost in its most brilliant period.   His acquaintance with the Piozzis began at the same time.

They were staying in the same hotel, and the landlord
having told them who Rogers was, and that Dr. Robertson,
Mr. Adam Smith, and Mr. H. Mackenzie had called
on him, Mr. and Mrs. Piozzi called and introduced themselves.   Rogers always said that one of the most memorable days in his life was the Sunday in Edinburgh, on
which he had breakfast with Dr. Robertson and heard him
preach in the morning, heard Dr. Blair in the afternoon,
took coffee with the Piozzis, and then supped with Adam
Smith in the evening.   The following is his journal : —

'*Edinburgh, Wednesday, July* 15, 1789. — Called on
Dr. Robertson.   In the parlor hung his portrait by Sir
Joshua Reynolds.   He soon entered, with his trumpet
in his hand.   His dress was remarkably neat, and his
countenance very open and pleasing.   Compared him with
the picture, but could not trace a very striking resem-
blance.   His eye has lost much of its fire, and age has
given a stoop to his figure.   The conversation began on
the English Universities, and the absurdity of proposing a
test to a poor boy of seventeen.   He said that Edinburgh
contained little worth notice, but that its situation was
very romantic ; that Gilpin had not done justice to the
Highlands ; he saw everything with the eye of a painter,
but many a scene gives pleasure which will not make a
good picture.   Richmond Hill is peculiarly striking to a
Scotchman for its richness and amenity, but is by no
means a fit subject for the artist.   Advised me to make
the home tour, but to revērse Mr. Gilpin's route, — to begin with Inverary and return by Dunkeld.   Said Mr. Gray
devoted a month to the lakes; that his cicerone, Hodg-
kins, who was a sensible fellow, described him as difficult
to be pleased, and peevish from ill-health ; that he could
not ride on horseback, and would not go on the water.
'*July* 16. — Called on Adam Smith, who was sitting
at breakfast with a plate of strawberries on the table.

Fruit, he said, was his favorite diet at this season.
Strawberries were a northern fruit. In the Orkneys and
in Sweden they were to perfection. Said that Edinburgh deserved little notice; that the old town had
given Scotland a bad name; that he was anxious to
move into the new town, and had set his heart on St.
George's Square; that Edinburgh was entirely supported
by the three Courts, — the Exchequer, the Excise, and
the Judiciary Courts; that Loch Lomond was the finest
lake in Great Britain, — the islands were very beautiful,
and formed a very striking contrast to the shores; that
the soil of Scotland was excellent, but that its harvests,
from the severity of the climate, were too often overtaken by winter; that the Scotch on the borders were
to this day in extreme poverty; and that when he first
left Scotland, he was on horseback, and was struck with
the transition as he approached Carlisle; that our late
refusal of corn to France must excite indignation and
contempt, — the quantity required was so trifling that
it would not support Edinburgh for a day. Said that
in Paris as well as in Edinburgh the houses were piled
one upon another. Spoke contemptuously of Sir John
Sinclair, but said that he never knew a man who was in
earnest and who did not do something at last. Said he
did not know Mrs. Piozzi, and believed her to be spoiled
by keeping company with odd people.

'*July* 19. — Called at two, when all the bells of the
kirk were ringing, to take leave of Adam Smith. His
chair was waiting to take him an airing. He met me at
the door. Asked me how I liked the Club. Had before
mentioned Bogle as very clever, and expressed pleasure
at the thought of his being there. He now said: "*That*
Bogle, I was sorry he talked so much, he spoiled the
evening." He seemed to apologize for him. Invited
me to supper and to dinner next day, as he had asked
Mackenzie to meet me. Who could refuse?

'Heard Dr. Robertson in the morning. An old church; sweet singing. His manner striking, but not graceful; his voice not unpleasing. He spoke and looked like a good man. The service began with a psalm, then a prayer, then a psalm, then a commentary on the first chapter of the Second Epistle to the Thessalonians, which lasted twenty-five minutes; then a short prayer, then the sermon, twenty-five minutes long. Text from Psalms, "Praise ye the Lord." The second part of a discourse on "Thanksgiving," then a psalm, and then a prayer. He seemed to direct himself particularly to us, and after church, when we joined him, he inquired my route, and said that if I kept anything of a journal, at night I should not find it dull. Reminded me of Lord Rosebery's park. "All good things attend you, sir." We parted.

'Heard Dr. Blair in the afternoon, but not distinctly. A hoarse, unpleasant voice. A very neat, elegant sermon on "Censoriousness," in which was a fine parallel between that vice and charity. Charity covereth a multitude of sins, censoriousness makes it its business to divulge them. Afterwards bowed to the corporation in the gallery on the right. Walked home with the Piozzis. Drank coffee with them and heard P. perform some of his music on the harpsichord.

'Repaired at nine to Mr. A. Smith's: present, all the company of Friday except Bogle and Macaulay. Mr. Playfair, a mathematician, and Mr. Muir from Göttingen were there. Talked of Junius. Adam Smith suspected "single speech" Hamilton to be the author. He was told by Gibbon that when Hamilton one day paid a visit at the Duke of Richmond's in Sussex, he told him that there was a devilish keen letter from Junius in the "Public Advertiser" of that day, and mentioned some of the passages. The duke was anxious to see it; but when the paper came there was an apology in it for its not appearing. It was a letter to the Duke of Richmond, and the last that appeared. As long as they were ascribed to Lord Lansdowne, Burke, Germaine, etc., they went on; but as soon as they were said to be Hamilton's they were dropped. Adam Smith said Turgot was an honest, well-meaning man, but unacquainted with the world and human nature; that it was his maxim (he mentioned it to Mr. Hume but never to Smith) that whatever is right may be done. He said that Nicholas Herbert, uncle to Lord Porchester, had read the list of the Eton boys and repeated them four years afterwards to Lord Porchester. He knew him well. He (A. Smith) had been in Voltaire's company five or six times. Voltaire had a great aversion to the States, and was rather attached to the king. [Said] that his old friend the Duke of Richelieu was a singular character, and that when he slipped down at Versailles a few years before his death, said it was the first *faux pas* he had ever made at Court. Dr. Smith said he had been bastilled more than once. Dr. Black said that when in Germany he [Duke of Richelieu] borrowed plate of the goldsmiths and gentlemen there, and never returned it. . . . Mrs. Piozzi said Pennant was her cousin. She should get me to introduce her to Mrs. Barbauld.

'*July* 20. — Heard a swindler tried in the Parliament House. Dined at Mr. Adam Smith's with Mr. Mackenzie, Mr. Muir, and Mr. McGowan. Mackenzie answered P.'s description, — of very soft and pleasing manners. Admired Mrs. Smith's sonnets and Mrs. Hunter's. Adam Smith said Blair was too much puffed off; was surprised at Johnson's reputation. Mackenzie inquired after Hannah More and admired her "Percy;" spoke slightly of Merry and [of] Blair's sermon on Sunday; said there were few in the Highlands who pretended to second sight; that there was a gentleman who pretended it to keep up authority and order there; that on going to see John O'Gaunt's house he was detained by rain in a cottage from nine to one, and heard some wonderful stories that would have lasted till now; mentioned an epigram on Mr. Smith's sleeping at the Royal Society; spoke well of "Emmeline" and of the "Sonnet on Shipboard" in it. Dr. Hutton drank tea with us, and we afterwards went to the Royal Society. Only seven persons there. Dr. Anderson read an essay on Debtors and the revision of the laws that respect them, written by himself, very long and dull. Mr. Commissioner Smith fell asleep. Mackenzie touched my elbow and smiled; afterwards said he should be glad to see me; sent him my book. Went afterwards to the play "Hippolita" and the "Romp." Sat in the box over the stage, shut in, in the Italian style, with Mr. and Mrs. Piozzi, Miss Thrale, Mr. Bruce, and a very handsome woman and her brother. Very lively and pleasant. Mrs. Jordan directed herself to the box.

'*July* 21. — Left Edinburgh at six. Rode through Lord Rosebery's park to Queensferry along the Forth, and there breakfasted. Walked in Lord Hopton's grounds, and was full of admiration. Had a delightful ride along the Forth to Falkirk; then saw the Carron works, five furnaces, each with four cylinders. A thousand men employed there. Saw the forges. Proceeded to Stirling; saw a beautiful valley on the right, bounded by the Athol hill; saw Falkirk moor, and Torwood, where Wallace and his men concealed themselves. Much struck with the first view of Stirling. The grandest and prettiest thing in the world.

'*July* 22. — Set out on a military road. The scene gradually grew wilder till we came to Dunblane, in a rich and pleasant valley. Saw the church, a monument of Knox's vengeance. It was built by one of the Davids. Rode through a wild country to Greenloaning, a mile and a half beyond which, on the right, is the finest Roman station in England, according to Dr. Robertson. It is encompassed with dykes and ramparts four deep, and contains three or four acres of ground. Just beyond Dunblane the field of battle in the year '15 was pointed out to me on a moor to the right. Arrived at Crieff, in a cultivated vale. There a girl sang me an Erse song over the washing-tub. She said it was made by a young man in praise of his sweetheart, but would not explain it. The notes were simple and melancholy, but without much harmony or sweetness. It lasted ten minutes, and was sung very fast. Left Crieff, and soon entered a deep valley that opened and closed as I advanced and receded. Very grand and awful. Left the Inverness Road at the tenth milestone, and soon passed along a considerable loch and several little villages among trees. Saw a woman extracting a thorn from the foot of an old Highlander, and a boy in his plaid watching sheep. Spoke to two who could not speak English. Observed the cottages with the smoke in them. Ascended a steep hill and soon came to a beautiful view. Taymouth Castle and park, through which the Tay ran, lay at my feet, and refreshed my aching eyes with the softest verdure. Behind rose hanging woods to a great height, and to the left opened Loch Tay in the bosom of the mountains, with the village church of Kenmore at the head of it. Dined on a trout. The village very fond of dancing. Waited on at dinner by a teacher of the art. Saw the castle and park. A walk on the banks of the Tay not equal to its fame. Had a sweet evening walk by the lake. Saw the fallow deer in the park.

'*July* 23. — Rode along the left bank of the lake. Saw the Hermitage and Fall, which rather disappointed me. The views down the lake very fine, particularly from the fifth stone. Gilpin rode on the other side, before this road was made. The lake had a line of surf that slanted

into the middle for a mile; imagined it to arise from a
hidden reef of rock. Several little clusters of cottages
on its banks.. Saw the inside of one. It was divided
into three apartments. The door opened into the first,
in which was a little lean cow. In the middle room was
the fire, over which was a hole in the roof, and on the
other side was the bedchamber. Came to Killin, through
which runs a rocky torrent into the lake. On the bank
of this were several women and girls dipping their
clothes into the river, and spreading them out on the
green margin, like kings' daughters of old. Saw a girl
stamping in a tub to wash. In the river is an island, —
the laird of McNab's burying-place. Saw a little girl of
four years old footing it in imitation of a reel. Breakfasted at Killin. The Reel Master mentioned before
comes here for two months in the year, and opens a
school for dancing. On weddings and holidays fifty are
sometimes collected to dance. Set off through rude,
rocky, and romantic country, with the river gliding on
my left hand; it changes its character several times.
Passed several hills with snow in the hollows on their
summits. From the hill before the inn at Killin saw
for miles up the glen Dr. Robertson mentioned. It is
romantic and woody, with a river running up it. It
extends ten miles; I saw about five of it. Called, on
my way to Tyndrum, at a cottage, and saw an old woman
at her spinning-wheel who answered me in Erse. Saw
several parties on their travels on foot, and a boy who
kept up with us for some time. A Highlander thinks
no more of a twenty-mile stage than of a walk for an
appetite before breakfast. Found afterwards from a
traveller that the old woman I called on was a widow,
and kept house for her son, who was a shepherd. She
said she supposed I had no Erse. Dined at Tyndrum on
trout, wild venison, and goat's cheese. At Killin saw a
hole said to be Fingal's grave. The laird had dug it up

to seek for the bones, but in vain. It is a fine situation for the grave of a hero, — at the foot of a mountain and in full view of a lake. At Tyndrum heard a Highlander whistle "The Ploughboy," produced but lately in the comic opera of "The Farmer." Have been waited upon everywhere but here by waiters in philibegs and maids without stockings.

'At eight left Tyndrum, looked into a hut and entered the door, where there was a room full of smoke and darkness. For some time could distinguish nothing, till I heard a voice that seemed to encourage me to come forward. Then I saw two women over a fire, and a man in bed. The man sat up, and one of the women — old, but of a pleasant countenance — spoke some Erse, and then, stepping out to a wooden box on the floor, took out a bowl of ewe's milk, and saying in broken confused sounds, "Here's health to you, sir," tasted and gave it to me. I tasted it, and she appeared dissatisfied, and wanted me to drink more. She then came out and offered it to the servant, saying, "Will you not drink some malk?" Her honest and hearty welcome affected me. I offered her a trifle, but she drew back her hand and at first refused to take it. Rode through a valley shut in with black mountains, and crossed, every half a mile, above ten torrents or channels of torrents. Passed only two villages. Arrived at Dalmally, a neat house, but they could give me no bread. After supper three young women came in, and each taking the corner of a napkin, sang their wild melody above half an hour, moving the napkin backwards and forwards. The verses were short and simple, and ended in a burden that was sung by two; the song by the other. Sang a song by a dairymaid to her herd in praise of her sweetheart; a song by a man at sea to his sweetheart; a song by a lovelorn maid. More melody here than at Crieff, but very melancholy and rude. They looked and sang sometimes like the weird sisters.

In my way from Killin met a man who seemed proud of
showing off a little English. Asked me if I came from
England and was going to Icolmkill, a place he said many
went to. I answered I was not. He said "Just so!" a
very common answer, as is "Indeed it is!"

'*July* 24.—Had a cold and dreary ride along Loch
Awe to Inverary, the glory of Scotland. Loch Fyne, an
arm of the sea above sixty miles in length, here forms a
bay, which, from the bold projection of the mountains
that rise abruptly round, has the appearance of a lake of
enchanting beauty. The flowing lines of the mountain
summits, and the frequent and natural curves formed in
the shore by their projection, have a fine effect. Add to
this the herring fishery, which impresses a busy character on the scene, with other vessels of greater size that
are continually sailing in the offing or anchored near the
bank. On a green lawn [surrounded] by hanging woods
the chieftains of the clan of the Campbells had fixed
their castle, and nearly on the site of that the Duke of
Argyll, their descendant, has erected an elegant house of
the same form, with turrets and battlements. He seems
possessed of far better taste than the rest of the Scotch
nobility, and has not attempted any little decorations,
thinking very properly that they would degrade the
dignity of the scene. In the house are pictures of the
present and the last Dukes of Hamilton, several Dukes
of Argyll, Lady Augusta, Lady Charlotte, the Marquis
and his brother, and a most bewitching portrait of the
Duchess of Argyll taken when she was Duchess of
Hamilton.

' Left Inverary with a sigh, the sun shining mildly on
as sweet a scene as it almost ever visited. Rode round
the bay, commanding beautiful views, particularly up
the loch, towards the sea, a fine vista of mountains, up
which a sail was coming. Drank tea at Cairndow, and
proceeded through Kinglas vale, smooth to the summits,

sprinkled with sheep, but dark from the clouds that formed above it. A beautiful retrospect towards Inverary, where the sun seemed smiling sweetly; before me clouds and darkness and black mountains. Took many a parting look.

'Entered Glen Croe: rude and romantic even beyond the pass through which I entered the Highlands. Enormous fragments lay on each side. Saw on the top between the two vales "Rest and be thankful," which Johnson and Gilpin describe. Gilpin is wrong in his account of the vales, — Kinglas is smooth and Glen Croe rough. Arrived at New Arrochar, a good inn, on the banks of Loch Long, where the herring-boats were busy. A sweet perspective down the loch. Saw a cormorant flying over it.

'*July* 25. — Had a very fine ride along Loch Lomond to Luss, the sun shining and the air calm. The reflection in the water not so vivid as in Cumberland. Walked in the churchyard at Luss. The minister's house a neat white house in a quiet secluded situation. His name was James Stewart, a very intelligent man, who furnished Pennant with natural history and Erse names of birds, etc. He made the tour of the northern lakes with Lord Mountmorres last summer. Was rowed by a boy and girl to Inchtavannach, and from the summit had a fine geographical view of the southern end of the lake, full of islands. Saw that where the osprey eagle builds, very small and tufted with trees. Sir James Colquhoun won't suffer the nest to be ever molested.

'Returned through a heavy rain. Dined and rode along the lake till I came to an obelisk with a Latin inscription to the memory of Dr. Smollett. On the left, a little removed from the road, is a single stone house in which he was born. Rode on to Dumbarton, where I saw the castle, and arrived at Glasgow in the evening. The steps in Dumbarton Castle are only 183, and not so many as Gilpin states them. J. Stewart at Luss preaches in English in the morning and in Erse in the afternoon. He translated the New Testament into Erse, and is now engaged on the Old. He has finished the Books of Moses. Saw only one eagle on Loch Lomond. The gardener at Inverary said he had seen twelve or fourteen sail over the week before in company. Saw the garden there, but found it to be only a kitchen garden. In it was a small greenhouse, erected for Lady Augusta, who is particularly fond of plants. The Duke is quite reconciled to the match. Inverary, Fort William, and Port Glasgow are the three rainiest places in Scotland.

'*July* 26. — Called in the morning on Mrs. Piozzi at the "Saracen's Head." She dined with Dr. Blair, who said that the Duke of Argyll, when in Scotland, was always pleased to hear that it rained in the south, and when somebody called the rain at Inverary a shower, another less polite said, "Then it is an everlasting shower." Walked round the town with Piozzi, stepped into the "Hart Inn" and saw some rooms. Afterwards dined with them, and then walked in the public walks. Mrs. Piozzi expressed great anxiety to see the reviews. Said she should look carefully into them now. Said Cadell had no reason to complain of his bargains with her, for he had always been sharp enough. Spoke rather slightly of Parsons, but highly of Merry and Greathed. Found Miss Cecilia Thrale was not more than twelve; appeared fifteen. Spoke of Carpenter coming 1,100 miles in nine days; that he slept an hour at Paris, another at Lyons, another at Florence; regretted she did not mention it in her books.

'*July* 27. — Called, and walked to the college and the old church with them; the first very handsome, the last bad. She talked much of Dr. Johnson. At three set off in the mail to Moffat, and arrived there through a wild country at half-past eleven. Saw Northern

Lights. Here are wells similar to but not so strong as
Harrogate.

'*July* 28. — Proceeded in a post-chaise with an English
gentleman to Dumfries, and there met my horses. The
country but little varied. Saw Linclouden College at a
distance. Dined and proceeded in a return chaise to
Annan along the frith, with distant views of Skiddaw,
and then to Gretna Green, through Solway Moss. This
is a pretty village in grove of trees. Here are two inns.
Slept at the wrong one. The right house is a small
house with some arms for the sign, and stands in Spring-
field, not Gretna Green. Saw the parson at the door, —
a tall, sottish, good-looking fellow. His name is Parsley,
or Parsfield, and he is a farmer. The man who used to
marry them filled peat and dung carts; his name was
James Long and his father's Peter. He signed his
name "James Long, Peter's son." Lord Westmoreland
was married at a small ale-house by the river between
Gretna and Annan, where a new bridge is now building.
They slept there afterwards. Mr. Henderson, a good-
natured old man, Lord Stormont's factor, left his bed
for them. Everybody goes back to Carlisle immediately
after the ceremony. An officer was obliged to pawn his
watch there in the last spring, not having £30, the
money exacted for it. The innkeeper from Carlisle
went with him to get it cheaply done, but he shared
with the parson. It was not the landlord of the
" Bush."

'*July* 29. — Crossed the sands in a boat, and my horse
was led over. Breakfasted again at Carlisle, and was
once more welcomed there with rain. Had a pleasant
ride from thence to Penrith. Piozzi said that Miss C.
Thrale was a good-tempered girl and companion to her
mother, "for the other daughters, you know — " Here
he stopped and shrugged his shoulders. She calls him
papa. Mrs. Piozzi talked of marriage, and said that it

was necessary to wait some time in a parish ; then turning
to Piozzi said, "You know, my dear, we waited twenty-
six days in Bath." Miss Thrale looks unhappy, but
brightens up sometimes. Mrs. Piozzi calls Piozzi her
master. Sadly out of sorts with the Scotch for sending
her to Carron; said one might as well go to one's own
brewery and then to see a steam-engine. Said, "You
know why the Scotch wish to send me to the Highlands?" Piozzi hinted it afterwards and said they
wanted her to contradict Dr. Johnson. Had a most
delicious ride to Appleby, a richly wooded valley running
on each side, bounded by mountains. Saw Countess
Pillar, a small octagon with her arms colored in front, a
sundial on each side, and the inscription behind. The
stone table is within a foot from the ground, and about
three yards from the pillar. It stands on a little hill
just beyond Brougham Castle, about two miles from
Penrith and opposite a milestone. Appleby is a small
mean town in a delightful valley, and consists chiefly of
one street running up the hill to the castle, the tower of
which forms a fine termination. In the castle hall are
three pictures of the countess, — when a child; when
married, with her husband, Lord Dorset, beside her;
and when married to Pembroke, a single whole length.
In a small room adjoining are four more pictures of her,
— when a child, when a young woman, in her first widow-
hood, and in her second. From all these she appears
very handsome. In the picture of Lord Dorset and herself are two children, one of whom alone survived her,
and upon it is written a very minute history of each.
In a room on the other side of the hall a small door is
opened, and in a closet appears the complete armor of
her father, Lord Clifford, richly gilt, his helmet, cuirass,
and saddle, with the stirrups lying at his foot. A curious
lock on his breast seems to keep it together. His gaunt-
lets are on. In the churchyard is a pretty epitaph on an

officer's wife who accompanied her husband through most parts of America, — "Who knew her living must lament her dead." Wandered till dusk.

'*July* 30. — Had a long but not very unpleasant ride over the mountains of Brough and Stainmore, having several distant views. Breakfasted at Bowes, and afterwards came to the spot whence James I. took his first view of England; then entered Leeming Lane, which runs in a direct line for some miles between shady hedge-rows, with rich enclosures on each side, till we came to a large heath whence we had a beautiful view of Richmond and its environs on the right and the county of Durham on the left. Dined at Catterick Bridge, and proceeded in the mail through a flat but rich country to Boroughbridge.

'*July* 31. — Had a pleasant ride in a return chaise for nine miles by Allerton, just purchased by Col. Thornton of the Duke of York. The house is very large, but not elegant. We had one view of it. Rode two miles on the left to the village of Cowthorp. The celebrated oak stands in a farmyard near the church. One half of it is bare of vegetation and shoots up its naked branches in a very fantastic manner; the other half is not so high, and is full of leaves. The cavity within is very spacious and lofty, about fifteen yards in circumference. In the oak-tree stands an immense block, detached from the tree, once the heart of it. Took away a relic. Saw there a gentleman from Harrogate, in the army, who measured it. Rode through Wetherby, a small town, and was confined for shelter under a tree for four hours with two sawyers, young men. Afterwards came on in a return chaise to Ferrybridge over a country I had seen between York and Leeds.

'*August* 1. — Rode through a flat but rich country to Doncaster. The church is of great antiquity, and its noble tower finely terminates almost every avenue to the town. Inquired here of Captain Stoven, my companion in the mail, and found that his father is just dead. Rode through a woody and pleasant tract of ground to Sandbeck Park (Earl of Scarborough's) through which I passed, having a full view of the house, an elegant stone structure, and proceeded to Roche Abbey, the last beautiful scene I shall visit. It stands in the centre of three valleys. One is wide, floated with a lake and finally terminated by Laughton spire. The others are close and woody, and meet each other in the same direction, being enlivened by a small river that forms frequent cascades. One of these last is finely hung round with high red rocks that are very beautiful, and are fringed with wood. But a small part of the abbey remains, and it is perfectly regular, being the east end. The parts are two and are detached, but are finely connected with trees. Behind is a building that was probably the abbot's apartment. This ruin afforded much employment to my glass. I spent an hour and a half there and left it with great regret. Had a charming ride through many rural scenes to Worksop. The moon shone and amused me with its shiftings.

'*August* 2. — Rode to Worksop Manor and Welbeck Park (Dukes of Norfolk and Portland) — neither of them very beautiful, the first the best. Breakfasted at Mansfield, a small, well-built town, and heard Mr. Catloe at Meeting, an ingenious young man and a pleasant speaker. The Unwins were there, and it was a funeral sermon for Mrs. Heywood of Nottingham, their relation. The road to Nottingham lies through Nottingham Forest, in a deep sand, with but few trees. Here and there we have a distant catch of the country on each side, the ground at Red Hill making rather a pleasant dip into the village of that name, and Nottingham in its first appearance is grand. The moon was up. A hot day.

'*August* 3. — Had a pleasant view from the castle, and set off from thence in the Leeds mail to Loughborough, Leicester, Northampton, and Newport Pagnel, — the greater part of the way in the guard's seat. From thence proceeded on the 4th in post-chaises to town with a Manchester gentleman.'

This Scottish journey, to which Rogers looked back with interest all his life, left one source of regret behind it. It enabled him to be introduced to some of the most eminent persons in the Scottish capital ; but he missed the most interesting of all in failing to visit Burns. The fame of the great peasant poet of Scotland had not then fully reached the ears of literary men in the south, though Burns himself had in August, 1787, addressed to Dr. Moore that striking biographical letter which is still the best extant account of his early days. Burns had visited Edinburgh in the autumn of 1786, where his coming had been prepared for by Henry Mackenzie in a paper in 'The Lounger,'— a short-lived literary journal of which Mackenzie was the editor. Burns had again visited the capital in the winter of 1787–88, when he had published the first Edinburgh edition of his poems. He was more fortunate than some other eminent writers, for he had received from his bookseller, Creech, nearly five hundred pounds, and had taken a farm at Ellisland, on the banks of the Nith, six miles above Dumfries, and settled down to the business of farming. Here Rogers might have found him in July, 1789, 'at times sauntering by the delightful wanderings of the Nith,' as he says in a letter to Mr. M'Auley, 'praying for seasonable weather or holding an intrigue with the Muses,— the only gypsies with whom I have now any intercourse.' It was a bright interval in the poet's life, and Rogers might have preserved for us a picture of him in his fields, or at home with his 'wife and twa wee laddies,' who, as he sang, 'maun hae brose and brats o' duddies,' and who had made him resolve that —

> 'To make a happy fireside clime
> To weans and wife,
> That's the true pathos and sublime
> Of human life.'

Burns, as we know from one of his letters to Mrs. Dunlop, had just been 'very busy with "Zeluco,"' the 'most sterling performance,' as he calls it, of his friend and Rogers's friend, Dr. Moore. He tells Mrs. Dunlop that he had been revolving in his mind some criticisms on novel-writing, which he found to be a depth beyond his research, and a year later he writes to Dr. Moore: 'I have gravely planned a comparative view of you, Fielding, Richardson, and Smollett, in your different qualities and merits as novel-writers.' This comparative view is only briefly hinted in a later letter to the author of 'Zeluco,' but his admiration for Moore's writings suggests a topic on which Rogers and he might have talked; and a most interesting conversation might have been added to the pleasant record of Rogers's Scottish visit. The opportunity thus lost never came again. Rogers did not revisit Scotland till 1803, when Burns had been dead seven years.

This first journey to Scotland was well-timed in other respects. Sixty years later, when the economical doctrines of Adam Smith had been established in Free Trade legislation, it was a satisfaction to Rogers that he had seen the author of 'The Wealth of Nations.' Mr. Dyce[1] records a story of him which is not in Rogers's Diary. 'Once in the course of conversation I happened,' said Rogers, 'to remark of some writer that he was rather superficial, a Voltaire.' 'Sir,' cried Adam Smith, striking the table with his hand, 'there has been but one Vol-

---

[1] Table Talk, p. 44.

7

taire.' Adam Smith died on the 17th of July, 1790, not quite a year after Rogers's interviews with him. Robertson lived three years longer. When Rogers breakfasted with him, and afterwards heard him preach, his 'History of Scotland' had been published thirty years, and he had been for as long a period one of the chief figures in the Scottish capital. Rogers always remembered the kindness with which the great historian had welcomed him, and told how he had taken down a map of Scotland, spread it on the floor, and, kneeling down upon it, had traced the route to be followed in the Highland tour on which Rogers was setting out. Robertson died in 1793. Henry Mackenzie, with whom a long friendship was begun on this meeting in Edinburgh, was then in middle age. He was born in Edinburgh, in August, 1745, on the very day on which Prince Charles Edward landed in Scotland. He had been in London in 1765, to study the modes of English Exchequer practice, as Sir Walter Scott tells us in his pleasant account of Mackenzie, in the 'Lives of the Novelists.' He had sketched the outlines of his principal work, 'The Man of Feeling,' during his residence in London, but had not finished and published it till 1771. It was anonymous, but it at once became the most popular novel of its time. Like George Eliot's 'Adam Bede,' it was the subject of a false claim. A man named Eccles transcribed the whole, made corrections, blottings, and interlineations in the manuscript thus produced, and pertinaciously declared himself to be the author of the book. Mackenzie was thus compelled to own and claim his offspring. His 'Man of the World' is regarded by Scott as a second part of 'The Man of Feeling,' while 'Julia de Roubigné' was written, Scott says, in some degree as a counterpart to the earlier work. Rogers had read and admired this pathetic story, and went to Edinburgh full of desire to see its author, who was then one of the most distinguished persons in the literary society of the Scottish capital. Rogers's feeling with respect to Mackenzie at this time was that with which a young writer regards an author of established fame. He first saw him at Adam Smith's dinner-table, and remarks in his diary on his soft and pleasing manners. Mackenzie was an admirable talker. Just thirty years after Rogers had first met him, Mr. Ticknor, the author of the 'History of Spanish Literature,' records in his diary that he had breakfasted one morning with Mackenzie at Lady Cumming's. 'He is now old,' says Ticknor, 'but a thin, active, lively little gentleman, talking fast and well upon all common subjects, and without the smallest indication of "The Man of Feeling" about him.' Rogers and he corresponded occasionally for five-and-forty years, and Mackenzie more than once visited Rogers in London. Their sympathy with each other was purely literary, for Mackenzie wrote against the French Revolution in the days when all liberal spirits in England were still hoping everything from it. He lived on through all the changes it brought, and saw the Monarchy of July and the agitation for English Reform before he died. In a letter announcing his death, in January, 1831, when he had got half-way through his eighty-sixth year, his son, Mr. J. H. Mackenzie, expressed gratitude to Rogers 'for your kind friendship to my father, which added so sensibly to the enjoyment of his declining years.' Mr. Joshua Henry Mackenzie afterwards became a judge of the Edinburgh Court of Session, and his daughter, Miss Mackenzie of Moray Place, Edinburgh, is now the sole descendant of 'The Man of Feeling.'

After his memorable stay in the Scottish capital Rogers was more than ever set on the attainment of literary distinction. He came back home to work hard at the poem by which he was to gain the fame he felt to be his right. He was always accumulating material for it, putting down happy thoughts and fortunate expressions, and polishing a line or a couplet into the perfect rhythm which distinguishes the poem. It was the chief subject in his thoughts, yet it is never mentioned in his letters or his diary. Perhaps it was because of this preoccupation with the work of this period of his life that there is no record of 1790, except one which he mentions in his 'Recollections.' It is a personal reminiscence of Burke. On the 10th December, 1790, Sir Joshua Reynolds delivered his fifteenth and last discourse at the Royal Academy. There was a crowded audience, and the front seats were reserved for persons of distinction, among whom was Burke. Younger and less known men, of whom Rogers was then one, were thus kept in the back of the room. Suddenly a beam under the floor gave way with a crash, and the people present rushed to the door. As there was no sign of further disaster the alarm was supposed to be a false one, and the audience struggled back to their places. Some of the younger got to the front, and Rogers was among them. Sir Joshua concluded his lecture with a striking passage : ' I feel a self-congratulation in knowing myself capable of such great sensations as he intended to excite. I reflect, not without vanity, that these discourses bear testimony of my admiration of that truly divine man, and I should desire that the last words I should pronounce in this Academy and from this place should be the name of Michael Angelo.' He came down from the desk to mingle with the audience, and Burke went up to him, and taking him by the hand repeated Milton's lines : —

> ' The Angel ended, and in Adam's ear
> So charming left his voice that he awhile
> Thought him still speaking, still stood fix'd to hear.'

' I was there,' writes Rogers, ' and heard it.'

CHAPTER V.

WHILE Rogers was enjoying the literary and social intercourse to which his friends had introduced him in the Scottish capital, events which greatly influenced the life of every prominent man in Europe were taking place in Paris. The destruction of the Bastille has made the 14th of July, 1789, a dividing line in history. It was the first great victory of the populace. The Bastille was at once the instrument and the symbol of despotism, and its fall announced to the world the overthrow of the ancient authority of a family and of a caste. The people of England rejoiced in the victory almost as much as the people of France. It was regarded by English Liberals as the formal entry of France on the career of constitutional government; as the proclamation of a new era, in which the old Whig toast of 'Civil and religious liberty all the world over' should come to complete realization. It is difficult in these days to enter very fully into the feeling of that already distant time. It is only by recollecting how completely the near future is veiled from us, how impossible it was in 1790 and 1791 to foresee the deeds of 1793 and 1794, that we can understand the enthusiasm which the first movements of the Revolution

aroused in men of liberal thought and training in
England and the United States. They beheld in 1789
and 1790 nothing but the rosy dawn ; they could not
foresee the storms which were so soon to obscure it and
blot the sky. Poets and philosophers, politicians and
divines, saw in the earliest movements of the Revolution
the power and the potency of all necessary ameliorations
in the lot of the great masses of mankind, and the pledge
of the quick coming of the better time in which Christendom, in spite of all disappointments, has passionately
believed and still passionately believes. Southey, Coleridge and Wordsworth, Price, Priestley and Mackintosh,
Charles Fox, Charles Grey, Whitbread, Francis, Erskine,
Sheridan, Windham and Stanhope, and all the men who,
like them, had been laboring in the popular cause, felt
upon their faces the light and warmth of a new morning
for the world. Wordsworth, looking back when he wrote
'The Prelude,' said of those days of illusive, yet not
wholly illusive, hope, —

> 'Bliss was it in that dawn to be alive,
> But to be young was very heaven.'

Coleridge, writing his 'Ode to France' in 1797, just after
the moment of worst disenchantment, sang of the time

> 'When France in wrath her giant limbs upreared,
> And, with an oath that smote air, earth, and sea,
> Stamped her strong foot and said she would be free.'

Even in those days Coleridge was not ashamed to
boast of 'the lofty gratulation' with which he could sing
'unawed among a slavish band' and 'bless the pæans
of delivered France.' All these men saw in the French
Revolution in 1790 what Milton had seen in the English
Revolution a hundred and thirty years before, — 'a noble
and puissant nation rousing herself like a strong man
after sleep.' Wordsworth exactly describes the almost

universal feeling at the time of his own first visit to France, in three lines of 'The Prelude' : —

'. . . Europe at that time was filled with joy,
France standing on the top of golden hours,
And human nature seeming born again.'

There were, however, other voices even then. In the autumn of 1789, John Adams, who had been the first Minister of the United States at the English Court, and who was afterwards the second President of the American Republic, expressed the opinion — I may almost say, uttered the striking prophecy — in a letter to Dr. Price, that nothing good could be expected of a nation of atheists, and that the probable result of the Revolution would be the destruction of a million of human lives. A great genius of our own land — a man who united in his own person the qualities of the statesman, the philosopher, the orator, and the prophet — was then writing the 'Reflections on the French Revolution' which were published in the following year. Burke, however, stood almost alone ; and when in April, 1791, Mackintosh, then a young and unknown man of six-and-twenty, issued his brilliant 'Vindiciæ Gallicæ' it was received with almost universal gratitude and admiration by the Whigs and the educated middle classes, as Paine's 'Rights of Man' was welcomed by less cultivated readers. Burke's eloquent lamentations over the disappearance of the age of chivalry embodied the feeling with which the Conservative section of the privileged classes regarded the Revolution. They saw in the scattering of a frightened *noblesse,* and the limitation of the arbitrary powers of the monarch, not the enfranchisement of a people whom king and aristocracy had utterly impoverished and grossly oppressed, but the overthrow of institutions based on privilege, which age had made venerable and picturesque. Paine, in the most eloquent passage in his 'Rights of

Man,' said of Burke's pathetic description of the sufferings of Marie Antoinette, that Burke pitied the plumage
but forgot the dying bird.   He and his friends mourned
over the troubles of the ornamental classes, but over-
looked the long patience of the people on whom they
preyed.

The great bulk of the English Dissenters, and of the
Whig aristocracy whose lead they gratefully acknowledged, were too much occupied with the progressive
establishment of Liberal institutions on the other side
of the Channel to think much of the cost at which the
enfranchisement was being purchased.   On the 4th of
November, 1789, the anniversary dinner of the 'Society
for Commemorating the English Revolution' was held
at the London Tavern, with Lord Stanhope in the chair.
Many of Rogers's friends were there, and Dr. Price — who
earlier in the day had preached to the members of the
Society, in the meeting-house in the Old Jewry, his great
discourse 'On the Love of Our Country' — moved a con-
gratulatory. address to the National Assembly of France.
This address congratulated the Assembly, so the resolution ran, 'on the revolution in that country, and on the
prospect it gives to the first two kingdoms in the world
of a common participation in the blessings of civil and
religious liberty.'   The Liberal triumph in France was
to lead to a similar Liberal triumph in England, and the
Whigs — who were the Radicals of the time — hoped to
see, in the words of Dr. Price's address, 'a general refor-
mation in the governments of Europe, and to make the
world free and happy.'   On the 14th of July, 1790, the
first anniversary of the taking of the Bastille, there was
a dinner at the Crown and Anchor, at which there is
reason to believe that Rogers was present.   Dr. Price
was one of the stewards of the dinner, and made the
speech which, together with his sermon in the Old Jewry
on the 4th of November, became the subject of some of

Burke's 'Reflections.' This speech, read in the light of
modern political ideas, suggests the wonder that any
human being could have felt anything but the fullest
and completest sympathy with its patriotic sentiment
and peaceful tone, or anything but appreciation for the
severe moderation of its language. It suggested an
alliance between the first two kingdoms of the world, for
promoting peace on earth and good-will to men. It was
eminently worthy to be, as it was, the last public testimony on behalf of civil and religious liberty borne by
one of the gentlest and purest spirits the eighteenth century produced. Dr. Price died before the second anniversary came round and brought with it the brutal attack
of the Birmingham mob on Dr. Priestley's house and
chapel, and before the angry clouds had risen which too
soon turned the golden hours to weeping. His name,
however, was known and honored in France, and he had
an extensive correspondence with some of the best men
of the early days of the Revolution. Dr. Price never
visited France himself, but his name was a passport to
the best society of revolutionary Paris, and to be known
as his friend was to be sure of a welcome in circles
where in 1790 and 1791 the chiefs of the movement were
to be met.

As Dr. Price's friend, and with letters from him and
many other well-known Whigs and sympathizers with the
Revolution, Rogers went over to Paris in the beginning
of 1791 to see the chief scenes and persons in the revolutionary drama. It had not yet become a tragedy; it was
not yet even apparently tending to tragic results. The
moment was one at which the hope and anticipation
raised in the previous summer had not yet died away.
The king and the National Assembly had come to an
understanding. He had accepted the new constitution,
and though he was almost a prisoner or a hostage in the
Tuileries, there were still reasons for hoping that the

Revolution might complete its course within the limits of constitutional forms. There were, indeed, signs of a different issue, but they were not discernible from afar. The king was already ceasing to desire final reconciliation with the Revolution and its leaders. Mirabeau, elected President of the Assembly while Rogers was in Paris, was within three months of the close of his career, and Lafayette was in retirement. It was most significant that when, on the 28th of January, Rogers and Boddington expressed to Lafayette their pleasure at finding everything so quiet, Lafayette made no reply, and that on the same evening Mr. Keay, their English friend in Paris, told them that the people were barbarous, and described how a few days before, when a mob was hurrying away a man they suspected to be a spy, a porkman rushed from his shop and ran a knife into his head. There was the germ of all the coming excesses in this event. But it was not likely that foreigners would discern the signs that were hidden from Frenchmen themselves. More than two months after Rogers's return from Paris, Fox spoke of the new constitution as the most glorious fabric ever raised by human ingenuity since the creation of man. So it seemed, regarded from afar. Like Mulciber's 'fabric huge' of Pandemonium in 'Paradise Lost,' it —

> 'Rose like an exhalation with the sound
> Of dulcet symphonies and voices sweet;'

and just at this moment —

> 'The ascending pile
> Stood fixed her stately height.'

But less than six months after Rogers saw Lafayette, and within ten weeks of the time at which Fox spoke, the king fled from Paris, and the prospect of transforming

France by peaceful change into a constitutional kingdom passed away like the baseless fabric of a vision.

Rogers went to Paris, full of the feeling with which all English Liberals regarded the Revolution, in January, 1791. He tells us, in the first page of his diary, that he regarded Calais as the shore which might 'soon, even to Englishmen, prove a welcome asylum.' He had as his companion Samuel Boddington, afterwards the partner in business of Richard Sharp.[1] The diary is a rough one. It was written on the evenings of his journey, and while each day's experiences and events were fresh in his recollection, and he probably intended to rewrite it afterwards. But it remains as it was written, and needs no other introduction than the reminder to the reader that Rogers was even more interested in the literary and social aspects of France than in its political state.

'*January* 18, 1791. — The hop-grounds and cherry-orchards of 'Kent were still pleasing amidst the dreariness of winter, and we had several fine catches of the Thames and its shipping. At Canterbury we snatched a passing view of the cathedral; and as we approached Dover the castle rose in all its majesty, and wore a chaste gray tint from the reflection of a storm that brooded over it.

'*20th*. — The wind being contrary we made a pilgrimage to the top of Shakspeare's cliff, which towers to a stupendous height from the edge of the ocean, and commands the town of Dover, shut in by mountains and only open to the sea. The French coast was not visible, but the sea was fresh and beautiful and spotted with white

---

[1] The name of the firm was Boddington, Sharp, and Phillips. Samuel Boddington's only child, Grace Boddington, married Sir Henry Webster, then a colonel in the army. Sir Henry Webster was the second son of Lady Holland and of her first husband, Sir Godfrey Webster, from whom she was divorced by Act of Parliament.

sails, and the air was so mild and elastic that it was a
luxury to breathe it. In the evening walked on the pier.
The brightness of the moonshine on the cliffs and the
water, the silver line of the horizon, and the old sailors
standing in groups on the beach, and conversing in their
long blue cloaks on the uncertainty of the weather,
formed an amusing scene.

'21*st*. — Set sail for Calais with a clear sky and calm
sunshine, and in two hours and forty minutes gained
that shore which may soon, even to Englishmen, prove
a welcome asylum. As we landed, the national troops
were parading in their white uniform, and several *gens
comme il faut* of both sexes were walking on the pier,
with large fox muffs. We were conducted across a
handsome square, built of white brick, and ornamented
with some good public buildings, the great church, the
Hôtel de Ville, etc., to the Silver Lion, where we dined
on *soupe*, *bouilli* and *perdrix*, and received a visit from
Father Martin, a Capuchin friar, who introduced himself
most cautiously to solicit alms for his convent. Proceeded afterwards to Boulogne, along a paved road
which ran in a direct line through a country well cultivated and uneven, and enlivened with many villages
scattered over it, but in some parts marshy and destitute
of trees. Our chaise was drawn by three horses abreast,
and the driver, a brisk pleasant fellow, wore a large
cocked hat and jack-boots, with deep ruffles, gilt earrings,
and an enormous *queue*. We afterwards changed horses
by the light of a blacksmith's shop, and in our own way
met the Calais stage, a huge monster, not much less than
Noah's Ark. It was heavily laden with trunks and passengers, and, though drawn by seven horses, rumbled
along at the rate of two miles an hour. Entered Boulogne by moonlight through a winding avenue of trees,
and after having ordered our *petit souper* at La Vignette,
we repaired to the theatre, a small oblong building with

a circular termination, the shape of every French theatre. It was very gayly painted, but miserably lighted, and it smelt of pomatum like a barber's shop. In the boxes were a few *abbés* and officers who left their seats between the acts and conversed familiarly with the actors on the stage behind the curtain. The comedy was admirably acted, and was often interrupted by the most rapturous bursts of applause. The entertainment began and concluded with a *pas de seul*.

'*January* 22.—The market-place at Montreuil was crowded as we passed through it. It was a busy scene, and exactly resembled a fair in a Flemish picture. The women wore a close cap, with no hat; and their muffs and powdered hair had a singular effect among baskets of eggs and stalls of gingerbread. The weather was now so fine—so superb, to speak the language of the country—that we could here contain ourselves no longer, and, leaving the chaise to follow us to the next *poste* we mounted our *bidets* and cantered away in jack-boots, as happy and as perpendicular as La Fleur himself. Our outset was, however, such as to have discouraged less enterprising spirits, for when we had accoutred ourselves for the ride, we could neither vault into the saddle nor even lift our feet into the stirrup, but tottered along with the hostler's assistance amidst the titterings of the landlady and her maids in the inn-yard. When we had passed through Abbeville—a large town in an extensive valley, and brimful of churches and convents, priests and beggars—we gradually ascended the heights of Picardy, whence we saw the Somme winding through green meadows on the left. The moon was rising when we entered Amiens through a deep gateway; the convent bells were tinkling, and the streets were lighted by lanterns suspended in the middle by a rope. Alighted at the Silver Lion, and were charmed by the *naïveté* and simplicity of the innkeeper's daughter, Flora, a sweet little girl

about ten years old. " Aimez-vous les Anglais ? " said I.
" J'aime tout le monde ! " " Avez-vous des sœurs ? "
" Oui, mais elles ont des maris." "Et vous serez mariée
de bonne heure ? " " Oh qu'oui, Monsieur."

'*January* 23. — When I descended into the parlor to
breakfast I was surprised to find there a little fellow
about fourteen years old, in a very fine coat, with
powdered hair and long *queue.* He advanced towards
me with his hands in an immense muff and with a profusion of bows and fine compliments. He proved to be
Flora's brother, and had been deputed by his mother to
conduct us over the town. Under his guidance, therefore, we sallied forth to the Cathedral, a most magnificent piece of Gothic. The clergy had not yet taken the
national oath, the gates that led to the high altar were
sealed, and Mass was performed in the aisle. "Où sont
les moines ? " said I, as we walked through the streets.
"Ils sont dans leur couvent à pleurer, Monsieur." The
ramparts form an amusing promenade round the town.
The Somme meanders on one side with convents and
manufactories on its banks; and on the other rise the
cathedral with its taper spire, of rich filagree work, and
a multitude of religious houses and *hôtels* of the *noblesse ;*
among these are small flower-gardens, each intersected
with espaliers and gravel walks, and furnished with a
marble fountain and an alcove of green trellis-work. As
we left Amiens we saw a fiddler perched up in the corner
of a street playing and singing, while he exhibited to a
crowded audience a scroll of pictures daubed in different
compartments. Proceeded through pleasant fields and
woods till the country made a grand fall, and presented
in front a very extensive plain, fading away into the
blue and purple tints of distance. At Breteuil we
passed a convent of Benedictines, with a very long and
elegant white front. It was a modern structure with
sash windows, the antique tower of its chapel rose beside

it, and it formed a very striking object for many miles.
At the door of an *auberge*, on a little hill, we were soon
afterwards stopped by the entreaties of the *aubergiste*,
who asked permission for an elderly well-dressed man to
ride a few leagues behind the chaise. "C'est mon ami,
c'est un officier, Messieurs." These arguments would
have been irresistible, if any had been necessary, and
he seated himself behind. We caught a glimpse of the
magnificent *château* of the Duc de Fitz-James, with a
lawn opening in front, and woods intersected with
avenues rising behind it.

'Neither the rattling of the carriage-wheels on the
pavi, nor the flats and sharps of the post-boy's whip,
could drown the brisk notes of a fiddle as we entered the
village of Clermont. It was a dance of the peasants,
and we immediately went to it, and were shown into a
large room, with a floor of red tile and a raftered roof.
There were three sets of *cotillons*, here called *contre-danse*, and never had we any idea of dancing before, —
such activity, so much soul in all their movements. We
were immediately pressed to dance. "Ne voulez-vous
pas danser, Messieurs?" resounded from all sides. It
was an invitation not to be resisted; and we danced
"Les Plaisirs des Loix" to the tune of "Ça ira." The
very *fille de chambre* who had conducted us from the inn
was already engaged in another set. Every man paid
three *liards* for two dances, and saluted his partner
when they were finished. On the hill was a dance of
the *bourgeois, très splendide*, but we chose the dance of
the peasants. The band consisted of two violins; and
some stools elevated on a table against the wall formed
the orchestra. Over the door was this inscription: "Ho-noré, Perruquier, tient salle de danse à la nation."
When I saw the innocent gayety of the villagers of Cler-mont, my heart bled to think of the oppressions which
so amiable and generous a people had so long endured.

Proceeded through an uneven country, with woods and vineyards on either hand, till we entered a long avenue that led to Chantilly, the seat of the Prince of Condé. Saw the house, the gardens, the stables, etc., altogether a most superb monument of bad taste. The gate of the stables is, however, a striking exception. The armor of Henri IV. and of the great Condé are here preserved with veneration. Continued through the woods of Chantilly, and passed through several villages. The country soon made another fall, and of equal grandeur with the former. As we changed horses at St. Denis, one of them was restive and broke the traces. "Ha, ha! Monsieur l'abbé Maury," said a boy as he passed by, "ne voulez-vous pas rester tranquille?" Over the arch of every nobleman's gateway the coat of arms was erased, and printed advertisements of the sale of the Church lands were fixed on every wall. As we approached Paris we saw an infinite number of avenues leading from it in all directions, like the radii of a circle. Passed at the foot of Montmartre, a hill of granite covered with windmills.

'The clumsy coaches of all shapes that rumble along without springs; the ladies hurrying out of their way with rouged cheeks and without hats; the gentlemen parading with their national cockades, immense muffs, and copper buckles; and the very beggars accosting us with a powdered head, a muff, and a cockade, — everything was new to an Englishman; but who could attend a moment to such *minutiæ* when so many thousands were beating as it were with one pulse in the cause of liberty and their country, and crowding every coffee-house and public walk to congratulate each other on an event so favorable in its consequences to the best interests of mankind?

'In the evening walked under the piazzas of the Palais Royal, a very elegant square, full of shops and coffee-houses, glittering with lights and crowded with belles and beaux who were taking their evening promenade.

'*January* 26. — Breakfasted in a coffee-house, where I could have passed hours in contemplating the various figures that were sipping their coffee and *càpillaire* around me, and dined at the Café des Quatre Nations, where the scene was so diverting and the dishes were all in masquerade. The moment we entered, one of the waiters with irresistible grace presented us with a printed bill of fare, including above two hundred different articles with the several prices affixed; from *fricassées, frican-deaus*, and *ragoûts* down to humble *bifteck*, so changed in name and nature that we could with difficulty recognize our old acquaintance. We afterwards repaired to the *cirque* in the middle of the Palais Royal, an elegant room, 300 feet by 50, lighted by a long skylight and designed for every species of entertainment. " Ce n'est pas un cirque," said I to a carpenter at work there. "C'est un cirque Français," said he, archly. Here we saw a faro-table surrounded by adventurers, and were soon called away from remarking their anxious and fluctuating spirits to view an assault between La Motte, a musician in the king's band, and several other fencers.

'*January* [1] 27. — " C'est une belle saison," said I to my hairdresser this morning. " C'est superbe, Monsieur," said he. Sallied forth with a smart *laquais de place*, Lefèvre, in a chariot driven by a coachman whose scarlet cloak formed a fine front screen ; over Pont Neuf, by the statue of Henri IV., to the Abbé Grenet,[2] a professor in the College of Richelieu, — a sensible, pleasant man, but an aristocrat; disapproved of the plan of juries now before

---

[1] Query Jan. 26.

[2] The Abbé Grenet was a celebrated writer on geography and professor of that science. He disappeared during the Revolution.

the National Assembly, and said it was unsuitable to the genius of the nation.   Proceeded afterwards to Monsieur Pétrie, member of the Assembly from Tobago, a gentleman and a man of sense.   He said he feared the Assembly had too many irons in the fire, and that the conduct of the clergy at Amiens had drawn a motion from Barnave to petition the king to appoint new bishops.   In the evening went to the theatre of the Grands Danseurs du Roi on the Boulevards, full of the *canaille*.   The first piece was the conduct of the Spaniards in Mexico, and when the priests were disgraced the laughter and shouts of the audience were very pointed.   Went afterwards to the *cirque*, and saw some *cotillons* danced by the *dames du Palais Royal* in a very capital style.

'*January* 27. — M. l'abbé Grenet breakfasted with us, and told us that the mob had last night threatened to burn the house of M. de Clermont-Tounerre,[1] and were proceeding to the *lanterne* with an officer of the police, but were prevented.   Said Marmontel[2] had changed his principles and disapproved of the new government; that the Abbé Raynal[3] was an *enragé*, and at Marseilles; that

---

[1] M. de Clermont-Tonnerre fell a victim to the populace in the succeeding August.

[2] The author of *Contes Moraux* was in his sixty-eighth year.   He had been Secretary of the Academy from D'Alembert's death in 1783, and on the suppression of the Academies in 1791 betook himself to the writing of new *Contes Moraux*.   He died in 1799.

[3] The Abbé Raynal was at that time the most celebrated French historian living.   In December, 1790, a severe criticism on the doings of the Assembly had appeared, entitled 'Lettre de l'abbé Raynal à l'Assemblée Nationale.'   It was by the Comte de Guibert, but embodied Raynal's sentiments.   In May, 1791, he wrote a letter to the President of the Assembly, which was read at one of its sittings, protesting against its proceedings and expressing regret that the writer had been 'one of those who, in expressing a generous indignation against arbitrary power, had perhaps put arms into the hands of license and anarchy.'   He did not emigrate, but lived in retirement through the Terror, and died in Paris in 1796, in his eighty-third year.

the Abbé Maury was the first man in France, and M.
Rabaut[1] the most dangerous ; that he was of Rousseau's
opinion that a republican form of government suited
small states only ; that M. d'Alembert, the great mathematician, could never draw a right angle with his com-
passes ; that M. l'abbé Maury had often appeased the
cry of "À la lauterne !" by saying, "You may take me
there, but will you see the clearer for it ? "[2] Sallied
forth afterwards and left our letters and cards at Lord
Gower's, the Duc de Rochefoucauld's,[3] de Liancourt's,[4]
etc. Called on M. de Kéralio,[5] printer of the *Mercure
National ;* saw his daughter, a very pleasing, sensible

---

[1] See note to page 179.

[2] The Abbé Maury was celebrated all through the Revolution for his
ready wit. ' I am going to shut up the Abbé Maury in a vicious circle,'
said Mirabeau one day in the Assembly. 'Then you are going to em-
brace me,' said the Abbé, to the great orator's confusion. Hearing that
he was proscribed he fled, but was brought back. On retaking his
place in the National Assembly he said, ' I shall perish in the Revolution or get a Cardinal's hat in fighting it.' He did not long fight the
Revolution, but fled again when the Constituent Assembly was dissolved,
and was made a bishop *in partibus* and afterwards a cardinal. He died
at Rome in 1817.

[3] The Duc de la Rochefoucauld was one of the early victims of the
Revolution. He was stoned to death at Gisors on the 14th of September, 1792, as he was on his way to take the waters at Forges. His
mother and his wife were with him.

[4] The Duc de Liancourt is the man who, two days before the fall of
the Bastille, had gone to Versailles to tell the king of the state of Paris.
' It is a revolt,' said the astonished Louis. ' No, sir,' replied the Duc
de Liancourt, ' it is a revolution.' He was for a time President of the
National Assembly. Not long after Rogers was at his house he fled to
England and took refuge with Arthur Young. On the death of his
cousin he took the title of La Rochefoucauld.

[5] M. de Kéralio, who had translated various works from English,
German, and Swedish, had translated in 1789 Dr. Price's sermon ' On
the Love of our Country.' He was one of the editors of the *Journal des
Savants* from 1785 till its suppression in 1792. He died at Grosley in
December, 1793.

woman.[1] Called at Perrégaux's,[2] and saw one of the partners, asked after Mr. Keay and heard he was in England. Dined at the coffee-house, and saw there an Englishman in the navy, a sceptic in religion, and in politics an aristocrat; went afterwards to the opera, — an ordinary house, full of the best company. All the boxes let except two. The *parterre* crowded, and the people there moved like ears of corn. The opera "Dido," Mallieux the first woman. Saw afterwards "Cupid and Psyche," — a beautiful ballet. Laboré and Nivelon wonderful dancers, the first more esteemed here than Vestris, only eighteen years old.

'*January* 28. — Called on Mr. Keay, who was out, — Hôtel des États Unis, Rue des Gaillons. Called on M. Hottingue and M. Rougemont,[3] and were politely received. Saw the Church of La Roche; the Italian theatre, with a beautiful Ionic colonnade in front; and the Théâtre de Monsieur, just finished, the front a circular colonnade.

'In the afternoon called at the Marquis de Lafayette's, and were introduced by M. de Châtelet,[4] through an anteroom where some officers were dining, into a large room where he sat at table with thirty or forty officers. He rose to receive us. We then passed on to another chamber, where several gentlemen were waiting. He soon entered with Madame de Lafayette, — a pleasing,

---

[1] Mdlle. de Kéralio was assisting her father in the editorship of the *Mercure National, ou Journal d'État et de Citoyen,* and soon after Rogers's visit married M. Robert, one of her father's colleagues. Robert became Danton's secretary, but escaped the proscription of the Dantonists. Madame Robert, like her father, was a voluminous translator, obtaining considerable celebrity. She died in 1821.

[2] The banker.

[3] M. Rougemont was a merchant to whom Rogers had received an introduction.

[4] This was probably the Duc du Châtelet, afterwards one of the generals in the army of the Republic. He was arrested as a Girondist, and poisoned himself in prison.

lively woman, but not handsome, who told us that we did her country honor to visit it when they were but in their infancy; that she could understand English, but was afraid to talk it. Lafayette then came up, a tall, handsome man about 35.[1] He inquired after Dr. Price, and asked whether he had any intention to visit Paris; said that most people could speak a little English and understand him. We expressed pleasure to find all things so tranquil; he made no answer. In this room was a picture of the Bastille. Invited us to dine with him to-morrow, and said he dined every day at four and should always be happy to see us. Went to the Théâtre de Monsieur and saw an Italian comedy, "La Pastorella," beautifully lighted in the centre with a transparency of Apollo and his rays. Came home, when Mr. Keay waited upon me and spent two hours with us. Said that Lafayette had nearly ruined his fortune, and would not touch his allowance from the Assembly; that the people were the most barbarous in the world; that when the mob on Thursday last were hurrying away the man they suspected to be a spy, a porkman rushed from his shop and dug his knife into his head; that Lafayette is no republican.

'*January* 29. — M. de Châtelet and another gentleman called this morning. M. de Châtelet invited us to the *Conversation de la mère du Duc de Rochefoucauld,* — a tall, thin woman, very animated. Advised us to attend the "Comedy," and said that we could acquire the language in two months; that Burke's letters were written to a M. Dupont, a young man, attached to the new constitution, who answered him with great spirit; that we might go to-morrow to the Assembly with M. Mirabeau, who was yesterday elected President. Wrote letters, and afterwards dined at M. de Lafayette's.

---

[1] He was born in 1757, and was therefore in his 34th year.

'Madame de Lafayette said they should come to see us after they had finished their Revolution; talked with rapture of Thomson and Gray, and thought the English language more difficult to learn than the French. Lafayette came late, inquired what news from England; said Pitt had a great majority and the confidence of, but was no friend to, the people; that every member of the Parliament had contributed more or less to increase the influence of the Crown; that Pitt did him the honor to dine with him on his return from Fontainebleau before he was Minister, in company with Dr. Franklin, and then told him that he had too much democracy in his principles for him.[1] There were about twenty-six people, chiefly officers, there. There were but two courses and a dessert. After dinner, retired into the drawing-room to drink coffee. Beyond this was another apartment, into which he frequently withdrew with some of the company. Went afterwards to the Théâtre François, and saw "Le Jaloux sans Amour" and Auguste and Théodore. The King of Prussia — very like Prince Henry — was much struck with it, and suggested some slight improvements in the costume. Saw there one of Lafayette's officers, who said that Lafayette, during the heat of the Revolution, kept eighty men at his own expense, and now supports nearly twenty besides the company at his own table; that he, the officer himself, had a shot through his hat at the taking of the Bastille.

'*January* 30. — Went at ten to the Salle Nationale; the tribune crowded, the subject uninteresting — respecting the alienation of the incomes of the hospitals. Barnave, Rochefoucauld, and Mirabeau spoke a few words; the last is the best speaker in the National Assembly.

[1] In a letter to his sister Sarah, dated the 4th of February, Rogers says that 'Lafayette said little about the French Revolution, but was very inquisitive respecting the state of politics in England.'

On the table was a bust of Monsieur Désiles, who fell a victim to the soldiery at Nancy. The bell rung frequently by the President Mirabeau to obtain silence. Walked afterwards in the Tuileries gardens, and saw the palaces of the Prince of Condé and of Monsieur. Dined with Mr. Keay (nobody else there), and at half-past five drove to M. de Condorcet's, formerly secretary to the Academy of Belle Lettres, and found Madame de Condorcet sitting in a little room with a girl of eight years of age. A charming woman with an oval face, very open and expressive, and very fair; a beautiful picture of two ladies painted in crayons by herself. Full of patriotism. Condorcet, being engaged below with Rochefoucauld, did not appear. Drove to the Théâtre François and saw "La Liberté conquise," — a simple representation of the taking of the Bastille, interspersed with noble sentiments but laid in a distant province. Between the acts "Ça ira" was played by the orchestra, and the audience beat time by clapping. When soldiers clubbed their arms and embraced their fellow-citizens the house resounded with shouts for some minutes. An English nobleman is introduced, who utters fine sentiments of liberty, and concludes the piece with this address, "François, vous avez conquis la liberté, tâchez de la conservir."

'Went from thence at nine to the Club of the year 1789, — an elegant room with sixty or seventy members there. Conversed with two, one of whom offered to supply me with facts if I would give him queries. They knew well that there were only two parties, — for the aristocracy and the crown. The apartments were three, leading into each other. Proceeded afterwards to sup at Madame de Canissy's Hôtel de Brienne, Rue St. Dominique, Faubourg St. Germain. Entered through several rooms into an elegant apartment, where were a lady and gentleman. The company consisted of Madame de Canissy, a very lively, talkative woman; her husband,

who resembled a Methodist minister; Châtelet; a bishop;
a Scotchman, a very pleasant, sensible man, rather dry;
a foreign Ambassador with a star and ribbon; two other
gentlemen, one of whom came in Châtelet's cabriolet;
and M. de Condorcet,[1] a very sensible but very plain
man, and his wife as enchanting as ever. In the room
was an elegant bed, with a portrait of a lady hung at the
head of it; and close by it was a couch on which was a
girl, who soon waked and was taken to the fire to warm
its little feet by Madame de Condorcet, and afterwards put
to bed again. The supper was brought in on the table,
at which few sat down, except the ladies, and afterwards
it was carried out in the same manner. Chemistry,
Shakspeare, Junius, Burke, animal magnetism, took
their turns. Châtelet said Dr. Priestley's "Answer" was
far below him; Condorcet, that water could be decomposed
into two substances; and the lady told a story of M. de
Clermont-Tonnerre, which all present confirmed as true,
that he actually believed and had certificates that a
certain woman "était accouchée par le diable."

'*February* 1. — Sallied forth with Mr. Keay. Saw the
Louvre with its most elegant front, the Place de Grève,
the Palais de Justice with the Sainte Chapelle, the
Church of S. Geneviève, the Church of Saint Sulpice,
the Palais de Monsieur, a Roman bath of the Emperor
Julian the Apostate, the Mint, and the statue of Henri
IV. on the Pont Neuf. M. Pétrie called and said that
Barnave, in a colonial committee to which he belonged,
— Barnave the leader of the Band, — said he hoped we
should be freer than England, but feared that in a few
years the National Assembly would become like the

---

[1] Mr. Hayward says : ' He had met Condorcet at Lafayette's table
in 1789.' Mr. Hayward is, of course, referring to this visit to Paris in
1791. The meeting with Condorcet, here recorded as taking place at
Madame de Canissy's, is clearly the first, and there is no trace in this
diary of Rogers's meeting Condorcet at Lafayette's at all.

Parliament of England; that he himself knew that several things had been carried by corruption. Dined at the Duc de Rochefoucauld's, with twelve or fourteen gentlemen, waited on at dinner by near twice the number of servants. Sat [Boddington and Rogers] on each side the Duke, a little man, continually winking his eyes, but with an air of great goodness, and very civil. During dinner came a letter from Lord George Gordon enclosing his remarks on the civic oath. Châtelet said that he was confined for a crime of which every man in France was guilty.[1] After dinner rose immediately, and withdrew to the other room with his wife. Mr. Morris from America, M. Chabot, brother to Madame, M. Châtelet, etc., were there. In came immediately the old duchess,— such a figure never seen now but in a picture-frame, lively and sensible, and a warm friend to the Revolution.[2] Drank coffee and went to Mr. Boyd's (a banker), Rue de Gramont, where we were soon set down to *brûlant*, — Mr. and Mrs. Boyd, General Campbell, Mr. and Miss Harris, and M. Pétrie. M. P. said that a considerable force was sent to the West Indies to quiet the contending parties there, that Barnave was completely led by a creole.

'*February* 2. — Went to the palace of M. d'Orléans, and saw his pictures: several of Raphael, Rubens, and Titian. Saw the duchess and all the children. Dined at the traiteur's, and saw "William Tell," a tragedy in which La Rive acted very well, and was afterwards called out to make his bow. The audience beat time to "Ça ira" with the same enthusiasm as before. After-

---

[1] He was in prison for libels on the Queen of France and the Empress of Russia.

[2] In a letter to his sister Sarah describing this part of his visit to Paris, Rogers says the Duchess Dowager said to him : 'I once wished to see England ; but now we are freer than you, and you must come to us, not we to you. I had many infirmities, but I have not felt them since the Revolution.'

wards " Le Fou par Amour." Went to the Club of '89.
A debate on three different motions to the same purpose,
the exclusion of the members of the Club Monarchique.
That of M. de Condorcet carried. Was afterwards told
that the Club Monarchique were friends to despotism
under the mask of moderation; [1] that the Club of '89
and that of the Jacobins are much the same in principle,
and act in concert in the Assembly, but that the first are
less precipitate in their measures, and that the leaders of
each have a degree of jealousy of each other; that a
motion had been made more than once to exclude those
of '89 from the Jacobins, but without success; that of '89
are about four hundred. The Jacobins much the largest.
M. Châtelet gave us tickets for the Jacobin Assembly.

'*February* 3. — Saw the pictures in the Louvre, chiefly
French. Observed a coachman with bag and muff.
Dined at M. de Liancourt's with about twenty-four men,
Châtelet,[2] Chabot,[3] Chapelier,[4] M. de Rochefoucauld, etc.

---

[1] The Club Monarchique was first called the Club des Impartiaux.

[2] This was probably Charles Louis Châtelet, who was a leading
member of the Jacobin Club. He adhered to Robespierre, became one
of the agents of the Reign of Terror, escaped on the 9th Thermidor, but
was arrested some months afterwards, tried, condemned, and in May,
1795, executed.

[3] François Chabot was in his thirty-second year. He had been a
Capuchin monk, and grand vicar of the constitutional Bishop of Blois.
He was at this time an enthusiastic clerical friend of the Revolution.
In the following September he was elected to the Legislative Assembly,
and speedily became one of the leaders of the ' Mountain' which owed
its name to him. He got the decree passed which turned the cathedral
of Paris into a temple of reason. Eventually he fell a victim to the
Terror, being guillotined on the 5th of April, 1794.

[4] Isaac René Chapelier, then thirty-seven years old, was a member
of the Committee on the Constitution, and drew up the decree for the
abolition of the *noblesse*. He broke with the party of violence, fled to
England, returned to save his property, was arrested, condemned by the
revolutionary tribunal, and guillotined with Thouret and Desprémenil
in April, 1794.

Very elegant rooms hung with good paintings and looking into the gardens of the Tuileries. Sat by him. A sumptuous dinner, — two courses and a dessert. Mirabeau no favorite, a man of *beaucoup d'esprit*, with no materials of his own, but possessed of the singular talent of availing himself of the ideas of other people. Three bishops have taken the oath. A revolution at Geneva. De Rochefoucauld twice excommunicated at Rome. Had seen Lord Stanhope when at Geneva, then very active with the patriots at the same time with Mr. Wilkes, but would not associate with him. "I admire his public principles," said Lord Stanhope; "I think him an oppressed man [at the time of the 'North Briton'], and would support his cause, but his private character is bad, and I don't want to become acquainted with him." Saw Adam Smith here and admired his "Wealth of Nations." The Jacobins above twelve hundred in Paris, with six hundred corresponding societies in the country; the Monarchique about four hundred, professing a desire to establish a constitution like that of England, but in fact something worse; that and the Club of '89 have no other branches in the country. Liancourt thought their vote of last night a bad one. Saw a fighting match with handkerchiefs. Afterwards at the Théâtre du Palais Royal saw "L'amant femme de chambre" and "Ruse contre ruse, ou Guerre ouverte."

'*February* 4. — Saw the king's library and his Cabinet des Estampes. Saw a Euripides with notes by Racine. Dined at the traiteur's, saw "Œdipe à Colonne" and the ballet of "Cupid and Psyche."[1] Went afterwards to sup with Madame de Condorcet. About twelve persons at supper; three rouged girls. After supper played at a game. The company fixed on a person distinguished in history or in the present age, and somebody not in the

---

[1] Is described in a letter. 'Such music, such scenery and dancing, I think could not be excelled.'

secret asked what advice they gave her or him (a lady if the asker be gentleman, and *vice versâ*). Que conseillerez-vous à mon ami ?

'Same day. — Saw the Place Vendôme; the Hôpital des Invalides, with a most beautiful dome; the military school and the Champ de Mars, the scaffold of which is still standing, with the elegant heights of the village Chaillot.

'In the centre of the area, on an eminence, is the *maison* in which the oath was administered; on one side is written this inscription: "C'est dans ce champ où ils venoient de jurer d'être fidèles à la Nation, à la Loi et au Roi."

'On the opposite side were these verses: —

> "Les mortels sont égaux; ce n'est pas leur naissance,
> C'est la seule vertu qui fait la différence.
> La loi dans tout état doit être universelle;
> Les mortels, quels qu'ils soient, sont égaux devant elle."

'Saw the Hôtel de Ville; the long room in the Louvre, 430 yards in length with the exhibition room. Went to Rougemont's, where were about fourteen people, two men from Neufchatel and an Italian chevalier who went with us to the Italian theatre. Saw "Selima and Azor" and "Le Convalescent de qualité" — a nobleman who, having been long confined by illness and being ignorant of the Revolution, is surprised to find his servants out of livery, but is told that *la loi l'a déchiré ;* finds that his daughter whom he had destined to a convent is in love with a *bourgeois*, and writes for a *lettre de cachet* to confine him; is insulted with the designation of his family name and an application to pay his debts, but is at last, after much point and *équivoque*, brought to reason. "Hé bien! demain Monsieur le Colonel, vous monterez la garde." English horses here at sixty and one hundred guineas.

'*February* 5.—Saw the family go to Mass through the apartments of the Louvre. The king came first with a good-humored unmeaning face, afterwards the queen bowing courteously to all about her, with the dauphin, a little pale-faced boy with a kind of nightcap on his head. She has a beautiful profile, but her eyes are heavy.[1] Then Monsieur, very like the king, his eldest brother, and his sister. Heard Mass,—a most beautiful concert. Raphael's "Cartoons" and his "Mass at Bolsena" in tapestry on the walls.

'Attempted to see the king dine, but could not, having frocks. In the evening at five went to Vespers, where a number of men in flannel gowns and hoods chanted for about half an hour in a very deep discordant tone. The king and queen were there; below were guards forming an avenue up to the altar. Afterwards, at the Théâtre de Madlle. de Montausier (who was there), saw "Le Sourd" inimitably well performed by an actor who imitated the Gascon dialect. Sat in the orchestra. Dined at the *table d'hôte* by myself, B. having a headache. Saw the hôtel of the Prince de Salm,[2] who asks 75,000 francs for it.

'*February* 6.—Called on Perigord.[3] Saw the remains of the Bastille, about ten feet high, in an area of three or four acres and surrounded by a fosse. In the centre a staircase that led into darkness; several cells open to daylight, one of which had a cross traced on the stone,— the melancholy amusement of some heavy hour. Perigord

---

[1] In the letter to his sister, Rogers thus describes the king and queen: 'The king is a very easy, good-humored man in appearance; but the queen, I think, has neither beauty nor good-humor. She has a fine profile, but her eyes are very heavy.'

[2] The Prince de Salm-Kirbourg was another of the victims of the Revolution. He was guillotined on the 23d of July, 1794, at the age of forty-eight. Fourteen months later his property was restored to his family. His hôtel became the headquarters of the Legion of Honor.

[3] Charles Maurice de Perigord, then bishop of Autun, afterwards Prince de Talleyrand.

knew Lafayette,—a man now forgotten, a courtier at
bottom, but a very amiable, well-meaning man. No other
could fill his place when he took it. He said handsomely
that he accepted it because he knew there was danger
in it. The delicacy of his constitution makes him observe
a regimen of rice and eggs. Waked often ten times in
a night, as every rumor is brought to him. P. said the
opera was once the finest thing in the world, on account of
its company, but now things were changed. Afterwards
saw the Gobelins tapestry, the coloring beautiful beyond
conception,—twenty years' practice before a workman
weaves figures. Saw a collection of Wouvermann's prints
at Bassan's, Rue Serpent; saw the Place Victoire, where
Victory is placing (or taking away) a wreath on the brow
of Louis XIV. Dined at the traiteur's, and afterwards
lingered away an hour at the Ambigu Comique, a kind
of Sadler's Wells on the Boulevards. Rode this morning
on part of them, and was charmed with the villas and
various buildings; they are planted on each side with
trees.

'*February* 7. — Rode along the avenue from the
Barrier, surrounded with *ginguettes pour faire des noces
et festins*, through La Chapelle to St. Denis. Saw among
a crowd of monarchs Henry IV., Francis I., Hugh Capet,
and Turenne; among the curiosities, the beautiful onyx
vase mentioned by Gray, on which is sculptured in *basso-
relievo* the rites of Bacchus, referred to the time of
Ptolemy. Saw relics of saints in abundance. A silver
bell most musical. Went at five to the Schools of
Painting in the Louvre, and saw about thirty students
drawing and moulding in terra-cotta the figure of a man
who lay naked in the centre in an oblique posture, his
right hand extended and his left shading his eyes. The
same number above drawing a man suspended by both
his arms in pulleys. Went afterwards to the Théâtre du
Palais Royal and saw the "Seigneur Supposé."

'*February* 8. — Rode with Mr. Keay along the road to Versailles. Passed Passy, the village from which Pilâtre de Rosier first ascended in a balloon, and saw the house in which Dr. Franklin lived, — a white house with green windows. At Sèvres saw the beautiful china in a princely house, and proceeded by several houses to Versailles, now a desert. Like the deserted town in the " Arabian Nights " silence has laid her finger on it. Saw amidst a number of statues Jupiter Stator before which Augustus and the Cæsars made vows. It had stood in the palace, but commanded too much respect there. Saw the " Witch of Endor " by Salvator Rosa, "Alexander in the Tent of Darius " by Le Brun, and "Charles I." by Vandyke; the Church of the Convent of the Augustines, and the room in which the Assembly first met, — all perfect in their kind. Some Swiss exercising there. Dined with Mr. Keay. Went afterwards to the Société des Amis de la Constitution. Passed through a long arched passage, and ascended by a stone staircase into a long narrow room, with a low vaulted roof, formerly the library of the Jacobins. Over the recesses for the books were written " Historiæ profanæ," " Interpretes Scripturæ," " SS. Patres," etc., with several portraits of nuns and abbots. An inquiry into the affair of La Chapelle was before them, the room full, 300 or 400 present. A fulmination against the Société Monarchique. The conquerors of the Bastille presented themselves, three plain modest men, thanked them for having been chosen members of their Society, presented them with a book, and desired leave to put themselves under the protection of the Society, as they had reason to expect every moment to be assassinated. The President replied that every citizen was under the protection of the law, that assassins seldom attacked men of true courage, that if they maintained that character they had hitherto borne they would be always dear to every friend of his country, and that

in the hour of danger every member of that Society
would stand foremost in the defence of men who deserved so well of their country.

'*February* 9. — Saw with Mr. Keay the chapel of the
Carmelites in which is a beautiful Guido, but ill-engraved
by Strange; and Madame La Vallière in the character of
a Magdalene, the *chef d'œuvre* of Le Brun. Le Val de
Grâce, a gaudy church, and the chapel of the Carthu-
sians, but Le Sueur's "History of St. Bruno" is removed
to the Louvre and lies packed up. Walked into the stone
quarries (near Val de Grâce) that undermine the city,—
three miles one way and a mile and a half the other;
walked above half an hour; saw a cavity into which
the nuns of Val de Grâce were let down when in disgrace, and fed with bread dropped down by a string.
Saw the workmen employed, several air-holes; could walk
for days a different route, many branches and turns;
were conducted by a pleasant lively fellow. At Notre
Dame heard Mass, saw a good picture of Le Sueur's, and
from the top of the great tower saw the city intersected by
the Seine and crowded with churches, convents, and palaces, the environs rich and woody and gay with châteaus
and villages, — a much better view than from St. Paul's.
The day favorable. The pavement of Paris bad, — the
stones being cut square and not oblong are soon worn
round by the feet of the horses; the lights of Paris dazzling, from their hanging in the centre before the eyes of
the coachman, but the lamp sooner cleaned and repaired
from its construction being an octagon with framed glass.

'Dined at Perigord's with Mr. Payn, Mr. Hartley, Mr.
Lockhart, and several Englishmen. Went to the opera,
and saw Renaud with a *divertissement*.

'*February* 10. — Rode with Mr. Keay by the Duke of
Orleans's English garden and a barrier, a very beautiful
Grecian Rotunda by the side of it, to Pont Neuilly, a
very elegant bridge, with six elliptical arches, on the top

of a direct plane. The country round it beautiful.
Rode through the Bois de Boulogne, chiefly young wood,
where the king generally rides every morning, to Bagatelle, Comte d'Artois's small house, not inelegant, with a
garden, a false imitation of the English. Passed Madrid,
a gothic *château* built by Francis I. after his return from
Spain, inlaid with porcelain, but now ruinous, and sentenced to fall by the National Assembly. Saw Long-
champs, a little hill with a nunnery on its summit, in
which are musical performances the last three days of
Passion week. A few years ago a favorite opera-singer
was engaged there, and the crowd from Paris was far too
great to be accommodated. The day being fine, numbers
amused themselves with riding in the Bois de Boulogne.
The thing took, and in these days every year all Paris in
its best equipages pours out to parade in the Bois de Boulogne. The palace of Versailles, almost entirely built
from a hunting-seat by Louis XIV., who did not like St.
Germain's (a finer situation), as it commanded St. Denis,
where he was to be buried. Saw St. Cloud, the queen's
house, where the king resided last summer, — a very elegant modern house; the gardens are in infamous taste.
A beautiful day. Walked with Mr. Keay in the Tuileries; full of company. Saw the dauphin's garden and
duckery at the end of it, in which his name was sown in
mustard-seed, — Louis Dauphin. Fair people always in-
constant and wavering. Went to the Bouche de Fer, a
debating society on the principles of Rousseau, in the
Circus, his bust before the President, the Abbé Mailly;
a numerous company. Afterwards saw "The Apothecary"
and "Sourd" at M. de Montpensier's, and looked into the
Society of '89; nothing doing. Went to the Jacobins,
but it was over. If one hundred millions have been
spent on building it, as much has been spent on going to
see it. Châtelet not at the Jacobins, because no favorite,
as his friend Lafayette is not popular.

9

'*February* 12. — A delicious day. Rode to Vincennes, where is a palace in a very pleasant park, in which our Henry V. died, and in which Louis XIV. first saw Madame La Vallière, — a chapel with beautiful painted windows (mentioned by Gray), and a State prison, chamber within chamber, lighted by a narrow grated window and carved on the walls of each, to chase *ennui* from the victims of tyranny. From the roof is a delicious view of the suburbs of Paris and the country, and round each story runs a gallery with a low parapet, into which some of the prisoners were taken for air. Who can sigh on seeing the still gloom that pervades Versailles, the grandest palace and the most elegant village in the world, — who can sigh on seeing the grass grow in the courts of the one and the streets of the other, when he recollects that so many dungeons share its downfall? Dined at the *table d'hôte*, and afterward walked along the Seine and saw La Sainte Chapelle; mixed in every group that was collected by the buffoon and the ballad-singer, and walked in the Tuileries, which were full of company. Saw "Cupid and Psyche."

'*February* 13. — At the Church of Notre Dame, from a gallery, saw three *curés* elected by the Electoral Assembly in the great aisle; each from the pulpit delivered a short discourse expressive of his attachment to the present constitution. He said that his office as preacher was to enlighten the people and give energy to the laws; that heaven approved of the Confederation, and that to inculcate these sentiments would be the last employment of his life. High Mass performed. Afterwards the king and queen, with the two children and Monsieur and Madame walked to chapel. Saw them at Mass afterwards. The Tuileries gardens very full of company. Attempted the National Assembly with Mirabeau's ticket, but was refused: nobody admitted there. Mr. Keay dined with us on frog pie, and we went to see

"Didon" and "Le Dévin du Village," an opera, the words and the music by Rousseau, the fable very simple, the music in general charming.   To-morrow leave Paris.

'*February* 14.—Mr. Keay called and spent an hour with us, and said the Protestants were numerous in this town, but that all calculations were very erroneous and that there was no place of public worship but the English Ambassador's chapel; that the king had allowed twenty thousand a year to the opera, but not now, and owing to this circumstance and the *noblesse* having thrown up their boxes, it was in debt fifty thousand to its tradesmen; the Théâtre de Monsieur also much in debt; that in one of the churches at Rouen he saw nobody but a woman flat on the ground apparently in the greatest agony; that he watched till she rose up and went out: he had the curiosity to see her face; it was the wickedest in the world. Said that Rousseau copied music at Paris, when he had about £100 a year, but would not accept anything more than his due, as he (Mr. Keay) was told last night by a lady who took him some to copy purposely to see him, but that when she offered to leave more his wife assured her that he would not suffer her to take it; that the Revolution was in great measure ascribed to his "Contrat Social," but that Voltaire with his winning vivacity first led the French to think on the subject; that he saw him when he was received at the French Comedy with great honors, just after the present king had refused to see him at Versailles, though in policy he should have gone to meet him, and that that affair was the first blow to the old government; that he knew Diderot perfectly, and saw him just before his death; his advice to him he should always observe: "Never let a Frenchman come nearer to you than this," said he, stretching out his arm to some distance in his usual emphatic manner. The air mild and pleasant as October, but cloudy. The country soon improved with some rich distances, and

villages everywhere on the horizon, but was still open
and flat on the foreground and intersected with roads
planted on each side with trees in straight lines. The
ground almost all tillage, and the farmers at the plough;
a single man guides it. It is drawn by two horses
abreast, and no other man attends with a whip, as in
England. Our post-boy had ruffles and earrings, and
drove as fast as in England. Recollect that in the Paris
houses there are no passages, but that we always passed
through the eating parlor in our way to the drawing-
room. Saw frequently two smiths shoeing one horse.
At Senlis, where are two or three old collegiate churches,
we walked along a pleasant promenade that runs beside
the town and saw near twenty women washing clothes in
the little river Nonette, and beating them with a wooden
trowel. From thence passed through the Prince de
Condé's woods, being now near Chantilly, along a serpen-
tine road to Pont St. Maxence, so called from an elegant
bridge with three elliptic arches on strong pillars, and
a good towing-path built by Maxence, who built Pont
Neuilly and is now engaged on Pont Louis Seize. The
view from the bridge very rich and woody on both sides.
On the roadside from Bourgot were frequently four
handsome stone pillars forming a square; on inquiring,
found they were gibbets. Walked in the village, full of
rosy, healthy children with black eyes and round, merry
faces. On stopping to admire them a woman pleasantly
asked us if we would have a coop to take some of them
away with us. At the church door saw two little fellows
striding over the pathway with spelling-books under their
arms. On the pillar that formed one side of the portico
was fixed a board full of nails, with several written
advertisements of wood and houses upon it, as in some
of the country churchyards in England. The river Oise
winds here very pleasantly through the valley. Arrived
here at half-past four, and on inquiry learned, with regret,

that last night there had been a dance of about two
hundred people, with three or four violins, in the "Grand
Salon " by the riverside, and eight dances at a time, — one
sous for each dance. Played *au noble jeu de billard*, a
favorite game among the townspeople. In the coffee-
house at Versailles the laboring people of both sexes
drank coffee and talked politics. Saw a drunken man
there, the only one I have seen.

'*February* 15. — Set out at half-past six through a
flat country and along a straight road. Near Gournay,
which lies in a hollow, the scene became more unequal
and woody. A *château* stands just without the town.
Here walked on, while the horses were changing, and
had an extensive but uniform view on the left, the larks
singing and the air mild and serene. The young corn
springing up in different streaks with the freshest verdure, and a file of beeches skirting the edge of the horizon on each side, while little plots of villages appeared
here and there. Beyond Couchy les Pots left the chaise,
and walked above a mile under a row of apple-trees that
were planted on the field-side, — the sun shining and the
larks still singing. Breakfasted at Roye, at the " Soleil
d'or," where we were waited on by some very handsome
young women, the younger sisters of our landlady at
Pont St. Maxence. Walked on a pleasant terrace, which
surrounds the village, and is dignified with the name of
a rampart. A *liard* was levied from us by some boys to
play for at top. At some little distance saw a convent
now nearly deserted by the monks of the Cordeliers. The
day soon turned to heavy rain, which lasted till within
a post of Péronne, but the country continued flat and
the prospect extensive, diversified with streaks of corn
and fallow ground melting away into the softest colors
through the harmonizing medium of a rainy atmosphere.
The crucifix rose frequently by the wayside, a windmill
was generally turning on an eminence, and several spires

were frequently visible at once above the horizon. Passed by several orchards and soon descended to Péronne, a fortified town round which the Somme is carried, and into which we entered through two gateways. Ascended the ramparts by a crucifix before which a well-dressed woman was devoutly kneeling; commanded on one side the outskirts of the town, and on the other a valley nearly half a mile wide and flooded with water, but broken into little islands planted with cabbages or covered with willows and rushes. Observed two little towers enclosed with strong square walls that were each washed by the water and comprehended about half an acre. Imagined they were castles, but found them to be summer-houses in which the *bourgeois* dine and drink tea. From one part looked up the great street and the market-place. Descended into the town by the crucifix; but the scene was changed, some children playing merrily before it. Every Sunday evening is here consecrated to the dance in which the *bourgeois* and the servants are regularly taught; an academy is open for the latter to-night.

'At Marché le Pot met the Brussels *diligence*, a long unwieldy vehicle, containing eight inside passengers in three rows, three in a kind of cabriolet in front, two in a basket at the top, and an immense [mass of] luggage behind and before. It was drawn by eight horses, two abreast, with two postilions on the first and third near horse. It had hardly moved ten yards when it fell into a deep rut; a cry of despair immediately issued from it, the passengers jumped out from the front and crawled from the top, and the women within desired with great fervency to be let out. Above twenty people flew with ropes to restore it to its proper centre, and with great efforts it was removed from the rut without a downfall. In the mean time a cheerful fellow, who had descended from his post in front with the same ease and unconcern that he would have crossed a threshold, walked up to

our chaise door and inquired what news from Paris and
whether we were going to London.   He said he was a
Dutchman, and a rope-dancer by profession; that he had
served under Astley in London and also at Sadler's
Wells, and was now engaged by him at Paris, to which
place he was going.   At Roye had left the *diligence*
from Paris to Brussels where it stood, — the gaze of the
market-place.   In the bookseller's shop in the Palais
Royal asked for the "History of the Bastille," and a
well-dressed man immediately opening it [the shopman]
and unfolding a plan of it, "There," said he, "was Marmontel confined, and that," he added with all the unconcern possible, "was my apartment."   "You, sir?"
"Yes, sir, I published something that gave offence,
and I passed eight months there."   "Were you well
treated?"   "Never better, sir."   Are lodged at the
Grand Cerf, kept by the eldest sister of those at Pont
St. Maxence and Roye.

'*February* 16. — Set off at six precisely, by owl-light,
through the same flat country, and were driven by a
phlegmatic Fleming with a large round hat and a pipe
in his mouth.   At Cambrai, a large handsome town
where we breakfasted, saw the cathedral, a large old
building, the gates of the chancel sealed, with the names
of the Commissioners affixed to them.   A woman had
torn off part of the paper, saying they should not keep
her God in jail.   Saw the tomb and bust of Fénelon,
with a very true Latin epitaph.   The palace contiguous,
very old, the most modern part built by him.   Went
through the cloisters of the convent of Chartreuse and
saw a picture, by Rubens, of our Saviour taken down
from the Cross, — very fine coloring, with some good
figures.   Was shown it by one of the Fathers, a mild
cheerful man about fifty.   We desired to see his apartment; he nodded assent and said it was but small.   We
followed him up a brick staircase, that led from the

cloisters, into a long narrow gallery into which their different cells opened with their names inscribed upon them. His was indeed small, and consisted of a bed-chamber and oratory, with a little casement to each; altogether about twelve feet by six. I stepped into his study; there were several little phials on his desk. There was but one book, — a missal. He said they dined at eleven, had no breakfast, but supped at six, went early to bed, and rose at twelve, when their matins lasted till one. There were but seventeen monks there. In a new church lower down saw some very good painting in bas-relief. The Hôtel de Ville, in the market-place, just finished and very elegant. Left the town on foot, having dismissed our guide, — an old man who once lived in England with Lord Stormont, — and pursued the road to Brussels, having a valley on the left in which was a village shaded with trees. The country soon opened again, the eye commanding a wide circle, diversified by no near objects, but frequently pointed with above eight spires at once. Valenciennes, which we soon approached, lay low, but appeared very considerable from its towers and steeples. It proved .the largest town we had seen except Paris, and was very strongly fortified. Walked on the ramparts, but were stopped by a shower when we had completed but half the circuit. Returned into the town and crossed a very handsome *place*, distinguished by a pedestrian statue of Louis XV., an *hôtel de ville*, and a theatre. Saw the Hospital for Orphans, and the Citadel, — a modern brick building. From the ramparts had a Flemish view, — cold, tame, and watery. Here Boddington bought a puppy of an apothecary. "Otez vos cockades, Messieurs."

'*February* 17. — Set off before seven, and soon entered the emperor's dominions, along a straight road planted with willows, raised above the country, and terminated with a church. The face of it soon improved. Mons, where we breakfasted, is a large fortified town, with a very handsome *place*, in which is the Hôtel de Ville, and where the Austrian troops were exercising. The faces of the people were here quite Flemish, and had lost all the French vivacity ; but there were many very pretty women. Between this and Valenciennes was a stone pillar to the memory of the Prince of Hainault. Casteau, the first post, was a very romantic village, the ground broken, and the huts one above another. The landscape now became English, a valley on each side full of farm-houses and enclosures, and bounded by hills dotted with wood. The road continued straight to Brussels. On each side were many Santa Marias, enclosed in a kind of sentry-box and peeping through an iron lattice. Met several strolling friars, one of whom was taken into a coach by a fat *abbé*. As we approached Brussels saw low carts drawn by four dogs abreast and a horse as leader. Austrian Flanders, at least that part which is near the capital, is far pleasanter and more varied than French Flanders. The post-horse which the man rides has bells. The uniform changed from blue and scarlet to scarlet and yellow, and they were less scrupulous in passing another traveller than in France. At Brussels saw "L'Amant jaloux," an opera, in an oblong theatre, the boxes partitioned from each other and lighted within, — their fronts of wood, painted white, with light gold ornaments, in compartments very cheerful and elegant. The *parterre* full of officers. French dukes, marquises, and counts here.'

The glimpses of revolutionary Paris in this diary are the more valuable because they give us its social rather than its political aspects. It is 'France standing on the top of golden hours,' as Wordsworth described it, though without many of the signs Wordsworth saw, of ' human nature seeming born again.' The hearty admiration of

England expressed to Rogers by some of the most prominent leaders of the movement in France, was repaid on
the English side by the sympathy which all liberal minds
felt with Frenchmen.   More than one illustration of this
feeling is given in Rogers's correspondence.   One of the
literary acquaintances he had made in London was Dr.
John Moore, the father of Sir John Moore and of Admiral
Sir Graham Moore, and then best known as the author
of 'Zeluco,' the most popular novel of its time.   Dr.
Moore had published, in 1779, 'Views of Society and
Manners in France, Switzerland, and Germany,' and in
1787 a similar book on Italy.   He had also written
'Medical Sketches,'—a work which may have suggested
Warren's 'Passages from the Diary of a late Physician,'
as 'Zeluco' is said to have kindled the fancy of Byron and
led to the production of 'Childe Harold.'   'Zeluco,' which
has as a second. title, 'Various Views of Human Nature
taken from Life and Manners, Foreign and Domestic,'
was published in 1789; and Mrs. Barbauld says in her
Memoir of the author that it at once placed him in the
first rank of writers of that class.   Rogers probably met
Dr. Moore at the house of Miss Helen Williams, and,
different as the two men were, a warm friendship sprang
up between them.   Dr. Moore was a large man, with
shaggy eyebrows and a most expressive countenance;
shrewd and humorous in conversation, full of knowledge
of men and things.   He had been with the army in
Flanders, had studied medicine in Paris, had then practised as a surgeon in Glasgow till he was forty, and had
afterwards travelled for five years with the Duke of
Hamilton.   He was in his sixtieth year when 'Zeluco'
was published.   Rogers had probably received some introductions from him when he went to Paris, and wrote
to him during his stay in that capital.   Dr. Moore's
reply illustrates both the character of the man and the
feelings and opinions which were current at the time.

Dr. Moore to S. Rogers.

'DEAR SIR, — I thank you very cordially for your letter,
which came à propos to destroy the effect of recent
rumors : of a counter revolution, of the king being in
danger of being ravished by two old princesses, of insur-
rections in all quarters, etc., — all of which your satisfactory and perspicuous letter dispersed, as the fogs and
clouds are dispersed by the rays of the sun.   The abettors
of despotism will be continually inventing stories of the
same kind, and we may expect to hear of Spaniards
jumping over the Pyrenean mountains ; of the Emperor
giving peace to the Turks by the Pope's orders, that he
may be at more leisure to make war on the Christians ;
of armies in disguise at the gates of Paris, and other
tales equally probable.   Why should they not still hope
for the restoration of the Bastille, and the return of a
monarch in all the splendor of unlimited power ?   Do
not the Jews still look for the coming of the Messiah ?

' I envy your present opportunity very much of being
an eye-witness to the most complete triumph over tyranny
and debasing prejudices that Philosophy and the free
spirit of man ever enjoyed.   I always loved the French
as an ingenious and amiable people ; I now admire them
as real and enlightened Franks, and am not surprised
— as many here seem to be — that the National Assembly
have made so little progress towards the establishment of
a steady free constitution, but I wonder rather that they
have made so much.   It ought to be remembered that it
was an unforeseen accident (the foolish attack of Lambert
in the Tuileries) that threw the power so rapidly in their
hands ; and although they had the spirit to seize it with
ability, yet they must have respect to the prejudices of
that very populace who were the immediate instruments
of transferring it to them.   This no doubt clogs and
retards their progress in the rearing a stable and com-

modious structure of Freedom, but with a little time
I am persuaded *ça ira à la dernière perfection*, and they
have my best wishes.   Make my best compliments to M.
de Lafayette, and tell him so.   If I can get over to Paris
in summer I shall carry letters to him from his friend
Colonel Fitzpatrick and the Duchess of Devonshire.

'I have not yet seen M. Dupont's answer to Mr.
Burke ; but you will bring what is most curious when
you come.

'There is nothing new here, only some people imagine
that Pitt intends to send his veto by the Baltic and the
Mediterranean against the Empress's seizing Constanti-
nople.   *Pour moi, je n'en sçai rien.*

'Adieu, my dear Rogers ! Believe me always, with
much esteem, sincerely yours,

'J. MOORE.

'CLIFFORD STREET, Feb. 10, 1791.'

Dr. Moore's letter fitly ends a chapter, the notes to
which may be fairly regarded as the disappointing answer
of history to the anticipations he expresses, — anticipations which Rogers, as his diary shows, fully shared.
The disillusion came quickly enough for them and for
Europe.   We have but to put ourselves in their position
to understand the revulsion of feeling which in this
country threw back the cause of social and political reform for forty years.   Rogers looked back on this visit
to Paris in 1791 with a feeling of horror.   He often
spoke of the men he had then seen, but he did not re-
fresh his memory by references to his diary, which he
seems to have put aside and almost forgotten.   To read
it would have been indeed to walk among ruins and
tombs.   He always recollected with a shudder that most
of the men he met were, at the very time he was talking
to them and sharing their glowing anticipations, standing,
as it were, with one foot in the grave.   There are, per-

haps, few more moving spectacles in history than that of
the old Duchess-dowager de la Rochefoucauld, ' a figure
never seen now but in a picture frame,' talking to Rogers
with enthusiasm of the Revolution, declaring that she
had not felt her many infirmities since it began, and then
within eighteen months driven into exile and called to
witness the massacre of her son by the angry populace
he had lived to serve. Rogers himself, Talleyrand, and
Lafayette were almost the only men whose names occur
in this chapter who lived to see any approach to the
rearing of that 'stable and commodious structure of
freedom' which Dr. Moore hoped the French would in a
little time bring to perfection. The whole political life
of Rogers's Whig friends in 1791, with the exception of
Richard Sharp, was spent under the cloud of public
disfavor and discouragement which settled down on all
political movements that seemed to look in the direction
of popular enfranchisement. It was not till the time
of the great Reform Bill that the English people fully
recovered from the frightful apprehension that triumphs
of philosophy and the free spirit of man over tyranny
and debasing prejudices, to use Dr. Moore's words,
might lead in England, as they had led in France, to a
Reign of Terror.

CHAPTER VI.

THE memorable visit to revolutionary Paris was only one of the events of this year which Rogers has left on record. On his return to London in the latter part of February, he naturally resumed his morning journeys from Stoke Newington to the banking-house in Freeman's Court. On one of these daily journeys an event happened of which he often spoke to his friends with some emotion. Mr. Dyce reports it in the 'Table Talk' in his usual bald and half-remembered manner; but the best and most vivid account is given in the postscript to a letter addressed by the Rev. John Mitford of Benhall to the 'Gentleman's Magazine,' soon after Rogers's death.[1] Mr. Mitford himself, in the letter, illustrates the premature confidence with which some of Rogers's friends spoke and wrote about him, by expressing the opinion that Rogers had left no diaries behind him. In the postscript Mr. Mitford says: —

'The last drive I ever took with Mr. Rogers in his chariot was one often previously made by us into the City, to pay one of his regular calls on his oldest friend, Mr. William Maltby of the London Institution, who had been his schoolfellow more than eighty years previous to this time, and who died a year or two before him, nearly at the same age. In returning by the City Road, he

---

[1] Gentleman's Magazine, vol. xlv. p. 147.

pulled the check-string opposite to the Bunhill Fields Burial-ground, and then desired me to get out and read the inscription on the stone which stands conspicuously over the grave of the well-known Thomas Hardy. This being done, he said: "You see that little chapel opposite; go and look carefully at the house which stands there to the left of it, and then come back and get in." This all duly performed, and again seated side by side, he said: "When I was a young man in the banking-house, and my father lived at Newington, I used every day in going into the City to pass by this place. One day in returning I saw a number of respectable persons of both sexes assembled here, all well dressed in mourning, and with very serious look and behavior. The door of the house was open, and they entered it in pairs. I thought that, without impropriety, I might join them; so we all walked upstairs, and came to a drawing-room in the midst of which was a table; on this table lay the body of a person dressed in a clergyman's robes, with bands, and his gray hair shading his face on either side. He was of small stature, and his countenance looked like wax. We all moved round the table, some of the party much affected, with our eyes fixed on the venerable figure that lay before us; and as we moved on, others came up and succeeded in like manner. After we had gone the round of the table in our lingering procession we descended as we came. The person that lay before us was the celebrated John Wesley, and at the earnest request of his congregation, they were permitted to take this pathetic and affectionate farewell of their beloved pastor." '

Wesley died on the 2d of March, 1791. Southey does not mention this lying-in-state in the house in the City Road, but only records that on the day before the funeral the body was carried into the chapel, 'and there lay in a kind of state becoming the person, dressed in his clerical habit, with gown, cassock, and band; the old clerical cap on his head, a Bible in one hand, and a white handkerchief in the other.' The crowds that flocked to see him were so great that the funeral was accelerated, and took place between five and six in the morning. The scene which Rogers so vividly remembered, in which he had been privileged to catch a glimpse of the great man's face as he lay dead, must have been an earlier and more private lying-in-state than that which Southey records.[1]

Two of Rogers's distinctive characteristics were his faculty of rapid and correct observation and his retentive memory. He used to say that Samuel Boddington, his companion in the visit to revolutionary Paris, attended a series of lectures on Memory, delivered by the Stokes of those days, Mr. Feinaigle, but on being asked the name of the lecturer, could not recollect it. Rogers was asked why he did not attend the series. He answered that he wished to learn the art of forgetting. The remarkable volume of his 'Recollections,' published by his nephew Mr. William Sharpe after his death, has shown the wonderful power he possessed of noting down the actual words he had heard in a long conversation. The earliest illustration which his diaries contain of this power of reproducing an evening's talk, is an account of a conversation at the house of Miss Helen Williams. At one of her literary parties he met Henry Mackenzie, whose acquaintance he had already made in Edinburgh, and a number of other men and women of letters, some of whom were then famous, but are now forgotten, and one or two of whom were then comparatively unknown, but are now familiar names after nearly a hundred years.

---

[1] Mr. Dyce in the last edition of his 'Table Talk' quotes Mr. Mitford's letter, and expresses the opinion that Rogers's memory had played him false. The view I have taken of the apparent discrepancy is, I think, far the most likely to be the true explanation.

'*April* 21, 1791.— At Miss Williams's.

'Mr. Mackenzie, a man of very mild and unassuming manners, was first announced, and began upon Edinburgh. "I believe," said he, "conversation is more cultivated there than here. In London the ardor of pursuit is greater. The merchant, the lawyer, and the physician are enveloped in their different professional engagements, but the Scotchman will retire early from the counter or the counting-house to lecture on Metaphysics, or make the grand tour of the arts and sciences. I believe we have a more contemplative turn than you, and it arises partly from a defect,— the little commerce and agriculture we have among us. We are also more national, and there is not a laborer among us that is not versed in the history of his country. Local history is what we are particularly fond of."

'"I had observed it," I said. "Not a Highlander I met but could give me the history of every pebble about his village."

'Mr. Mackenzie: "I remember an innocent trick that was once played on an Englishman. When Dr. Roebuck was riding in Scotland, he was assured by a friend that every peasant knew Greek. 'Let us visit, for instance, that farmhouse!' Dr. Roebuck assented. It belonged to Wilkie, the celebrated author of the 'Epigoniad,' and he was at work as usual in the dress of a laborer. Dr. Roebuck made an observation on tillage. 'Yes, sir,' said Wilkie, 'but in Sicily there was once a different method,' and he quoted Theocritus. Dr. Roebuck was thunder-struck. Wilkie was an original character. He had conversed so long with the ancients that he had lost every trace of the modern in his composition. When he paid Edinburgh a visit at a time that party ran high on some particular subject, he attacked the leading wits of the day in a large circle with such spirit that he set them to flight, and when his hearers, who were struck

10

with the uncouthness of his look and gesture, expressed
their surprise at his courage : 'Shall I,' said he, 'who
have kept company so long with Agamemnon, the king
of men, shall I shrink from a contest with such a puny
race?' But after all," said Mr. Mackenzie, returning
to his subject, "Dr. Johnson was perhaps right when he
said of us that every man had a taste, and no man a
bellyful."

'"And yet you will allow that there are many exceptions to the last part of the rule, sir?" said Miss Baillie,
a very pretty woman with a very broad Scotch accent.
"Mr. Adam Smith —"

'"Yes, ma'am," Mr. Mackenzie interrupted, with a
warmth he seldom discovered, "Mr. Smith was an exception. He had twice Dr. Johnson's learning — who
only knew one language well, the Latin — though he
had none of his affectation of it. He was one of the
mildest and most amiable of men, a good son, an affectionate brother, and a sincere friend. The last time we
met was at a club which was held every Sunday evening
at his own house (I had once the pleasure to see you
there, sir).[1] He was very cheerful, but we persuaded
him not to sup with us, and he said, about half-past
nine, as he left the room : 'I love your company, gentlemen, but I believe I must leave you — to go to another
world.' He died a few hours after. Before I came that
evening he had burned, with the assistance of Dr. Black,
sixteen volumes in manuscript on Jurisprudence — the
sum of one course of his Lectures at Glasgow, as was
the 'Wealth of Nations' of another; but these had not
received his last corrections, and from what he had seen
he had formed a mean opinion of posthumous publications in general. With a most retentive memory his
conversation was solid beyond that of any man. I have

---

[1] See Rogers's visit to Edinburgh, p. 85.

often told him after half-an-hour's conversation — 'Sir, you have said enough to make a book.' Dr. Blair by these means introduced many of Adam Smith's thoughts on Jurisprudence into his lectures, but when I told him of it — 'He is very welcome,' said he, 'there is enough left.' "

' I inquired after his old servant.

'Mr. Mackenzie: "He was provided with a place in the Custom House at the request of everybody. Mr. Smith left the bulk of his fortune to his nephew, a very clever young man. But perhaps the Scotch cannot claim him entirely, for he received part of his education at Oxford."

'During this conversation came Dr. Cadogan, Mr. Jerningham, Dr. Baillie, and Cadell with his daughter. Tea now walked in, and drew a disquisition on its merits from Dr. Cadogan. Dr. Johnson's immoderate love of it was mentioned, and the remark brought him again upon the carpet. Lord Monboddo's contempt of his Dictionary was mentioned. Mr. Seward (who now introduced Mr. Merry, a very genteel, handsome man) said he had silenced him with quoting James Harris's high opinion of it, and that when somebody had given Johnson a list of its imperfections — "Are those all?" said he; "I thought there had been a thousand more." Mr. Mackenzie said Johnson's greatest fault was in rejecting every word from the Saxon.

' As the tea went round, the sugar suggested the slave-trade and the late debate.

' Dr. Cadogan thought it the most disgraceful evening ever spent by the House of Commons.

' Mr. Mackenzie thought the immediate abolition dangerous in its consequences in the islands. So did Dr. Baillie and Mr. Cadell. Mr. Cadell said a whole people was not chargeable with any solitary acts of cruelty, and instanced a late case of a chimney-sweeper's apprentice.

'Mr. Mackenzie: "You should consider not the act itself, but its impression on the minds of the people. An English mob would, I doubt not, massacre the chimney-sweeper in a moment; but I fear the Jamaica people view barbarity with unconcern."

'Mr. Merry said he believed it indeed, and he blushed for his country.

'The company then rose up to read a small poem of Mr. Day's, of which Mr. Seward proposed an emendation —

"Turns on his hunters and then valiant falls."

'There were different opinions; and different groups were formed. Mr. Jerningham asked me concerning the fate of Mr. Merry's play. I fear, said he, that his style is too artificial for tragedy.

'In another place stood Dr. Moore, Mr. Merry, and Cadell on Boswell and Johnson and Piozzi; and in another stood Seward and Mackenzie and Dr. Kippis in judgment on the poem. Mr. Mackenzie said that Robert Burns had lately written a beautiful poem in Scotch, called the "Kirk of Alloa."[1] It fell flat towards the conclusion.

'Mr. Mackenzie: "The same young man who wrote the German tragedy mentioned in the Edinburgh Trans-actions, has since published another, full of uncommon merit and more regular, the last scene particularly striking. A nobleman's son in love with a musician's daughter is induced by his father, who is an enemy to the match, to think her false, and in a frenzy he stabs her. Her innocence then appears, and he stabs his father and himself. The German works appear to great disadvantage here, as they are translated from the French only, which is very bad, the translators gliding over

---

[1] This is 'Tam o' Shanter.' It was written for Captain Grose in return for a drawing of Alloway Kirk, and published in Grose's 'Antiquities of Scotland.'

every difficulty. I have learned a little German since
that paper of mine appeared, and I am now struck with
their tragedies particularly, though the unities are not
observed."

'I said, only one of those was of consequence, — unity
of character.

'Mr. Mackenzie: "Mr. Smith wrote a charming piece
on that subject in a periodical paper at Glasgow, in
which Lord Loughborough engaged, but which was soon
dropped, the parties being discovered."

'Mr. Jerningham inquired after Dr. Beattie.

'Mr. Mackenzie said his spirits were naturally low,
and were now still lower from family affliction, the confinement of his wife, and the death of his son. He then
adverted to Lord Monboddo. He is a friend of the slave
trade because the ancients encouraged it. He bathes
every morning in a cold and a hot bath, and afterwards
anoints himself because they did so.

'"Ay," said Mr. Seward, "I remember that circumstance drew a pun from Johnson, notwithstanding his
aversion to puns. 'That man of Grease,' said he. I
laughed at it, and he affected to be angry, and said he
did not intend a pun."

'Mr. Mackenzie: "When I congratulated him [Lord
Monboddo] on his recovery from a fever, he assured me
it was not one of your modern nervous fevers but a true
Roman fever, a burning fever. He complains that the
present race have no voice now he grows deaf, and often
desires the barristers to speak up."

'Mr. Seward: "He is come to town partly to buy an
orang-outang, that he may take him to Edinburgh and
teach him to talk and think."

'Mr. Mackenzie: "He has been often imposed upon
with baboons which have passed for that species, particularly with one which had been taught to walk with a
stick and was afterwards shown in Edinburgh."

'I observed that Lord Monboddo had that day se'ennight asserted that no man in the House of Commons
could make or deliver a period but Mr. Pitt, and no man
recite Milton but the Lord Chancellor.

'Dr. Kippis: "He is a great enemy to short sentences, but he is wrong in his notion of the sentence of
the ancients."

'Mr. Mackenzie: "His admiration of Milton is now
so high, that he begins to think it unintelligible to the
vulgar. He once set Macklin to read it, but found so
much fault with him, that he threw the book to his
lordship saying, 'Do read it yourself.' He admires Mrs.
Siddons, but does not think she does justice to Milton.
He once saw her act the lady in Comus."

'The circle now contracted to Mr. Jerningham, Mr.
Merry, Mr. Seward, Dr. Moore, the ladies, and myself.

'Mr. Merry said he should pass the summer in France,
and that he knew Madame de Condorcet. Asked me if
I had ever played at a kind of question and answer at
her house with the Abbé Sieyès. Mentioned also another
game similar to our blind-man's-buff. He said Condorcet's house was charmingly seated on the Seine, of
which I knew nothing, as I had paid my visits there at
night.

'Mr. Jerningham asked me doubtingly if Paris was
quiet.

'Mr. Merry said he had walked at midnight to his
lodgings from the Palais Royal frequently with no
alarm.

'I said I admired Madame de Condorcet, and that if
I left England again it would be with Sir Charles Gran-
dison's resolution to form no attachment.

'Mr. Merry: "Sir Charles is translated into Italian and
universally laughed at by the Italian ladies, among whom
there are no Clementinas. Sir Charles wore a wig, and
the coach and six are continually coming in. Do you

remember Sir Charles's wig? Lovelace's wig fell off in a most affecting situation. Wig-stealing was once a very lucrative profession, when wigs sold for fifty pounds apiece. Many a man has had his wig snatched off, when he put his head out of the coach window to speak to his coachman."

'Mr. Jerningham said Richardson was ridiculed at Florence when he was there.

'Dr. Moore mentioned Voltaire's contempt of Clarissa, who thought Tomlinson and — which was the good character? "Lovelace," said Merry — a laugh.

'Miss Williams said that Mrs. Siddons read Clarissa at Streatham last autumn for the first time, and was much struck with it.

'Mr. Merry asked if she felt on the stage. I said she had assured me she did.

'Dr. Moore: "It is impossible. Good acting requires a cool judgment and a clear memory. It is not acting your own part but another's. What a burden must so many different characters be to the memory! Yet an old actor will forget his lesson of last night, and learn another for this evening, as easily as you can change your clothes. What is very singular, they never want more than their part of the dialogue."

'The conversation now turned upon feeling.

'Dr. Moore: "We are struck differently by the same thing. 'I remember,' says Rousseau, 'a fine picture by Le Sueur; the subject, Alexander drinking the physic prescribed by Philip, at the same time that he puts a letter into that physician's hand, — a letter which accuses him of an intention to poison him. Everybody was struck with the piece, but particularly a boy who shuddered at the sight. Upon being questioned concerning the reason, he said it was to think that he could drink so black a dose.'"

'Mr. Jerningham took his leave, and it was observed

that he was aristocratic, though one of his brothers who lived at Náples has been obliged to leave it on account of the freedom of his language.

'Mr. Seward: "Mrs. Montagu, too, is an aristocrat and a friend to the slave trade. But I suspect her of art. She has often diverted me with instances of Dr. Price's simplicity."

'I said Mrs. Montagu was a composition of art. She has so long been attached to the trick and show of life, as Mrs. Piozzi expressed it of her, that she has no taste for the simplicity of a great mind. The genuine soul of nature has forsaken her.[1]

'"What a beautiful expression is that of Paine!" said Mr. Merry; and the next — "His hero or his heroine must be a tragedy victim," etc. — and again "We have dropped our baby-clothes and breeched ourselves in manhood." He seemed a warm admirer of Paine.

'On the feeling of actors Mr. Seward observed that Garrick affected to feel his part deeply, and that one night when Johnson spoke loud between the scenes, Garrick, who was acting Richard, cried out, "Don't talk so loud, you disturb my feelings!" "Pooh!" said Johnson, "can *Ponch* [as he pronounced it always] feel?"'

The Mr. Seward mentioned in the above conversation was not the Rev. Mr. Seward of Lichfield, the father of Miss Seward the poetess, a man whom Johnson de-

---

[1] This was not the general opinion respecting Mrs. Montagu, though it is a most striking circumstance that two observers like Mackenzie and Rogers should have agreed in it. Lord Bath, as we learn from a note of Croker's, said of Mrs. Montagu that he did not believe a more perfect human being was ever created. Sir Joshua Reynolds repeated the words to Burke with the observation that Lord Bath could not have said more. 'And I do not think that he said a word too much,' was Burke's reply. Rogers knew Mrs. Montagu in her old age. She was more than seventy when this conversation at Miss Williams's took place, and she died in 1800 at the age of eighty.

scribed as having the ambition to be a fine talker, and as
going to Buxton and such places where he might find
companies to listen to him.   It was Mr. William Seward,
F.R.S., of whom Johnson had spoken in a letter to Boswell in 1777 as a great favorite at Streatham, who
had edited a book entitled 'Anecdotes of Distinguished
Persons.'   Boswell acknowledges indebtedness to him for
several communications concerning Johnson.   He was
forty-four at the time of the above conversation, and
died eight years later, in 1799.   Robert Merry is chiefly
remembered as one of the writers attacked by Gifford in
the 'Baviad' and the 'Mæviad.'   He was the Della
Crusca of Gifford's preface.   He had been educated at
Harrow and Christ's College, Cambridge; had studied
for the bar, and then joined the army as an officer in the
Guards.   Having gone to Florence, where a group of
British poetasters were writing poems to one another in
the 'Florence Miscellany,' he entered into the scheme,
and on his return to England became one of the leaders
of a school.   With curious appropriateness they took
their name from the Della Cruscan Academy in Florence,
— a Society formed in 1582 to winnow the chaff from the
Italian language and leave the pure wheat behind.   The
English Della Cruscans were chaff without grain, bran
with the least possible admixture of flour: the mere
refuse the signature Della Crusca implied.   Yet for a
moment they met the public taste.   Macaulay, in his
'Essay on Byron,' speaks of them as signs that a literary
revolution was at hand.   'There was a ferment' — he
tells us — 'in the minds of men, a vague craving for
something new, a disposition to hail with delight anything that might at first sight wear the appearance of
originality.'   Hence the temporary success of writers
now utterly forgotten.   'Anything which could break the
dull monotony of the correct school was acceptable.'
'Macpherson and Della Crusca were to the true reformers

of English poetry what Knipperdoling was to Luther or Clootz to Turgot.'[1] The Della Cruscans were the Spasmodics of their time. Gifford in the 'Baviad' speaks of 'Merry's Moorfields[2] whine,' and rhymes it with 'Greathead's idiot line.' In the 'Mæviad' he writes:

> '. . . while Merry and his nurslings die,
> Thrill'd with the liquid peril of an eye,
> Gasp at a recollection, and drop down
> At the long streamy lightning of a frown.'

Mr. Jerningham's criticism of Merry's play that his style was too artificial for tragedy was the gentle view of one of his friends. Mr. Jerningham was himself one of the Della Cruscans. Gifford writes:—

> 'See snivelling Jerningham at fifty weep
> O'er lovelorn oxen and deserted sheep,'

and speaks of him as 'a gentleman with the physiognomie d'un mouton qui rêve.' He pours worse contempt on Este and Topham, the parson and captain who between them edited 'The World,' and who were literary arbiters in the days when Gifford was beating pieces of leather smooth, and working problems on them with a blunted awl. Rogers used to say that he felt great pleasure when told that Este had said of him: 'A child of Goldsmith, sir;' and that, as reader at Whitehall, Este read the service so beautifully that Mrs. Siddons used to go to the Chapel Royal to listen to his elocution. Gifford's lash fell on this school in 1794 and 1796, and scattered it to the winds. Merry went to America, and Este died insane.

Rogers was now in his twenty-eighth year, and was quietly at work in most of his leisure hours polishing

---

[1] Essays, vol. ii. pp. 334, 335.

[2] The great Bethlehem Hospital — the Bedlam of popular tradition — stood in Moorfields.

his second poem to perfection. Yet his life seems to have been so full of business, visiting, and travel, that there was little space left for serious work. His health was still weak, and he was advised to take exercise on horseback. During the early summer of this year, 1791, he made a journey in this fashion through a great part of Wales. His quick observation and retentive memory have enabled him to hand down some valuable sketches of South Wales as it was in the days of our great-grandfathers.

The diary of this journey is broken into two parts, the first extending from the 17th to the 30th of June, and the second from the 19th to the 22d of July. The volume containing the intervening period has probably been lost. The entries chiefly consist of descriptions of the scenery; but there are now and then glimpses of contemporary manners and of passing events. He begins by noting the solitude of the London streets at four in the morning, which was the hour of starting, and anticipates a common remark of travellers in these days of railways, by saying that the rapidity of a stage-coach allows no time for observation, so that the architecture of an Adam or the statuary of a Damer, Sion Gate, and the Keystone of Henley Bridge were equally unnoticed. He says that Abingdon market-place, and Fairford church, where he probably stopped to see the windows, left pleasing traces on his memory. 'In the evening walked in the classic park of Lord Bathurst.' The day's stage seems therefore to have been from London, by way of Henley and Abingdon, to Cirencester. The next day he 'rode with the keeper through Lord Bathurst's woods and saw a favorite seat of Pope,' and then on to Birdlip Hill, from which the counties of Worcester, Hereford, and Gloucester 'spread like a carpet beneath' him. Thence through a delicious country to Ross, finding there a very agreeable and intelligent

apothecary, Mr. Pope, and sleeping in the house of the
' Man of Ross.'   The diary next day records a row upon
the river.

'19th. — Left Ross at ten in a small boat with two
oars.   The church bells chimed most musically, and the
sound came floating among the hills down the river long
after the spire had disappeared.   Passed under the
bridge, and in a few minutes saw Wilton Castle just
above us on a green bank on the left, its round tower and
grated window mantled with ivy.   These ruins have no
majesty, but they are very soothing, and strike the mind
as a first object.   A little line of cottages lies below them,
— the village of Wilton.   Glided down the stream under
a sedgy shore on the right, the left fringed with willows,
and on the surface of the water floated white flowers,
here called greeds. . . .   Ross spire continually sinks and
rises to the eye of the voyager, and the river, having
formed a noble curve, now returns almost up to it.   A
walk from the churchyard, called Kyrle's Walk, runs
down to a summer-house which here overlooks the river.
A very steep and rich eminence, intersected with hedge-
rows, among which are several cottages and a little farmhouse called Weir-end, with its appendages — a barn, a
poultry-yard, and a haystack — now presents itself, but
soon sinks to the left, and is succeeded by the humble
village of Groson, a cluster of thatched huts by the
waterside, with their hanging gardens and a succession
of green enclosures ascending rapidly above them.   Before the most conspicuous of these huts lay several loose
and newly-felled trunks of trees, and a vessel lay moored
near the spot.   The boatman dignified it with the name
of a timber-yard.   So far the scene had never risen above
the simple and humble style of pastoral beauty, but its
character soon changed.   In front, and sweeping round
to the right, a superb amphitheatre of wood and pasture

unfolded; the Friary, a little farm half discovering itself
near the summit; and on the left, near the base, Goodrich Castle, with its towers and battlements, gave a
glimpse of the grandeur which soon burst upon us. . . .
Landed at the ferry, and, crossing a meadow, ascended
through a glade of ancient elms to the ruin. The port-
cullises, the pointed windows, the round towers were
hung with large masses of ivy. The structure in its
present state is very extensive. Elm and ash trees of
considerable height have taken possession of its internal
courts. The daws were very clamorous at our intrusion,
and a white owl fluttered from the fractured mouldings
of a window. The view from it in front is very rich
and extensive. Directly in front, and not above two
miles off, is Ross spire, with the Chase, a long woody
ridge, in the background. Behind are hanging meadows.
Returned to the boat. In our course we continually
passed the fisher, with his wicker basket on his back,
angling for salmon-fry and grayling knee-deep in the
water. The left bank, which had as yet been low, became now very steep, with cottages perched one above
another, half sheltered with wood, and often discovered
only by the blue wreaths of smoke that ascended from
them. One of the most observable was a basket-maker's.
In his little garden, which was almost a precipice, hung
linen to dry on a line, and his threshold was strewed
with heaps of rushes in the sun. Everything wore the
face of cheerful industry. Passed a fisherman's hut,
which had a very fresco appearance behind a clump of
trees. A brown pitcher had been left on the landing-
place, and against the bank rested a coracle, a small
leathern boat. The man mentioned by Gilpin, who navi-
gated the Wye and reached the Bristol Channel in one
of these vessels, was Luke Hughes. Near Bristol, a mile
beyond the river's mouth, he was hailed by the king's
yacht stationed there, the crew thinking that he floated

on a cask. ' He went on board, and was made welcome, but returned to his nutshell. From either hand shoots up a high promontory. On the left is a chain of orchards, the apple-trees twisting into a thousand forms, with beautiful cows grazing on the shore. Pass on the right the coal wharf at Lidbrook, a busy scene, but properly softened down by the woods that nearly envelop it. On the left in a meadow a plain old house called Courtfield. On this spot Henry V. is said to have been nursed. An ancestor of Mr. Vaughan, to whom it now belongs, kept the ferry-boat at Goodrich, and when Henry IV. came disguised on his way to Monmouth, where the queen lay in, he first learned from the ferryman the birth of his son Henry, and was invited by him with honest exultation to drink at the alehouse kept there. The king gave him this estate. This is the boatman's tale. The little church of Welsh Bicknor to which Henry IV. gave gold communion plate, rose now by the green hillside, with yews in its churchyard and the parsonage built of gray stone close by it. Red and blue cornflowers fringed the opposite bank. It was a scene of great simplicity. A succession of cottages on the left, with their orchards grazed by horses, several of which were standing in different groups in the water; the water wagtail running and flying along the shelving rocks on the right. A blue volume of smoke now spread itself over the pointed wood which announced Coldwell Rocks. . . . Here we came to anchor, and the boatmen drawing water from a fine spring on the bank, which gives the name to this part of the river, I dined in full view of this charming perspective. While they were at their repast I wandered half a mile along the river, till I came directly opposite the rocks. Cottages and orchards were hanging near their bases; in the centre was a lime-kiln, into which the sheep had retreated from the sun, and not a single sound was heard but the tinkling of the wether's bell, when I

was roused from a delightful reverie by the appearance
of one of the boatmen, who immediately hallooed to his
comrades, who were dispersed in pursuit of me. The
echo among the old woods gave immediate life to the
scene. Re-embarked, and wound round these majestic
rocks. Others soon towered above the wood on the left,
less bold, but correspondent. The village on the right is
called Coldnose, the sun seldom shining upon it. . . .
Landed here on the opposite side, and half a mile from
the spring, and was conducted by a woman who showed
me her orchard, garden, and cottage, in which was a poor
solitary jay in a wicker basket up the rocks. She lived
by spinning, brewed and baked for herself, made her own
cider, and kept only a few ducks. Said the cottagers on
each side often ferried over to visit one another, that
winter was very dreary, but the boats which passed in
summer were a great amusement to them. Attended by
a little nephew and two girls she led me up a winding
path to the green summit of a projecting rock called
Symond's Yat, which commanded a cluster of wooded
hills in the foreground, the distant and whimsical windings of the Wye and a wide stretch of cultivated country
fading away in the blue and purple tints of distance.
Directly before us was an immense hill, round which the
Wye made a circuit of above three miles. Descended,
and embarked at the New Weir, an iron forge, where the
rocks on each side tower to an immense height, often in
very grotesque forms. Here the river makes a considerable fall, and we descend by a lock. This scenery continued about a mile, with nearly the grandeur of Matlock
and the solitude of Dovedale. Passed a small house, the
greatest fishery on the river, with a long shed to hang
the coracles in, and several barked trunks, on which the
nets are spread. The coracles go down the river two at
a time, one on each side, drawing the net along to sweep
the river. . These pairs succeed each other every ten min-

utes. The Dean Forest still hung on our right, and we
now came to what is called Slaughterhouse Stream, the
deer, many head of which are still in the Forest, having
been formerly shot here by the bowmen as they came
down to drink. The rocks continued like ruined towers
mantled with ivy and brushwood, till at St. Martin's
Pool, where was the deepest water in our course, they
died away. . . . Threaded several reefs that raised a
surf in the river, and shot rapidly by Dixon Church, a
humble and solitary white building on the left shore.
A magnificent wood now rose in front and seemed to
preclude all further progress. As we advanced it withdrew to the right, and on the left rose Monmouth spire.
The bridge and the town above it appeared soon afterwards, and at six in the evening we concluded the
voyage.'

The next day he records a ride to Raglan, 'a beggarly
village,' with a neat inn; a visit to the Castle, 'a most
noble ruin;' and on to Usk, where there was a village
fair. Continuing his ride he describes the view of the
Bristol Channel with the Steep and Flat Holms and
here and there a sail. At Newport — which he describes
as 'a neat town on the side of a hill, the church, like
most others near the coast, a conspicuous landmark' —
he 'saw several boats waiting to catch the coal at low
water which is washed in flakes from the mountains.'
This was the coal trade of Newport in 1791. The journey continues over the hills and through the marsh to
Cardiff, where he walks round the Castle with 'a sensible
little fellow, my landlord's son at the " Cardiff Arms." '
Next day to Llandaff, with its ruined Cathedral, 'part of
it included in the modern Cathedral, a strange medley of
Grecian and Gothic.' Then on to Caerphilly Castle, 'less
picturesque and less perfect than Raglan, but with more
traces of magnificence and on an infinitely larger scale;'

and thence along the banks of the Taff and over the hills to Cowbridge. On the way —

'On Newbridge Hill was overtaken by two good-natured, pleasant men on one horse, who had come from a large foundry twelve miles from Pontypridd — or bridge built of the earth — and who accompanied me to Cowbridge. From them I learned several anecdotes. The Welsh are a very joyous social people. At weddings they often muster friends and relations to the number of fifty on horseback; and often make what is called "a bidding." Each gives a crown, or some trifle, to the newly-married couple, and the sum has amounted to one hundred pounds. When a family are in distress there is very often "a pye." The good woman of the house makes a great many pies, and on a Sunday a considerable number will meet and dine and dance, and afterwards make her a present. The relator of this story had often been of the party. At weddings the bagpipe is often played, as in Scotland, and at funerals the church singers always lead the procession with a psalm. The women here wear black beaver hats, gowns of blue or blue-and-red check, which descend to the knee, and a blue or black petticoat. The men and boys also wear a jacket and often trousers of check. About Cardigan the women wear wooden shoes. The sudden drop they make in curtseying and the familiar nod are very diverting. From Easter to Whitsuntide the peasantry dance every Saturday night. The clergyman frequently translates his text into Welsh. . . . Curacies are about £30 or £25 per annum here.'

The journal of the next two days records the continuation of the ride to Swansea and Carmarthen, summarized in a letter to his father.

S. Rogers to his Father.

' Saturday, June 25, [Postmark] 1791.

'DEAR SIR, — I received your kind letter to-day, as
well as Martha's enclosing a very long and entertaining
one from Mrs. Piozzi. She says an account of her little
fête will overtake me in the newspapers before I reach
Monmouth, but I have not seen it in any of them. All
I learn from them is that Mr. Sergeant Bond has with-
drawn his name from the list of stewards. I wrote to
you from Pill. Margam next morning gave me great
pleasure, but the orangery is in decay, and the view
along the sea-coast rather dreary. At Neath, which is
most charmingly situated, there was a fair. I dined
with the farmers, — as I had done the day before with
the collectors of excise at Bridgend, — and there met
with a gentlemanlike, sensible young man, an attorney
from Swansea. He offered to ride over with me, and as
I found him to be a man of good character I accepted
this offer. He offered also to go with me to the ball
at Swansea in the evening, and through him I danced
with the surgeon's wife, a very pretty woman about
twenty who has just left the Quakers. The harp was
the principal instrument. My sisters will smile to
hear that I have been kicking my heels at a Welsh
Assembly.

' Sir Herbert Mackworth's house at Neath commands
a very beautiful stretch of country, but just before his
parlor windows he has erected a steam-engine and large
copper-works. They are actually on the lawn before his
house : but if they are a source of profit he may think
them the finest objects which it commands. Yesterday
I had a most delicious ride of twenty-five miles to Llan-
dilo, where I saw the ruins of Carreg Cennin, an impregnable fortress, and the fairy scenes round Dynevor

Castle. I find that Mr. Rice, the member for the county and owner of this enchanting spot, is brother-in-law to Mr. M. Dorrien.[1]

'To-day I made a pilgrimage to the top of Grongar Hill,[2] but a mizzling rain came on before I had reached it. I rode through the delightful Vale of Towy to Carmarthen, which was crowded with market people. Welsh is everywhere the current language, and it is curious to hear children that have just left the cradle conversing in sounds that are as unintelligible to me as the Sphinx's enigma. I am now on my way to Tenby, where I shall stop to-morrow. . . .

'Sunday, 26th June.

'To-night I mean to sleep at Tenby, to-morrow at Haverfordwest, Tuesday at St. David's, Wednesday at Cardigan, Thursday at Aberystwith, Friday at Dolgelly, and Saturday at Carnarvon,—at which last town I hope to find a letter from the Green, at farthest, but flatter myself I shall hear sooner. The weather is now cold and blustering, which, I find, agrees best with me. The hot days have prevented my making any progress. Pray give my love to all, and believe me to be, dear Sir,

'Your dutiful and affectionate son,

'SAML. ROGERS.'

The account in the diary of Neath fair and the farmers' dinner, gives further glimpses of South Wales in the days of our great-grandfathers:—

'In one street were numbers of farmers, etc., cantering and trotting and walking horses of every size and color to attract the notice of those who came to buy; in another was the trumpet sounding for the puppet-show, with bas-

---

[1] The banker in Finch Lane, Lombard Street.
[2] Made classic ground by John Dyer's poem, published in 1726.

kets of gingerbread, etc., carried by rosy-cheeked girls.
In another street were booths for gloves and hats and
every article of dress.   Here stood an old woman with a
roll of flannel under her arms, the product of her spinning-
wheel, and there were baskets of fleece and goose-wings
in abundance.   The concert of voices in the Welsh language was very diverting.   I think it more sonorous and
grand than the Erse.   Heard a man thunder at his cow,
and thought it had a very philippic air.   Every woman
wore the black hat and flannel check, which lasts three
or four years in constant wear washed in cold water with
but little soap.'

The dinner was with seven or eight farmers, and
their talk is briefly recorded : —

'Lambs destroyed by bad land in half an hour,
thin soil never to be tilled, fern strewed in a farmyard the best manure, — these were the principal topics.
Duels also had their turn, owing to a late fray at Swansea between two farmers.   A lusty man had affronted
a thin one, who challenged him.   "No," said he, "I
am too broad a mark, it will be unfair."   "Then," said
the thin one, "I will stand close to you, and my size
shall be chalked on your body, and if I don't hit within
the line it shall go for nothing." '

He speaks of the country on the way to Swansea as
even then 'deformed with forges.'   At Swansea the
dance was at the Mackworth Arms, and the sensible
attorney's name is given in the diary as Mr. Mansfield,
and the pretty wife of the surgeon is Mrs. Seycombe,
described as 'a most beautiful woman.'   At Carreg
Cennin Castle, 'a ruined citadel, the Gibraltar of former
times,' a story was told him illustrative of the popular
superstitions of the time.   The young man who conducted him over the ruins led him —

'back to a cottage at the foot of a rock, from which he had borrowed a lantern to explore the well. At the door we saw one old woman, who looked like a "poster of the sea and land." I walked in, and pointing to a human form which sat in the chimney of a dark room he said, in a low voice, that it was that woman who sixteen years ago lost her sight the instant she looked on some old pieces of coin which she discovered at the Castle ; that she was driving the horses of a plough when the coins were turned up, and that the man who guided it and who pillaged great part of them and took them to a Jew at Swansea to melt shared the same fate. He added with great seriousness that his father and grandfather had told him that several other instances of the same nature had occurred near the Castle. . . . Near Carreg Cennin is a cavern, called in Welsh the "Eyes of the River Loughor," branching into innumerable others, which branch some over some under the river which issues quietly into day, but within dashes along with the noise of thunder. Is not this Merlin's cave in the "Faëry Queen" ? '

At Carmarthen it was market day, the streets and roads were crowded, and some of the women on the road were walking barefooted with their shoes in their hands; others moved briskly along knitting as they went. He slept that night at Tavern Spite, a neat house on a furzy heath, and continued his journey in the morning, going to church on the way, as it was Sunday, and hearing there a good sermon. The church was hung round with flowers. Tenby was reached in the afternoon, and his description of it as it was in 1791 is worth quoting in his own words : —

'The church and village of Tenby are situated on a low cliff, hung with ivy and other vegetable tints. On the left the shore is high and rocky, and a distant reach

of land projects into the sea beyond it, though not equal
in grandeur to the mountainous shore on the left of
Swansea. On the right, seated on a small but lofty
promontory which is united by a narrow isthmus to the
shore, are the ruins of a castle, half mantled with ivy.
This promontory forms a beautiful bay.   Beyond it,
still farther to the right, within two hundred yards is an
insulated rock, tufted with herbage, on which are the ruins
of a house and where hung a few goats. The rock is of
rich gamboge color, and through it the waves have per-
forated a small archway. Half a league beyond this,
still farther to the right behind the town, is Caldy Island
with a farmhouse on it, but with no trees. The vessels
in the harbor and the offing gave cheerfulness to the
scene. Walked to the Castle and saw a clergyman drawing the insulated rock with a camera; a boat was rowing
under it; on the extreme point of the promontory is a
lofty single tower from which the sailors were looking out.
Walked by a little path to the cliffs on the opposite shore
(the fashionable walk) and also on the sands. The scene
beautiful in every point of view, the church spire rising
nearly in the centre, and drawing the village to an apex.
From the little by-path which connects the front cliff
with the left is perhaps the best view. . . . Tenby was
once very strong. The walls that guarded the two sides
next the sea are now nearly demolished, but sufficient
vestiges are left to trace them. On the two sides next
the land it is guarded by a high wall in perfect preservation, with strong round and square towers at a small
distance from each other, richly hung in many parts
with ivy. . . . Walked again to the Castle; the clergyman was still employed on his sketch. In the strait
below lay some boatmen on their oars, and along the
perpendicular sides of the rock two sea boys of their
party were chasing for diversion where I would not have
stood for fifty worlds.'

The day at Tenby did not include a visit to Giltar rocks; and on the next day Rogers resumed his journey over the Ridgeway to Pembroke. Thence the way lay through shady green lanes to the ferry across Milford Haven, on which magnificent sheet of water, 'blue as ultra-marine,' he notes ships in full sail in different directions before the wind. On to Haverfordwest, — 'the largest town I have yet seen in Wales, with the dirt and gloom of a large town,' and thence on towards St. David's. On the way he 'was surprised to meet a lady with a veil, and a pretty woman, with an air of some elegance, washing linen in a rivulet with her bare feet, though only two hovels were in sight.' He describes St. David's as a poor village. 'Except two or three neat little houses belonging to the clergy of the Cathedral, no house habitable by civilized beings.' He had to put up at a hovel of an inn, 'the canon residentiary, Mr. Holcombe, whose hospitable genius has raised a *caravanserai* in the desert, and whose musical and elegant family gave an air of enchantment to the reception of the desolate traveller, being now in London.' Riding next day through the cornfields the larks were so numerous that 'every stalk and ear of corn seemed full of melody. Never in my life was I so struck with their music. It was above, below, and around.' On the way to Cardigan is the Castle of Cilgerran, which was reached by a boat up the Towy River. At the village near the Castle, which was solely inhabited by fishermen, were several coracles. He measured one of the smallest with his handkerchief. It was exactly the breadth of the handkerchief, but an inch more in length. At one point of the voyage a fisherman came down with his coracle on his back and his paddle in his hand, to go out for the night. 'They suffer themselves to be carried down by the tide, and when they wish to return paddle ashore and walk home with their vessels on their backs.' Next day he

was 'stopped by the rain at three cottages, the first best,
the last worst but cheerful, with a colt neighing in one
of its divisions, the second dark as night, a spinning-
wheel in each.' A little English was spoken in one cottage, none in the other two. At a wayside inn, called
the 'New Inn'—'was entertained by a sweet little girl
with some Welsh songs; she had a very pleasing voice
and the tunes were equally so. They were of the cheerful kind. Her elder sister, a very modest, reserved,
pretty girl, told me that the harper from Aberystwith
often slept there in his musical peregrinations through
the country, and that they sat up the whole night to
listen to him.' On arriving at Aberystwith itself 'in
the hall of the inn a poor blind girl was playing on the
harp most exquisitely, such airs as made Gray put his
last hand to the unfinished ode of "The Bard."'

There are here eighteen days missing from the journal,
but there is evidence that these were spent in Central
and Northern Wales. The journal opens again on the
19th of July, when he is on the way out of Herefordshire
to Brecknock. He is up betimes, making a ride of several miles before breakfast. One day he is on horseback
by six in the morning, the next at half-past five, and the
shades of evening are usually falling when he concludes
his day's wanderings. The journey along the road from
Leominster to Brecknock is, at first, 'through a succession of hop-grounds, orchards, and villages,' not particularly beautiful in themselves, but chiefly so 'from the
ideas of cheerfulness and comfort and plenty which were
everywhere excited.' Passing the old hall of Kynnersley
the road soon approaches the Wye —

'Here we were presented,' he says, 'with a striking
image of desolation, the wreck of a bridge. It had consisted of several arches, and had been very elegant, but
fell in last spring, having had a bad foundation. Three

of its arches were still standing on one side, but all further progress was abruptly broken off, and the river
rushed triumphantly over the shattered pieces of the
rest. The toll-house on the other side, the lane that led
from it, and the sweeping approach all reminded us of
the communication which now existed no longer. The
ferry-boat was unfit for horses, and we were obliged to
follow at some distance the course of the river. We
were soon rewarded with a beautiful reach between
woody banks, and soon afterwards with another less
woody but more extensive and distinguished by the
ruins of a castle on a green eminence over the river.
We had now ascended to high ground, and presently saw
before us a rich and extensive valley, skirted by distant
mountains and disclosing here and there a faint catch of
the Wye in its passage from Plinlimmon. Descended,
and by a narrow bridge entered The Hay, a long scattered
town on its banks, with very fine woody hills behind it.
The old village-like church hangs beautifully on a green
knoll over the river, which there makes a curve to meet
it. Above it is a forlorn castle, part of which is glazed
and tenanted. As we left The Hay the same chain of
hills with wood accompanied us on the left; and on the
right in a delicious valley wound the Wye, but seldom
an object of sight, though its banks were almost level
with its surface. Beyond it rose green and shady hills,
with hamlets and spires and scattered farms below them.
At the fourth stone the Wye made a bold turn to the
right and left us among the hills. . . . Nothing could be
more beautifully retired than the descent into Brecknock.
We wound between woody declivities, above which in
front rose the double tower of the Priory. On the right
rushed the little river Honddu over mossy fragments of
rock. In the course of half a mile we came to a few
cottages and a water-mill, and presently we discovered a
rude stone arch. We then entered Brecknock. From

this bridge is the most enchanting view. The eye is carried up the dell along the foaming current of the stream, which is closely fringed with shrubwood and darkly overhung with foliage of the freshest verdure, but of different shades. It appears to work its way through the windings of a wood. On the left, loftily seated behind the trees, is the Priory, a noble Gothic structure now converted into a church.

'Ascended to the Priory and pursued a delightful path along the edge of the woody precipice which overhangs the glen, the little torrent gleaming through the trees below, and soothing the ear with the dash of its waters. Here and there a humble hut stands solitarily on the margin or hangs on the opposite declivity, with a little cabbage-garden running along a ledge of the rock, and literally on a level with the ridge of its thatched roof. As I proceeded, the path descended gradually towards the level of the river, and the glen along which the Leominster road had at first wound now contracted to the breadth of its current. At a forge which is near a mile from the Priory this beautiful scenery ended. In a little shady cove, half-way down the precipice, and not far beyond the Priory, a clear spring gushes out of the rock and falling over a rude ledge hurries down to the river. An oblique path through the fern and shrubwood descends to it on each side. It is a favorite resort for water. I could have passed hours here to observe the children that descend almost every minute into this beautiful recess. It was once, according to Homer, the occupation of king's daughters, and, as we are told with a beautiful simplicity in Holy Writ, the charms of Rachel suffered no diminution from it. That golden age is gone; but the visitors of a spring are still interesting to a contemplative mind; the fair and ruddy complexions of the country, with that simple and open expression which is soon lost in the less retired walks of life,

arc to me more interesting than the most beautiful scenery. Their action always pleases and is generally
graceful because it is natural and unaffected. I have
seen a ragged shepherd boy, particularly near St.
David's, throw himself down in an attitude that Raphael
would not have disdained to copy; and I have often
stopped, especially between Bala and Berwyn, to admire
the firm and graceful step of a girl with a brown pitcher
on her head. A little beyond the bridge the Honddu
enters the Usk, which forms a semicircle round the ruins
of a castle which stands on a rock. Part of the round
tower of the citadel crowns the highest point; below on
the other side is the College, a small Gothic building
belonging to St. David's; part of it is employed as a
school-room. As I returned from the forge to the Priory
had a beautiful glimpse of the valley and mountains over
the town. From the Castle Hill commanded the whole
valley, which is nearly circular, and but small, rounded
by green hills on three of its sides, and on the other,
opening to the Vale of Usk between the foldings of the
mountains. The evening was close and damp, with now
and then a drizzling rain.

'*July* 20. — Set off at half-past five — a pleasant gray
morning — and immediately entered the Vale of Usk,
which was at first mountainous, but afterwards sank into
cultivated uplands. On the right side ran a chain of
mountains, sometimes woody, sometimes richly cultivated.
Along the valley murmured the Usk in the sweetest
meadows through its fringed banks, with little farms and
villas scattered around it. It was Nature in her neatest
attire. About the sixth stone ascended from the Vale
behind a high hill, looking down directly on the windings
of the river, and commanding a rich review of its progress
from Brecknock. At the summit were agreeably surprised with the view of another valley with a small lake
(Langor's Pool) gleaming in the centre of it. As we

descended round the hill we passed Tretower Castle, with its gray round tower and battlements, at the foot of a hill, and there re-entered the Vale of Usk, the little river winding close to the road which now ran along the middle of the valley. The valley grew wider, and the river still more rapid; and considerable woods masked the hills on the left. It was diversified with noble promontories and insulated hills, cultivated to the very summit. The road now regained the left side and taking a higher direction wound along a green terrace over the river, the banks of which were now indeed sometimes exposed, but which ran in a noble stream. We here passed a little bridge over a tributary stream that turned a mill as it entered the Usk, and soon came to Crickhowell, a village deliciously seated on a gentle eminence near the Usk, looking up and down the Vale for some miles. Here again are the remains of a castle on the river, and though not very considerable they have a beautiful yellow tint and are in good preservation. The Vale soon afterwards contracted and grew more woody and less cultivated as we entered Monmouthshire, but a duskiness, arising perhaps from the heat, spread itself over the scenes we had left. As we approached Brecknock it opened on the right, and on the left the hills were of great beauty, especially the Sugar Loaf, which is cast perhaps in too correct a mould for picturesqueness, but is cultivated almost to the very summit, where it is green with shrubwood. The cheerful little villages that were blended in beautiful confusion along the sides of the opposite mountains, and the incessant bursts of wood and cultivation which enriched them continually, varied the scene. As we left Abergavenny — its hills forming a grand screen on the left, and lofty mountains hung with wood projecting into the Vale on the right — a magnificent pass presented itself through which we looked back towards Brecknock. Continued along the Vale. On the left were the green swells of a park belonging to Mr. Hanbury Williams, and on the right ran the mountains finely clothed with wood. These, however, soon shifted behind us; but the Usk still accompanied us, not often visible indeed, between rich uplands with little villages on its banks. At the sixth stone it makes a sudden bend to the road, and then, taking its farewell both of eye and ear, it turns off to the right between close woody declivities, and after a pleasant journey of five miles arrives at Usk, where I first found it. The scene soon closes on the right, but a sweet valley, deficient only in water, unfolds itself on the left, bounded by the Abergavenny hills, among which the Sugar Loaf lifts its pointed summit. The views on each side are at last reduced to the compass of a few fields, when Raglan Castle appears, with its walls and towers at a small distance, but with no great degree of elevation. The Vale of Usk extends from Brecknock to Abergavenny, a tract twenty miles in length. This is its first and finest part. It then turns on the right eleven miles to Usk, and from thence to Newport, ten miles, a tract of equal extent. The river there loses itself in the sea. Dined at Raglan, and afterwards stole a parting glance at the Castle, still beautiful as ever, not magnificent as a distant object, but in itself, when viewed at hand, the most picturesque I ever saw. The deep pointed arch of the gateway, half obscured by the network of ivy that hangs from it, the rich Gothic workmanship of the windows and abutments, the elegance of the banqueting-hall, — these still please and must ever please. Returned, as I went, in haste, to the great and loud merriment of a party at a cottage door, particularly an arch, black-eyed girl of sixteen. Rode on high ground and had a succession of the most beautiful views, little hills on each side melting into most delicious valleys and falling into each other with the most varied forms and

with the softest swells. Such a charming interchange
of wood and valley, meadow, corn and fallow ground, all
in miniature, and all in the most enchanting confusion,
is only equalled between Monmouth and Raglan, and
scarcely even there.   From several higher points we
commanded in retrospect an extensive valley bounded by
a noble amphitheatre of distant mountains.

'Left the turnpike road, and turning through a farmer's fields soon arrived at a very striking spot. On
the right was a deep glen, so deep that the tufted tops
of very high trees were far, very far, below me, and a
torrent rushed along through them with fury, but was
not an object of sight. The wood on the opposite side
of it rose very majestically to a considerable height, and
on the left, directly above me was a woody declivity.
As I descended the depth decreased and cottages were seen
clinging to its sides. At last a forge appeared with its
gigantic hammers and its sheet of red flame, but the
wood around, above, and below it was as luxuriant as
ever. Down this glen, the sides of which folded over
each other in perspective very finely, I was let down
gradually among hanging cottages till a lofty wood
ascended in front with the Wye winding calmly round
it. On its green and level margin stands Tintern Abbey.
The church is built, as indeed all abbeys are, in the
form of a cross. The west window is entire, and its rich
framework is clear of ivy, but within is finely hung, and
ivy in large masses and with the freshest verdure hangs
everywhere over it. The arch of the south window,
which has lost its framework, is so deeply fringed with
ivy that it scarcely admits the light, and the external
wall of the south aisle is entirely overspread with it.
Roger de Montgomery, the founder, lies entombed there.
But a very small part of the cloisters is now to be traced.
Adjoining to what is called the Monk's cell a poor
woman has furnished a melancholy apartment.   The

vault and its tenant correspond with Mr. Gilpin's description, but are not the same. The woman he mentions died in the workhouse. A poor girl was weeding the fragments on the green floor. The head of a monk and the body of a virgin are scattered there among mouldings and cornices. A little path leads directly to the river, which is shut in on all sides by high hanging woods. Ascended by a by-path, taking leave of this venerable ruin through the trees. Nothing can be more imposing than the perspective through its aisles when the west door is thrown open. Its outside is almost wholly [hidden] by the cottages that surround it. Ascended up a hanging wood. On the left was the rocky bed of some winter torrent, and the path itself was little better. It soon closed and the trees overarched it. It was now near ten, and the gloom was awful. It was here that I met a figure which I at first thought was an ancient tenant of the abbey. It wore a flannel gown which hung like a hood over the head. Not a lock of hair appeared over a pallid but striking countenance. A small black beaver hat was in one hand, and the other held a staff. I asked with some degree of hesitation the way to Chepstow, when it appeared to be an old woman. My question drew an appeal to my charity. She was returning home from the surgeon with a strengthening plaster and could scarcely crawl. Gained the heights, and saw the Severn with its wide waters before me; but the night was cloudy and I could but just distinguish a park on my left as I entered Chepstow. There I was regaled with songs by a cheerful young man of the town who was entertaining the landlord's daughters — fine girls, particularly the youngest — in the bar. Read an account of the riots at Birmingham.'

The journey was continued in the same manner to Bristol and Bath. Having dined at Beachley Passage

House he crossed the Severn, two miles, in six minutes
and a half, landing on a rough rock covered with sea-
weed, it being half-tide, and went by King's Weston,
paying a visit to the point in Lord Clifton's park from
which the celebrated view is to be seen, and thence on
over Durdham Down to Clifton. He notes the villages
and villas which spot the country, the sprinkling of
carriages and horses on the downs, the 'close and awful
pass' through which the sails rapidly succeed each other
along the Avon; the Hot Wells, 'and the walks full of
walkers, French staymakers, Pall Mall milliners, and
all the finery and impertinence of life;' and adds: 'I
was sorry to renew my acquaintance with it.' Next day
he notes the picturesque aspect of St. Vincent's rocks,
tastes the water at the Hot Wells, and notes the young
women, many apparently consumptive, who were there,
and one girl who 'drank her glass on the mail pillion.'
He complains of being 'enveloped in black dust on the
road to Bath, where the Royal Crescent on the hillside
strikes him with its simplicity and beauty as he enters
the city, which, however, 'wants the domes and turrets
of public buildings to give it magnificence' at a distance.

The month in which Rogers had thus been enjoying
the delights of home travel, which made him sorry to
return to all the finery and impertinence of life, had been
one of great anxiety to many of his personal friends.
His brief record on the 20th of July — 'Read an account
of the riots at Birmingham' — is like that of an outside
spectator of a serious social and political crisis. There
is no need to tell in this place the painful and disgraceful story of the sack of Dr. Priestley's house, the destruction of his philosophical apparatus and library, and
the burning by a drunken mob of the meeting-house in
which he preached. If on the other side of the Channel
crimes were being committed, as Madame Roland afterwards exclaimed, in the name of liberty, these outrages

were perpetrated in the England of Pitt and George III. in the supposed interests of church and king. Rogers was in full sympathy with those against whom this violence was directed, but poetry and not politics was still the uppermost thought in his mind. During the Welsh journey he corresponded with Mrs. Barbauld, among other friends, and just before the ominous entry in his diary he had received from her a letter expressive of her enthusiastic adherence to the Liberal side. It was written on the day before the second celebration of the fall of the Bastille, and the occurrence of the Birmingham riots.

Mrs. Barbauld to S. Rogers,

'DEAR SIR,—For your very entertaining as well as very friendly letter I thank you with all sincerity, and am truly sensible of the favor you do me by writing when you are surrounded by such charming scenes that while you bend your eyes upon paper you must lose a landscape. But why do you bid me write who have nothing to communicate, where there are neither harps nor Druids ? We have a lady, indeed, and she is a pretty lady, who sings a Welsh song most enchantingly, but then she has not the advantage of singing in a cottage; and, moreover, she is a married woman. I have been trying in my own mind whether Miss Hagen, with her fingers upon her harp, will bear any comparison with an ancient Druid sweeping his with his flowing beard; but I find her so infinitely inferior in the sublime, that I am obliged to drop the similitude. I know of no news to tell you but that Mr. George Maltby was at meeting yesterday, looking very happy, and that the family of the Websters set off to-morrow for Devonshire, to our great regret, as I suppose they quit Hampstead entirely.

'But pray, sir, what have you to say in your defence for rambling amongst fairy streams and hanging woods

instead of being at the "Crown and Anchor," as you and
every good patriot ought to be on the 14th of July?
What do you say to that? Do not you deserve at least as
severe a philippic as the Welsh farmer gave his cow?

> 'Muse, thy thrilling numbers dart
>   Through his ear and through his heart;
>   Chide the youth who holds his stay
>   Far from Freedom's band away.

> 'Hanging woods and fairy streams
>   Inspirers of poetic dreams,
>   Must not now the soul enthrall
>   While dungeons burst and despots fall.

> 'Shall peals of village bells prevail,
>   Floating on the summer gale,
>   While the Tocsin sounds afar,
>   Breathing arms and glorious war?

> 'Think when woods of brownest shades
>   Open bright to sunny glades,
>   Such the gloom and such the light
>   Of Freedom's noon and Slavery's night.

> 'Harps of Mona, sound once more,
>   With strong vibrations shake the shore,
>   Ne'er did your solemn chords relate
>   Eventful scenes so big with fate.

> 'Now stretched at hoary Snowdon's base
>   Hide in shades thy long disgrace,
>   And blush that Freedom's child should be
>   Far from Freedom's Jubilee.

'You see how envious I am, not being able to transport myself to those delightful scenes you so well describe.
I am maliciously endeavoring to disturb the harmony of
your sensations, but I dare say you will disappoint my
malice. . . . I hope when you return we shall have the

pleasure of seeing you soon, as we shall go into Norfolk, I believe, about the beginning of August.

'M. Rabaud[1] has sent a second address to the people of England. It is an exhortation to peace, and urges sentiments of national justice, which I hope we are not disposed to controvert.

'Perhaps you know that Mrs. Williams and Cecilia are set out for France, and that Helen and the rest of the family are soon to follow. They pay a visit to their old friends at Rouen before they settle at Orleans.

'Mr. Barbauld, who has shared in the entertainment of your letter, desires to join in thanks for it and in affectionate remembrance,

'I am, dear Sir,
'Your obliged friend and faithful servant,
'A. L. BARBAULD.

'HAMPSTEAD, July 13th. [Postmark 1791.]'

The excitement which the Birmingham riots produced spread more or less violently all through the country. Thomas Rogers was well known to be in full sympathy with Dr. Priestley and his friends, and there were reasons to fear an attack by the mob on the house at 'The Hill,' where his sisters, Samuel Rogers's aunts, continued to live. Happily the danger passed over. Thomas Rogers was there, as usual, in the summer, and in a letter to his son, dated the 21st of September, speaks of the state of feeling which then existed at Stourbridge:—

'I am sorry to say in answer to your postscript respecting the party spirit at Stourbridge, that there is some truth in the report, though the conduct of the church is not quite so bad as the report makes it. Mr. Parker, Jr., a grocer in the town, received a parcel by

---

[1] M. Rabaud St. Étienne, a deputy of the National Assembly. He was a Protestant clergyman and correspondent of Dr. Price.

the common carrier of the obnoxious handbill.[1] He owns that he gave one of them to a clergyman in the neighborhood, but at [the] same time expressed his disapprobation of it, and his determination to burn the remainder. He declares solemnly that he burned all the other copies immediately afterwards; but one of them having been left in the public library and another stuck up in the coffee-room at the "Talbot," and about six more having been sent under cover from the post-office in Stourbridge to as many gentlemen in the neighborhood, the whole of this, notwithstanding his denial, is laid to his charge. This brought the young man into disgrace, and many of his customers immediately sent for their bills and paid them off and left his shop. Some others of the Dissenters have also suffered in their business. . . . The flame the handbill has occasioned is scarcely to be conceived, and the violent charge the whole body of Dissenters with entertaining the same sentiments, and wishing for a revolution in this country, and conduct themselves accordingly; but it is said that at Birmingham and Stourbridge they are softening apace. Many of my acquaintance seem to be more attentive to me than usual.'

In a postscript he adds: —

'I am inclined to think Dr. Priestley will not return to Birmingham. All the respectable part of the congregation, except about two or three, signed a very warm request for his return, but he had not returned his answer on Wednesday last. Mr. Taylor and Mr. John Ryland were among the opponents. When I saw Mr.

---

[1] This was an address from the assembled deputies and delegates of the Protestant Dissenters of England to the Protestant Dissenters of Birmingham who suffered from the riots. It expressed the astonishment and horror the outrages had excited, and assured the Birmingham Dissenters of their warmest affection and steadiest support.

Stone at Brighton he intimated that it was the wish of many of the Hackney gentlemen to invite the doctor to Hackney, and that Mr. William Morgan approved of the idea. He said also if Jones went to Birmingham, where he was likely to be invited, that perhaps Dr. P. would be prevailed on to give chemical and philosophical lectures at the College.'

The Jones mentioned in this letter seems to have gone to Birmingham as Mr. Morgan expected. He appears also to have kept up a connection with the house at Newington Green. Samuel Rogers's advice to him to call on Dr. Parr was the origin of one of the familiar stories told by him and not very correctly reported by Mr. Hayward in the 'Edinburgh Review' article in which Mr. Dyce's inaccuracies are severely rebuked. The story is told by the Rev. D. Jones himself in the following letter : —

An Interview with Dr. Parr.

'Bm., 13th Novr., 1793.

'DEAR SIR, — Do not be surprised by the trouble I now give you. Perhaps you recollect a part of our conversation which turned upon Dr. Parr, and your advising me to introduce myself to him. This advice I took the first opportunity of putting in practice. The next Saturday after seeing you I set out for Warwick. Hatton, the Doctor's residence, lies in the way. I arrived at the place, fastened my horse to the gate, knocked at the door, inquired for the Doctor, and learned that he was at dinner. I told the servant I would wait while he dined, when I should be glad to speak to him. I was turned into a parlor where was the Doctor's picture; it set him off to the best advantage. Here I waited half an hour, contemplating the oddness of the adventure. The door opens, I prepare to make my bow and my speech — behold, it is a servant girl come to ask my name! Presently again the handle of the door moves, I make the same preparations — behold, it is a young lady whom I took to be Miss Parr, and who proved to be her! She requests me to walk into the parlor. This I decline, stating that I had not the honor of being known to the Doctor, but that when he was perfectly at leisure I should be glad to speak a few words with him. I judged it better to introduce myself to him alone than before company. The young lady soon left me, and she had hardly been gone any time before the great man ushered himself in. I was cool and composed. I approached him and thus accosted him: "I hope, sir, I have not interrupted your dinner; I begged that I might wait till you were perfectly at leisure?" "Not at all, sir." "My name is Jones; I am a Dissenting minister at Birmingham. Being on my road to Warwick I could not resist the inclination I felt to pay my respects to Dr. Parr." I had hardly uttered these words but the Doctor's eyes glistened. He took me by the hand, squeezing it heartily, leading me round the room, and asking me several times how I did. He begged I would stay the evening with him, and offered to send to Warwick to apprise my friends of it. I closed with the offer, as I was not expected at Warwick. He then introduced me to Mrs. and Miss Parr as a man of piety, sense, etc.; to another lady and gentleman as "a thorough Whig, no Tory, but one who had successfully opposed them in his writings." This was about four o'clock, and the Doctor entertained me till one in the morning. I was highly pleased with him. He possesses first-rate conversational powers. He speaks of Dr. Priestley in the highest terms. "Ma'am," said he to a lady there, "he has done more to promote human knowledge than any man in Europe." I have since written to him, and received a very friendly reply, and have a general invitation to his house, of which I mean to avail myself.

'I think not very highly of Brissot and his party, but there was no necessity for putting so many people to death. The account shocked me greatly. I do not mean to try to draw you into a correspondence, but if you could let me know, in a few words, how I am to conceive of that event it would oblige me much. I do not urge this, as it will not be long ere I see you. I thought that the relation of this adventure, suggested by yourself, may amuse you. Excuse the freedom, and believe me with unfeigned esteem to be sincerely yours,

'D. JONES.

'SAMUEL ROGERS, Esq.,
'Newington Green.'

CHAPTER VII.

MRS. BARBAULD'S rebuke to Rogers for being away in Wales, 'far from Freedom's Jubilee,' on the second anniversary of the capture of the Bastille need not be held to indicate any want of sympathy on his part with the great Liberal movements of the time. His nephew Samuel Sharpe reminds us that 'poetry was the uppermost thought in his mind;' and he was at that time just bringing his chief poem to completion. He had been occupied with it for more than six years. It was begun in 1785, as soon as the 'Ode to Superstition' was complete, and in the summer of 1791 he was just sending it to the press. It had been written in the same manner as his earlier poems. It was literally the recreation of a man of business, his 'leisure's best resource,' as he calls it in the lines prefixed to the fifth edition. With the exception of his holidays, which the state of his health made somewhat more frequent than they might otherwise have been, his whole life during these years was that of a junior partner in the bank. He went into the City in the morning, spent the day there, dined early with the other partners at the banking-house, and rode or walked home when business was over. He had, of late years, been more away from home in the evening, going with Dr. Kippis to literary parties or to some literary club, or to the Hampstead Assemblies, or following up his acquaintance with Mrs. Barbauld or the

Baillies, the Piozzis, the Williamses, or Dr. Moore. But
as a rule his evenings were spent in diligent reading or
in equally diligent composition. The only verses which
he published during these years seem to have been the
little poem 'On a Tear,' which in his works bears the
date of 1791. It was apparently printed in Este's journal, 'The World,' and reissued in 1791 in a 12mo volume
entitled 'The Poetry of *The World*,' and published by
Ridgeway. In a review of two of these volumes in the
'Monthly Review' for September, 1791, the managers of
the paper are thanked 'for the exertions which they
have made to rescue newspaper poetry from disgrace by
inviting some acknowledged favorites of the Muses to
decorate their. pages.' The favorites whose names are
mentioned are Mr. Sheridan, Mr. Merry, Mrs. Cowley,
Mr. Andrews, Mr. Jerningham, Mr. Colman, Mrs. Robinson, Captain Broome, and Captain Topham. Most of
these belonged to the Della Cruscan school, and all but
Sheridan are forgotten. But the critic quotes none of
them. He deprecates criticism as 'breaking butterflies
on the wheel,' and adds, 'instead of assisting our readers
to detect little faults we will tempt them to admire by
transcribing the following beautiful stanzas.' He then
quotes the six verses 'On a Tear,' which have almost
ever since kept their place in collections of popular
poetry.

'The Pleasures of Memory' was published by Mr.
Cadell early in 1792. It was described as by the author of
the 'Ode to Superstition.' Only two hundred and fifty
copies were printed, and they were disposed of at once. A
long review of the poem appeared in the 'Critical Review'
for April, 1792, in which it was rather severely criticised,
though with the admission that its defects were over-
powered by its beauties. 'The flame of genius,' said the
critic, 'which pervaded, and so brightly glowed in the
"Ode to Superstition," demanded our applause, which we

shall not withhold from the present poem, though exhibiting less splendid marks of poetical inspiration ; more
argumentative and metaphysical.' In June the 'Monthly
Review' made the poem the subject of its first article, and
spoke of it with unstinted praise.   'If the author of this
poem be thought happy in the choice of a copious and
fertile theme, which has yet by no means been exhausted,
he is equally so in the manner in which he has treated it.
Correctness of thought, delicacy of sentiment, variety of
imagery, and harmony of versification are the characters
which distinguish this beautiful poem in a degree that
cannot fail to insure its success.' This is a perfectly
just account of the poem, and does not need the
slightest change at the end of nearly a hundred years.
In the same month in which it appeared the 'Critical
Review' in a short notice said that though neither the
fiery stream of passion nor the electric sparks of fancy
burn along the lines, yet a mellow tasteful tint shed over
it renders many of the sentiments interesting and the
whole soothing.   These two views are curiously blended
by Mr. Hayward in the article written sixty-four years
later in the 'Edinburgh Review.' He there said of Rogers
that 'from the moment he discovered that he was destined to excel by grace, elegance, subdued sentiment, and
chastened fancy — not by fervid passion, lofty imagination or deep feeling — his poetic fortune was made.'[1]
Sir Egerton Brydges, who had just published a little
volume of sonnets and poems, records in his 'Autobiography' that a year or two after he entered the lists 'came
out Rogers's "Pleasures of Memory," which instantly
became popular, especially among the ladies. The lines
have something of a cast between Tickell, Shenstone,
and Goldsmith.'[2] The popularity of the poem was

---

[1] Edinburgh Review, July, 1856.
[2] Autobiography, vol. i. p. 87.

by no means confined to ladies. Critics, authors, philosophers, and statesmen united in its praise. The first
editions seem to have been sold as soon as they were
published. Rogers's early friend, William Maltby, writes
to him while he was travelling in the south of England
in July, telling him that he had called at Cadell's and
learned from Lawless that the whole impression was
sold before the 'Monthly Review' came out, and adding
'he lamented that two hundred and fifty copies only were
printed, as twice the number might have been sold.'
This may possibly refer to a second edition, as the work
was out, and copies were sent to the author's friends
early in January. Robert Merry, the almost forgotten
author of 'Lorenzo' and 'Fénelon,' writes to Rogers
from 35 Gerrard Street on the 18th of January, 1792,
thanking him for a copy of the poem, telling him that
he had gone to Mr. Cadell and found out the author,
and urging him to put his name to it at once. During
the first twelve or fourteen months after its issue four
editions of the poem, probably of two hundred and fifty
copies each, were disposed of, and its popularity and
success were already established. In May, 1793, a fifth
edition was published, and it was thought wise to venture
on printing a thousand copies. These were all dis-
tributed in the course of the year. This fifth edition
was a duodecimo of a hundred and twenty-four pages,
and was published at six shillings. It was prefaced by
the introductory lines which have ever since stood as
the preface to all editions of his poems.

It is only fair to Rogers that I should point out how
completely these lines embody the spirit and express
the motive of his poetry. He could not have sat at
Dr. Price's feet, or been Priestley's friend, or breathed
for thirty years the moral and spiritual atmosphere of
blended Puritanism and latitudinarianism which pervaded his Stoke Newington home, without learning to

feel a high sense of moral responsibility for what he wrote.

> 'Oh, could my mind, unfolded in my page,
> Enlighten climes and mould a future age ;
> There as it glowed, with noblest frenzy fraught,
> Dispense the treasures of exalted thought;
> To Virtue wake the pulses of the heart,
> And bid the tear of emulation start !
> Oh, could it still, through each succeeding year,
> My life, my manners, and my name endear,
> And, when the poet sleeps in silent dust,
> Still hold communion with the wise and just ! —
> Yet should this Verse, my leisure's best resource,
> When through the world it steals its secret course,
> Revive but once a generous wish supprest,
> Chase but a sigh, or charm a care to rest;
> In one good deed a fleeting hour employ,
> Or flush one faded cheek with honest joy, —
> Blest were my lines, though limited their sphere,
> Though short their date as his who traced them here.'

In this last line he gives expression to the feeling his frail health produced. He had less expectation and less reason for the expectation of long life than young men usually have. These lines were published before he had completed his thirtieth year, and he lived for nearly sixty-three years after they were written. He lived to know that 'The Pleasures of Memory ' had taken its place as an English classic. The fifth edition, to which this preface was affixed, was illustrated with a couple of whole-page woodcuts from drawings by T. Stothard : the first a group of children to illustrate the line —

> ' 'T was here we chas'd the slipper by its sound ; '

and the second, the Shipwreck, with the ' faint and faded Julia,' in her lover's arms on the shore, and the father kneeling behind, his white hairs strewed in the wind. This edition contained the ' Ode to Superstition,' and five small poems which like the 'Ode' had been previously published. These were, 'The Sailor,' 'Verses on a Tear,' 'Sketch of the Alps at Daybreak.' 'A Wish,' and 'An Italian Song.' The 'Ode' was illustrated by two woodcuts from pictures by R. Westall: the first, of the Fates 'wrapt in clouds, in tempests tost;' and the second to illustrate the lines —

> ' In cloistered solitude she sits and sighs,
> While from each shrine still small responses rise.'

Each engraving bears the words 'Published May 29th, 1793, by T. Cadell, Strand.' The world has been so often told that Rogers got his poems beautifully illustrated because they had ceased to sell, that it is needful to point out how early he began to associate his poetry with the best examples of the engraver's art. Nearly all the editions of his poems contained engravings, if it were only, as in the edition of 1816, pretty vignettes by Stothard, engraved by Clennell, to fill blank pages and the spaces at the beginning and end of a poem. The popularity of ' The Pleasures of Memory,' shown by the issue of the fifth edition within sixteen months, continued to increase year by year. He did not put his name on the titlepage even of the fifth edition, but he signed the prefatory lines with his initials, and the binder labelled the volume on the back ' Rogers's Poems.' From this time, therefore, he was known, and wherever he went was acknowledged as the popular poet of ' The Pleasures of Memory.' In 1794 a sixth and a seventh edition, each of a thousand copies, were published. In 1797 appeared the eighth edition, also of a thousand; a ninth in 1798, and a tenth and eleventh in 1799. In 1801 a twelfth edition was called for, and the number printed was raised to fifteen hundred, in addition to which a hundred copies were printed on large paper; in 1802 the thirteenth edition, also of fifteen hundred, was issued. On the fourteenth edition being called for in 1803 the number printed was raised to two thousand; in 1806 the fifteenth edition was printed, also of two thousand. The sale continued at much the same rate, and the edition of 1816, already mentioned, was the nineteenth. Omitting the sales of the first four editions, of which no clear record is preserved, but which consisted of very small numbers, and including the large paper copies, of which a hundred were printed in 1801 and two hundred and fifty in 1810, the total issue of the work — from the publication of the fifth edition in 1793 to the nineteenth in 1816 — was 22,350 copies. This was one of the greatest literary successes of the time. When we recollect how small the educated and reading world then was, and to how narrow an audience a poem of culture and not of passion was addressed, the steady and increasing demand for 'The Pleasures of Memory' is a remarkable sign of the poetical taste of the period, and of Rogers's success in meeting and satisfying it. These large numbers may be compared with the small sale of Wordsworth's 'Excursion,' of which the first edition, published in 1814, consisted of only five hundred copies and sufficed for six years, when another edition of the same number was issued, and lasted seven years. The favor with which Rogers's poem was received was, moreover, not that of the unreflecting multitude. The letters published in these volumes, and similar letters and notices which are scattered all through the biographies of Rogers's eminent contemporaries, show the universal appreciation in which his 'Pleasures of Memory' was held by men of taste and culture. It was totally unlike anything that was appearing at the time. The period had just passed of which Macaulay speaks when he says that 'poetry had fallen into such decay that Mr. Hayley was considered a great poet.' Cowper, whose Life is the work by which Hayley best deserves to be remembered, had already published most of his poems; and his translation of Homer, in which Rogers delighted as Thomas Campbell also did, had come out in the year before. 'The Task,' which had been the most popular of his poems, had appeared in 1785; but large and rapid as its sale had been, — so large that Johnson the publisher told Rogers he had been induced to make a handsome present to its author, — it did not by any means reach the success of 'The Pleasures of Memory.' Hayley's popularity had already faded away before that of Cowper, and the sentimental school to which he belonged, and of which he had been the foremost representative, had disappeared in the new love of simplicity and naturalness which Cowper had awakened. The Della Cruscans were the degenerate descendants of the sentimental school, and were only waiting for Gifford's rough heel to crush them finally. Other poets were still in embryo. Tom Moore, then a boy of fourteen, though, as he calls himself, 'a determined rhymester,' had not sent his first rhymes to the 'Anthologia Hibernica,' in which magazine he first read Rogers's poem in the numbers for January and February, 1793, — little dreaming, he says in his memoirs of himself, that he should one day become the intimate friend of the author; 'and such an impression did it then make on me,' he adds, 'that the particular type in which it is there printed, and the very color of the paper are associated with every line of it in my memory.' Byron was a child just four years old. Wordsworth was in France looking on at the Revolution, riveted to the spot, as his biographer tells us, by a mysterious spell, longing to remain in Paris, but obliged by circumstances to return, or, as he says in 'The Prelude,' —

'Dragged by a chain of harsh necessity,
   So seemed it — now I thankfully acknowledge
   Forced by the gracious Providence of Heaven' —

and thus escaping the proscription which swept away his
friends the Brissotins, with whom he says he should
have made common cause, and —

> ' . . . haply perished, too,
> A poor mistaken and bewildered offering,
> Should to the breast of Nature have gone back
> With all my resolutions, all my hopes,
> A Poet only to myself.'

Wordsworth's first little volume of ' Descriptive Sketches '
came out in the year after ' The Pleasures of Memory.'
Coleridge was at Cambridge, where he had just gained
the medal for a Greek ode, and where he was regarded
only as the revolutionist in politics and the heretic in
religion.   Southey had not yet entered at Balliol, where
he was afterwards regarded in precisely the same light
as that in which Coleridge stood at Cambridge.   Of those
who may properly be described as his contemporaries,
Rogers was, therefore, some years in advance.   He had
come to fame before any one of them had been heard of,
and he survived them all.

The published criticisms on ' The Pleasures of Memory ' in the periodicals of the day have already been
spoken of.   The chief objection urged was that of the
' Critical Review,' which discovered bad grammar in the
eight lines, now only six, which describe ' the intrepid
Swiss that guards a foreign shore ; ' and strongly objected to the lines, —

> ' That hall where once in antiquated state
> The chair of justice held the grave debate ; '

on the ground that figuratively speaking the chair of
justice might *hear*, but could not ' *hold*, the debate.'
Rogers, however, appears to have taken the same view
of the recommendations of critics which was taken by
Burns.

When Mr. Ramsay of Ochtertyre asked Burns whether the literary men of Edinburgh had improved his poems by their criticisms, 'Sir,' said the poet, 'these gentlemen remind me of some spinsters in my country who spin their thread so fine that it is neither fit for weft nor woof.' He said he had not changed a word, except one to please Dr. Blair. Rogers probably changed a few words,— not to please Dr. Parr, but in consequence of Dr. Parr's criticisms. He sent the Doctor an illustrated edition of the poem in 1796, and received the following characteristic letter of acknowledgment and criticism : —

Dr. Parr to S. Rogers.

'HATTON, June 14, 1796.

'DEAR SIR, — With pleasure — no, it was often with delight, it was sometimes even with ecstasy, it was with approbation almost always, that I have read your poem on Memory. The topics are, indeed, chosen most pertinently and even happily. The imagery is rich and varied, the versification is near perfection, — and so near that I must entreat you with a little revisal and a little effort to make it quite perfect. Your Muse is so gay without levity, and so serious without gloominess, that she would have tamed the surly genius of Johnson himself. She holds, and has a right to hold, converse with the spirits of Shenstone and Goldsmith and Gray. Believe me, dear sir, when I tell you that my mind, jaded as it has been even to indifference and insensibility upon the common objects of poetry when treated of by common minds, was roused and refreshed by the uncommon excellencies of your most charming poem. I love the work and I love the artist so well that without further preamble I will tell him of the passages which do not satisfy me.

13

'Page 15: "resigned" is surely a feeble epithet to happiness, nay, it is an improper one. Resignation may make us happy, but happiness does not make us resigned.[1]

'Page 17.[2] What do you mean by "the Sibyl's muttered call," and who is the Sibyl? And by "muttered" call do you mean a call that was given in a muttering tone? To me this is quite enigmatical.

'In the same page —

" To learn the color of my future years."

Does the word "learn" quite harmonize with the word "color"? Each expression is good by itself, but they are not well joined together here, and the transition is too violent from a dignified literal word "learn" to the vivid metaphorical word "color."

---

[1] 'As when in ocean sinks the orb of day,
    Long on the wave reflected lustres play ;
    Thy tempered gleams of happiness resigned
    Glance on the darkened mirror of the mind.'

[2] 'Down by yon hazel copse, at evening, blazed
    The Gypsy's fagot ; there we stood and gazed, —
    Gazed on her sunburnt face with silent awe,
    Her tattered mantle, and her hood of straw ;
    Her moving lips, her caldron brimming o'er ;
    The drowsy brood that on her back she bore,
    Imps, in the barn with mousing owlet bred,
    From rifled roost at nightly revel fed ;
    Whose dark eyes flashed through locks of blackest shade,
    When in the breeze the distant watch-dog bayed:—
    And heroes fled the Sibyl's muttered call,
    Whose elfin-prowess scaled the orchard-wall.
    As o'er my palm the silver piece she drew,
    And traced the line of life with searching view,
    How throbbed my fluttering pulse with hopes and fears,
    To learn the color of my future years !'

'Page 18 : —

> " Unconscious of the kindred earth
>   That faintly echoed to the voice of mirth." [1]

I really do not know what you mean by "the kindred
earth" which faintly echoes, etc.

'Page 19 : —

> " . . . whose every word enlightened." [2]

The use of "every" is rather too pretty; and, indeed, is
the only prettyism I have seen, and therefore it strikes
the more, as being more contrary to the general purity
and elegance of the style.

'Page 21 : —

> " . . . yet all with magic art
> Control the latent fibres of the heart." [3]

---

[1] 'On yon gray stone, that fronts the chancel door,
Worn smooth by busy feet now seen no more,
Each eve we shot the marble through the ring,
When the heart danced, and life was in its spring ;
Alas ! unconscious of the kindred earth,
That faintly echoed to the voice of mirth.'

[2] 'Guides of my life ! Instructors of my youth !
Who first unveiled the hallowed form of Truth !
Whose every word enlightened and endeared,
In age beloved, in poverty revered,
In Friendship's silent register ye live,
Nor ask the vain memorial Art can give.'

[3] 'Lulled in the countless chambers of the brain,
Our thoughts are linked by many a hidden chain.
Awake but one, and lo, what myriads rise !
Each stamps its image as the other flies.
Each, as the various avenues of sense
Delight or sorrow to the soul dispense,
Brightens or fades ; yet all with magic art
Control the latent fibres of the heart.'

The philosophy is here better than the poetry; each thought "stamps its image," each "brightens or fades." Here we have imagery, very just and distinct and yet varied. But is not the imagery rather too remote from that which precedes, when we are told that thoughts "control the latent fibres"? My friend, you do not lead my fancy, but you drag it after you here. Perhaps, too, I am not quite pleased with the word "dispense" as applied to the "varied avenues of sense;" avenues do not dispense.

  ‘Page 24 : —

  " All touched the talisman's resistless spring." [1]

This line, though intelligible, is obscure. I have many objections, and will state them to you. In the two pre- ceding lines we have ornamental description, and orna- ment, too, which throws over the mind many strong images, well adapted to the scenery, as it affects the senses; but, my friend, is there not danger of confusion, when, having recalled such images so pleasing to the senses, you proceed in bold metaphor to speak of the operations of the mind? To me it is quite enigmatical. And consider, too, after the metaphor of the talisman we have another metaphor of "busy tribes" that are "on the wing," and do you think that touching a spring leads us to think of beings on the wing? I think these meta- phors do not follow one another well, and when two metaphors immediately succeed such vivid description of natural scenery I feel my mind confounded and fatigued.

---

[1] ‘So Scotia's Queen, as slowly dawned the day,
    Rose on her couch, and gazed her soul away.
    Her eyes had blessed the beacon's glimmering height,
    That faintly tipped the feathery surge with light ;
    But now the morn with Orient hues portrayed
    Each castled cliff and brown monastic shade ;
    All touched the talisman's resistless spring,
    And lo, what busy tribes were instant on the wing !’

'Page 26 : —

"When at his feet . . . the sage . . . reposed." [1]

If you use "when" it should be when Tully found him reposing; if you put "where" the passage will be right. Perhaps you were frightened by seeing the word "where" follow so close in the next sentence. I am not quite satisfied with the line where you say that "his youth in sweet delusion hung." [2] To hang in delusion is at least unusual, and though it be a fact that this happened when Cicero was young, yet the circumstance of youth does not add to the effect; therefore I would have avoided the word "youth," and have endeavored to express it in a plainer way as that which happened while he was young. His mind felt the charming delusion when he was young.

'Page 27 : —

"What though the fiend's torpedo-touch arrest!"

Dear sir, this line shocked me. The character of a fiend is accompanied by an idea of violence with which "torpedo-touch" ill accords; and again I do not like the word "arrest" as joined to "torpedo-touch;" for surely to arrest suggests some notion of vehemence and force which is very ill-connected with the touch of a torpedo. No touch can arrest, so far as touch is a slight operation; and then a torpedo-touch conveys to me, as I

[1] '. . . As now at Virgil's tomb
We bless the shade, and bid the verdure bloom ;
So Tully paused, amid the wrecks of Time,
On the rude stone to trace the truth sublime ;
When at his feet, in honored dust disclosed,
The immortal Sage of Syracuse reposed.'

[2] The line was altered. It now reads —
'And as he long in sweet delusion hung.'

told you before, an idea of benumbing properties [1] rather than of those which arrest or seize, and by seizing stop the motions of the mind. I know you can say that a torpor seizes, but I should not say the touch of a torpor seizes, nor should I choose to say that this act of seizing had checked any preceding emotion, whether habitual or not. When we so use the word " seize," we mean to express the *suddenness* of the effect, rather than the vehemence of the cause. Again, in the same page I do not find the word "erase" very appropriate to the word "school," though it agrees well enough with the epithet "iron." [2] Still, my friend, you must not have the properties of the subject merged in the properties of the adjunct; and wishing the subject were better adapted to the *action* of erasing, I must beg leave to express my doubt on the propriety of the epithet "iron" as applied under any circumstances to the subject "school." I cannot admit the transposition of "iron school of war" for the "school of iron war," except in dithyrambic, nonsensical, meteoric odes.

'Page 30 : —

> " And win each wavering purpose to relent
>   With warmth so mild, so gently violent."

I don't understand these two lines. We generally say that a *stubborn,* not a *wavering,* purpose *relents ;* and

---

[1] It may be desirable to remind a younger generation of readers that the torpedo of their grandfathers is an electrical ray-fish (*Torpedo vulgaris*), commonly called ' the cramp fish.'

[2] The lines here criticised are —

> ' What though the iron school of War erase
>   Each milder virtue and each softer grace ;
>   What though the fiend's torpedo-touch arrest
>   Each gentler, purer impulse of the breast ;
>   Still shall this active principle preside,
>   And wake the tear to Pity's self denied.'

pray what do you mean by "with warmth so mild, so gently violent"? I am all confusion about it.

'Page 31 : —

> "These, when to guard Misfortune's sacred grave,
> Will firm Fidelity exult to brave."

The first line is obscure. You mean to say when employed, or when designing, to guard the grave, but you have *not* said it ; and after not finding your meaning in the first line we expect to find it in the second, and expecting to find it [not finding it, is clearly the meaning] in the second we are driven back to the first, and even there we cannot find it without an effort, — without supplying something which is not expressed. This effort is made more painful from the structure of the second line, which is very artificial. "These, will firm Fidelity exult to brave," I could understand pretty well, if the other construction, "when to guard Misfortune's sacred grave," did not intervene. But the passage so intervening makes me look for aid from the second, which aid is not furnished ; and the second, where the ideas are thrown at a distance from the subject to which it relates, finds embarrassment upon embarrassment, — embarrassment from the intervening passage, and embarrassment from its own inverted position in tracing its way back to that which Fidelity exults to brave. Besides, my friend, I do not relish the personification of Fidelity, nor do I much admire the epithet "firm," nor do I much approve of the word "exult." Do you think that exultation is a very obvious property of fidelity ? And if it is not obvious what are the circumstances which make it proper on this occasion ? I see none. Pray reconsider the lines.[1]

---

[1] It may be well to quote the whole passage, to the last two lines of which this criticism applies : —

> 'Recall the traveller, whose altered form
> Has borne the buffet of the mountain storm ;

'Page 45 : —

    ". . . presumes its base control."

Is this quite accurate ? I think otherwise.[1]
'Page 50 : —

    "So richly cultured, every native grace
     Its scanty limits he forgets to trace."

My ear is hurt with *its* scanty *limits*, and my understanding is totally at a loss to conjecture what you mean.[2]

    " Time's sombrous touches soon correct the piece,
     Mellow each tint, and bid each discord cease;
     A softer tone of light pervades the whole,
     And breathes a pensive languor o'er the soul."

My mind, I am sure, feels here a very strange discord
indeed. Again and again I have had occasion to tell
authors that one metaphor never can be worked into another. I remember in a famous speech of Lord Mansfield's about Wilkes he was guilty of confounding two
metaphors. He spoke of " the color of his life," and so
far was well. But he added to the word " color " some

    And who will first his fond impatience meet ?
    His faithful dog 's already at his feet!
    Yes, though the porter spurn him from the door,
    Tho' all that knew him, know his face no more,
    His faithful dog shall tell his joy to each,
    With that mute eloquence which passes speech. —
    And see, the master but returns to die!
    Yet who shall bid the watchful servant fly ?
    The blasts of heaven, the drenching dews of earth,
    The wanton insults of unfeeling mirth,
    These, when to guard Misfortune's sacred grave,
    Will firm Fidelity exult to brave.'

[1] The line is altered to — ' assumes its base control.'

[2] The lines now read, —

    'So rich the culture, tho' so small the space,
     Its scanty limits he forgets to trace.'

other metaphorical term, completely heterogeneous. I
forget what it was, and am a dunce for forgetting it,
though at this moment I remember a stupid attempt of
a stupid antiquarian to vindicate the learned judge by
supposing that he alluded to Heraldry. Lord Mansfield's
speech was for a time admired, and when I attacked it,
I never found a man of sense undertake its defence.
Having fetched, like Parson Adams, a stride across the
room, and brandished my pipe, I suddenly experience
the "Pleasures of Memory." Lord Mansfield's word was
"armed" — "has armed the color of my life." His life
might be armed, but the color of it could not be. I
return from Lord Mansfield to a better man and a better
writer. My friend, you pass too quickly from painting to
music; from the sense of seeing to the sense of hearing. There are, it is true, some words which, belonging
originally to one sense, are without violence transferred
to another. So, sweet, from taste, is applied to sound,
and even to the features of a countenance; so, soft, from
feeling, is applied both to notes and pictures. I allow
much to the laws and even caprices of association; I
allow much to the authority of custom, which predomi-
nates not only in the cases just now mentioned, but in
many other metaphorical words, which having originally
a mere literal sense are also used in a metaphorical sense
with such frequency that we hardly perceive them to be
metaphorical. But none of these concessions will avail
towards your justification. My concessions go to single
words. But in your poem we have more than single
words: we have a train of images, we have a succession
of metaphors; and when the first metaphor has been
preserved pure, many of its appropriate terms are inter-
mingled with a second, and a distinct and quite heterogeneous metaphor. I cannot bear the expression of "a
tone of light." A soft tone can, but a soft light cannot,
"breathe a pensive languor." Well, but even supposing

that you had preserved the second metaphor from sound
from all mixture of terms borrowed from music, still I
should say that to pass so suddenly from one metaphor
to another, from the effects of one sense to the effects of
another sense, would be a faulty accumulation of imagery :
for you will observe that you are not speaking literally
of sound or literally of colors, but of both metaphori-
cally, and according to my judgment metaphors so
remote ought not to succeed each other so closely, more
especially they ought not, because they are applied to
one and the same subject, — the mind; and because in
truth they are describing one and the same operation
or affection of that mind.   Take either of them away,
leave the picture and remove the music, or leave the music and remove the picture, and in either case you will
have sufficiently expressed your meaning.   I see what
it was which produced this confusion.   The unlucky
word "discord" has produced all this discord.   My
friend, I have observed in poets, and indeed in all
speakers, that the mention of one metaphorical word
leads the writer or speaker into the expansion of the correspondent metaphor at full.   Thus in "Cymbeline," —

> " *Second Gentleman.*   You speak him far.
>   *First Gentleman.* — I do extend him, sir, within himself,
> Crush him together rather than unfold
> His measure duly."

So in Horace, Sat. i. —

> " Dum ex parvo nobis tantundem *haurire* relinquas,
>   Cur tua plus laudes cumeris granaria nostris ? "

Having dropped the word *haurire* he goes on with the
metaphor suggested by it at full, —

> " Ut, tibi si sit opus *liquidi* non amplius *urnâ*,
>   Vel *cyatho*, et dicas ; Magno de *flumine* mallem
>   Quam ex hoc *fonticulo* tantundem sumere."

I could quote you several other instances, but these are enough for my purpose, and will show you the train of your own ideas. What you have in common with Shakspeare and Horace is that one metaphorical term led you on to a complete metaphor. A difference between you is that they preserve the metaphor well, and that you have not preserved it. You run on from discordant tints to discordant sounds, to both of which you meant to apply the correction of time, and unfortunately when you got to the sounds you mingled with them the terms which belonged to the tints.[1]

'Page 54: "As the stern" and "as when" in the third line afterwards, seem to me unfinished writing.[2]

'Page 59: "Tenderer tints." The comparative here is very harsh to my ear, and surely it is unusual.[3]

'The close of the tale of Florio is admirably to your purpose, and is well told; but the introduction to it is far too long and too much encumbered with circumstantial description. Florio, by accident as it afterwards appears, meets the lady. But what was he doing before? Was he merely wandering? So it should seem. But why, then, so much description lavished on the scenery? There

---

[1] The line was altered, and now reads —

'And steals a pensive languor o'er the soul.'

[2] This, too, was altered, and the lines now read —

'As the stern grandeur of a Gothic tower
Awes us less deeply in its morning hour,
Than when the shades of Time serenely fall,
On every broken arch and ivied wall.'

[3] The lines are —

'Fair was her form; but who can hope to trace
The pensive softness of her angel face?
Can Virgil's verse, can Raphael's touch, impart
Those finer features of the feeling heart,
Those tenderer tints that shun the careless eye,
And in the world's contagious climate die?'

is no interest awakened about Florio for near two pages, because we do not see any purpose he had in view. It is a charming tale; pray reconsider the introductory parts.

'Page 67 : —

> " Each ready flight at Mercy's call Divine
> To distant worlds that undiscovered shine.''

What is the meaning of "each ready flight"? To me it is nearly unintelligible. The structure, too, displeases me. My friend, let us suppose this passage right. Every particular introduced by the word "each" has certain effects separately assigned to it. Very well! But when you come to the last line to describe their joint effects my mind is not sufficiently severed from the particular cause and effects immediately preceding, on which you have bestowed three lines. (On looking again I suspect " undiscovered shine" refers to "worlds." Be it so. What is a "ready flight," and how does a flight " fling its living rays "? My mistake is a proof that you have not written clearly.)[1] Where the particulars in detail are so fully detailed you

---

[1] The passage referred to in the above criticism is as follows. Speaking of 'the enchantress Memory' the poet says : —

> 'But is her magic only felt below?
> Say thro' what brighter realms she bids it flow?
> To what pure beings, in a nobler sphere,
> She yields delight but faintly imaged here:
> All that till now their rapt researches knew,
> Not called in slow succession to review;
> But, as a landscape meets the eye of day,
> At once presented to their glad survey!

> 'Each scene of bliss revealed, since chaos fled,
> And dawning light its dazzling glories spread;
> Each chain of wonders that sublimely glowed,
> Since first Creation's choral anthem flowed;
> Each ready flight, at Mercy's call Divine
> To distant, worlds that undiscovered shine;
> Full on her tablet flings its living rays,
> And all, combined, with blest effulgence blaze.'

should not have included under the same couplet a part
of one particular effect and the aggregate effect of all
the preceding particulars.   There is something awkward
in this.   And so much by way of stricture, were I to put
my commendations on paper they would fill six sheets.

'Not knowing your address I write to you at Dr.
Bancroft's, and pray present my best respects to him.

'I am, most sincerely yours,

'S. PARR.'

Another letter from one of the best known men of
his time seems to have been called forth by a present
from Rogers similar to that sent to Dr. Parr.   The Rev.
William Gilpin writes : —

'VICARSHILL, July 23, 1796.

'I received, my dear sir, your agreeable packet, and
return you many thanks for it, both as it was a token
of your esteem and as it was the vehicle of much real
pleasure and amusement.   I am a great lover of nature,
and find it is an instrument on which you have the art of
playing many a pleasant tune.

'But now, my dear sir, you must not call my taste in
question for not having read your poem before.   Heard
of it I often have.   But as I rarely go out of my own
parish, and live in a neighborhood which, though a very
agreeable one, is not very literary, I have seldom the
opportunity of seeing anything new but what I purchase
myself ; and I have been so often disappointed with new
publications that I have at length learned a frugal lesson, — that of bridling my curiosity, which, though often
the handmaid of science, is as often the companion of
folly.   From the little acquaintance, however, I had with
you, I conceived I should not be disappointed in the
present case, and therefore sent for a copy, which I
received the day after I got yours.

'Scaleby Castle came often into my mind as I read it; which, though in some degree faded, is still a well-colored picture in my memory. The *old mansion frowning through the trees — once the calm scene of many a simple sport — the hollow tower — the hospitable hall — the dusky furniture — the garden's desert path — the martin's old hereditary nest* — are all ideas familiar to me: *starting to life and whispering of the past.*

'I believe I did not tell you why Mrs. Gilpin's recollection and mine presented Scaleby Castle to us in such different colors.   It was equally familiar to us both in our youth.   But I knew it chiefly in its cheerful days. She was a witness of its distressed state, when an uncle of ours, the possessor of it, through mere imprudence (cause enough, you will say) but without any vicious propensity, became an unhappy, embarrassed man, and was obliged to sell it.

'I cannot conclude my letter without saying I think the artist who has adorned your volume is a very considerable master both of picturesque composition and expression.

'Mrs. Gilpin desires me to add her best respects to those of, dear sir,

'Your most obedient and obliged humble servant,

'WILL. GILPIN.'

One criticism on the poem which gave Rogers unfailing amusement appeared in the 'English Review,' in the notice of the fifth edition.   The writer quotes the lines describing the Gypsy, beginning 'Down by yon hazel copse at evening blazed,' with the approving statement that 'Cowper's Gypsy is not portrayed in livelier colors.' He then marks the alliterations in the passage, and adds: 'We have no objection to alliteration, but this writer is too fond of it.'   In a note on this subject of alliteration

the reviewer says: 'The second part opens with these
lines, —

> "Sweet Memory, wafted by thy gentle gale
> Oft up the *t*ide of *t*ime I *t*urn my sail."

Allured by the alliteration we are almost tempted to *t*urn
our *t*ail.'

The extracts I have given from the poem in the notes
to Dr. Parr's letter will sufficiently exhibit its character
to readers who may as yet be unfamiliar with it.   Mr.
Hayward, one of the most genial and generous of Rogers's
later critics, thinks there is no reason for surprise at its
immediate success.   It struck, he says, into the happy
medium between the precise and conventional style and
the free and natural one.   Rogers's only formidable
competitor was Cowper.   Crabbe's fame was then limited,
Darwin never had much, and Burns was little known.
Mr. Hayward points out with great force the absence
from the poem of any passages which cling to the
memory, which haunt and startle and waylay.   Although
it has long taken its place as an English classic, he says,
none of its mellifluous verses or polished images are
freshly remembered like the 'coming events cast their
shadows before' of Campbell, or Scott's 'Oh, woman, in
our hours of ease!' or Moore's 'Oh, ever thus from
childhood's hour!' or Byron's 'He who hath bent him
o'er the dead,' or Wordsworth's —

> '. . . creature not too bright or good
> For human nature's daily food.'

In spite, however, of this shrewd and just criticism, I
must point out that there are many expressions borrowed
from Rogers's 'Pleasures of Memory' which have passed
into literature, though their original source may be
forgotten.   The 'treasured tales of legendary lore,' the
'dreams of innocent repose,' the admirable line —

> 'And the heart promised what the fancy drew;'

and the further line —

> 'And breathe the soul of inspiration round;'

are illustrations from the first page or two of expressions
which have passed into common use. The lines — 151 to
156 — which commemorate the virtues of Dr. Price and
other of Rogers's early teachers have a familiar sound
to readers who know not whence they come: —

> 'Guides of my life! Instructors of my youth!
> Who first unveiled the hallowed form of Truth!
> Whose every word enlightened and endeared;
> In age beloved, in poverty revered;
> In Friendship's silent register ye live,
> Nor ask the vain memorial Art can give.'

Mr. Hayward says that in the passage beginning,—

> 'So Scotia's Queen, as slowly dawned the day,
> Rose on her couch and gazed her soul away' —

Rogers has never been excelled in the art of blending
fancy and feeling with historic incident and philosophical reflection. Mackintosh thought the closing lines of
'The Pleasures of Memory' equal to those of 'The Dunciad,' which Mr. Hayward says is like comparing Virgil's
'Apostrophe to Marcellus' with Homer's 'Battle of the
Gods.' He quotes the lines : —

> 'Ah! who can tell the triumphs of the mind
> By truth illumined, and by taste refined?
> When age has quenched the eye, and closed the ear,
> Still nerved for action in her native sphere,
> Oft will she rise — with searching glance pursue
> Some long-loved image vanished from her view;
> Dart thro' the deep recesses of the Past,
> O'er dusky forms in chains of slumber cast;
> With giant-grasp fling back the folds of night,
> And snatch the faithless fugitive to light.

So through the grove the impatient mother flies,
Each sunless glade, each secret pathway tries ;
Till the thin leaves the truant boy disclose,
Long on the wood-moss stretched in sweet repose.'

He asks why verses like these have failed to lay fast
and durable hold of the public imagination, and thinks
the answer is that the linked sweetness is too long and
elaborately drawn out, and that the very symmetry and
artistic finish of a production may militate against its
general popularity. But this criticism begs the question.
Mr. Hayward did not know how largely ' The Pleasures
of Memory ' was circulated in the generation to which it
was first addressed. It did attain general popularity.
It is now a classic ; and classics are almost always for
the few. Rogers's poems are poems of taste and culture.
They are adapted rather to smooth the raven down of
darkness till it smiles, than to stir the blood and nerve
the arm and set the soul on fire. Madame d'Arblay acci-
dentally uses the fit expression with respect to ' The
Pleasures of Memory ' when she describes it as ' that
most sweet poem.' It rendered literature, as Mr. Hayward says, an ' invaluable service by its purity of
language and chasteness of tone — which immediately
became the objects of improving imitation and elevating
rivalry.'

14

CHAPTER VIII

THE success of 'The Pleasures of Memory' gave Rogers
at once a high position in the literary society of the time.
He soon begins to be spoken of by contemporaries as
'the poet Rogers,' or as 'Mr. Rogers, the admired poet.'
His society was sought; and wherever he went he was
pointed out as the author of the poem everybody was
reading. This was just the kind of fame for which he
longed. He had found the direction in which his strength
lay. It was not in the noise and hurry of dithyrambic
odes, but in smooth and polished versification; not in
bursts of passion or in great flights of bold imagination,
but in graceful elegance of movement and restrained
feeling, that he was able to excel his contemporaries.
The time, moreover, was singularly fortunate. The most
barren era of English poetry was just drawing to its
close. The laureateship which Spenser had adorned in
the sixteenth century, and Ben Jonson and Dryden in
the seventeenth, had fallen in the eighteenth to Colley
Cibber and William Whitehead and Henry James Pye,
and through the whole century never rose above the
level of Pye's immediate predecessor, the Rev. Thomas
Warton, who had just succeeded to Whitehead when
Rogers's first poem came out. It was true that Gray
had declined it in 1757 and Mason in 1785; as Rogers

himself was destined to do in 1850. But Gray had been in his grave in Stoke Poges churchyard for more than twenty years, and Mason was chiefly known as his biographer, when 'The Pleasures of Memory' appeared. Cowper — who divides with Rogers the true poetical chieftainship of the times, but whose popularity was never as great among the cultivated classes as that of Rogers — was out of society, cowering in the gloom of religious melancholy. It is only possible to understand the high position which the success of this comparatively short poem gave to Rogers when we recollect that he was educated in the eighteenth century, but in the midst of the men by whom and the influences by which the nineteenth century was moulded; and that he wrote the poem by which he was best known in later times before the Lake School had risen, or Scott had been heard of, or Tennyson was born.

It is quite possible that the title of the poem — 'The Pleasures of Memory' — was suggested by Akenside's 'Pleasures of Imagination;' and it is quite certain that the success of Rogers's poem suggested to Campbell his 'Pleasures of Hope.' There were the usual inquiries as to its authorship, and in those days it was a surprise to be told that the new poet was a young banker in the City. When Lord Eldon, then Sir John Scott, was told of it, he exclaimed: 'If Old Gozzy [head of the firm of Goslings, with whom he banked] even so much as says a good thing, let alone writing, I will close my account with him the next morning.' Neither the partners nor the customers of the firm of which Rogers was the youngest member had this feeling. His father's letters are full of matters of business, all of which he seems to have intrusted to his poetic son without the least fear that his pursuit of poetry, as the happy occupation of his well-earned leisure, would in any way interfere with his application to business. The best business man is perhaps the one who thinks least about it, and gets farthest away from it when business is over.

In these early days of his fame he kept a diary of his occasional visits to literary people and conversations with them. The habit was unfortunately not continued long; but as in the records of his Edinburgh visit, and his conversation at Miss Williams's, so in the diary for 1792 and 1793 we catch glimpses of interesting and sometimes of eminent persons.

'1792. — Paid two visits at Streatham this winter. Walked back to London the first time with Lysons, who said Lord Orford would never go to Houghton, as it would remind him of the sale of the pictures. The last time saw Miss Harriet Lee and Mr. Ray, a very sensible and engaging man. Danced a blind minuet with Cecilia, and footed another with her mother. Mrs. Piozzi read me an opera called "The Fountains" in blank verse interspersed with songs. Scene Dovedale. It contained some touching sentiments, particularly a line in a woman's mouth —

"For independent only means forlorn."

'In January dined at Dilly's with Parr, Cumberland, Hoole, Reed, Priestley, etc.

'Parr: "I have written a Latin epitaph for Johnson, and the knowing ones will be taken in. They expect it to be pompous, as it is written for Pomposo, and by Pomposo the Second." He mentioned *tangere* as unclassically used in Goldsmith's epitaph, and thundered against the round-robin addressed to Johnson to persuade him to write it in English. He was shocked to see Tom Warton's name in so Gothic a business. Speaking of a lie against Watson's charge: "It was begot by Prejudice on Ignorance, and Malice was its godfather." He spoke very contemptuously of Dr. Ash.

'Cumberland spoke of his grandfather Bentley as gentle and fond of children. He would never count money, but desired it always to be placed in piles of twenty guineas on the table, and he would run his hand over them to feel that they were all of a height. When a thief was arrested in his pantry, he (Bentley) said: "You see you can't succeed in this trade; go and try a better." When remonstrated with for dismissing him, he said mildly: "What more should be done with the fellow? He has failed so egregiously in this instance he will never think of thieving again." Just before he died, his wife said: "I wish you had harassed yourself less with criticism and controversy, and written more on other subjects." He sat musing for a little while, and then burst into tears.

'Somebody mentioned Griffiths, editor of the "Monthly Review." Cumberland said he did not envy him his place, it was like the keeper of a bridewell. Cumberland has often found it a House of Correction. Tweddell said if he had a new comedy he should sit in the pit. "No," said Cumberland, "sit in the green-room, and now and then take a peep between the scenes to feel the pulse of the house. If it is in good humor, well; if not — why, take a walk!"

'Parr was afterwards in a rage with Cumberland. "Why did Dilly ask me to meet such a scoundrel? He shall tell me who I am to meet next time. To tell Priestley that to attack him was to attack philosophy, and when his back was turned to abuse him as a firebrand, an innovator, and a disturber! Did the fellow think I should forget his words? And then to bring up his Epic Poem. How could I tell it was his? I might have found fault with every line of it."[1]

[1] William Maltby was at this party, and Dr. Parr met him a few days afterwards and let off his anger at Cumberland's treatment of Priestley in similar terms to those recorded by Rogers. 'Only to think

'I desired Dilly afterwards to give Hoole and Cumberland my poem. Hoole wrote a civil note.[1] Cumberland called to thank me and tell me of its faults — faults which he himself had committed, and which he hoped I would hear from an old writer — " too rich, and too much alliteration," and "the story too obscure." He afterwards sent me "Calvary."

'At Tuffin's, in the winter, met Romney, Horne Tooke, and Priestley. Romney very animated at times. Speaking of Pitt — "That man," said he, "has a nose turned up at all mankind." Of Horne Tooke he said: "His brain has starved his nose." Spoke of Hayley's agitation at the acting of Eudoxa. "I thought I should have sunk," said he; "I did not dare to look at him."

'The next day with Sharpe and Tuffin; saw Banks's statues, called at Romney's and saw him, and also saw Townley's collection; and dined at the Grecian.

'In the autumn of last year Dr. Priestley, Dr. Kippis, Dr. Moore, Mr. Merry, Captain Brown, Major Montfort, Mr. Sharpe, and Captain Moore dined with me. When I published my poem Merry wrote me a very flattering letter, and I dined with him and his wife. He is Count of the Holy Roman Empire, which the Abbé Grenet procured for him. It cost ten guineas, and his patent of creation hangs in a frame in his parlor. He mentioned Sir James Murray, who by twelve questions could get at your thoughts.

'In February, passed the evening at Stone's with Fox,

of Mr. Cumberland, that he should have presumed to talk *before me, before me*, sir, in such terms of *my* friend Dr. Priestley. Pray, sir, let Mr. Dilly know my opinion of Mr. Cumberland, — that his ignorance is only equalled by his impertinence, and that both are exceeded by his malice.' — Mr. Dyce's *Porsoniana*, p. 314.

[1] The note is among Rogers's letters. It is dated from 28 Pall Mall, and expresses 'the great pleasure he has received from the perusal of his elegant performance, which has given pleasure to all Mr. Hoole's friends who have seen it.'

Sheridan, O'Brien, the Bishop of Autun, Madame de
Sillery, Pamela,— supposed to be her daughter,— Adèle
Princess of Orleans, and Henriette, her niece. Fox said:
" All titles are equally ridiculous. I believe Hume wrote
up the Stuarts from a spirit of opposition, because it was
the fashion to write them down." He spoke French
fluently; said his son (who is dumb) had ideas before he
had words, talked to him with his fingers, and when he
first entered the room flew to receive him with the most
lively pleasure. In conversation his (Fox's) countenance
brightens, and his voice assumes a pleasant tone. Dr.
Priestley said afterwards he was improved in manners
since he saw him at Shelburne House ten years ago,
when he spat on the carpet and hurt Lord Shelburne,
who is a man of great neatness. "Charles," said Sheridan, " have you read Parr's letter?" "I read it last
week," said Fox. "Charles," said Sheridan, "received a
long letter from Parr, to dissuade him from moving for
the repeal of the Test Act. But as he began with not
requiring him to answer it, Charles thought he would go
a step farther and not read it."

'Madame de Sillery has an air of vivacity. She said
Marmontel was an affected writer, of no taste or genius,
but cried up by a set of admirers in Paris. I mentioned
this afterwards to Blanchisserie, secretary to the Embassy,
an aristocrat. "Tell her," said he, " to write as well. Her
best works are her daughters." They are fine women.
He owned afterwards that he thought himself slighted
by her. He has bought Sir Isaac Newton's house in
St. Martin's Lane, and intends to ornament the front.
Pamela excited Sheridan's notice. (Mirabeau used to be
at her feet.) She has fine black eyes, and her skin is of
a dazzling whiteness, but Adèle struck me more, having
more softness in look and manner. Her fine light hair
descended below her knees. She plays delightfully on
the harp. Pamela draws. Saw them afterwards at the

exhibition. Dr. Priestley said afterwards that he had
often heard Marmontel read his tales at Madame de
[? Seran's] at Paris, where the *literati* met every Wednesday evening, and that his action was so violent he was
afraid of sitting near him. It was there also he heard
D'Alembert deliver his famous *éloge* on Voltaire.

'In March Dr. Aikin called upon me. On the 20th
of April dined with Paine at William Morgan's, a silent
man, but very strong and emphatic in his language.
The memory of Joshua was given as a toast. "I would
not treat kings like Joshua,"[1] said Paine: "I'm of the
Scotch parson's opinion when he prayed against Louis
XIV., — 'Lord, shake him over the mouth of hell, but
don't let him drop!'" He gave in his turn "The Republic of the World," — a sublime idea.

'On the 23d dined with the Antiquarian Society.
Nothing occurred of moment. Sat by Lysons, and con-
versed with Marsh on Shakspeare. Townley, Daines
Barrington,[2] and Dr. Douglas, the bishop,[3] were there.

'On the 24th dined at Sharpe's with Porson, who read
Will Whiston's trial with some humor. On the 26th
with Lord Dacre at Edison's, and attended the "Friends
of the People" at Freemasons' Hall. On the 27th with
Dr. Aikin and Dr. Priestley at College dinner; Dr. A.
thinks Molière far superior to any comic writer in this
country.

'On the 28th of May dined with Dr. Bates and
Marsden and Major Montfort at Mr. Raper's. Marsden
thinks our words derived from the Latin at second hand
through the French. Dr. Bates said that the fish caught

---

[1] See Joshua, chaps. x., xi., xii.

[2] The Hon. Daines Barrington, fourth son of the first Lord Barrington, a lawyer and an antiquary. He died in 1800.

[3] Dr. John Douglas, then in his seventy-first year. He was made
bishop of Carlisle in 1787, translated to Salisbury in June, 1791, and
died in 1807.

in the Italian seas were often boiled by being dropped
into the current of a warm spring some fathoms below
the surface, and mentioned a curious sacrifice to a saint
in Sicily.

'In June, dined at home with the Barbaulds and Dr.
Bates. Dr. B. had heard a celebrated singer sing an
ode of Anacreon at Angelica Kauffman's at Rome. In
Sicily a lover must write an ode to his mistress before
she will listen to him.

'*June* 21. — Set off for Salisbury Cathedral, Stonehenge, Wilton, Bryanston, Portland Quarries, Lulworth
Castle, Lulworth Cove, Corfe Castle, etc.; and met Sharp
at Southampton.'

This is the first clear mention of Richard Sharp.
The Sharpe named in the earlier portions of the diary
is Sutton Sharpe, of Nottingham Place, who afterwards
married Maria Rogers. Sutton Sharpe was then a
widower, living with his only daughter, Catharine Sharpe,
the heroic story of whose after-life I have told in another
volume,[1] in which also Sutton Sharpe's melancholy history is briefly narrated. He was a man of much taste
and culture, and at this time of considerable wealth
as a brewer. He had studied drawing at the Royal
Academy, and lived on terms of intimate friendship with
Opie, Shee, Stothard, Flaxman, Bewick, Holloway, and
others. At his house Rogers made the acquaintance of
these eminent artists, and learned that love of art which
distinguished him in after-life. Boddington, Richard
Sharp's partner, once remarked to Rogers in the hearing
of William Maltby : ' You know, Rogers, we owe all these
tastes to Sutton Sharpe;' and Rogers himself, speaking
to Sutton Sharpe's fourth son, the late Mr. William
Sharpe, said, 'William, all I know of art I learned from
your father.' A pencil drawing by Flaxman shows

---

[1] Samuel Sharpe ; Egyptologist and Translator of the Bible.

Sutton Sharpe to have been a person of singularly noble presence, though perhaps with more taste and sensibility than resolution or energy. He was an intimate friend of Porson, and among his frequent visitors were William Maltby, Samuel Boddington, Richard Sharp, and Horne Tooke.

The journey which is summarized in the last entry taken from Rogers's diary, is more fully described in another of his journals, and the account is worth reproducing as a sketch of southern England in the early days of the French Revolution, and before the Napoleonic wars.

'*June* 21, 1792. — Went in a post-coach from London to Salisbury. The Cathedral is the lightest and most elegant piece of Gothic extant. It is, indeed, so light as to lose in some degree that grandeur which is attached to magnitude. The spectator at first sight thinks he could almost "hang it to his watch." ·Not that the masonry is so very curiously wrought, for in rich filagree work York Minster and the Cathedral at Amiens far excel it; but the style of its architecture is so beautiful, and the whole is so happily put together and so neatly finished, that for a moment we forget the sublime simplicity of the Grecian school and pronounce it to be perfection itself. When viewed from several parts of the close, it has a very pleasing and picturesque effect through the trees.

'*22d.* — Rode nine miles across Salisbury Plain to Stonehenge. At the sixth stone, or soon afterwards, it presents itself on a small elevation. As we approach it it becomes an object of importance, and is indeed most interesting to a contemplative mind. When we consider its great antiquity and the inexplicable mystery in which its story is involved—its many barbarous purposes, among which was most probably the sacrifice of human beings, the sacrifice of Romans; the shapeless masses that compose it, their gigantic size and rude arrangement; and, to close all, its solitary station in the desert, which unites on all sides with the sky — we must acknowledge it to be a very sublime and imposing piece of scenery. Proceeded to Wilton. What I thought there most admirable were: a Venus extracting a thorn from her foot — her half-closed eyelids are strikingly expressive of acute pain; the busts of Hannibal and Brutus — the last is evidently a likeness, and its lineaments are sufficient alone to tell his history, the face of a man who could stab his friend to save his country; a statue of Bacchus with a cup in his hand and poppies hanging from his shoulders; and a bust of Sappho which is exquisitely beautiful. The " Assumption of the Virgin " by Raphael, and a Madonna by Carlo Dolci (her veil colored with ultra-marine) equal to any piece of that master, even to Domenichino's portrait of his mistress, or the picture of " Christ Blessing the Elements " at Burleigh. Continued through an open and hilly country to Dorchester. Mr. Portman's walk at Bryanston, near Blandford, gave me, however, some relief. It was along a very high green bank, near a mile in length, in many parts perpendicular and hung with noble firs and forest trees. The Stour winds below it through the soft lawns of the Park, and then, skirting the uplands on the opposite side, makes its exit with the accompaniment of a little rock scenery. Dorchester is nearly encircled with a pleasant sycamore walk. Its foundations are an inexhaustible mine of Roman antiquities. I left it in the evening, and soon ascending Ridgway Hill (so called from a village that shelters itself under it), was agreeably surprised at its summit with a beautiful view of Weymouth Bay, and the Isle of Portland rising with its mountainous ridge near the entrance of it.

'24th. — Went to church, and heard a rustic band of

singers accompanied by the bassoon. In the evening
rode on the sands, the Corso of Weymouth; and afterwards, from the brow of a little eminence that overlooks
Weymouth, saw Portland and the windings of the coast
as far as Lyme to great advantage. It is an evening
view, and the setting sun had shed its richest hues
over it.

'27th. — Rode to Upwey, a retired village near Ridgway, to visit a friend who had just chosen it as a retreat
from the bustle and glitter of Paris. It was there that
I saw him last, and the contrast of the present scene
struck me forcibly. At dinner, however, he regaled
me with *soup bouilli* and an *omelette;* and his parrot
Jacquant, his dog Azor, and an old French horse on
which he exercised in the Bois de Boulogne are still his
favorite companions. Rode with him along a noble terrace near a mile in length, and commanding the sea, and
the adjacent downs pastured with sheep and swelling
everywhere into *tumuli.* Within a few yards of his garden, under a green hill and overshadowed with aged
trees, is the fountain-head of the river Wey.

'28th. — Passed the ruins of Sandford Castle, which
are situated on the edge of a cliff, and when viewed from
a low point make a good picture. Ferried over to Portland, ascended through several villages, crossed the
island, and came to a very romantic scene. The cliffs
were here very lofty, and formed a small semicircular
recess. Towards their summits they were partly hewn
into quarries, the white diagonal strata of which con-
trasted with the gray and rugged crags interspersed
among them. It was a busy scene. A team of horses
were continually ascending and descending by an almost
perpendicular path, and a boat was employed in conveying the stone to a small vessel that lay moored at the
entrance. Above, on the extreme verge of the precipice,
were the ruins of an old church and of a still older castle.

'29th. — Rode to East Lulworth, through a well-cultivated country, the beauties of which were blurred and almost blotted out by a wet mist that overspread them. Lulworth Castle is very ancient and has an air of great dignity. It consists of a quadrangle, with a round tower at each corner, and the gray hue of its stone finely chastens the fresh green of the trees in the park around it. The village church has a very handsome tower, and stands just beside it. The effect of the whole is beautiful, but some of the parts offend. A Grecian portico with Ionic pillars forms a singular entrance to an old castle. The balustrade that runs round it, and the Grecian portico are modern additions, and correspond but ill with the sullen grandeur of the old structure. Proceeded to East Lulworth Cove, a small basin nearly encircled with high cliffs, which affords a secure asylum to the little coasting vessels that frequent it, and is, indeed, a very singular and romantic scene. Proceeded over hills whitened with sheep to Corfe Castle, the situation of which is high and commanding. Two drawbridges and as many gateways lead to the citadel, and its extensive walls give ample testimony to its ancient consequence. One of its round towers is fearfully inclined from its base and overhangs a road that is already strewed with tremendous fragments. A girl assured me that from her infancy she had never passed it but at full speed. From hence to Wimborne there is a chain of black and melancholy heaths. Here and there, indeed, we were relieved with a little woodland scenery, and on the left we had an almost uninterrupted view of Poole Harbor stretching across the country like some magnificent river; the sea-gulls were flying over it, and its banks were bare and desolate. Slept at Wimborne, and saw the Minster, which has two square towers and is very ancient. Entered the New Forest, which is at first dreary and black with furze, but improves beyond Ring-

wood, and at Stony Cross presents some grand distances.
The wood increased as we approached Southampton, and
the deer and other forest cattle enlivened the scenery.

'In the evening rowed down to Netley Abbey. The
ground on which it stands is finely formed; and ivied
windows and fractured arches, and the daw and the owl,
excited nameless sensations. A door in a dark passage
half-intimidated my fellow-travellers. Returned by moonlight, through its old woods catching delicious views of
the river; ferried over the Itchen.

'*July* 1. — Sailed down the river by a fine breeze to
Cowes, breakfasted and proceeded in a chaise to Newport.
Went in another to Ashey Down,[1] whence we saw the
Channel from the mouth of the Beaulieu River to Portsmouth and along the Arundel coast. To Nunwell Down,
commanding Brading Haven, running up the island (now
at low water). Shanklin Chine and village, the first a
rocky romantic glen that opens to the sea and affords
shelter to some hanging cottages, — the last a most retired rural spot, the ground charmingly tumbled about
and varied with little woods and dingles. Passed John
Wilkes's, and dined at Steeple. The shore is here finely
broken and shut in by a semicircular range of gray rocks
that not very boldly but very picturesquely overhang the
village. Returned by Sir Rd. Worsley's, and from the
Obelisk hill in the park commanded nearly the whole
island. The general face of the country was rich, varied
with little hills and woods and villages.

'*July* 2. — Had a pleasant view from a hill above
Newport commanding the course of the river towards the
sea. Walked along the banks to Hurst Stake, its bold
and beautiful twin. The succession of close wood and
high meadow, the cattle near the brink, the sails gliding

---

[1] This part of the journey was taken in company with Richard
Sharp, whom he had met at Southampton.

round the hills, the soft uplands on the opposite side, and Newport church tower among the trees,— these were its principal beauties.   Proceeded round Carisbrook Castle, which rises on an elevated bank, and has some dignity; had several grand reaches of the channel, crossed Afton Down and from a field near Freshwater had a foreshortened view of Yarmouth River; it was low water.   Sailed from Yarmouth to Lymington in forty minutes, the prospect of the island and the mainland very amusing.   Lymington falls to the river; the church-window that looks down it, and the green meadows that rise directly in front, make the perspective of its street beautiful.   From the Angel yard the river is seen winding among the trees in the valley below, and losing itself in the forest.   On the opposite side of the street there runs a pleasant lime-walk, commanding the Isle of Wight and the Needles.   The path to the baths has the same view, and lies through the fields.

'3d. — Rode to Hordle, and had a distant view of Lord Bute's.   The coast here forms a grand semicircle in full view of the Needles, but it is bare and desolate.

'4th. — Rode to Rope Hill and had a foreshortened view of the river in its course through a rich valley to the sea; a fine grove of trees formed the foreground.   Proceeded to Mr. Morant's, and from the front of his house were enchanted.   Passed through Whitley Ridge woods which are very fine, and crossing Heathy Dilton, returned by Vicar's Hill, from which we saw a very fine and well-wooded bank of Sir H. Burrard's.

'5th. — Passed Vicar's Hill, and soon afterwards by turning a little to the right saw a beautiful lake of Sir H. Burrard's, fringed with wood.   Passed Doyley Park and Pilewall; not a thing worth mentioning except the neat cottage of a clergyman's widow, shaded with willow-trees and hung with jessamine; and proceeded to Sooley (or Sowley) Pond — that from the farthest end presents a fine reach — but here the Channel on the right, and the mountainous ridge of the Isle of Wight softened down by distance, very maliciously arrested our attention. Returned through Norley Wood, full of encroaching cottages and now nearly felled, and descended to Boldre Bridge that commands a beautiful home view of the river now reduced to a humble brook and winding among the sedges. Came home by Rope Hill.

'6th. — Followed the same track to Sowley Pond. Passed a slitting-mill, and at Bucklershard had a most magnificent view of Beaulieu River sweeping boldly round hanging woods, with the busy scene of a dockyard on its shore. Dined at Beaulieu; it was high water, and the lake above and below the bridge and the walk among old oaks on the abbey side of the river detained us two hours. Proceeded by the Fighting Cocks and through the wild wood scenes; passed over Culverley Heath, commanding a circular sweep of forest, very grand and extensive; of Denny Walk, a very rich and secluded scene, to the Lyndhurst road, which we entered at the sixth stone, — in the grand avenue that extends to Brockenhurst. Followed the turnpike road by Rope Hill to Lymington.

'7th. — From Lymington turnpike, turned directly through a gate on the left, and after having ridden a little among some woody scenes, traversed a cheerless heath for many miles, leaving Wilverley Lodge, a lonely and melancholy object, on the left, the Isle of Wight visible on the horizon. At last from Burley Hill saw a cultivated valley skirted with a chain of hanging woods. Turned through a long narrow tract of shrubwood, and crossing Markway bottom flat and marshy, in which the cattle were well grouped near some water, ascended to Rhinefield Lodge, which is seated among old oaks on a circular knoll and commands noble views over the wooded scenes of the forest. It is less rich and extensive than the Burley view, less grand and simple than Morant's, but formed a noble station for a forest lodge. The buckhounds sallied out at our approach, and one of the under-keepers led us into the Brockenhurst road; over a heath we proceeded to that village, and there entered the turnpike road from Lyndhurst to Lymington. From Rope Hill there is a delightful mile, commanding the river in the valley with Vicar's Hill, and Sir H. Burrard's plantations on the opposite heights; the Channel and the Isle of Wight in the distance.

'8th. — Rode by Rope Hill and over Boldre Bridge to Boldre Church, which is seated on a hill and commands pleasant views round it. Gilpin read the service and preached: " Commune with your own hearts." His manner was familiar and unaffected; his language simple and correct. " But, you say, it is now your custom to swear; you may soon make it your custom not to swear." His figure apostolical, his head bald, a short man. Several fine heads in the church, and the band of singers full of rough harmony. Returned by Mr. Morant's and Brockenhurst and Battramsley.

'In the front of Mr. Morant's the lawn is skirted with aged oaks, and falls with a fine swell into a wide uncultivated valley, beyond which rise the dark woods of the forest, extending like a magnificent curtain to right and left as far as the eye can reach.

'July 9. — Rode by Boldre churchyard, in which are two inscriptions written by the vicar.

'July 10. — Went in a chaise through a beautiful country to Lyndhurst. Proceeded on horseback by Minstead, and through several woods full of lawns and sudden declivities to Bramble Hill Lodge, seated on a green hill, — on the brow of which a herd of deer was assembled. A long ridge runs far above it which commands Mr. Gilpin's celebrated view. The foreground falls with a fine sweep, and discovers a grand extent of

15

forest-wood below, with Southampton and its river, in which the mouth of the Itchen was very visible, and the Channel and the Isle of Wight in the distance.

'At Lyndhurst is the King's Lodge, and here generally resides the Ranger. His table is often during the venison season furnished with twelve haunches that are served up in succession; such are the refinements of luxury. In a lawn near Whitley Ridge Lodge I saw a forest girl with some lettuces in a basket. When dressed with verjuice, — the fermented juice of the crab-apple, — they were to furnish a dinner to a family with the humble addition of oat-bread. It was only on a Sunday that they could indulge themselves with meat! What a contrast!

'*July* 11. — Rain.

'12*th*. — Rain.

'13*th*. — The waters of the river above the bridge were out, and it now presented the appearance of a noble lake, fringed on every side with the trees that skirt the uplands. Rode by Walhampton and Vicar's Hill, and returned over Boldre Bridge, where there was a ferry for foot-passengers.

'14*th*. — Rode in a chaise to Beaulieu, and proceeded through Exbury woods, commanding a catch of the river and Bucklershard, and a noble view of its course from the sea into the forest. Its shores were wild and well-wooded, and gave the idea of an unexplored and uninhabited country. Rode along the sea-shore opposite the Isle of Wight and turned off to Cadlands: the lawn beautiful, the garden towards the river very inferior, but the situation and ground admirable. From hence to Dibden, exquisitely fine. Stobland Common and Butt's Ash Farm particularly delightful. At Dibden met the chaise and returned by Totton along the Lyndhurst road.

'15*th*. — Rode to Boldre and heard Gilpin. "Therefore, my beloved brethren, cleanse yourselves from all filthiness," etc.

'16th. — Proceeded through the forest to Southampton; a sultry day, concluded with a thunder-storm.

'17th. — Came by Botley, Titchfield, and Fareham to Gosport, twenty-five miles. The country rich and well-wooded, exhibiting several beautiful distances on the left, and on the right once or twice a noble catch of Southampton Water. Titchfield Abbey is a venerable, square, castle-like mansion, with an octagon tower at each corner. Its offices and gateways are in a similar style, and its elevated position, when viewed from some points, gives it an air of dignity. From Fareham Common had a lengthened and broken view of the Channel and its shipping, with the Isle of Wight beyond it. The foreground was rich and woody, and the multitude of masts that rose in some parts above the trees had a singular effect. Ferried over and walked on Portsmouth ramparts, which nearly encircle the town, commanding the Isle of Wight, here variegated with woods. Walked there again in the evening. The green and leafy island in front, and the busy vessels in the offing, were finely made out by the evening sun. On the left, seated on the extreme edge of a promontory, lay a castle, the whole of which was in shadow, and the outline of its turrets and battlements was distinctly marked. The general character of the scene was softened, but now and then a transient gleam of sunshine caught a white sail and called it out into the landscape. It was the annual fair, and all was mirth and mummery.

'18th. — Through a rich country, with woody distances on the left and frequent sea-views on the right, proceeded to Chichester. The spire is almost equal to that at Salisbury in point of elegance and lightness. Passed through a beautiful country, the Goodwood plantations festooning the woods on the left, and village spires among the trees on the right. I turned aside to East-ham, a very pleasant and retired village. In the churchyard, which commands fields and woody hills, are three epitaphs of Hayley's. His shrubbery runs beside it, and he has a walk that looks down into a deep and woody valley, glen soon afterwards, and commands the rich wealds of Sussex. Rode among woods to Arundel. Passed a cricket match,—the country people, in scarlet cloaks and white wagoner's frocks, forming an amusing line along the field in which it was played. Saw Arundel Castle, the deep fosse, now a romantic glen full of trees; the round tower, a fragment mantled with a grand mass of ivy; the castle-yard, skirted on one side by the venerable gallery, etc., and on the other by the shell of the chapel. In the chapel a fine head of Rubens, by himself. The church ancient, with some old ivied walls behind it.

'Rode among woods and over downs with frequent views of the sea on the right to Worthing.'

When this pleasant summer journey was taken, 'The Pleasures of Memory' was just beginning to receive that public recognition which soon made its author famous. He speaks of Gilpin and Hayley, but he had not yet made the personal acquaintance of either of them. Gilpin was then old. He had been the guide of a whole generation to the picturesque scenery of their own country, and Rogers had probably travelled through the New Forest with his volume in his hand. Hayley, too, was then in the full enjoyment of his evanescent fame, and Rogers had not yet heard through Mr. Cadell of that approval which gave him so much pleasure and pride. On his return to London — which was always early, in order that his father might get away on his own long summer holiday — he naturally found himself the object of increased interest. People were talking about him, and his poem was being praised in the reviews and was selling fast. He did not allow himself to be much more tempted into society, but continued as usual to spend

his days in the city, and his evenings chiefly in his Stoke
Newington home. He was already contemplating his
next poem, or at least laying up the material for it. A
few pages of his diary record his social experiences
during the next eighteen months.

'*August* 11.—Rode to Sevenoaks with Sharp and
Cooper; saw Knole and worshipped a statue of Demos-
thenes. West told Sharp: "I never showed a young
artist a picture he liked, but he asked me where I bought
my colors; and Sir Joshua said a picture never pleased
him till after he had labored at it again and again."

'*August* 13.—Dined at Tuffin's with Cooper, Tooke,
Dr. Priestley, Dr. Crawford, etc. Politics. Whether man
has any natural right to property, and a free government
is friendly to the Arts; decided in the affirmative.

'*August* 15.—Dr. Priestley, Dr. Aikin, Cooper, Fell,
etc., dined at the Green. Dr. Priestley said De Luc,
when in London, said he knew it better than Priestley
(though Priestley lived there) and he would be his guide.
"He took me," said Priestley, "to the Old Bailey, the
only time I was ever there, and bade me observe the
criminals at the bar. 'Did you ever,' said he, 'meet
elsewhere with the same lines of character? An English
blackguard is not to be found out of England: insolent
and brutal — with a trait of generosity. I was once
walking in the street with Mr. Howard, when a baker
dropped some pies and he damned their souls to eter-
nity!'" Mentioned a singular escape he had in his
laboratory at Warrington, and another he experienced
that very morning. The American Indians must be ex-
terminated; cannot be civilized. America not peopled
a thousand years ago. Man created long after other
animals, — few human bones in a fossil state; many
animal bones. Coal is vegetable in a decayed state, and
must be exhausted in time. Cooper said America was

not in being a thousand years ago.   Aikin and Priestley
said it must have been.   Cooper replied that an island
might be raised in a night with a mountain on it.
Priestley: "But not with the Andes on it!"   Cooper
said: "Those are European experiments — America
works on a grander scale."

'*November* 6. — First meeting of the Club.   Argument
between Aikin and Sharpe on the principles of Beauty.
A. maintained that the Greeks were inferior in their
combinations to nature.   S. said that statuary could
soar above her by selecting and proportioning her best
features.

'*November* 13. — Dined at Sharpe's and met Boddington and Stothard.   Stothard said: "If the Pantheon were
in London I think I should be a happier man.   I often
take an evening walk in the park in summer to observe
the figures, and at a distance they portion themselves
into those bold simple forms that were the delight of the
Grecian artists."

'*November* 19. — Drank tea at Dr. Garshore's.   Present: Dr. Gillies, Dr. Bates, Mr. Planta, Dr. Kippis, Mr.
Parsons, Major Rennell, Mr. Marsden, etc.   Talked politics with Gillies, who said he should publish Aristotle's
political works with a commentary.

'*November* 24. — Dined at W. Vaughan's, with Priestley, B. Vaughan, Aikin, Christie, etc.   A. gave a good
motto for a Peerage Book, —

> " The air hath bubbles as the water hath,
> And these are of them."

'*27th*. — Second meeting of Club.   Dispute respecting
Capital Punishments.   The objects of punishment are to
deter by example, to reform the offender, and contrive
that he should make reparation to society for the injury
he has done her.   The last two cannot be attained by
capital punishments.

' "A case occurs," says Sharp, "in which the first — and most important — cannot be accomplished without them : A soldier runs away; the influence of fear in that man is irresistible — it overcomes the sense of shame. As you cannot restrain it you must make it subservient to your own purposes. He flies to escape the *chance* of dying : make *certainty* of death the consequence of his flight."

' *December 2.* — Rode to Streatham and slept there. Present : Mr. and Mrs. Broadhead.

' *7th.* — Dined at the Athenæum Club. Introduced by Sharp. Present : Murphy, Carr, Ogle, Blake, Parsons, etc. Murphy very rancorous on politics. Said the old English writers had great strength, such as Hooker, etc. — but they all wrote according to the Latin Syntax. Then came a new set — Temple, Dryden, etc. — who were grounded on the English Syntax. Dr. Johnson returned to the Latin, and so did the Scotch except Robertson. Spoke with enthusiasm of Garrick. "Were he to act to-night none of you would have been here !" said he. "He had his faults as a man, but on the stage he was a demigod. Prior and Swift would have made a Fontaine between them. Swift approached near to him."

' *18th.* — Third night of the Club. Was at Paine's trial, and heard Erskine.

' *19th.* — Saw Stothard at Sharpe's, who said Dr. Bates had tried to purchase the Temple at Tivoli and transport it to England.

' *29th.* — At Parndon met James Martin and Jackson Barwis. Mrs. Martin had met and conversed with Mrs. Armstead (Fox's *chère amie*, and originally Mrs. Abbington's maid) unknowingly at Hastings's trial, and thought her a charming woman. Said that Boehm, the traveller, once left his hat as a pledge at a barrier in Sweden in consequence of a wrangle about a fee, and

that he walked without a hat through the country, re-
solving not to purchase another where he had been so
imposed upon.

. 1793, '*January* 14. — Dined at McMurdo's, with
Hinkley and Dr. Priestley. The dialogue turned on
distressing situations. Dr. Priestley remarked that Dr.
Franklin said of Dibbs: "If that man is not damned,
the devil's kept for nothing!"

'*January* 15. — Mr. Raper dined at Newington Green.
Said that the Jesuits at Macao, when they took their
siesta after dinner, held an ivory ball in their hands and
a brass basin between their feet; that the instant the
ball dropped the noise wakened them, that they then
knew they had slept, and held one wink of sleep to be
sufficient refreshment; that when a European visited a
great man at Canton he often walked in in his waistcoat —
a servant carrying behind him his coat, hat, and sword;
and that was considered a visit of ceremony.

'*February* 7. — Went to the Club and met Priestley,
Cooper, etc. Cooper, speaking of Louis's execution, said
he died well enough.

'*February* 9; *Sunday*. — Went with Sharp, Cooper,
Tuffin, and Weston to Stothard's, and afterwards to
Romney's. Saw him and his statues and pictures; a
warm democrat, and his gallery full of beauty, — Mrs.
Tickell, Lady E. Fitzgerald, Mrs. Siddons, Lady Hamilton, etc. Afterwards walked to the Park and saw the
line of carriages. Sharpe told Lady Hamilton's history —
Joseph Boydell's cook, afterwards Greville's mistress —
the masquerade scene: "What's the matter, Greville?
Not well? I know what it is;" threw the dress on the
fire; her vow to Sir William not to be his wife till he had
educated her. Dined at the Grecian: Politics, the arts,
travelling, picturesque beauty, etc.

' . . . Dined at Sharpe's. Dr. Aikin said that when
a Hungarian officer came to London with a letter of

recommendation to Mr. Howard, Howard walked the streets with him; and his first exclamation on seeing the wealth and comfort around him was: "What a fine city to plunder!"

'*May* 3. — Danced at Smith's ball.

'*May* 6. — Was introduced by Dr. Gillies to the Athenian. Present: Dr. Bancroft, Dr. Gillies, Dr. Griffiths, Dr. Franklin's grandson, and myself. Dr. Franklin used to say that when a tradesman was tired of business, he left off and went into the country to retire.

'*December* 9. — Dr. Priestley at the Hackney Club: "When I was dining at Paris, fifteen years ago, at Turgot's table, M. de Chatelleux, — author of 'Travels through America,' — in answer to an inquiry, said that the two gentlemen opposite to me were the Bishop of Aix and the Archbishop of Toulouse; 'but,' said he, 'they are no more believers than you or I.'[1] I assured him I was a believer, but he would not believe me; and Le Roi, the philosopher, told me that I was the only man of sense he knew that was a Christian. A young man of family called upon me and said, with tears of joy in his eyes, that he heard I was a believer. 'Yes,' said I; 'but I am a great heretic, not such a believer as you.' 'Still,' said he, 'you are a believer.'"

'Dr. Franklin's receipt for a verdict in your favor: "Have reason on your side, procure an eloquent attorney to state it, an impartial judge to try it; and then, if you have great luck, you may gain your cause." Franklin said a man once came into the country where he lived who asked: "What! do you bury lawyers? We place them in an arm-chair at the top of the stairs, and they are always gone before morning — the devil takes them."

'A Spanish judge satisfied everybody with his sen-

---

[1] The story is told in Mr. Dyce's 'Table Talk,' but the fact that the two gentlemen were eminent ecclesiastics — the point of the story — is omitted.

tences: his son who succeeded him satisfied nobody.
" What did you do, father? I read their cases with all
possible care." "I did no such thing. I received their
papers till each party was tired of sending them in. I
then piled them in my pair of scales, and the heaviest
scale had it." (Franklin.)

'" When I [Priestley] was at Bowood the last Lord
Lyttelton, son of the author, called on me and was surprised to find me a believer. 'You ascribe all things to a
cause,' said he; 'so far is reasonable, but what produced
that cause? Why not sit down with things as we find
them?'"

'An inn in Yorkshire had this sign: On one side a
smart young man with this inscription — "I am going to
law." On the other side the young man in rags — "I've
gained my cause."

'There was a sect at Philadelphia, Franklin says,
which believed that a violent death was a sure passport
to heaven, and many of them committed murder in order
to be hanged. One of these enthusiasts set off into the
fields early one morning with a determination to shoot
the first man he met. It proved to be a Quaker, who
saluted him so civilly that it disarmed him. He met
nobody else; and, returning into the town, turned into
a billiard-room where some persons were at play. There
he stood for some time resting on his gun. At last one
of the players struck the ball into the pocket: "That was
a good aim," said his antagonist. "But this is a better,"
said the enthusiast, as he raised his gun and shot him
dead. The astonishment of the company was great, as
you may imagine. "Poor man!" said the enthusiast,
taking the dead man by the hand, "I meant you no
harm." He declared his motive triumphantly, and was
hanged. "And what steps did the Government take?"
I asked Dr. Franklin. "Why," said he, "the sect was
very small, and it was thought better to hang them up as

they committed such crimes than to interfere publicly to crush them."

'*Dec.* [no date]. — Dined at Dilly's with Reid, Pinckerton, Butler, Thomson, Boswell, Sharpe,[1] and Tuffin.

'*Dec.* 19. — Dined at the Eumelean. Murphy preferred Swift's verses on his own death to all his other poems and his polite conversation. Said that the theatres charged an author one hundred and forty guineas for the expenses of his night, and he was never charged in Garrick's time (when there *were* actors) more than seventy. Said Johnson recited well, and would often at night leave the house at Streatham, and, seating himself on one of the garden seats and turning it on its pivot from the storm, would roar and bellow Latin hexameters and English heroics for the hour together; that he would do the same at Brighton in one of the machines, and could be heard at Thrale's on the cliff. Said the "Confederacy" was translated from a dull French play; that he and Tooke one summer evening, after they had dined together, walked along Oxford Street, and ordering a pot of porter at a small alehouse they sat down on the bench before the door. "This is the grandeur of human life. Those scoundrels in their carriages have no taste for happiness." Wrote Johnson's "Life" at the "Dog" alehouse, near Richmond Bridge, where I kept close for a month, and hardly ever put on my shoes.'

Arthur Murphy, the biographer of Fielding and Garrick, the friend and first biographer of Johnson, — to whose 'talents, literature, and gentleman-like manners' Boswell bears witness, — formed with Rogers, as he had previously done with Johnson, a friendship which was never broken. Rogers had first met him at the house of the Piozzis. Murphy was then in poverty. He had spent the wealth his popular plays — such as the 'Upholster-

---

[1] Sharpe is, in all cases, Sutton Sharpe; Sharp is Richard Sharp.

ers,' 'All in the Wrong,' the 'Grecian Daughter,' and
'Know your own Mind' — had brought him, and was
living by miscellaneous literary work.   He was in debt
everywhere.   Like Cumberland and others he soon began
to borrow money of Rogers, for which Rogers got nothing but dishonored bills.   He had once lent him two
hundred pounds; and asking Murphy when he meant to
repay him, Murphy went back with him to his chambers
in the Temple and used all his persuasive arts to induce
Rogers to lend him more.   At a later time he assigned
the stock and copyrights of his works as security for a
loan, when they had been already sold to the bookseller.
But he had no desire to deceive, and made so humble an
apology that he was easily forgiven.   In 1803 a pension
was given him, and he died in 1805, at the age of seventy-
eight.   Rogers always spoke kindly of him, repeated his
mot that the theatres were a fourth estate of the realm;
and told to his credit that when an actress with whom he
had lived left him her money, he gave it all up to her
relations.

A few further scraps of Murphy's conversation are
recorded by Rogers in his Commonplace Book : —

' "I should like to use that story of yours, Sheridan,"
said Lord Lauderdale.   "Would you?" said Sheridan.
"Then I must be on my guard in future, for a joke in
your hands is no laughing matter."   Murphy considers
Cowley as Addison's model.   Thinks "Boadicca," by
Glover, is, in point of style, the best tragedy since
Shakspeare.   It has a bad fifth act.   The opening of
the "Alchemist" is a model of dramatic writing for
effect, though never followed.   Close your acts well, and
have a good fifth act, and your play must succeed.   Also,
always give a counter turn, a surprise in the fifth, so
that nobody shall foresee the conclusion.   Was first
struck by Dryden's criticisms on the "Silent Woman"

in his preface to his plays, and afterwards read it carefully with the play. Had not then thought of the stage.
Afterwards read Ricciboni on Molière, D'Alembert's
" Life of Des Touches," etc. Used to compose walking
about Bagnigge Wells and New River Head, and then
call in at an alehouse to write down a thought. Used to
make three or four chairs pass for his people on the
stage, and would say " that chair has continued too long
silent." Kept a memorandum book for good things.
When French died without leaving him anything he
said to himself: " I have got by him, however," —
having put him into " Sir Bashful Constant " and the
" Citizen."

'Murphy had two inscriptions on the collar of his
dog : —

> " My name is Prince, of honest fame :
> Let other Princes say the same."

> " My name is Prince, from vice and debts I 'm free ;
> I want no Parliament to pay for me."

' " Am I not in Heaven ? " said a girl at High Mass.
" No, my dear," said Murphy, " there are not so many
bishops in Heaven." '

Murphy was full of stories of Foote, some of which
Rogers has written down in his early memorandum
book : —

' " Great as Foote was on the stage," said Murphy,
" he was greater in the green-room, and there I loved
to attend him. One night when I was there the last
Duke of Cumberland hurried in, saying: 'I come every
night to swallow all your good things.' 'Do you?' said
Foote; 'you must have a damned good digestion, for you
never bring them up again.' "

' In his cause before Lord Mansfield, when Lord
Mansfield, who had continued firm on his side through-

out, was at last brought over to his opponent: "Damn
the trial," says he to Murphy, " what a crane-necked turn
it has taken ! It has been tried twenty times at Caen
Wood, and gained the verdict in my favor."

' When Foote proposed a venison feast at the " Crown
and Anchor" to Murphy and Garrick, Dr. Schonberg
and two other lawyers were engaged to it. None came
but Foote, Murphy, and Garrick. The bill came to three
guineas a head, and Foote wrote to the absentees for
their shares. When Foote paid his, the waiter said:
"This is a bad shilling, sir." "Is it?" replied Foote,
"look at it, Davy." ' Garrick, who was half-tipsy, said it
was and threw it away. "Do you change it for him,"
said Foote, "you can make it go as far as anybody !"

' When a collection for the poor players was proposed,
all but Garrick attended the meeting. "He did set out,"
says Foote, " but as he turned the corner of the Adelphi
he met the ghost of a shilling."

' When L——, who had been sentenced to the pillory,
saw Foote in the pump-room at Bath, whither he had
been ordered for the jaundice, " Your looks mend," says
L——. " Yes," says Foote, " I am washing the eggs
from my face."

' Murphy said : " I meant Foote in my character of
Dashwold, where I have used his *bon-mot* to the Duke
of Cumberland."

' Murphy met Costello at Lord Camden's. "My wife
and I," said Costello, "quarrelled, and we agreed to
divide. I said to her—'I will take one side of the
house and you the other.' I took the inside and she
took the outside." '

CHAPTER IX.

THE turning-point in Rogers's life had now come. At
the beginning of his thirtieth year he had found himself
recognized as a popular poet, and had begun to enjoy
the kind of fame for which he longed. But no thought
of the social celebrity he was afterwards to attain had
as yet come into his mind. He was still the junior partner in the bank, and day by day was occupied with its
business. He was on the unpopular side both in politics
and in religion, and his prospects of wealth were remote.
'While his father lived,' says Samuel Sharpe, 'Mr. Rogers's friends had been as much chosen for their politics
as for their literature,' and in the diary quoted in the
previous chapter we find him frequently in the company
of some of the chief Liberal politicians of that exciting
and agitated time. The house at Stoke Newington
was one in which Liberal politicians and Liberal divines
— Whigs, latitudinarians, and Unitarians — found themselves at home. The elder Rogers was, in words which
came into use at a later day, 'a Whig and something
more.' Among the signatures to the celebrated Declaration of the 'Society instituted for the purpose of obtaining a Parliamentary Reform' under the title of 'Friends

of the People,' that of Thomas Rogers comes immediately before that of the Hon. Thomas Erskine, M.P.,
and Samuel Rogers directly follows on the Right Hon.
Lord John Russell, M.P. The names of John Towgood,
who had married Samuel Rogers's eldest sister Martha,
and of his friends Dr. Kippis and Richard Sharp, also
appear with those of Grey and Lambton and Sheridan
and Mackintosh and Whitbread, among the hundred
which constitute this illustrious catalogue.   Dr. Priestley
had come to London in the autumn of 1791; and the
elder Rogers first, and his son afterwards, opened the
house at Newington Green to the persecuted philosopher
and divine. Thomas Rogers in one of his last letters to
his son expresses constant sympathy with the French,
but writing on the 13th of September, 1792, about the subscription for France which Horne Tooke and his friends
were getting up, he reasons conclusively against it, and
tells his son: 'I would wish you not to have anything
to do with it. It is of a piece with the rest of Horne
Tooke's politics, which are more of the bravado than the
man of true wisdom.' This is not the criticism of an
opponent, but of a friend. It need not be taken to indicate any difference between father and son. In politics,
as in religion and business, there seems to have been to
the last the fullest confidence and sympathy between
Thomas Rogers and his son Samuel. The beginning
of the year 1793, to which part of the diary given in
the previous chapter belongs, found Samuel Rogers still
living at Stoke Newington with his father, sisters, and
younger brother, without any thought of change or any
desire for it on his part or theirs.

This state of things might to all appearance have
lasted many years longer, and had it done so the world
might never have known Samuel Rogers as the munifi-
cent patron of art and literature he afterwards became.
But in the spring of 1793 his father was seized with a

fatal illness, and died on the 1st of June. Thomas Rogers had not been a strong man, but his death in his fifty-eighth year was premature. There are no references to it in his son's diaries, nor in the family letters. It was the custom of the family to be silent on such events. There are, however, in the poems two stanzas headed 'Written in a Sick Chamber,' and dated 1793, which give the only account of his illness.

> 'There in that bed so closely curtained round,
> Worn to a shade, and wan with slow decay,
> A father sleeps. Oh, hushed be every sound,
> Soft may we breathe the midnight hours away!
>   He stirs — yet still he sleeps. May heavenly dreams
> Long o'er his smooth and settled pillow rise —
> Nor fly, till morning through the shutter streams,
> And on the hearth the glimmering rushlight dies!'

It is a remarkable testimony to Samuel Rogers's business faculty that so excellent a man of business as his father should have left him his own share in the bank and his estates. Thomas Rogers's will practically disinherited his eldest son Daniel in favor of his third son Samuel, who thus became head of the banking firm, and practically head of the family. He now found himself in possession of about five thousand a year, partly derived from estates and investments, but chiefly from the bank in Freeman's Court. This was a considerable fortune in 1793, and gave Rogers the opportunity which probably woke the desire to live in the society of London. He soon felt that its possession set him free to follow the career to which — as he was not long in discovering — his inclination, his social talents, and his ambition led him. He had formed no definite plan. He probably found that the residence at Stoke Newington was a hindrance to the cultivation of the literary society in which he delighted, and therefore, without breaking away from the

old home on the Green, he took chambers in Paper Buildings. The rooms had been previously occupied by Lord
Ellenborough, and the range of buildings in which they
stood has since been pulled down and a new one erected
on the site. Rogers lived in these chambers between
six and seven years. During this period he became intimate with many well-known persons, and particularly
with four men, of different types of character, who probably exerted the greatest influence on his life. These
were Fox, Sheridan, Tooke, and Richard Sharp. Rogers
not only belonged to Fox's school in politics, but was a
devoted admirer of the great Whig statesman and orator.
His 'Recollections' of Fox are among the most interesting and valuable of the treasures his tenacious memory
has allowed him to preserve from oblivion and to hand
down to posterity. His intimate association with the
Whig leaders for the first fifty years of this century
was begun by his acquaintance with Fox, if it may not
be said to have arisen out of it. With Sheridan his
connection was of another kind. The great orator and
dramatist became the recipient of much assistance from
the poet, who stood by him to the last when the great
world had left him to die in poverty and neglect. Richard Sharp was destined to become Rogers's closest and
most intimate friend. He had much to do in making
Rogers's life what it afterwards became, and had more
influence on his poetry, as well as on his character, than
any other of the friends of his maturer years. This
admirable and popular person was already widely known
among men of letters for that critical force which made
Mackintosh call him the best critic he knew, and for
those remarkable conversational powers to which he
afterwards owed his chief authority and fame. He was
born in Newfoundland in 1759, and was therefore about
four years older than Rogers. He had written in 1784 a
very able essay on English style as a preface to a gram-

mar published by his old schoolmaster, the Rev. John
Fell. He had been the intimate friend of Henderson, the
actor, and at his request had gone in 1785 — the year in
which Henderson died — to see the new 'Hamlet,' whose
provincial fame had preceded him to London.   In 1787
he read an admirable paper before the Manchester Society, 'On the Nature and Utility of Eloquence.'   He was
a strong advocate of a simple style as opposed to the
prevalent Johnsonian pedantry.   'Johnsonism,' he said,
'has become almost a general disease;' and he laughed
at 'Mr. B. and Dr. P. strutting about in Johnson's bulky
clothes, as if a couple of Liliputians had bought their
great-coats at a rag-fair in Brobdingnag.'   He contemplated, at a later period, the writing of a history of the
establishment of 'American Independence,' and was encouraged to do so by his intimate friend, Mr. Adams,
afterwards President of the United States.   He had fixed
on the period between 1775 and 1783, but Mr. Adams
assured him that those were 'by no means the most important nor the most interesting eight years of the Revolution, which had in fact been effected, so far as the
minds of the people were concerned, in the period from
1761 to 1775.'   The design of the history was abandoned,
and Mr. Sharp is only known to literature by a small
volume of 'Letters and Essays in Prose and Verse,'[1]
which he published towards the close of his long and
interesting life.

The acquaintance between Rogers and Richard Sharp
began in the spring of 1792.   They were introduced to
each other by William Maltby, and soon became close
friends.   Rogers always said that he did not know Richard Sharp till after 'The Pleasures of Memory' was published, but in the July of the year in which the poem

---

[1] This book was made the subject of a very laudatory article in the
'Quarterly Review' in 1834, vol. li.

appeared they travelled together in the Isle of Wight. Richard Sharp's first letter to Rogers is one acknowledging the gift of the volume, and recommending Rogers to read one of his favorite books, Usher's 'Clio.'   It is the letter of a comparative stranger.   Rogers wrote to Maltby during their stay in the Isle of Wight in praise of his new friend; and Maltby, writing a letter of literary gossip[1] on the 13th of July, 1792, concludes by asking to be remembered to Sharp, 'who deserves everything-you say of him, and can never be praised too much.'   This was not merely the enthusiastic expression of an admiring friend.   It was a simple statement of the impression Richard Sharp produced on his contemporaries. Mackintosh's biographer speaks of Richard Sharp as a friend whose good opinion Sir James Mackintosh always considered a sufficient counterbalance to any amount of general misrepresentation, and Mackintosh himself said that he never quitted him without feeling himself better, and in better humor with the world.   'I owe much to your society,' says Mackintosh in a letter to Sharp in January, 1804.   'Your conversation has not only pleased and instructed me, but it has most materially contributed to refine my taste, to multiply my innocent and independent pleasures, and to make my mind more tranquil and reasonable.   I think you have produced more effect on my character than any man with whom I have lived.'[2] Francis Horner, writing to Lady Mackintosh in 1805, says: 'Sharp I respect and love more and more every day; he has every day new talents and new virtues to show.'[3]   Sydney Smith, in a letter to Allen in 1809, says: 'Let the child learn principles from Dumont, Sharp

---

[1] One item of the news is 'that Mr. Gibbon is coming to England, and brings with him a work prepared for the press; the subject of it is not yet known.'

[2] Life of Sir James Mackintosh, vol. i. p. 196.

[3] Life of Francis Horner, vol. i. p. 297.

shall teach him ease and nature;'[1] and Miss Caroline
Fox records in her diary in 1840 that John Mill spoke
with much interest of 'Conversation' Sharp, and said:
'It was a fine thing for me to hear him and my father
converse.' These testimonies to his character and genius
are borne out by the letters and statements of all his
friends, — and his friends included nearly every distinguished author, statesman, and man of society for forty
years. His life has not been written, but his name is
prominent in most of the memoirs of men who lived in
the first thirty-five years of the present century. It is
an honor to Rogers that such a man should have been his
fast friend till death divided them.

At the time this friendship was first formed Richard
Sharp was in business in the City, and the letters to
him bear the address of Fish-street Hill. He was already a figure in society, where his great conversational
powers and his unbounded goodness of heart made him
universally welcome. His judgment was trusted by all
who knew him, and in later years statesmen went to him
for counsel and advice. It would scarcely be too much
to say that he was the most popular man in London
society in his time. His familiar *sobriquet* of 'Conversation' Sharp indicated only his most striking faculty;
but his power of sympathy, his insight, his large reading
and culture, more forcibly impressed themselves on his
friends than even his conversational powers. He soon
perceived the social faculty of his friend Rogers, and
when the death of his father left Rogers master of a
fortune, urged him to leave the distant suburb of Stoke
Newington, and to establish himself in London. Rogers
felt the force of his friend's reasoning, enforced as it was
by that friend's example. There was an evident struggle
in his mind between the love of home and the love of
society, and he turned it into poetry as a poet should.

[1] Letters of Sydney Smith, p. 63.

It was the origin of his next poem, 'An Epistle to a Friend.' But while writing this, which many regard as the most finished and beautiful of his productions, he took up his abode more and more in London. The 'Epistle to a Friend' was the mental protest with which he yielded to the social forces which pressed him to take advantage of his fame; and he had done his six years' work upon it, completed it and published it, before he finally gave up Stoke Newington, and made a solitary home, first in his chambers in Paper Buildings, afterwards in lodgings in Prince's Street, Hanover Square, and finally in the well-known house in St. James's Place.

Some of Rogers's literary friends had already discovered his amiable willingness to help them by counsel, or personal service, or money. There is an enthusiastic letter from Richard Cumberland which, though without date, may be mentioned here. It is written in the large bold hand which well became Cumberland's character. Rogers had given him some pecuniary assistance, and the old dramatist, in writing his thanks, finds it difficult to moderate his gratitude. 'Your bounty surprised me,' he says; 'I hurried back on discovering its amount, resolved for the moment to entreat you to moderate your benefaction.' On second thoughts, however, he kept the money, lest his motive in returning it should be misunderstood; and he declares his uniform and unalterable esteem and love for his generous friend. The declaration was no doubt sincere, and the esteem was mutual. Rogers always spoke of Cumberland as a pleasant companion and an excellent and entertaining talker. He was full of recollections of the stage, epecially of Garrick, whose 'Lear' Cumberland regarded as the greatest piece of acting he had seen. Rogers records that he linked with this high praise Henderson's 'Falstaff' and Cooke's 'Iago.' Garrick said of Cumberland that he was a man without a skin. Cumberland used to repeat Garrick's advice to him : 'Make your hero expected with impatience.' He told the story, too, of Garrick playing the water wagtail on the lawn at Hampton, to the great delight of Cumberland's children, 'as they stood round him one year under another.' Another of Cumberland's remarks, put on record in Rogers's Commonplace Book, was of the greatest possible benefit to Rogers : 'I hope it will be put on my tomb,' said Cumberland, '"Patron of the Flesh-brush." I have not caught cold since I used it.' Rogers took the hint and acted on it. In his later years he spoke of the use of the flesh-brush as the art of living forever, and said he had learned it from Cumberland. The old playwright thus amply repaid Rogers's kindness to him. He had led a life of immense variety and adventure, but had a grievance against the Government, and became something of a sycophant in his latter days.

There is a letter of this period from a friend of Robert Merry's, who, though utterly unknown to Rogers, makes a pathetic appeal for help. Rogers sent him the money he asked for. Robert Merry himself seems to have been under similar obligations. It is, indeed, a striking feature in the correspondence between Rogers and his political and literary friends of three generations that his readiness to do them all kinds of service is constantly assumed and acted upon. Criticism of manuscripts, negotiations with publishers, advice on business or travel, advances of money, are forms of help constantly asked and as constantly given. There are several letters from Robert Merry in the autumn of 1793 which show both Rogers's helpfulness and his political associations. Merry left London in September to go to Geneva with his wife and Charles Pigott, — another of the men who got pecuniary assistance from Rogers. At Harwich, however, they heard so much of the difficulties and dan-

gers of travel in Holland and on the Rhine that they
turned back; and Merry went to Scarborough, whence he
writes to Rogers on the 17th of October. He is as quiet
there, he says, as if he had gone among the Alps. He
has an excellent ready-furnished abode, 'looking boldly
and bleakly to the sea,' for little more than a guinea a
week, though in the summer it lets for from ten to fourteen. He promises Rogers, if he will go down by the
Scarborough mail, 'a good bed, a good fire, and capital
Yorkshire stingo.' He is finishing his novel, and will
send it to Rogers for approval and to arrange with
Cadell, or any other bookseller, to bring it out. He
asks for all the news. 'What is the situation of Toulon,
Lyons, La Vendée, Mauberge, and the Duke of York's
army?' He has had but two letters since he left London, and both of them had been opened, so he is to be
addressed under cover to somebody else. Rogers is to
tell nobody that he is still in England. As no answer
came at once he wrote again, fearing that his letter had
been seized in the Post Office. In a third letter on the
8th of December he makes a political reference written
for the edification of Pitt's Post Office spies: 'It is with
much sorrow that I find those licentious and abandoned
regicides, the French, have been of late successful. God
grant that the justice of our endeavors may meet with
its due reward!' He is also 'much afflicted to discover
that even here a turbulent democratic spirit too much
prevails.' On the 12th of December he writes again, to
enclose a little theatrical piece for Mr. Harris, of Covent
Garden theatre. He conceals his name as author —'not
to be exposed to Aristocratic Malice.' He further describes the piece as the French play of 'Fénelon,' reduced
to three acts. He urges Rogers to get it published if
Harris will not take it, but not to let the name of the
translator be known —'as the name of a Republican
would damn any performance at this time.' 'If Hayley

is a furious democrat,' he asks, 'what must be the scale
of patriotism in this country?' This letter had begun in
Della Cruscan style : 'If you knew the pleasure I receive
in reading your letters you would not be sparing of them.
They allure me from a boisterous sea of Politics to the
mild abode of Poetry and Peace. It is in solitude alone
we learn properly to estimate our comforts, and prove
how sweetly the voice of friendship breathing instruction and delight affects the soul. I, here, am tolerably
secluded from the world, and scarcely view a living crea-
ture except the hovering sea-gull or the lonely cormorant
traversing the distant waves. Yet still am I troubled by
the Revolutionary Struggle; the great object of human
happiness is never long removed from my sight. Oh
that I could sleep for two centuries like the youths of
Ephesus and then awake to a new order of things! But
alas! our existence must be passed amidst the storm;
the fair season will be for posterity.' Ten months later,
on the 11th of October, 1794, he writes in London — but
giving his address as Post Office, Norwich — regretting
to have missed a talk with Rogers 'on the existing
circumstances which seem to me,' he says, 'to be advancing to some great catastrophe.' As things stood he
felt some inclination to go with Mrs. Merry to America,
asks Rogers to put him in the way how to proceed, and
promises to call shortly to replace a few pounds he
feared he had overdrawn at the bank. He and his wife
afterwards went to America, where he died in 1798.
Gifford's 'Baviad,' published in 1794, may have had
something to do with this resolution; but the 'aristocratic malice' to which he referred in the year before its
issue — meaning by that the disfavor and unpopularity
of advanced Liberal views in those days, and the personal
danger to those who held them — was the predisposing
cause of his exile.

Two letters from Priestley's friend, Thomas Cooper,

further illustrate the political characteristics of the times and Rogers's relation to political movements. Cooper was a Manchester man who seems to have thought it necessary to go where the expression of opinion was freer than it was at that time in England. He had dined with Rogers at the Stock Exchange just before leaving London, and wrote to him from Deal about a commission of Priestley's [1] that he had forgotten. The letter is dated Sunday, August the 24th, 1793, 5 o'clock; and he says: 'I am not yet on board, but you may conclude that the receipt of this letter at your house insures to you my safe delivery on board ship.' On the 14th of December he writes from Philadelphia: 'I will be at your house in February or March: *incog.* like other great men. Mention this, with strong injunctions of secrecy, to Tuffin and Sharp. I wish the enclosed letters to be duly and safely conveyed, and having to write to you to send Russell his letter, I do not write to Tuffin or Sharp. Russell, Priestley, and T. Walker (not R. Walker nor any other of my friends or my family) know of my intention. I hope to come over with a sufficient inducement for others to return with me.' This inducement was a scheme which had been got up by Joseph Priestley, Cooper himself, and some other English emigrants for an English settlement in Pennsylvania, near the head of the Susquehanna River. As there seemed to be some likelihood that his sons might fix themselves there, Dr. Priestley himself, on his arrival in the United States, went on from New York to Philadelphia, and thence a hundred and thirty miles up the country to Northumberland. This was a small town at the confluence of the east and west branches of the Susquehanna, and fifty miles from the proposed settlement. The scheme had to

---

[1] Probably Joseph Priestley, son of the philosopher, who with his two brothers was already settled in America.

be abandoned; but Dr. Priestley remained at Northumberland, where he died on the 6th of February, 1804.

Merry's opened letters and Cooper's secrecy illustrate the dangers of that martyr age of Reform. Dr. Priestley himself left London in April, 1794, urged to do so by numerous friends, who felt that he might at any moment be seized as the next victim under the White Terror which the frightful doings in France had conjured up in England. Dr. Price had died in April, 1791; and Dr. Priestley had succeeded him as preacher at Hackney at the close of the year. Some account of conversations in which Dr. Priestley, Cooper, and other Liberals took part in the few years of his residence in London, has already been given in extracts from Rogers's diary in the preceding chapter. After the iniquitous sentence of seven years' transportation. which had been passed on the Rev. Thomas Fyshe Palmer, a Unitarian minister in Dundee, it was felt that no Liberal was safe. A few poor men in that town, imitating the influential body in London, had formed a society of Friends of the People. They prepared an address to their fellow-citizens to which Mr. Palmer had given literary form. It is most moderate in tone and just in sentiment; but Mr. Palmer was prosecuted for sedition, and at a trial in which the judge allowed his religious opinions to be urged as grounds for his condemnation on a political charge, was found guilty and sentenced, and the sentence was rigorously carried out. Dr. Priestley's friends were naturally alarmed lest he should fall a victim to the same malevolent tyranny, and it seems probable that he was not too early in placing himself beyond King George's beneficent sway. It was one of Rogers's boasts that the exiled philosopher and divine spent his last night in England under his roof.

Dr. Priestley had scarcely been gone six weeks when two of Rogers's intimate friends were arrested for high

treason.   On the 14th of May, Mr. William Stone was
arrested, and after various examinations, was committed
to Newgate.   Horne Tooke was carried to the Tower under
circumstances which he has himself put on record in a
memorandum in a volume he afterwards gave to Rogers.
This memorandum is published as a note to Rogers's
' Recollections '[1] of his friend.   'I was apprehended,'
says Horne Tooke, 'at Wimbledon, Friday, May 16,
conducted to the Tower, Monday, May 19, 1794, without any charge; nor can I conjecture their pretence of
charge.   Mr. Dundas, Secretary of State, told me in the
Privy Council that " It was *conceived* that I was guilty of
treasonable practices."   He refused to tell me by whom
it was conceived.'   Horne Tooke was tried in November,
and Rogers was present.   He often told the story in
later days, especially dwelling on Erskine's incomparable
pantomime.[2]   The attorney-general, Sir John Scott, in
replying for the Crown, used arguments for which Erskine
was not prepared, and to which he would have no opportunity of reply.   Erskine drew the attention of the jury
to himself, and by shrugs of the shoulders, shakings of
the head, and other significant gestures conveyed to
them his sense of the astonishing audacity and worthless-
ness of his opponent's statements.   Horne Tooke was
acquitted; and as he left the court a lady, who described
herself as a daughter of one of the jurymen, came up and
asked to be introduced to him.   He shook her warmly
by the hand and said: 'Then give me leave, madam,
to call you sister, for your father has just given me
life.'   Juries like that which acquitted Horne Tooke,
not only saved the lives of the men they refused to con-

---

[1] Rogers's ' Recollections,' p. 140.

[2] Mr. Hayward (Ed. Rev. July, 1856) quotes Mr. Dyce's account of
Rogers telling the story, as an illustration of the carelessness by which
Mr. Dyce 'has repeatedly made Rogers use phraseology he notoriously
disliked, and fall into errors of which he would have been ashamed.'

vict, but saved the country itself from being compelled to choose between despotism and revolution. Rogers heartily sympathized with his persecuted political friends. Twenty years later — when Horne Tooke had been some time dead, and Rogers had seen much of him in that quiet old age in which Rogers afterwards said his manners and conversation reminded him of a calm sunset in October — he turned the circumstances of the trial into poetry. Horne Tooke was evidently in his mind when he wrote his 'Human Life.'

It was more than a year before Rogers's friend, Mr. William Stone, at whose house at Hackney he had met Paine, and who had introduced him to Fox, was brought up for trial. One day in January, 1796, Rogers read in the morning paper at breakfast that a summons had been issued to bring him before the Privy Council. His horse was ready to take him as usual to the bank, and he rode at once into town and then drove in a coach to Downing Street. He asked for Mr. Dundas, and was shown into the presence of that Minister. He inquired with some nervousness what was the meaning of the announcement he had seen in the papers. Dundas replied by asking what conveyance he had with him, and learning that it was a hackney coach proposed to go with him to the Home Office. There Rogers was told that he was required as a witness in the trial of William Stone for high treason. In March, 1794, Stone had met him in the Strand, and told him a gentleman had applied to him to learn the sentiments of the people of England as to an invasion from France. 'I rather declined the conversation,' said Rogers in his evidence. 'I was in a hurry, and I told him I had no wish to take part in any political transactions at that time. It was a time of general alarm, and I wished to shun even the shadow of an imputation, — as I knew when the minds of men were agitated, as I thought they then were, the

most innocent intentions were liable to misconstruction.'
In reply to further questions he said that Stone had
afterwards called on him with a paper, in which it was
shown that, however the English people might differ
among themselves, they would unite to repel an invasion;
and he had expressed the opinion that he should do his
duty if by stating this, which he believed to be true, he
could save his country from invasion. Mr. Stone was
acquitted, but one result of the trial was that Rogers —
who, though always an ardent Liberal, had no passion for
politics — was less inclined than ever to take any active
part in the political agitations of a time when the Habeas
Corpus Act was suspended and there was a reign of
terror in England. 'You will infect me like the plague,'
he had said to his friend Stone during the conversation
which was the subject of his evidence; and he avoided
the infection, though not by keeping away from his
friends. The political danger may have been one cause
of the discontinuance of the diary which recorded the
conversation at their dinner-tables. The brief record of
the toasts drunk at Mr. Morgan's table,[1] and of Paine's
remarks on kings, might have been made evidence against
him had the Ministers of the day known that it was in
existence.

It is pleasant to turn from the gloomy aspect of
public affairs in those miserable times to the brighter
world of poetry in which Rogers loved to dwell, and to
the social intercourse with pleasant people he diligently
cultivated. As we look back to those years we can
scarcely wonder that Wordsworth gave up some of his
earlier aspirations, or that Southey went over to the
reactionary side. It is to Rogers's lasting credit that
he never forsook his political friends. Poetry, and not
politics, was his pursuit; but he kept to the Liberal side
through all the weary years of its depression and dis-

---

[1] Chap. VIII. p. 216.

couragement. Wordsworth in the most beautiful of his
early poems [1] speaks of the 'tranquil restoration' which
the dim recollection of Nature's beauties had brought;
and of —

> '. . . that blessed mood
> In which the burden and the mystery,
> In which the heavy and the weary weight
> Of all this unintelligible world,
> Is lightened' —

which contact with Nature produced. Rogers felt the
same tranquil restoration in talk with authors and
literary men on the literary topics of the time, and in
poetry itself. He was writing his 'Epistle to a Friend,'
and in this year wrote the lines — which were published
in the earlier editions, but were afterwards omitted — in
which he pays his first tribute to Fox, and speaks of
Horne Tooke, who had just been defeated in his second
candidature for Westminster, with a reverence that in
those days few would have paid him : —

> ' Hail, sweet Society ! in crowds unknown,
>   Though the vain world would claim thee for its own,
>   Still where thy small and cheerful converse flows
>   Be mine to enter, ere the circle close.
>   When in retreat Fox lays his thunder by,
>   And Wit and Taste their mingled charms supply ;
>   When Siddons, born to melt and freeze the heart,
>   Performs at home her more endearing part;
>   When he, who best interprets to mankind
>   The wingèd messengers from mind to mind,
>   Leans on his spade, and playful as profound
>   His genius sheds its evening sunshine round ;
>   Be mine to listen, pleased yet not elate,
>   Ever too modest or too proud to rate
>   Myself by my companions ; self-compelled
>   To earn the station that in life I held.'

[1] Tintern Abbey.

He was often with Horne Tooke at Wimbledon in these years, and the talks with him in his garden, as he leaned upon his spade, supplied some of the material of the 'Recollections.' An illustration of Fox laying his thunder by has been given in the preceding chapter in the extract from the diary which records the evening spent with Fox and Sheridan at the house of Mr. Stone. There are many other examples of the great orator's familiar moods in the 'Recollections,' which, as Rogers himself says, 'show his playfulness, his love of letters, and his good nature in unbending himself to a young man.'

Rogers had long known Mrs. Siddons where she performed 'her more endearing part,' and in the year before the lines in the 'Epistle' were written she had asked him to write an epilogue to be spoken by her on her benefit night. The 'Epilogue' as published in the Poems is said in a note to have been spoken by Mrs. Siddons 'after a tragedy performed for her benefit at the Theatre Royal, Drury Lane, April 27, 1795.' The stanzas are printed as they were written, not as they were spoken. Mrs. Siddons made some changes and abbreviations in them, for which she apologizes in the following letter : —

Mrs. Siddons to S. Rogers.

'MY DEAR MR. ROGERS, — I know your goodness will pardon the liberties I have taken of curtailing and a little altering the "Epilogue," and tho' my having two long parts to perform upon my benefit night will make it painful to *me* to *speak* more of it, yet as you will probably let that appear among your other elegant productions, you will unquestionably *print* it as it was originally written. I'm afraid my friends will think they have too much of a good thing, for I am desired by those whom I must not refuse to play Emmeline in " Edgar and Emme-

line " (a fairy tale) and to speak the epilogue to it ; so I
think they will have *enough* of me, and all this (beside
my part in the play which is quite new to me) I have
got to learn. Pity and pardon and believe me, my dear
sir,

> 'Your very much obliged
>> 'And affectionate humble servant,
>>> 'S. Siddons.

'I send you the original "Epilogue " to compare with
the copy ; and as I think the trifling alterations I have,
presuming on your kindness, made, will have a rather
better stage effect, I hope they will not be disagreeable to
you. Pray have the goodness to return it immediately,
for, as Mr. S. Lysons would say : "I must begin and study
like a dragon ! "'

Another letter from the great actress, written on an
ample sheet of the old-fashioned letter paper, contains a
ticket bearing the words : 'Mrs. Siddons's Night, Theatre
Royal Drury Lane Company.' It bears her monogram
and her written initials, for Box No. 664 : —

'With Mrs. Siddons' comps. & thanks to Mr. Rogers.
With respect to the Verses —

" Never let your noble courage be cast down. "

'April 25, 1795.'

He did not let his noble courage be cast down, though
he was free from the conceit which buoys up the spirits
of many inferior men, and was never quite content with
what he had written. The 'Epilogue' is certainly none
the worse for the absence of that careful elaboration
which he gave to some of his poems, and it associated
his name with one of the greatest reputations of the time.
Mrs. Siddons spoke it after the play of 'Mahomet the Impostor,' in which she acted the part of Palmyra. Speak-

17

ing of the 'Occasional Address' which followed the play,
the 'True Briton' said: 'We know not which most to
praise, its poetical merits or her delivery of it.' The
changes made by Mrs. Siddons are recorded in Rogers's
Commonplace Book. They are simply such as make it
more personal and direct.

> 'I wake, I breathe and am myself again,'

becomes —

> 'I wake, I breathe, I am myself again.'

And —

> 'Ah no! she scorns the trappings of her Art,
> No theme but truth, no prompter but the heart!'

became —

> 'Oh no, I scorn the trappings of my Art,
> My theme is truth, my prompter is my heart.'

The two lines —

> 'Thus Woman makes her entrance and her exit,
> Not least an actress when she least suspects it;'

were delivered —

> 'Yes, fair ones, you've your entrance and your exit,
> And most you're acting when you least suspect it.'

And the last four —

> '*Thus*, from her mind all artifice she flings,
> All skill, all practice — now unmeaning things.
> To you, unchecked, each genuine feeling flows,
> For all that life endears to you she owes;'

were delivered —

> 'No! from her heart all artifice she flings,
> All skill, all practice, now unmeaning things,
> Unbounded now each genuine feeling flows
> For all that life endears — to you she owes.'

The cordial reception accorded to this 'Epilogue' was rightly regarded by its author as a sign that his literary position was already fully established. 'His society,' says his nephew, 'was eagerly sought for by ladies of fashion as well as by men of letters. His father when young, and living in Worcestershire, had mixed with the men of rank in his own neighborhood. He had been intimate with the Earl of Stamford and Warrington and that excellent man the first Lord Lyttelton, the poet, and his son-in-law Lord Valentia, the father of the traveller. But though such society had been cultivated by the grandfather at "The Hill," it was by no means to the father's taste. On settling in Newington Green he was glad to drop his titled acquaintance; and he gave his son the strong advice : "Never go near them, Sam !" But their doors were now open to the young and wealthy poet, and he did not refuse to enter.' At this period he was just beginning to shake himself free from business. His brother Henry came of age in the summer of 1795, and was at once made a partner in the bank, and gradually intrusted with its management. He proved to be an excellent man of business, and the elder brother soon saw that he could with the utmost confidence leave everything in his hands. Thus year by year the way seemed to be opening to Samuel Rogers into the life of cultivated ease, of literary and artistic friendships, and of social celebrity and success of which he had only dimly dreamed in earlier days. 'We never go so far,' says Guizot, 'as when we know not whither we are going;' and Rogers exemplified the axiom. He was gradually detaching himself from business on the one hand, and from the home at Stoke Newington on the other; and circumstances concurred in a striking manner to urge him forward in the course to which his tastes inclined him, but with which his old associations were in conflict. The home at Stoke Newington was breaking up. Mary Worthington, the 'Milly' of the family letters, who had lived with Thomas Rogers and his wife, and had always been the oldest of the familiar faces in the Stoke Newington home, died in November, 1795. Samuel Rogers had entered her name in his own hand in the family Bible, under the family list: 'Mary Worthington, born November 27, 1716, died 2d of November, 1795.' In the same year his sister Maria had been married to his friend Sutton Sharpe. There remained at home only his brother Henry, his sister Sarah, and Miss Mitchell, who, as has been previously stated, lived with the family till her death in 1812.

Among the few relics of a large correspondence with literary and other friends at this period are, a very characteristic letter from Dr. Moore to Rogers, and one from Rogers to his friend Richard Sharp. The two letters curiously exhibit the relations in which he stood towards these very different men. The author of 'Zeluco' had sent Rogers a manuscript to read and criticise; and Rogers, as was his wont even then, had kept it so long that the author became anxious for its safety. The manuscript was, in all probability, that of Dr. Moore's work published in the next year under the title of 'A View of the Causes and Progress of the French Revolution.'

'CLIFFORD STREET, Sept. 17, 1794.

'DEAR SIR, — Your letter of the 16th gave me great pleasure, because I really thought some mischief had come on the manuscript, not one page of which could I have ever renewed. I am now easy, and I beg you will not put yourself to the least hurry, as I can now wait with patience and tranquillity till it is convenient for you.

'As for your verbal criticisms I would not give a damn for them, because I have always been subject to forget

words and letters in writing; and I am more careless
in what goes to the press than in a letter to a friend,
because my compositor is the most accurate man on
earth.   What I expect from you are alterations of more
importance, which affect the truth and justness of the
observations and the spirit of the composition.   If I did
not value your judgment in those particulars I should
not have troubled you on the subject, and if you do not
think I am able to bear the severest remark that you can
make with good humor, you do me injustice.   Although
I might think your remarks ill-founded it would not destroy my friendship for you,— which is founded on another
unalterable basis besides my opinion of your taste in
works of literature.

'Yours sincerely,

'J. MOORE.

'P.S. — Do not show the MS.'

The letter to Richard Sharp is a year later.   It is
the earliest part of the correspondence between these two
friends which has been preserved; but it must not be
regarded as indicating the full nature of their intercourse.
They had common political relations, such as letters
from other persons have already indicated, and large
correspondence on literary topics.   But they were both
young and both unmarried, and yet neither of them had
given up the intention of matrimony, — though Rogers, at
least, was not engaged.   He was, of course, regarded as
an eligible person, he had much of the susceptibility of
the poet, and there is evidence in this letter, as well as
in others, that he had been more than once in love.   He
would naturally tell the story of his social successes to
the friend who was most in his confidence, — and that
friend was Richard Sharp.

S. Rogers to Richard Sharp.

'MARGATE [Oct. 15, 1795].

'MY DEAR SHARP, — Surely I am the most miserable dog alive, the most dependent on the opinion of others, in heaven to-day, sent *ad inferos* to-morrow, — now sleepless from ecstasy, now from despondency. I will live so no longer. *Badinage* apart, I have been making experiments on my own heart in this great laboratory by the sea-side. I dropped it into the crucible, and when I looked for it again, it was — shall I say not there? No, but it was not so sound as I left it. I have been fooling away a fortnight, and am neither better nor happier for it. Yet how long is the retrospect! In this foolish place every day is a little drama. My first week was almost entirely spent in the company of a girl whose face you know, whose beauty you must have felt, — at least I did. She seemed sinking, and I could have wept when I looked at her; but she left Margate, and I looked about for somebody else. My second has passed miscellaneously. Mrs. Gillies has some beauty from Dover Street, and I have been flattered, amused, and tortured successively beyond description. On Saturday when I dined there it was actual war, and I did not mean to open my lips to her High Mightiness again; but to-day she made me go with her to the painter's to make my criticisms on her miniature. The white flag has resumed its place, and I think will hardly be taken down again. She goes to-morrow with Dr.[1] and Mrs. G[illies].

'But what will you say when I tell you that I was at the last ball introduced, by her own desire and previous arrangement, to a girl whose face distracted me at the opera concert last winter, but whose name I did not know, and whose face and fortune together have turned

---

[1] Dr. John Gillies, the historian of Greece and translator of Aristotle.

all the heads in the island? To-day, though I had not exchanged three words with her, she walked several yards up to me at a review, and conversed half an hour, as I sat on horseback, by the clock of St. Peter's. She is, indeed, the most touching girl now left in the island, but I fear she amuses herself at the expense of other people, and therefore stand on the defensive. Roger Palmer has been giving her dinners innumerable at Peg-well, and Miles P. Andrews,[1] who has been driving about his four horses, has been making love to her these six weeks, and has made me the confidant of his hopes and fears. But the last is just gone, full of love and hope. These, you will say, are neither of them very formidable rivals, nor, I believe, has the first any thought of it. When I have reconnoitred the ground a little you shall know more.

'Mrs. Cowley[2] is here, and is really a very agreeable woman. Reynolds the dramatist is also here, and is a very good-humored fellow, though a little out of spirits from having singed his wings at the flame above-mentioned. Colonel Barré[3] is here, and Mackintosh is at Broadstairs, so that I find tolerable society. I live alone in a small cottage, with a vine over the front and benches at the door, very cheerfully looking into a field,

---

[1] Mr. Miles Peter Andrews was a member of the celebrated firm of gunpowder manufacturers at Dartford. He entered Parliament as Member for Bewdley in 1790, and was re-elected without opposition in 1796, 1802, 1806, and 1807. He had been an intimate friend of Garrick and Foote, and of the 'wicked Lord Lyttelton,' who left him a bequest in his will. He was the author of a number of comedies and some operas. His 'Mysteries of the Castle; a Dramatic Tale in three Acts,' had been performed at Covent Garden Theatre with a strong cast in the January before Rogers met him at Margate. He bought Lord Grenville's house and became a prominent man of fashion. He died in 1814.

[2] Mrs. Cowley, the Della Cruscan poetess.

[3] Colonel Barré had been a personal and political friend of Dr. Price.

and furnishing more room than I want at a guinea per week. Parsons is not here, nor do I now expect him. Weston was here for a day or two, but caught the spleen and vanished before I came. My Muse is neither asleep nor awake, she is very stupid. I thank you most sincerely for your good wishes, but am sorry to say they are not yet fulfilled. I shall, however, return with such a magazine of female freaks and follies as will serve to furnish many a sublime speculation when we sit in council together. Adieu! You wrote me a charming letter about myself, and I blush to think that I have confined myself to the same subject. If ever you should pass near the precincts of the Temple, will you visit my nutshell and take a peep at our architectural experiments? The sublime dreams of a Piranesi vanish before them.

    'Yours at all times and in all places,

                                  'S. R.

 'Wednesday morning.'

The reply to this letter has not been preserved, and here, for a couple of years, the correspondence ceases. The intercourse between the friends was constant, and was necessarily greatly facilitated by Rogers's removal from his remote suburban home to chambers in the Temple. Among the friends he made in this period of his life was Mackintosh. The brilliant author of 'Vindiciæ Gallicæ' had been eating his way to the bar, to which he was called in 1795. He and Richard Sharp were in the habit of meeting each other at Rogers's lodgings, where, as he told Mr. Dyce, they would stay for hours talking metaphysics. Rogers made no secret of his dislike of the subject, though he was far from indifferent to some of the most fascinating themes of transcendental speculation. The only two occasions of offence between him and Sharp arose out of Sharp's fondness for metaphysics.

One day at Rogers's chambers, Mackintosh and Sharp were so intent on the abstract considerations into which he did not care to plunge that he went out, paid a visit, and returned to find them still so absorbed that they did not know he had been away. He was angry, and sat down to write his letters. On a later occasion Sharp and Rogers were together at Ulleswater, and Rogers made a remark on the favorite topic of his friend. 'There are only two men in England with whom I ever talk on metaphysics,' said Sharp. Rogers took no offence, though his sister Sarah, who was at the Lakes with him, said he should have left him at once.

The friendship of these two men was not to be broken off by so paltry a misunderstanding. If they could not talk metaphysics together, they talked of everything else, politics and theology included. Rogers, however, knew but little of his friend's early history. He used to tell a story of a curious meeting at Glencoe between Richard Sharp and a friend of his father's. Sharp and a friend had found the inn crammed, and had been sent by the landlord to the house of a laird who was willing to give hospitality to travellers. They were cordially received, and in the evening talked with their host of people and places they knew. The host mentioned Newfoundland. 'Have you been there?' asked his guest. 'I spent some time there when I was in the army,' answered the host, 'and the dearest friend I ever had was a gentleman I knew there of the name of Sharp.' 'I am his son,' said Sharp with much emotion; at which the laird embraced him with a warmth which found expression in tears.

There are about this date some entries in Rogers's Commonplace Book which give glimpses of the talk of his numerous literary friends.

Dr. Price was told by Mr. Hume that when Rousseau came with him to England he suspected that he was seduced over to be poisoned; and on the way one night, as they lay in separate rooms divided by a single partition, Rousseau heard Mr. Hume cry out in his sleep: 'I 've got you, Rousseau; I 've got you!' Rousseau left him and went off into Derbyshire, where he took it into his head that the people of England had entered into a con- spiracy against him, and wrote up to the Minister for a guard to escort him out of the kingdom.   Hume, with much difficulty, pre- vailed on the king to grant Rousseau a pension of £100 a year; but when he was informed of it, he spurned it as an affront.   He stayed here two years.   Voltaire said of him that he believed half the world were employed in raising a statue to him and the other half in beating it down again.

The Duke of Bedford regretted to leave his steward's house by the park-side where he had resided while his fortune was at nurse : *in parvis maxima voluptas.*

Du Tens, the writer, possesses an invaluable copy of Madame du Barry's 'Memoirs.'   She says, she was caught by a shower in the garden at Versailles when walking with the king, and that they were wet through.   The Duke of Richelieu has in this copy written this marginal note — 'That is not true, for I was with them and held an umbrella over her.'

Mackintosh has just paid a visit of two days at Beaconsfield, and was well received.   M. acknowledged that, when he wrote his book, he was misinformed as to the facts.

Burke often complained of the discord and intractability of our language.

[Asked] Is he an important man, Warton [answered] 'I never knew anything in an important man.'

Collins's first performance at school contained this line — 'And every grammar clapt its leathern wings.'   Warton admired Sheri- dan's parliamentary speeches, not his 'School for Scandal,' first written in. two acts — a number of people met together, uncon- nected, and not aiding the plot.   Johnson always abused 'Para- dise Lost,' and said, 'None of you can read it;' afterwards did not dare to attack the public opinion.   'Comus' perhaps his finest piece.   Fuseli thought the passage, 'And from his horrid hair shakes pestilence and war' worth all 'Comus.'[1] Warton thought Johnson's criticisms would soon lose all weight. Talked with great affection and good humor of his brother (dead). Thought the philosophical Dyer wrote 'Junius,' and Mason certainly wrote the 'Heroic Epistle.'[2] February, 1795.

Collins, says Warton, is very fine in 'Who shall wake the Spartan Fife?' Armstrong thought little of him, as he complained to Warton. Not generally admired.

These contemporary criticisms stand in curious contrast to the verdicts of posterity. Fuseli's preference of the account of Satan's conflict with the 'grisly Terror' to the whole of 'Comus' is characteristic of his gloomy genius. It is a striking instance of unconscious self-revelation. Warton's criticism on Sheridan's 'School for Scandal,' may be compared with that of Jekyll, who, on seeing the piece, said, 'Why don't all these people leave off talking and let the play begin;' and both are instructive instances of the weakness and shallowness of contemporary judgments. Armstrong thinking little of Collins will suggest to many in these days the question who Armstrong was. Millions who read with admiration Collins's 'Ode to the Passions' have never heard of the author of 'The Art of Preserving Health,' and would probably expect to find under that title a medical treatise rather than a didactic poem. Collins is better known now than Warton, and is more generally admired than he was a century ago.

[1] Incens'd with indignation, Satan stood
Unterrified, and like a comet burn'd,
That fires the length of Ophiuchus huge
In th' arctic sky, and from his horrid hair
Shakes pestilence and war. — *Paradise Lost*, Book ii.

[2] 'An Heroic Epistle to Sir William Chambers, Knight, 1773, by Malcolm Macgregor.' It was afterwards acknowledged by Mason.

Here are some further recollections : —

Dr. Parr. — I heard Horsley at St. Margaret's Church. He saw me as he went up into the pulpit. He sat down and sweated. I darted my eye at him, and through the whole of his sermon there was a most entertaining contest between his fury and his fears. I was never near enough to Mr. Pitt, but I always dart my eye at him. He has often bullied and abused me, but he could never look me in the face. At Nando's, 19th April, '96.

In walking up Hampstead Hill I was solicited by a beggar woman with some fine children for alms, and I had only a bad sixpence. I told her so; she said she would pass it in the night. What should I have done? I said to myself, 'Society are her aggressors,' and I gave it to her. Mr. Smith and Mr. Barbauld thought I was wrong. Dr. Parr thought I acted right, and said the man who could have done otherwise would have kept it to pass it himself. 19th Octr. '96.

I asked Sir George Staunton when 'The Embassy'[1] would be published. He did not seem to know, and therefore I would not ask him again. I never ask a *great* man a question which he cannot answer. He never forgives you for it. — *Dr. Gillies,* 24 Oc. '96.

' God bless your voice !' said an old blind man when I answered a question concerning the way this morning. 25 Octr. '96.

Some other entries in the Commonplace Book, to which no date is attached, but which evidently belong to a comparatively early period of Rogers's life, may be conveniently added here. Some of them are curious as showing the remuneration which was given to some well-known people who edited or contributed to the literary periodicals of the time.

In 'The Adventurer' A was Bonnel Thornton, Z was Warton according to Mr. Ryland, Dr. Hawkesworth's brother. H. had

---

[1] 'The Authentic Account of the Embassy of Lord Macartney and Sir George Staunton to China in 1792,' was published in 1797. It was in two volumes quarto.

£2 2s. for each 'Adventurer.'   Moore had £3 3s. for each 'World.'
A coalition was attempted by Mr. R., but nothing could be done
but printing on different days.   Hill had 7s. 6d. for each 'In-
spector.'   Dr. Hawkesworth was incapable of reading the mottoes
prefixed to 'The Adventurer;' they were chosen for him.

In an anonymous preface to the edition of 'The
Adventurer' published in 1823, we are told that Dr.
Richard Bathurst, who was one of the members of
Dr. Johnson's Ivy Lane Club, is said to have written
the eight papers marked 'A.'   Dr. Joseph Warton wrote
twenty-four papers, and Dr. Johnson is known to have
written twenty-nine.   Rogers's statement about Dr.
Hawkesworth is rendered probable by the fact that
his degree was a Lambeth one, conferred by Archbishop
Herring, and that he was a man of no early education.
It is difficult nowadays to understand the esteem in
which 'The Adventurer' was held.   Horne Tooke told
Rogers that he could never forget the pleasure he felt
in retiring to read it at the age of seventeen; and Dr.
Burney tells us that in his day it was in every one's
library.   The scale of remuneration for it belongs to the
day of small things for periodical literature.

Here are other items bearing on the same subject : —

Griffiths has 42s. per sheet (printed) for the authorship of
the 'Monthly Review.' — Dr. Gillies.

Millar gave £100 for 'Joseph Andrews,' Fielding's first
novel. — Cadell.

Warburton wrote the preface to the first edition of 'Clarissa.'

Warton wrote the essay 'On the Use and Abuse of Poetry,'
quoted in 'Essay on Pope,' vol. i.

Colman read the 'School for Scandal' before it was acted to
Burke, Reynolds, Windham, etc. — Windham.

Sheridan of Pitt: His is a brain that never works but when
his tongue is set a-going, like some machines that are set in
motion by a pendulum or some such thing.

Gray made Nicholls promise before he went abroad that he would not call upon Voltaire. — *Nicholls.*   Lord Hampden's father did the same. — *Ld. H.*

When Sir C. Wren's plan for rebuilding London after the fire was rejected — ' A set of blockheads,' he exclaimed ; ' they don't deserve to have their city burnt.' — *Priestley.*

Lord Chesterfield willing away £50,000 to the Dean and Chapter of Westminster (with whom he had had a lawsuit) in case his nephew could be proved to have ever been in Italy or at Newmarket.

Garrick and Reynolds entering Rome — the first out on the coach-box, the last unable to sit up or look out of the window.

When Wilkes's windows were broken he smiled and said: ' Some of my own journeymen set up for themselves.'

Lord Chesterfield in person compared to a stunted giant. When driving out slowly in the Park in his old age said he was rehearsing.

Mrs. Warburton, provoked by the bishop's silence, once threw a book at his head — ' If you won't answer me you 'll answer a book.'

Dr. Douglas in the bishop's palace at Salisbury said to the archbishop of Narbonne: ' Your Grace should not be discouraged when you recollect that the house in which you now are, was for fourteen years a public inn ' [during the Commonwealth].

Dr. Franklin had a mirror obliquely fixed near his window by which he could see the person that knocked at his door, and deny himself or not accordingly. — *Este.*

Florence is so pretty a town it should be only seen on a Sunday. — *Un François.*

A young man who is undazzled and unattracted by the glitter of life is either above or below the common level, and he is generally below it.   Such a man was the Duke of Hamilton. We may call it a love of ease, but it generally shows a want of energy. — *Aikin.*

A regiment in France had a great regard for the memory of their *old* Colonel, and when asked why, replied: 'He said, "Allons, mes amis!" the present says, "Allez, mes amis!"'

Barwell lost an election by canvassing with his gloves on.

Boswell drunk at Lord Falmouth's in Cornwall, kicking about his bed at midnight, swearing at the house in which he said there was no bed to lie on, and no wine to drink.

Of papers the old duke of Cumberland said: 'D—n them, they breed!'

When Sheridan is writing he requires a great many lights. —*Spencer.*

I will make you a Baronet. Baron, if you please. The net at the end is a net only to catch fools with.

His forte was fancy — his foible was ignorance. — *Burke on Lord Chatham. Grattan.*

The following appear to be Rogers's own reflections; some of them recur in his poems, and some in letters to his friends : —

Plant nettles on the grave of a satirist — stinging nettles.

We cannot compare places, we only compare impressions. 'T is thus we deceive ourselves.

Mountains, like fine ladies, are subject to vapors.

Close to the earth there is a refreshing fragrance — lost when you elevate yourself. Remark in a clover field.

More *ennui* in society than out of it.

Men of fashion are mannerists, and all manner is bad; a natural character, manners ever varying with the thoughts and feelings, how superior to that uniform and monotonous thing called high breeding!

Women are ever ready to make confidants of each other in everything but love.

Poets the best prose writers: Shakspeare, Cowley, Milton, Dryden, Pope, Gray, and Addison.   Burke and Rousseau began with poetry, as did also Voltaire.

The heart, like a musical instrument, has a thousand rich melodies, which may slumber there forever if not called forth by the various offices and duties of social and domestic life; each of which excites its peculiar set of feelings and sympathies.

> The soul of music slumbers in the shell
> Till waked to rapture by the master's spell;
> And thy young heart, when rightly touched, shall pour
> A thousand melodies unheard before.

A few items of chat, attributed to Richard Sharp will appropriately conclude the extracts from the Commonplace Book : —

Sir Joshua Reynolds told Sharp that he never painted a picture, or part of a picture, well till he had done it several times.

Hoppner drew the waterfall at Melincourt, near Neath, and slept at a miller's near the spot.   At night through a crevice of his chamber he saw his host breaking off a piece of his chalk, which he had left with his sketch below, and slyly treasuring it up in his bureau.

Terror is a powerful engine, but when overstrained is the weakest of all.   Inspire a man with fear and you are his master ; with despair, and he is yours.

A nation in a state of despotism is like a giant asleep, with his arms intrusted to a dwarf.

In the spring of 1795 Dr. Parr called public attention to a misstatement of Boswell's as to the interview which Dr. Johnson and Dr. Priestley had with each other at the house of Mr. Paradise.[1]   Boswell in a note to a new edition of his third volume declared his firm belief that the two men never met.   He based this

---

[1] Mr. Paradise was a member of Johnson's evening club at the ' Essex Head.'

conviction on two circumstances : firstly, that his 'illustrious friend was particularly resolute in not giving countenance to men whose writings he considered. as pernicious to society;' and secondly, that when one day at Oxford Dr. Price came into a room where Johnson was, Johnson instantly left the room. Dr. Parr thereupon wrote to Dr. E. Johnstone of Birmingham, where in 1790 he had heard Priestley speak of the interview, and Dr. Johnstone at once wrote to say that he remembered Dr. Priestley's statement that he met Johnson under the idea that Johnson had sought the interview and that it was mutually satisfactory. Mr. Bearcroft wrote from Francis Street that he had only in April or May, 1794, heard Dr. Priestley remind Mr. Paradise of the particular civility with which Dr. Johnson had behaved towards him when they dined together at Mr. Paradise's house. Mr. Bearcroft adds that 'having mentioned the subject this afternoon to Mr. Paradise, he told me that, though he did not clearly recollect the motive by which he had been induced to bring Dr. Johnson and Dr. Priestley together, he very well remembered Dr. Johnson having been previously informed that Dr. Priestley would be one of the company, and his having manifested great civility to the latter on that occasion.' To this testimony Rogers was able to add his own in the following letter —

S. Rogers to Dr. Parr.

'NEWINGTON GREEN, February 23, 1795.

'DEAR SIR, — I can answer your several questions distinctly. I heard of the interview between Dr. Johnson and Dr. Priestley from Dr. Priestley himself. I have heard it mentioned more than once. I understood that it was not solicited by Dr. Priestley, and that if any overture was made for that purpose it came from Dr.

Johnson.   I found that Dr. Priestley thought Dr. Johnson's behavior such as it ought to have been from one man of letters to another.   Johnson was very civil.

'I hope that I have written satisfactorily, and am happy in the opportunity which you have given me of assuring you with what respect

'I am, dear Sir,

' Your most obedient servant,

'SAMUEL ROGERS.'

There were various signs in the periodicals of 1794, 1795, and 1796 of the esteem in which the author of 'The Pleasures of Memory' was already held by his literary contemporaries.   A poem on his poem appeared in the 'European Magazine,' which contained the lines —

> ' With more attractive charm the verse appears
> Whose magic power calls back our fleeting years,
> And binds with Memory's tenacious chain
> The airy forms of pleasure and of pain.'

In another of the magazines appeared a poem in Spenserian language 'on his ordering a great-coat called a Spenser.'   One of the verses ran —

> ' O precious *Impe* of *Fame*, Sam Rogers *hight*,
>   Who chauntest *Memorie* in dulcett straine,
> Filling our eares and harts with such delight
>   Entraunced we live past pleasaunce o'er againe ;
> This *amplest* theme, by others minc'd in vaine,
>   Was by the sacred sisters nyne withheld,
> *Immortal guerdon* for *thy browes* to gaine.
>   *Certes* old Humber's Bard, and he who dwel'd
> *Whylome* in *daintie* Leasowes, are by thee excel'd.'

The last references are to Mason's and Shenstone's Odes to Memory.   A more amusing reference to him and to a number of his friends is contained in a short poem entitled 'My Club,' which appeared in the 'European Magazine' in July, 1795 : —

> ' With M[arsden] I would trust my life,
> With L[awrence] all my civil strife,
> And steal him from Justinian's code
> To make him sport another ode ;
> With B . . . . write in purest Latin
> From classic Celsus to Guy Patin ;
> From B . . . . catch some emendation
> Of Aristotle or of Tatian.
> Impromptu P[arsons] shall rehearse
> With ready pen in easy verse,
> While R[ennell] tells how Agamemnon,
> Diomede and Ajax Telamon,
> Forced out from Holland and from Flanders
> The Dutch and English Alexanders.
> S[harp], too, the subtle and acute,
> Shall quickly settle the dispute,
> And mightiest Stagirites among,
> Leave his opponents in the wrong.
> Meek R[ogers], whom the Muses love,
> Unites the serpent and the dove ;
> In business, as in rhyming terse,
> Can talk of agio or of verse.
> S[eward], of anecdotes a storehouse,
> Lays gratis all he hears before us,
> And tells the whole long ere 't is seen
> In th' " European Magazine ; "
> B[erdmore], no common politician,
> At once is chymist and physician ;
> And of the Roman as was said,
> He knows his art but not his trade.
> R. C . . . , whose active mind ne'er still is,
> Loves Greek, we 're sure, but not like G[illies] ;
> Tom Warton, merry wight — ah, no !
> Death envied us, but left us Jo.'

Another very satisfactory sign of the recognized place he had taken in literature was given in the reception

accorded by the critics to the Rev. R. Polwhele's dull
poem called 'The Influence of Local Attachment with
Respect to Home.' So much was said by the reviewers
of the similarity of this poem in some parts to the beautiful poem, as they all called it, 'The Pleasures of Memory,' that Mr. Polwhele was obliged to come forward
with a labored vindication. His apology was in the
form of a *tu quoque*. He had been accused of copying
some of Rogers's notes verbatim, and he admitted that
he had written his own notes hastily with Rogers's before
him. But as to plagiarism, had not Rogers borrowed from
him ? He had written an 'Epistle to a College Friend,'
which he was almost inclined to consider as the proto-
type of the first part of 'The Pleasures of Memory.'
Only one of his comparisons need be given. He had
written in his 'Epistle to a College Friend' —

> 'While yet 't is mine to trace the feeling hour,
> And win young Fancy from the Muse's bower
> Ere pressing cares, too numerous, intervene
> To disenchant the bosom-soothing scene,
> Come, nor too soon, alas! to memory fade,
> Ye views fast fainting into sombre shade!'

The passage with which Polwhele compares this — which
he intimates was suggested by it — is this : speaking of
childhood's loved group ,revisiting every scene, 'the tan-
gled wood-walk and the tufted green,' Rogers proceeds —

> 'Indulgent Memory wakes, and lo, they live !
> Clothed with far softer hues than Light can give.
> Thou first, best friend that Heaven assigns below,
> To soothe and sweeten all the cares we know ;
> Whose glad suggestions still each vain alarm
> When Nature fades and life forgets to charm ;
> Thee would the Muse invoke! to thee belong
> The sage's precept and the poet's song.
> What softened views thy magic glass reveals,
> When o'er the landscape Time's meek twilight steals!'

The comparison of these passages — and they are put in juxtaposition by Mr. Polwhele himself — not only shows the ridiculous nature of his suggestion of plagiarism, but conclusively and sufficiently exhibits the immense superiority of Rogers's poem to the boasted productions of the poetasters of the time.

CHAPTER X.

THERE are but few signs at this period of that lively interest in public affairs which characterized Rogers in earlier days. Many of his first friends were gone. Dr. Price was dead; Dr. Priestley was in exile; William Stone had only lately been acquitted on a charge of high treason for which he had lain two years in Newgate untried; Horne Tooke was cultivating his garden at Wimbledon, after his defeat in the Westminster election; and Fox, though he had headed the poll in the same election, was in a state of discouragement at the gloomy aspect of public affairs; Sheridan was enjoying the temporary relief from pecuniary troubles which his new wife's five thousand pounds had given him; and Sharp, Mackintosh, and others of his political friends and acquaintances were keeping comparatively quiet in the vain hope of better days. In the autumn of 1795 there had been a great agitation in the country for reform in Parliament and peace with France. This agitation had been purely political, but there had gone on side by side with it a social movement which had serious results. There was almost a famine in the land, and the utmost distress prevailed among the laboring classes. The papers contained frequent reports of death by starvation, and the populace, with just instinct, regarded the war as the chief cause of their sufferings. There had been a great meeting on Copenhagen Fields on the 26th ·of October, 1795, when a remonstrance to the king had been resolved on, complaining of the neglect and contempt his ministers had shown for an address presented to them some time before. On the 29th an unparalleled multitude, estimated at two hundred thousand, ten times as great, it was said, as had ever been seen before, assembled to see the king go to the House of Lords to open Parliament, which had been called together earlier than usual in consequence of the prevailing distress. While waiting for the king the crowd hissed Lord Chatham and the Duke of Gloucester as they passed, hooted the Duke of Portland, and made hostile demonstrations against other well-known members of the House of Lords. When the king's carriage appeared a storm of hisses and groans broke forth, mingled with loud cries of ' Bread, bread!' 'Peace, peace !' and ' Down with Pitt !' Opposite the Ordnance Office a stone struck one of the windows of the state carriage and broke it, and the king thought he had been fired at. When the king arrived at the House of Lords he exclaimed to the Lord Chancellor : ' My Lord, I have been shot at.' Later in the afternoon Lord Westmoreland informed the House of Lords that the king had been treated with insult and outrage by the mob, and that the glass of the carriage had been broken by a shot fired from an air-gun from the bow window of a house adjoining the Ordnance Office, with the object of assassinating his majesty.

These events had most painful results. The fears of the sovereign and his advisers had magnified a bread riot into a rebellion, as Louis XVI. had mistaken a revolution for an *émeute*. The meeting in Copenhagen Fields on Monday was associated with the riot of the following

Thursday, and proclamations were issued offering rewards for the apprehension of the ringleaders of the riot, and urging well-affected people to assist in putting down such gatherings as that of Monday, and in preventing the dissemination of 'seditious writings.' The Marquis of Lansdowne courageously accused the Ministry of intending to seize the opportunity to work on the fears of the public in order to get repressive laws passed, and to increase their own power at the expense of freedom. Two bills were brought in and passed, one entitled 'An Act for the safety and preservation of his majesty's person and government against treasonable and seditious practices and attempts;' and the other 'for the more effectually preventing seditious meetings and assemblies.' The Whig leaders protested against these Acts, but did not even succeed in shortening their duration, which extended in the first case to the whole life of the king, and in the second to three years. The Duke of Norfolk declared that the family of Brunswick owed its possession of the throne to the principle of resistance; the Duke of Bedford said the measures constituted a direct attack on the liberty of Englishmen; and Mr. Fox maintained that the bills totally annihilated liberty. They were passed, however, and they were not allowed to remain as a dead letter on the statute-book. The first result was to render the Government intensely unpopular, and the second was to discourage all Liberal political action and movement. To these two measures, and to the prosecutions which followed on them, we may attribute the temporary suspension of political action on the part of Rogers and his friends, though the complete discontinuation of his diary, so far as political persons and movements are concerned, dates from a time just previous to the arrest of his friend William Stone on the charge of high treason, in May, 1794.

His 'Recollections of Fox' in the volume edited by

Mr. William Sharpe begin with a dinner at Mr. William Smith's on the 19th of March, 1796. There was a great gathering of Whigs: Tierney, Courtenay, Sir Francis Baring, Dr. Aikin, Mackintosh, Sir Philip Francis, and Dr. Parr, but the talk seems to have been of everything but politics. At Sergeant Heywood's on the 10th of December, Lord Derby, Lord Stanley, Lord Lauderdale, Lambton, Aikin, Smith, and Brogden were present with Fox, and still the talk seems to have been chiefly literary. It is significant, however, that what Fox is reported by Rogers to have said bearing on the politics of the time was pitched in a key of the most profound despondency. 'I always say, and always think,' said Fox to Rogers, 'that of all the countries in Europe, England will be the last to be free. Russia will be free before England.' A bad prophecy, but a good indication of the feeling of the time. On the same evening Lord Lauderdale said: 'I wish I was Member for Westminster.' 'And I wish I was a Scotch Peer,' answered Fox. 'Why so?' he was asked. 'I should then be disqualified,' replied Fox. This was said just six months after his triumphant return for Westminster at the head of the poll. That election was the last in which Rogers gave a vote for two-and-twenty years; and he gave it not only on the Whig but on what may be described as the Radical side.[1] Rogers voted for Horne Tooke, who was seconded on the hustings by his brother-in-law, Sutton Sharpe. Rogers also voted for Mr. Fox. In an edition of the speeches delivered by Horne Tooke at this election, which had come into Rogers's hands, there is a note in Horne Tooke's handwriting giving the number of days he had been in prison. I copy it precisely as it stands: —

---

[1] The poll closed on Monday the 13th of June, the fifteenth day of the polling, and the numbers were: Fox 5,160; Sir Alan Gardner 4,814; Horne Tooke 2,819.

1774	H. of Commons	2 days
1777–1778	K.'s Bench	336 "
1794	Privy Council	3 "
"	Tower	148 "
"	Newgate	30 "

	In Prison . .	519 days

There is a curious reckoning, too, in Horne Tooke's writing, which shows that he had spoken from three and a half to four hours during the fifteen days, and that he had made two hundred and twenty-seven points against the government, or about one point every minute.   The pamphlet further contains the speech made by Mr. Fox to the electors at the close of the poll on Saturday the 11th of June, the fourteenth day of the voting. Mr. Fox spoke quite as strongly as Horne Tooke.   ' The law that was passed in the last session of Parliament,' said Fox, ' has made it impossible for more than fifty persons to meet without being subject to the interference of a magistrate.   If you take my advice the law will not disturb your meeting.   Meet ! Meet !   Act in obedience to the law, which does not forbid your meeting, it only empowers the magistrate to commit you if you act improperly. Meet, then, I say ; conduct yourselves with propriety, and see whether any one will dare to oppose you.'   This advice was received with great cheering.   Mr. Fox concluded by saying : ' Gentlemen, I have spoken plainly and openly to you, and I will conclude by repeating that in my conscience I believe that [the character of the] Government has been by none exaggerated.   A more detestable one never existed in British history ; and not to detain you any longer I will sum up its character in two words. This Government has destroyed more human beings in its foreign wars than Louis XIV., and attempted the lives of more innocent men at home than Henry VIII.'   In these words Fox expressed a feeling which Rogers and his friends fully shared, and to which Rogers frequently gave expression in later and happier times.

The Westminster election probably left some soreness behind it, for at one of William Smith's dinner parties, at which Rogers was present with Fox and Tooke, he noticed, with much pain, that Fox tried to ignore Tooke. At another of these dinners, Tierney and others were speaking disparagingly of Pitt, and declaring that he was not in earnest about the slave-trade, when Fox rebuked them. Wilberforce had just at this time brought himself into much unpopularity by voting for the ministerial measures for the suspension of freedom. The Liberals were profoundly depressed. They seemed conscious that they were just entering on their long journey through the wilderness. There was none of the buoyant confidence which distinguished them in the halcyon days when the French Revolution was young. The shadow of the Terror had already rolled away from France, but it had settled down on England.

Unpopular as the war was, it necessarily created an interest of its own. Dr. Moore, for example, was one of its opponents, but he naturally felt, as every patriotic man feels, a certain pride in the successes of his country-men, even when the country is in the wrong. This feeling spread. Dislike of a struggle which multitudes of the best Englishmen regarded as needless and wicked, conflicted in the public mind with pride in their country's prowess, and that pride eventually came uppermost. Dr. Moore had personal and family interests in the war. He had two heroic sons actively engaged, each destined to win honors, and one immortal fame. In the following letter he refers both to his own literary work, and to the success of one of his sons.

Dr. Moore to S. Rogers.

'Monday.

'MY DEAR ROGERS,—I will be happy to accompany you to Mr. Smith's on the first Monday in Christmas, provided my son Graham does not come to town at that time. You will see by last night's "Gazette" that he has brought a fine French corvette to Spithead. Mrs. Moore and I have scarcely had a fortnight of him since the war. He is the most delightful fellow alive, and I cannot lose a day of him, but I will know when he is to come and inform you. The "Melampus" needs repair.

'I am glad you like Edward. I am told he is thought too much of a common man for a hero. Though I tried to make him something of a man of this world and not quite an ideal being, yet I heartily wish that heroes as well as common men were more like him. I am not much of a misanthrope, but I have a notion that all men of humanity are a little so. That you should think all Edward's conduct very natural does not surprise me; that some who rank him with common men should think so, does.

'Adieu!

'J. MOORE.

'Do you ever see my Charles?'

Edward was the hero of Dr. Moore's second novel, which Mrs. Barbauld regards as much inferior to 'Zeluco' but as having many amusing conversation pieces. Charles was the youngest of his five sons. Graham was the third. He was a year younger than Rogers, had joined the navy in 1777, had been made a post-captain in 1794, and in 1795 had succeeded Sir Richard Strachan in the 'Melampus.' In this vessel he served for five years with great distinction, and then came home invalided to his father's house, where the Peace of Amiens found him. When the war broke out again he was appointed to the 'Indefatigable,' and after twelve years of active service was made a K.C.B. Other deserved honors followed, and in 1837 he was promoted to the rank of admiral. He died at Chobham, in November, 1843. A brief memoir of him was written in 1844, by Major-General Sir Robert Gardiner.

The kind of life Rogers was living at this period when his greatness was ripening is shown in some family letters. The first is from his sister Sarah. She was visiting Mrs. Rogers at Whitehall near Stourbridge, and wrote to him on the 28th of November, 1796 : —

'Here I am at such a distance from all of you that I seem quite in another world, and want very much to know what you are doing in yours. . . . Your time is, I suppose, entirely taken up with engagements, attending clubs, reading papers of which I have heard, etc., while I have little to do but to watch for the time of the post coming in that I may hear a little of what you are about. . . . Wherever I go I hear a great deal about you. We drank tea a few nights ago at "The Hill." Miss Hopkins was there; she looked very handsome, and if you had heard her conversation, you would have thought her still more so. But I shall make you too vain if I go on and repeat to you what she said; for though you are sufficiently used to compliments, yet, coming from the mouth of so pretty a woman, I don't know what the effect might be.'

In a letter from Nottingham Place on the 10th of December, 1796, Mrs. Sharpe tells her sister Sarah :

'On Sunday Sam called, and with him Mr. Hoppner, who took Mr. Sharpe to see a collection of pictures of a Mr. des Enfans,[1] where there were some fine ones. . . .

---

[1] This is the collection which now forms the Dulwich Gallery.

On Thursday Sam engaged to dine here, so Mr. Sharpe got some other gentlemen, Mr. Tuffin, Mr. Cline, Mr. S. Boddington, W. Maltby, and Stothard. . . . Yesterday Mr. Sharpe dined at Mr. Cline's, where were Horne Tooke and a party of gentlemen. He was not home till past twelve, so late are parties now.'

The men named in this letter were all celebrities in their time. Mr. Tuffin is now forgotten, but for many years he was one of the liveliest and most interesting talkers of a circle of men who made conversation a study and an art. An octogenarian friend of mine still remembers his white head and his amusing talk, and the story he told that his hair had turned white in a single night in which he had been shut up by accident in one of the vaults at Windsor. Hoppner was the well-known artist already mentioned in an extract from Rogers's Commonplace Book; Cline was the celebrated surgeon who afterwards tapped Fox for the dropsy, and was consulted by Windham respecting the tumor which cost that statesman his life. Of the others it is needless to speak. Sutton Sharpe had married Rogers's sister Maria in 1795, and the result of this closer connection between him and Rogers was, as I have already said, that Rogers was brought into more frequent and familiar intercourse with the chief artists of the time. It was this intercourse, together with Sutton Sharpe's own direct instructions and influence, which gave Rogers the knowledge of art which made him eventually the chief authority of his time on questions of taste.

These letters show, not only what his private and family life was at this period, but the very affectionate relations he maintained with the members of his family. These relations are further illustrated by a letter to his sister Sarah : —

Samuel Rogers to Sarah Rogers.

'TEMPLE, 10 March, 1797.

' MY DEAR SARAH, — Surely the wildest dream of Mad
Bess herself must have been dull and insipid when compared to what is passing in this planet of ours! At
present things are indeed a little too interesting, and I
am not yet half recovered from the stunning blow we
received last week.   I hint this by way of apology ; you
will shake your head at it and pronounce it a lame one,
but I have been really so harassed for the last month or
two that I have even wanted spirits for a pun.   Of you,
however, I often think, and again and again have I
begun an invocation to your friendly but fugitive spirit
(when will you take your flight to us ?) but in vain.   A
thousand cares and follies have interposed to prevent
me.   But how shall I answer you in your own style ?
Really, child, you have an admirable way of charming
people out of their senses ; you must surely have dipped
your pen, not into ink, but into some sweet intoxicating
spirit, prepared no doubt (for they abound in it) from
the old family receipt book at Cheadle.   But what are
you about ?   Are you indoctrinating yourself into the
sublime mysteries of a cotton mill ?   Or, like Bonaparte's
cannon, are you dealing havoc among the beaux of the
north ?   Some sylph or sylphid has indeed whispered
strange things ; what she said I dare not say, but her
voice was so musical that we " think her still speaking,
still stand fixed to hear."

' This morning I had a visitor to breakfast with me,
a noble stranger whom I long to introduce to your
acquaintance.   Elegant, animated, and modest, with a
look of sentiment, a fine form, and the *coiffure grèc*, in
short, another Imogene, — the dear brother of Clementina,
and of as noble a family, his father being Doge of
Genoa.   What do you say ? and yet I should not like

to lose you neither. But do answer, child: would you like to sport a veil and a train, and receive incense as her Serenissima the Marchesa Brignola among tables of massive gold and curtains of crimson velvet? In your next pray say yes or no. I cannot finish this subject without hinting that he talks of visiting Manchester. Perhaps he may suit somebody's taste at Cheadle. With regard to our domestic annals you are in correspondence with those who are far better qualified than I am to inform you on that subject. The *petites histoires* of Charlotte Street and Nottingham Place are in better hands. My own memoirs are dull enough, and have no pretensions even to furnish a little light summer reading for a cit's daughter at a watering-place. I feel, my dearest Sarah, that your mind will be in a very unfit state for the stuff I have just scrawled, when you hear what I have just heard while I was writing, that *Patty has this morning* lost her little boy. A few days ago he *had a slight relapse,* but no great danger was apprehended. The poor little object of all their anxieties is now, however, no more. I have not yet heard the particulars; you will, I suppose, by this post receive them from Maria or Mr. T[owgood]. Pray remember me very particularly to all the family at Cheadle. To two of that family I am at a loss how to express myself. I have deposited the little epistle in lavender, and shall often turn to it with pride and pleasure. It is some consolation to a man as he advances in life that he sometimes receives expressions of kindness and friendship from the young and the lovely, which are withheld, or at least concealed, from the gayer and younger candidates for their favor. Pray give my sincere and unalterable love to the fair personage above alluded to. Adieu, my dear girl,

'And believe me, ever,

'Most affectionately yours,

'S. R.

'A thousand inquiries were made about you at the last City assembly. Miss Edison said she should have called upon you, but she heard you were gone to the north of Europe.'

In the correspondence with Richard Sharp which took place during Rogers's absence from town in the autumn of this year, there are references which throw light on some parts of the life of both the writers. It is incomplete, of course, for it only fills a gap in that personal intercourse which at this period was constant and intimate, and by its constancy and intimacy escaped all such record. In October, 1797, Rogers was at Brighton, and Richard Sharp replies to an urgent invitation to get out of business for a time and pay his friend a visit. Richard Sharp pleads his mother's illness, the approaching death of a friend who he fears has left him as executor, and a fortnight's laborious employment that a West India merchant has sent him, which, he says, 'will occupy the last two months of this distressing year.' The letter continues : —

'I never knew before the full value of a taste for reading. During the last twelve months I have had no opportunity of gratifying myself in any other amusement. Books are always at hand, and though I never meddle with them before night, yet then they transport me from unpleasant scenes into other worlds, and interpose a pleasant hour between the insipid or painful occupations of the day. Johnson would have burned this letter before he had read the first page; for he hated complaining people. Your querulous fellow is always selfish, and generally finds more delight in talking of his own pains than in sympathizing with the pleasures of others. I am not so far gone as to have lost my relish for your occupations, and am sincerely rejoiced when I

19

think how completely the sea air seems to have restored to you both your health and your spirit. Seize the precious moment; consult your solid interest by increasing your present name. Publish as soon as you can, that you may run round the only circles where you can now wish to move, and that you may be able early in life to enjoy the highest possible of all intellectual pleasures, — that of living with the few friends you may have selected from every class and every rank. For a delicate and discriminating man it is necessary that he should see all, to select, alas! a very few.'

This letter appropriately illustrates the influence which Richard Sharp exerted on his friend. He had a high opinion of Rogers's literary powers, and shows a constant anxiety that those powers should not rust in him unused. He was constantly urging him along the road which his faculties and his ambition marked out, but which ill-health, a too fastidious taste, and a great love of social intercourse, threatened to block. Rogers owed him much in the way of stimulus and encouragement; he probably owed him almost as much in the way of suggestion and criticism. There must have been another letter from Richard Sharp, announcing the death of his friend, and telling Rogers something of his own troubles and difficulties, as is shown in Rogers's reply.

Samuel Rogers to Richard Sharp.

'Surely, my dear friend, you must have conceived a very sublime idea of my philosophy to think it equal to such trials. But, not to reproach where no reproach is due, let me express my great concern, not at my disappointment, but at the events which have occasioned it, and let me hope that you will not suffer your spirits to sink under such an accumulation of troubles.

'The loss of such a friend as the last, from whom you had experienced such an uninterrupted succession of good and kind offices, must indeed have greatly affected you.   After all, there is nothing so attaching as kindness; indeed, nothing else is worth living for in this world.

'That friend has, indeed, left you in a very delicate and embarrassing situation, and of the motives for his doing so there can be no doubt.   You will, of course, take no step till after you have maturely weighed it, and then, whatever it is, I am sure it must be right.

'With regard to myself, I live on here stupidly enough, knowing nobody and not wishing to know anybody.   My taste, as you well know, has been too fastidious for my happiness, and it has now become more so than ever.   Aikin[1] was a great comfort while he stayed.   He began his operations with great spirit; the weather was delightful, our situation no less so, and indeed the whole scene was sufficient to intoxicate even a man of his complexion.   He over-fatigued himself presently, a hemorrhage came on, and he left me (though not sooner than he first intended) in a very melancholy state indeed.   I never knew half his value before.   Hoole and his son live within a mile of me, and are a very pleasant acquisition.   Mathias[2] has also given me great pleasure, and G. Morgan[3] made two days pass very ,smoothly.   But the translator of "Ariosto" is now ill, and the last two have vanished.   The Prince and his little court left us on Monday for the season.   The place is

[1] Dr. Aikin's health, as Lucy Aikin tells us, had visibly declined all this year.   He was writing the first volume of ' General Biography,' and editing the 'Monthly Magazine.'   On the day this letter was written, Aikin's friend, Dr. Enfield, died.   His painful illness had exerted a very depressing effect on Aikin's spirits.

[2] T. J. Mathias, author of ' The Pursuits of Literature.'

[3] George Morgan, nephew of Dr. Price and brother of William Morgan, who wrote Dr. Price's life.

now joyless and deserted, and the Steyne, which was lately crowded with the young and the gay, is now resigned to the nets of the fishermen. In the mean time I bustle about, and my regimen consists of large draughts every morning of a certain pure ether, to be taken only on the South Downs, and which is sweetened by the effluvia that escape from the wild thyme now in full blow: I had flattered myself that you would have shared it with me, *mais n'importe.* I must bear it as I can. Give me leave to hope that the alarm was a false one, and that your mother is gradually advancing to be what you wish her.

'Adieu! and believe me to be, ever,

'Yours very affectionately,

'S. R.

'BRIGHTON, Friday, Novr. 3, 1797.'

Richard Sharp's answer to this letter is dated the 10th of November, 1797. A great crisis had occurred in his life, the outline of which can only be dimly traced in his correspondence with Rogers, but which seems to have been as important as that which gave Rogers himself the wealth he was now enjoying. In this letter he announces the change. His friend was dead, and had left him as one of his executors and he had assumed the trust. After speaking of some private matters which throw no light on his personal history and have no public interest, Richard Sharp says:—

'It turns out that my deceased friend, as well as the living brother, have always wished that I should be the representative in this world of themselves and all their immense property. This I never supposed, though I had reasons undoubtedly to think so. Their conduct has been so singularly affectionate and so unspeakably respectful to me in this matter, that I should be the most ungrateful of the human race if I did not do whatever they have desired I should do. Two men, who have desired to unite me to their only child and to more than £150,000 are entitled to command me, and all that is mine, in every case and to every possible extent. I shall, however, have but little employment in the trust at present, nor will it be ever complicated or difficult. . . . Last night I read a paper at our Society, 'On the Sublime and Beautiful in External Objects,' in sounds, colors, forms, and language. We were a full Club, which is rather uncommon on the first night of the season.

'Boddington extols your situation at Brighton; but your picture of the Steyne and of the Downs interested me more than his panegyrics. I hope you write, as well as ride and read. I hope, too, yet I know the perils of the wish, that you have found stronger inducements to stay by the sea than the desire of health or amusement. Are you determined (without my excuses) to waste your youth as I have done? With all that can invite and satisfy in manners, fortune, and character, will you defer the chief scene of life till you must perform it under many disadvantages? Remember your own illustration, — the rivulet that became a river, and the river that widened into a sea.

'I have not been in my place either in the Strand or in Bond Street. Favell gave me a dull dinner with Horne Tooke on Monday. He was never kinder, but the spring of this curious machine seems to have lost its elasticity. . . . I have learned from you, I suppose, to be very jocose and entertaining "dum angor intus, et ipse meum cor edens incedo." If I go on for another year thus, I shall eclipse you in gayety by mere dint of melancholy, and shall be as sentimental and as interesting as the most inspired poet can desire. If you do not mean to envy as well as admire me, you must come soon to

Town, and, by cheering me with your presence, bring me back 'again to the natural stupidity and serenity of my character.'

Rogers's reply to this letter, written from Brighton on the 14th of November, 1797, contained the following passage : —

'Yes, my dear friend, I am indeed of your opinion (though I fear you were not aware of the full meaning of your words) that you would be very blamable if you did not do whatever they have desired you to do. I believe I have delicacy, I know I have pride, and yet, were such an alternative placed before me, I think I should not hesitate. But why should I say anything ? I was once more than pleased with her. I could again, I am persuaded, love her better than ever ; and if I have sometimes affected to resent the little sallies of a lively and open temper, it was in order to disguise them to my own vanity as the effects of a pique at the discontinuance 'of attentions which I am now convinced she never cared for, and has entirely forgotten. If she were to become the wife of my friend I am very sure we should fall desperately in love with each other in a fortnight. So, beware ! '

The self-revelation of this passage makes it an important contribution to Rogers's early history. It shows, at least, that he did not deliberately lay out his life from the first on the plan of bachelor freedom. He makes no further reply to Richard Sharp's hint as to deferring 'the chief scene of life,' unless indeed the tone of the rest of the letter, especially the reference to his flirtation, may be regarded as a kind of escape from a subject which had unwelcome associations. He continues, —

'I have nothing to send you but a diary of the weather and a chronicle of visits ; I am reading French novels with relentless fury, and though I am not, like you, the hero of a romance, I am often acting a part in one, though a very subordinate part.

'Did I tell you of my flirtation with a very celebrated countess? . . . How I dined alone with her, rode alone with her, spent an evening alone with her, the last she spent in Brighton, and how I was domesticated with her daughters? And such daughters — but *n'importe!* I shall only observe *en passant* that if you think you have any notion of what perfection a woman can attain to you are quite mistaken, and should be punished for your presumption. I hope the Prince is jealous of me, for I am most furiously so of him.

'The Hooles dined with me yesterday, and beg to be remembered to you.

'We have had the most delicious weather, — an Italian sky, and the air clear as crystal from sunrise to sunset. Deserted as we are, we are still cheerful, tho' we make no effort to be gay. A regiment-band plays twice a day under my window; and we form the pleasantest little supper-parties imaginable, a *mélange* of cards and conversation, music and macaroni. Last night it was held *chez* the Thompsons; to-night Mrs. Hope opens her rooms; and to-morrow night Mrs. Dawson, a lady of great beauty and accomplishments, who cost Erskine a duel some years ago. To tell you a *secret*, I am in fashion just now, — arrangements are made to see me, and the favor will last three days. The great Pétrie is here (a Parisian acquaintance), and his wife, who trails about in her equipage of four horses, has invited me to Gatton; so I shall call in my transit to town. But I have played the egotist long enough, and shall only add that you are in no present danger of losing the picture; my pulse beats very temperately.

'I am sorry I was not present the other night. Why did not you send an express for me? . The Society will recover itself in my opinion; if it discovers a little respect for us, I shall require no more.

'Adieu, my dear Friend!

'Ever yours,

'S. R.'

The countess to whom he thus humorously alludes was Lady Jersey [1] whose acquaintance he had made during this visit, and whom he continued to visit in after years. Her intimacy with the Prince of Wales was one of the Court scandals of the time. It need only be referred to here by way of annotation on Rogers's letter. It was about this time that he wrote the lines to Lady Jersey's youngest daughter Harriet. Her elder sister was about to be married, and the younger sister had written some lines on the coming event. Rogers remonstrates in the following stanzas : —

> 'Ah! why with tell-tale tongue reveal
> What most her blushes would conceal?
> Why lift that modest veil to trace
> The seraph sweetness of her face?
> Some fairer, better sport prefer,
> And feel for us, if not for her.
> For this presumption, soon or late,
> Know thine shall be a kindred fate.
> Another shall in vengeance rise,
> Sing Harriet's cheeks, and Harriet's eyes;
> And, echoing back her woodnotes wild,
> Trace all the mother in the child.'

It was to Lady Jersey that Rogers once expressed his regret that he was not married, — a regret that he

---

[1] Frances Twysden, daughter and heiress of the bishop of Raphoe wife of the fourth earl of Jersey, whom she married in 1770. She was therefore much older than Rogers. Miss Frampton (Journal, p. 84) describes her as 'clever and unprincipled, but beautiful and fascinating.'

often felt and expressed, especially in his later years. 'If I had a wife,' he said, 'I should have somebody to care about me.' 'How could you be sure,' asked Lady Jersey in reply, 'that your wife would not care more about somebody else than about you?' Why he never married is not known. Lady Morgan, some time after his death, published a statement that he had made 'a formal proposition for the hand and fortune' of Cecilia Thrale before she had attained her fifteenth year. She tells the story in order to support the ridiculous falsehood that Rogers resented his refusal and consequently accused Mrs. Thrale's daughters of neglecting her after her marriage with Piozzi. There is not the slightest foundation for Lady Morgan's story in any documents Rogers has left behind. He made the acquaintance of Cecilia Thrale at Edinburgh in 1789, and expresses surprise at finding her to be only twelve years old. He did not become acquainted with the other daughters till January, 1801, as will be seen by a letter to his sister in the next chapter, which letter he writes 'after dining with Mrs. Mostyn (my old friend Cecilia Thrale).' The whole of the references to the Piozzis in the diaries already given disprove the insinuation that Rogers stood in any such relations with them as a scornful rejection by Cecilia Thrale in her girlhood would have brought about. The only traces of a susceptible period in his life are those which occur in his correspondence with Richard Sharp, in the years between 1795 and 1801.

To the letter which contains the hint of love and disappointment Richard Sharp replies in a long confidential epistle, further continuing his own romantic story. Of this romance there is no continuation. In Richard Sharp's next letter he says his life 'for the last eight days has been a stagnant pool, after tumbling down cataracts and making a furious noise to very little purpose.' He continues: —

'My romance will not finish, I apprehend, either in a church or in a churchyard, as all others do, but will terminate in some poor vapid conclusion, or break off suddenly, yet not before there is evidence enough of a want of ability and resources to carry it on to any interesting end. If men and women, too, insist upon it that I must play an old part before I have run the round of younger characters, why I must submit — unless I choose to be hissed off the scene — to perform what others may approve, how much soever it may be against my own inclination. The town would not hear even Garrick in "Romeo," but called him to be the merry bachelor "Mercutio," or the melancholy and sententious "Hamlet." If I am not to be the happy man in a regular comedy, I hope still to retain the old fellow in a farce, or the clown in a pantomime. Tragedy is not to my taste.'

There the romance ends, and we hear no more of it. He had recovered his spirits, and turned at once to give his friend that excellent advice for which he was distinguished all his life. He says: 'Flirting with countesses is sadly anti-matrimonial. The French opera spoils the taste for Molière or Racine. . . . I do not like this regularity of your pulse, except as it is a proof that your blood is not to be warmed by the brilliancy of fashion or the fever of dissipation.' There is a curious hint, too, in this letter, that even at this early period Rogers had thought of 'Columbus' as the subject of a poem. 'Ah!' writes Richard Sharp, 'I hear nothing of the "Epistle." The watering-place obliterates the happy valley's picture. You are so busy in discovering new worlds at home that "Columbus" is forgotten.' 'Columbus' was not finished till many years later. It was printed in 1810 and published in 1812. The 'Epistle' was very familiar to Richard Sharp. He had been consulted as to many of

its lines, and was an approving critic. Samuel Sharpe
tells us that when Rogers showed it to his friend from
time to time he would say: 'Let it alone, it can't be
better.' But Mr. Rogers was not so easily satisfied, and
continued to recast and to mend the rugged lines, and
when he again showed it to his critic, Sharp would say:
'It is quite another thing.'

In this early correspondence with Richard Sharp there
are further hints which show that, at this period, when
he was between the ages of thirty and thirty-five, Rogers
contemplated matrimony, not only as a distant possi-
bility, but as a near and probable event. I have pointed
out some of these hints in letters already given; but if
we go forward another year, there is what amounts almost
to the statement that he was actually engaged. Mr.
Hayward, in his affectionate and appreciative memorial
article on Rogers in the 'Edinburgh Review,' says that
'his own version of his nearest approximation to the
nuptial tie was that when a young man he admired and
sedulously sought the society of the most beautiful girl
he then and still thought he had ever seen. At the end
of the London season she said to him at a ball: "I go to-
morrow to Worthing. Are you coming there?" He did
not go. Some months afterwards being at Ranelagh he
saw that the attention of every one was drawn towards
a large party that had just entered, in the centre of
which was a lady leaning on the arm of her husband.
Stepping forward to see this wonderful beauty, he found
it was his love. She merely said: "You never came to
Worthing."' This story rests on the sole authority of
Mr. Hayward. Whether it was 'his nearest approximation to the nuptial tie' seems a little doubtful when
we read some of his confidential communications on the
subject to his friend Richard Sharp. In the autumn of
1798 he was again at Brighton, and his letters to his
sister Sarah and to his friend Sharp give a vivid picture

of a Brighton season at the close of the eighteenth century, at the same time that they throw further light on the personal history both of Sharp and Rogers.

S. Rogers to Richard Sharp.

'My dear Friend, — I have nothing to send to you; but having said I should write, I shall keep my promise by reminding you of yours. On my arrival here I threw myself into a temporary lodging, and then flew to Worthing, where I spent three very pleasant days with the Ellises. On my return I found Parsons in full cry after me, and by him was persuaded to adopt a plan of life which I relished little, though it has turned out tolerably well. We have taken a house on the cliff, every room of which is like the cabin of an Indiaman, commanding nothing but blue sea, and there we dwell *à la* Gibbon, having separate parlors, and breakfasting separately, but dining together when we have neither of us any engagement. This you will imagine occurs not very frequently. When it does we generally invite a friend or two. Mr. Matthew, a most elegant and *accomplished* man of family (I use the language of the world), Mr. Walpole, our minister at Munich, and Mr. Gray, the Resident at Dresden, of whom I must have spoken to you, have been our occasional guests. With the company I have mixed but little, not wishing to open my campaign seriously till your arrival, and I have nothing to relate, though I have had a dinner with Francis, a conversation with Jekyll, and a most sumptuous entertainment with some *Cognoscenti* at Concannon's. In the morning I walk on the Steyne to military music, and afterwards take a gallop with the hounds or the ladies. At three there is a full promenade, and the evening takes care of itself. When may I expect you to join us? We have a bed reserved for you, and you must be

my guest. Indeed, you were uppermost in my thoughts
when the house was taken. When will you come that
we may make our criticisms together on the beauties
of the Steyne, and afterwards steal away along the cliff
to open our hearts and minds to each other, and form
schemes of happiness out of the materials before us?
Schemes, did I say? Are we still scheming? Little
did we think, when we first entered the world and
ranked ourselves as men, that twenty years afterwards
we should be still only planning how to live, and busy-
ing ourselves with projects of happiness. Come, my
dear friend ; lose no time, for my sake and your own.
Come and find me as ever,

'Your most faithful friend,

'S. R.

'BRIGHTON, Octr. 26, 1798.
'No. 8 Marine Parade.

'Parsons desires me to say everything for him.'

S. Rogers to R. Sharp.

'BRIGHTON, 5 Novr. 1798.

'MY DEAR FRIEND, — A thousand thanks for your kind
letters. L——'s demands are indeed exorbitant! Had
he asked £350 we might have listened to him. Our rent
would even then for the first 13 years be £40 — the sum
he was contented to receive for it in its best state from
a casual tenant while the furniture was comparatively
new, which together with the house will grow worse and
worse as the rent increases. I resign my claim to our
friend Tuffin, but should he also decline it, and L——
continue firm, we may at least solicit to become yearly
tenants or for a short lease. Could you procure me a
sight of it on my way to town ? [1]

---

[1] They seem to have contemplated taking a house together near
Mickleham in 'our valley' as he calls it in this letter on page 303.

'Your first letter gave me concern; I will not say disappointment, for you have long taught me not to be sanguine. I lament exceedingly the very delicate and embarrassing situation in which you are placed, but doubt not that you will extricate yourself even to your own satisfaction. Remember the first break of day on our return out of the cavern at Castleton. What a recompense for our labors! I wish I could tantalize you with a description of the life I lead here, of Mrs. Schollet's evening parties, where the young and the gay assemble nightly, to laugh, and to sing, and to play at "my lady's toilet," and where I have more than once found myself alone among six or seven beautiful girls, who paint, and play on the harp divinely, who devour the books you recommend to them, and who accost you with that voice, cette voix argentée de la jeunesse — mais n'importe; nor will I describe their form très mignonne et très formée, ce qui est pour une fille le plus beau moment. Suffice it to say that I have been charmed out of my senses, and I have made one acquaintance which, I hope, will last for life. Interpret this last expression as you please. Oh that I had you here!

'I have read a novel which has enchanted me: "Clara" [by] Du Plessis. Have you? If not, pray do. I have also read the "Confessions," against which I had conceived a prejudice, I don't know why. I now rave about them, to the astonishment of Parsons, who says he has Rousseau by heart, but never could like him. But is he right? Different minds find different things in the same book. The same letters and syllables pass in review before the eye, but what different feelings and associations are excited. In what a different sense is it often confidently said in company, "I have read that book." What a charming frankness runs through the "Confessions"! How admirably he describes his silence before those he loved, his suffering "un gros butor de

valet" to pick up Mme. de Breil's glove, his first and last
interview with Mme. de Warens, and above all his day's
adventure with the two girls at Toune; his want of words,
yet his rage for talking; his journeys on foot, "le grand
air, le grand appétit," though I could never enter into
"la liberté du cabaret;" his night spent in the open air
near Lyons — what a heavenly climate!— his notion of a
fine country "des torrens, des precipices," not that I ever
loved to "contempler au fond, et gagner des vertiges
tout à mon aise;" his castle-building on the Lake of
Geneva, "absolument au bord de ce lac et non pas d'un
autre." Cannot we say the same of our valley? "Son
goût vif pour les dejeunés" [sic]. Oh that he had been
a Templar! His portraits, particularly that of Venture,
his whole employment at Paris "à y chercher des res-
sources pour se mettre en état d'en vivre éloigné." But
enough, I must have worn you out. I have a thousand
things to say, a thousand stories to tell, among others
that of our fair hostesses at Llangollen, but adieu! the
sun shines, the music plays, and a lady has sent her
groom to say that she is already on horseback.

> 'Yours most affect',
>
>   'S. R.

'The ladies, I see, have dismounted for five minutes
at Lady Lucan's, and I may proceed. I wish you joy
of your correspondent. May the conversion be mutual!
Poor Morgan! he will certainly die of some experiment.
When you see Boddington tell him I hope to see him.
Who but Cumberland could write an epic at a public
place? À propos of Miss C., she has written a play and
is writing a novel in concert with another girl. Who
could have thought it? But your coy girls are up to
anything. I wish you could see Matthew. He answers
Parsons's idea of a perfect man of fashion, and indeed he
deserves it. No attitudes, no conceit, very simple and

very easy; but after all, men of fashion are mannerists,
and all manner is bad. A natural character, manners
forever varying with the thoughts and feelings, how
superior to that uniform and monotonous thing called
high breeding! You will say I am growing *sensible,* and
that it comes from living with P.   I can assure you
I never knew before that I was so unlike him, though I
must confess that I sometimes envy him, and indeed
a thousand others who elbow their way on in the world.
A hard nature frequently imposes itself on the world
for a superior nature.   Its confidence seems to confirm
its claims, and its insensibility to place it above (and
not below) the reach of sufferings by which a feeling
and shrinking nature is continually harassed and obstructed in the commerce of life.   I never made this
stale remark so feelingly to myself as I have done since
I came here.   I must away, to ride with two pretty
women, and then dress for Mr. Hope's dinner and Lord
Carrington's ball.   You will think me very gay, but I
have long found that there is at least as much if not
more *ennui* in society than out of it.'

A letter to his sister, written four days later, continues
the description of the gayeties of Brighton in 1798 : —

Samuel Rogers to Sarah Rogers.

'BRIGHTON, 9th Novr. 1798.

' No, he has not forgotten her, nor ever will cease to
remember her, he can truly say, with pride and pleasure.
In all his castles (and night and day he is building them)
she still has a place ; and when all his wanderings are
over (as they soon will be) he hopes and trusts that she
will not shut her heart against him, but will welcome
back one who is ever the same, and whose regard for
her is, if possible, increased, not lessened, by absence.

Yes, my dear Sarah, you are indeed often in my thoughts, and whenever I shall have a home let me hope you will sometimes at least deign to grace it. Its door will always fly open to welcome you. Here — though perhaps you will smile when I say so — I feel alone in a crowd, as a thousand gay images are passing continually by me; but, like the *ombres chinoises*, they leave no trace, nothing for the heart to fix upon, or the mind to recall with any real satisfaction to itself. Yet as you wish me to send you a register of the follies of the place, I must obey; though, were I to do them justice, I should exhaust reams of paper, and ruin you in postage. But where shall I begin? With Concannon's supper-parties, where there is charming music, which you are not compelled to listen to, where French dishes are served up on silver *chiffoirs*, and where champagne goes round with glees and *bon mots* to an early hour; or with Mrs. Schollet's humbler though merrier meetings, where there is more beauty though less fashion, and where "my lady's toilet" and a thousand whimseys fill the room with noise and disorder; or with Miss Haldimaud's *conversationes*, where I was introduced on the first evening blindfold, and where Miss Cleaver, a relation of the Huttons, plays divinely on the harp, and looks as divinely; or with Lord Carrington's ball, where I spent last night among Lady Marys and Lady Bettys, where the supper shone most splendidly with youth and beauty, and jellied meats and grapes and pine-apples? No, my dear Sarah, I will begin with a list of the *dramatis personæ* here, and leave my whereabouts for another chapter. Here is Mrs. Armstead (Fox is pheasant-shooting in Norfolk), who lives in a small cabin with a man and a maid, and who is reading "Emily Montagu" for the third time; Mrs. Bristow, who still dances *à l'opéra*, but is now in a little disguise, having last winter got rid of a dropsy in a remarkable manner; Mrs. Horsley, who looks very dull and rather

20

old ; a Miss Grant, who is seldom seen, but who, without
entering into these gayeties, looks very cheerful and very
well, and makes many kind inquiries after her friends ;
Miss Hunt, who was once to have been married to Lord
Wycombe, and who has three mines in Cornwall with
3,000 lamps burning night and day in each of them ;
Tommy Onslow, who is one instant seen in his phaeton
and six, and the very next on a docktail pony, with
his skirts pinned up, and his hat in his hand, bumping
along the London road at the rate of twelve miles an
hour ; General Manners, who follows the hounds in a
low chair, which he says he gave eight guineas for
twelve years ago, and which is dragged up and down
the hills by a tall white coach-horse ; Miss White, a
most charming and elegant woman about thirty-five,
who, after having long excited the admiration of the
Pump Room by her wit and her talents, shut herself up
in her father's sick-room for two long years, but he is
now dead, and she lives at present in Sir J. Reynolds's
house at Richmond on an independency of £1,200 per
annum — you must know her ; Lady Lucan, who is illu-
minating a Shakspeare with her beautiful drawings,
and who sleeps every night in her little steel travelling-
bed, lest she should feel any difference between at home
and abroad ; and Mrs. Hope, who turns up her nose
alike at English peeresses and English [customs], and
whose little girls come in regularly with the dessert
after dinner, with earrings, and necklaces, and white
gloves.   But I could continue my list till Christmas, and
shall conclude with Mr. Spencer, who is a nephew of the
Duke of Marlboro', who translated " Leonora," and who
married rather oddly.   When he was at Heidelberg, a
mutual attachment took place between him and the wife
of an ex-German nobleman, who became uneasy at it,
and Mr. S. left the place.   She was an Englishwoman
born there.   On his departure she solicited leave of her

husband to hear once a year from Mr. S. The Baron
consented, and immediately wrote to Mr. S. to meet
him at an inn on the road. Mr. S. came and found him
dead; he had shot himself, and had left a letter on the
table, recommending his wife as a most amiable and
excellent woman to the regard and protection of Mr.
Spencer. Mrs. S., who has nothing remarkable about
her, is just here. *A propos*, I have just received a letter
from Brignola; he is well, but low in spirits, at Florence,
and desires his homage to you. Parsons and myself
are here on the edge of old Ocean, who has been taken
rather fractious lately. The spray wets our windows,
and the wind rocks our beds, and the door sometimes
requires three men to shut it. We live like Gibbon and
Deyverdun (in only one respect, I fear), breakfasting
separately and dining together, when disengaged. We
then sometimes indulge ourselves with a *partie carrée;*
and Mr. Walpole, the Munich minister, and Mr. Gray,
our Resident at Dresden, have formed it frequently with
us. We have a decent cook, and P.'s Frenchman is
just equal to an *omelette* or a *fricassee*. P. bathes most
furiously, and parades along the cliff in a flannel robe
and pantaloons. By some he is taken for the Pope, who
has emigrated; by others for a Carthusian friar. Your
More returns her best thanks for kind inquiries. She
still excites a little notice, and is forever scampering
with the hounds or the ladies. But adieu! my dear
Sarah. I must prepare myself for Lady Clark's supper, where there is to be a general insurrection this
evening. Remember me to everybody at Aspleyns and
Amersham.

'Affectionately yours,

'S. R.'

CHAPTER XI.

THE 'Epistle to a Friend' was already finished when, in the autumn of 1797, Richard Sharp inquired about it. It had in all probability originated in conversations with him, and it may be regarded as a poetical reply to the arguments he had used to induce Rogers to leave his suburban home and plunge into the social life of the West End of London. His nephew, Samuel Sharpe, speaks of it as 'a picture of his mind at the age of thirty-five, as "The Pleasures of Memory" shows his mind at the age of twenty-nine. The "Epistle to a Friend" describes his views of life and his feelings on Art, on Literature, and on Society, as one who valued cheap pleasures, who had lived out of town, and was separated from London's round of gayety and glitter.' Readers of my account of Rogers's early days will have no difficulty in understanding the truth of this statement. I have previously said that there was a struggle in his own mind which he turned into poetry. This praise of country life from the point of view of a dweller in the town is an old theme. So Horace wrote to Fuscus and Petrarch to Colonna. Dr. Aikin, as S. Sharpe points out, had just translated the 'Epistle of Frascatorius' in praise of a country life. It is the object of 'An Epistle to a Friend.' Yet the life at Stoke Newington had scarcely been country life. It was life on the verge of London, with many opportunities of mingling in the whirl. Rogers had seen true country life, such, for example, as Gilpin lived it at Vicar's Hill, only as a spectator, or at the very most as a visitor, but that may only make his praise of it the more sincere. He had not failed to read Cowper, the true poet of country life, and he could not read him without feeling a profound sense of the quiet which a close and constant communion with Nature brings into the mind. He appreciated what Cowper calls —

> 'an unambitious mind, content
> In the low vale of life; '

yet said to his soul —

> 'Be thine to blend — nor thine a vulgar aim —
> Repose with dignity; with Quiet fame.'

There is a good deal in the poem to indicate what his early home had been. The partial pencil, which, as he says, must —

> 'love to dwell
> On the home prospects of my hermit cell,'

needed the guidance of the poet's fancy, though he probably drew the picture from recollections of Gilpin's parsonage at Vicar's Hill. But the library demanded no flight of imagination. It is the very place where on many an evening he had sat amid the studious silence of brothers and sisters, reading ancient books and dreaming inspiring dreams.

> 'Selected shelves shall claim thy studious hours;
> There shall thy ranging mind be fed on flowers! [1]

---

[1] Rogers's note on this line is as follows: —

> . . . apis Matinæ
> More modoque
> Grata carpentis thyma. — *Hor.*

> There, while the shaded lamp's mild lustre streams,
> Read ancient books or dream inspiring dreams;
> And, when a sage's bust arrests thee there,
> Pause, and his features with his thoughts compare.
> — Ah, most that art my grateful rapture calls,
> Which breathes a soul into the silent walls;
> Which gathers round the Wise of every Tongue,
> All on whose words departed nations hung
> Still prompt to charm with many a converse sweet;
> Guides in the world, companions in retreat.'

There are other home touches. He had spoken in 'The
Pleasures of Memory' of the family portraits —

> ' Those once loved forms still breathing through their dust,
> Still from the frame in mould gigantic cast,
> Starting to life — all whisper of the past.'

In the new poem the thought is again taken up and
further expanded : —

> But could thine erring friend so long forget
> (Sweet source of pensive joy and fond regret)
> That here its warmest hues the pencil flings,
> Lo, here the lost restores, the absent brings;
> And still the Few best loved and most revered
> Rise round the board their social smile endeared.'

His nephew points out that whereas in the earlier
poem the family portraits are the only works of art spoken of, and were 'almost the only works of art known
in his father's house,' in the later poem we find that he
' had gained a knowledge and love of art of the highest
class, and understood the beauties of Greek sculpture
and Italian painting.' He had imbibed this love of art,
as has been already said, from his sister's husband, Sutton Sharpe, but he had not yet dreamed of indulging it
as a rich man may. The villa in the 'Epistle' is a small
country house, plainly and economically furnished.

> ' Here no state chambers in long line unfold,
> Bright with broad mirrors, rough with fretted gold;
> Yet modest ornament, with use combined,
> Attracts the eye, to exercise the mind!
> Small change of scene, small space his home requires,
> Who leads a life of satisfied desires.'

The very object of the 'Epistle,' as he says in his
'Preface,' is to show how little True Taste requires to
secure ' not only the comforts, but even the elegancies of
life.' 'True Taste,' he says, ' is an excellent Economist.
She confines her choice to few objects, and delights in
producing great effects by small means ; while False
Taste is forever sighing for the new and rare, and reminds us, in her works, of the Scholar of Apelles, who
not being able to paint his Helen beautiful, determined
to make her fine.' Hence, in the imaginary villa, where
the aim was to blend —

> ' Repose with dignity ; with Quiet fame,'

a severe economy reigned.

> ' What tho' no marble breathes, no canvas glows
> From every point a ray of genius flows.
> Be mine to bless the more mechanic skill
> That stamps, renews, and multiplies at will ;
> And cheaply circulates, thro' distant climes,
> The fairest relics of the purest times.
> Here from the mould to conscious being start
> Those finer forms, the miracles of art ;
> Here chosen gems, imprest on sulphur, shine,
> That slept for ages in a second mine ;
> And here the faithful graver dares to trace
> A Michael's grandeur and a Raphael's grace!
> Thy gallery, Florence, gilds my humble walls;
> And my low roof the Vatican recalls!'

In pursuance of his habit of taking counsel with his
friends on his works before they were published, Rogers

sent the unfinished manuscript of this poem to Dr.
Joseph Warton,[1] and afterwards in its completed state
to the Rev. William Gilpin. Dr. Warton returned it
with the following letter : —

Dr. J. Warton to Samuel Rogers.

'April 9, 1797.

'My DEAR SIR, — I should ill deserve the friendship I
hope to cultivate with you if I wrote you a letter of
mere compliment on the poem you have so obligingly
sent to me. I must assure you, with strict truth, that
I like it much. There is in it uncommon elegance and
simplicity both of style and sentiment, and the notes
are very pertinent and proper. It is more to show you
that I have read it with attention than to wish you to
alter a word or two, that I venture to carp a little at the
following words : Page 1, "*unvalued* hours," "*ambush 'd*
gate," a good image certainly, but the word seems harsh.[2]
Page 7, "Fountain *flings*."[3]   Page 8, "*woo* dreams," why
not *wait?* 9, "*unfelt*," the idea is excellent, and I cannot
suggest another word, yet doubt of *unfelt*. I lay no sort
of stress on these seeming blemishes, nor think them of
much consequence. I cannot forbear adding that I am
extremely struck with the concluding lines as well as
with the Plan and Design of the whole, and hope you
will finish it immediately. Own, my dear sir, that I

---

[1] Warton had just then finished his edition of Pope, on which it is
said he had been engaged for sixteen years. He was in his old age.
He had resigned the head mastership of Winchester School in 1793, and
was living at Wickham, of which parish he was rector, where he died in
February, 1800.

[2] It now reads 'the sheltered gate.'

[3] There is now no such expression in the poem. The line is —

'That here its warmest hues the pencil flings.'

have treated you with the freedom you are pleased to desire, and believe me,

'Very faithfully and sincerely yours,

'J. WARTON.'

Rogers did right in retaining both the 'unvalued hours' and the 'unfelt current.' The latter is compared to life —

'which still as we survey,
Seems motionless, yet ever glides away!'

Mr. Gilpin's criticisms were more important than those of Dr. Warton, and more influential. As Rogers had spent his own life chiefly in the immediate neighborhood of London, he probably felt some diffidence in describing country life, and passing a eulogy upon it without taking counsel of some authority. He therefore sent the manuscript of the 'Epistle' to the Rev. William Gilpin, inviting him to make free remarks and criticisms upon it. Mr. Gilpin, like Dr. Warton, was then drawing towards the close of a lengthened life. He was universally known as the great authority on Picturesque Beauty. Rogers has already described him in his diary of a journey in the south of England in 1792. He speaks there of 'Mr. Gilpin's celebrated view.' Mr. Gilpin was a lineal descendant of Bernard Gilpin, 'the Northern Apostle,' whose life he wrote and published ten years before Rogers was born. He had long been known as a faithful country clergyman and a writer of religious and biographical books when, in 1790, he published his 'Observations on Picturesque Beauty.' A series of works from his pen on the same subject followed in rapid succession, and before the close of the century Mr. Gilpin had been universally acknowledged as the great modern authority on the Picturesque. In Mr. Green's pleasant 'Diary of a Lover of Literature' there is a glimpse of his parsonage in 1798 which is in har-

mony with the sketch of the 'Villa' in Rogers's poem.
'Crossed the river by a causeway, and pursued its
course by an agreeable walk along its banks up to
Boldre, and returning by the upper road, struck down
into a woody dell at the back of Vicar's Hill, Mr. Gilpin's parsonage, the object of our pilgrimage; shrouded,
together with its gardens, in thick foliage. Contemplated, with much interest, the residence of a gentleman
by whose pen and by whose pencil I have been almost
equally delighted, and who, with an originality that almost always accompanies true genius, may be considered
as having opened a new sense of enjoyment in survey-
ing the works of Nature.' It is more than likely that
Rogers in writing the 'Epistle' had Mr. Gilpin and his
parsonage, with the forest scenery around it, present to
his memory. He had been in the neighborhood, and
he had written a diary of his visit, just as he was beginning to write the poem; and he probably sent the
manuscript to Mr. Gilpin because of his personal connection with it. Mr. Gilpin's letter, in sending it back,
is interesting in itself, and is still more so as indicating
Rogers's willingness to take the advice of so experienced
an observer of Nature.

Rev. W. Gilpin to Samuel Rogers.

'VICAR's HILL, July 7, 1797.

'DEAR SIR, — I have read your little poem two or three
times over, with great pleasure : I should say with increased pleasure, for that is the truth. I have seldom
met with, in so short a space, so many beautiful lines.
But though you check criticism in a printed work, it is
expected you should treat a manuscript with more freedom. I'll tell you, therefore, frankly, all that occurred
to me.

'With regard to the whole, you seem to me (what

is certainly a fault, if it be one, on the better side) too
concise.   I think your subject would not only have
allowed more, but disappoints us in not having more,
—particularly in the description of the *cottage* and the
library.   In describing your cottage, instead of alluring
us by its near and distant scenery, you give us only a
view of the *pales* and *footpath*.   If it be a picture taken
from the life, and have no distant scenery, you might
perhaps (if you did not choose to raise the *idea*, by
telling us *what it had not*) give us a few reflections on
the advantages of a cottage entirely sequestered.   I
think, too, you might have dwelt a little more on the
worthies that adorn the study; and as a poet might have
specified a few poets.   A friend told me, the other day, he
had paid a visit to Lord Muncaster in the north; and that
he had adorned, or intended to adorn, a room with one of
the chief worthies of every profession.   I thought the
idea a pleasing one.   Lastly, I was not quite pleased with
the conclusion of your poem.   I thought it might have
ended better with a few pertinent moral reflections.

'So much for the *whole*.   With regard to the *parts*,
I have not much to say.   Most of the lines, I think,
are unexceptionably beautiful.   *Point out the green lane*
appears to me rather prosaic; and I do not think you
have chosen picturesque figures to adorn your footpath.
The *panniered ass* I allow.   But the *pedler* is injured by
his profession.   The *satchelled schoolboy* is neither a
novel nor a pleasing idea.   The *red-hooded* maid is less
so: and the *cry of cresses* has too much of London in it.
Perhaps a man of *studious hours* would not be contented
to *feed on flowers*, if he were in a place, as I suppose he
was, which afforded more *solid nutriment*.   Some of the
lines, too, on the ice-house I think are rather too heroic.

'But now, my dear sir, I must inform you that Mason
used to tell me I was among the worst poetical critics
he consulted; and I believe he was very right.   But

as it is not my end at present to display my critical abilities, but to show my sincerity, I have no doubt but your
candor will accept what I have said in good part; and
that you will believe me to be on this, and every other
occasion,

'Your very sincere and most obedt. humble servant,

'WILL. GILPIN.'

Some of the lines and expressions here objected to
did not appear in the published poem, and some of
the omissions noted are supplied. There is now the
full recognition of distant scenery which Mr. Gilpin
suggests —

> 'Far to the south a mountain vale retires,
> Rich in its groves, and glens, and village spires,
> Its upland lawns, and cliffs with foliage hung,
> Its wizard stream, nor nameless nor unsung.
> And through the various year, the various day,
> What scenes of glory burst and melt away !'

But there is no pedler now in the poem, no satchelled
schoolboy, the red-hooded maid becomes 'in her kerchief
blue, the cottage maid;' and the cry of cresses — which
as Mr. Gilpin truly says has too much of London in it
— has given place to the 'brimming pitcher from the
shadowy glade.' The lines about the ice-house were re-
tained in the earlier editions, but they were afterwards
excised and placed in the notes, and every reader will
agree with Mr. Gilpin's criticism that they 'are rather
too heroic.' When the poem had been published it was
sent to Mr. Gilpin, who returned the following letter —

Rev. William Gilpin to Samuel Rogers.

VICAR'S HILL, Ap. 16, 1798.

'DEAR SIR, — At the time I received your first letter,
and long after, I was so ill that few things in any degree
attracted my attention. I was so ill that, to tell you the

truth, I was not overjoyed at the idea of having all the suffering I had undergone, or something like it, to undergo again at some future period. It hath pleased God, however, to give me a wonderful restoration, which I should wish to return with a greater degree of religious gratitude than I fear the confirmed habits of old age will in general allow. I am still, however, far from being well; though I am as well as I ever expect to be, unless, on the return of the zephyrs and swallows I may now and then perhaps be enabled to breathe a little more freely.

'Having thus talked of myself through a page, it is now time to come to your villa, for the sight of which I am much obliged to you. I entered your gate impressed with those just sentiments which you had so justly raised. I admired the view from your windows — I thought you had collected your prints with great judgment. Many of your sulphur-gems I had never seen before. Your portraits and books I thought the happiest appendages of the place. I then sat down with you to your elegant *closet-supper*. Of all kinds of food, the *dapes inemptæ* please me most: and, as it fortunately happened I am now ordered to drink wine (which I almost never before tasted), I drank two bumpers of your excellent Falernian. In short, you have entertained me like a prince, and I once more return you many thanks. I must not forget that, as I left your villa, I met a bride going to church, whose beautiful simplicity and varied sensibilities were very interesting. "There," said I, "is Nature in its pleasing innocence;" and I could not help thinking what a happy subject it would have been for you. We painters very sparingly, if ever, introduce the mixed passions into the same face; but you would have had the advantage of us, and might have introduced a thousand varieties of delicate emotions almost at once.

'Cadell has in hand one of my books of picturesque travels. I sell him the copy, tho' our bargain is not yet struck. The money is to be funded, as the beginning of a fund for the posthumous use of my school; so that they who do not purchase from a motive of choice may please themselves with purchasing from a motive of charity. With Mrs. G.'s best respects,

'Believe me, dear Sir,

'Very sincerely and cordially yours,

'WILL GILPIN.'

The bride whom Gilpin met going to church was in Rogers's volume in the short poem, 'To a Friend on his Marriage.' It is dated 1798. There were two other short poems in the volume: the lines 'To a Gnat,' and the five verses, written in 1797, entitled 'A Farewell.'

It might, perhaps, not be altogether impossible to construct out of the slight materials furnished by these two poems — the 'Farewell' and the 'Lines to a Friend on his Marriage' — taken together with the hint in his letter to his friend Richard Sharp,[1] a romantic episode in Rogers's life. But beyond those vague hints and the story told by the 'Edinburgh Review'[2] there are no further traces of his having really experienced the feelings the 'Farewell' expresses. It is only the most prosaic criticism which essays to trace the events of a man's life in his imaginative writings. One of the chief marks of the true poet is the possession of the power of realizing situations in which he was never personally placed, and of giving expression to feelings which he never seriously experienced. It has not been proved that Shakspeare's mental history is to be found, as some tell us, in his sonnets; nor that Sidney, though he looked into his heart and wrote, really passed through all the feelings so exquisitely described in his 'Astrophel and Stella'

---

[1] Chap. X. p. 302.　　　[2] Page 299.

sonnets. It was probably never literally true of him
that, —

> ' the race
> Of all my thoughts had neither stop nor start,
> But only Stella's eyes and Stella's heart ; '

nor of his friend Fulke Greville that he wrote in
'Caelica' the romance of his own life. There is, of
course, no such passion in Rogers's few lines as these great
Elizabethan writers express. It is only the imaginative
experience which is the same, and that is the essence of
such poetry. He was never engaged to be married, and
there is no evidence that he ever made any woman an
offer of marriage.[1] The nearest approach, in any of his
letters, to the utterance of any feeling of disappointment is in those from Margate and Brighton already
quoted ; and it is just worthy of notice that the last of
these was written in the same year as the 'Farewell.'

It is not to be wondered at, however, if some of his
friends suspected that these little poems had an autobio-
graphic character. The Rev. William Gilpin expresses
this suspicion in a very characteristic letter. He had
returned the compliment Rogers had paid him in consulting him about the 'Epistle to a Friend,' by sending
to Rogers the manuscript of a work on North Wales
for his criticism and remarks. Rogers kept it so long
that Gilpin became anxious about it and wrote to inquire whether he had asked his friend, after reading it,
to send it to Cadell and Davies. Rogers, whom Gilpin
had described as 'such an ubiquitarian that I know not
where to find you' wrote from Exmouth apologizing for
the delay, and promising to send the manuscript forth-
with. Mr. Gilpin then sent him the following letter:

---

[1] I have already discussed the ridiculous statement of Lady Morgan with respect to Cecilia Thrale, which is exactly on a par with her
hint as to a similar offer to her niece in the days when Rogers's memory
had failed him.

Rev. William Gilpin to Samuel Rogers.

'VICAR'S HILL, Nov. 29, 1799.

'I hope, my dear sir, you read my letter in the same honest, sincere spirit in which it was written. I certainly neither wanted my papers, nor in the least doubted your care. But I had entirely forgotten whether I had desired you to leave them at any place, and under that forgetfulness might have suffered them to lie I knew not where, nor how long. You gratified me much with what you said of them; but I should have been more gratified if you had made any remarks that would have led to amendment. I shall, however, I doubt not, when I receive the papers, find a few remarks bundled up with them. If not, do not again hypocritically call me *friend.* It has always been my chief endeavor, in all my picturesque exhibitions, to bring the objects I describe, as much as I can, before the eye of my reader; remembering our old friend's remark that things brought before the eye affect us more than things only described. How far I have succeeded *I* am not the person to judge. There is, I think, another great criterion of excellence in works of fancy; and that is the power of exciting *feelings.* But this belongs rather to animate than inanimate objects. Gray's "Elegy" will be *felt* when Dr. Johnson's cold criticisms on words and syllables are neglected. I have often read with much pleasure, among other pieces which pleased me, a little poem on the "Marriage of a Friend." It is wonderfully wrought up with that sort of sensibility which excites feeling; and to me, who have so often, as my duty led, seen it realized, it appears an admirable portrait from the life. It is followed *so immediately* by another poem, called the "Farewell" (which also I like much), that I cannot help thinking there is some connection between them. If you are

acquainted with the author perhaps you can tell me
whether any history belongs to them. By the way, I
think the Marriage Service in our Liturgy is not quite
so delicate as it might be. I see no reason for entering
so minutely into the causes of matrimony : and I think
I should rather have spared the young lady her hesitat-
ing speech. Her coming to the altar with her friends
and signing her name seem sufficient. But the other
parts of the Service (except one prayer) I think extremely fine. You write cheerfully, and I hope you are
well ; but I want to know why you have been sent to
Exmouth ; and your saying so significantly that you are
sorry your sister is not with you seems to have a meaning. Let me hear. With regard to myself, a degree of
health is a blessing at the age of 76, and I have great
reason to bless God for it. Coughs and a few other infirmities summon me to a change, which I would gladly
persuade myself I do not regret. God bless you !

'And believe me to be

'Your affect. and sincere

'WILL GILPIN.

'Mrs. G.'s best respects.'

'An Epistle to a Friend' was published in the spring
of 1798, a year and a half before the above letter of
Gilpin's was written. It had occupied Rogers, with the
notes, half-a-dozen years, and had undergone, as these
letters show, much patient elaboration and critical review before it took its final shape. It seems to have
been received with some differences of opinion among
Rogers's friends. Soon after it was published he wrote
to Richard Sharp in apparent despair : —

Samuel Rogers to Richard Sharp.

'MY DEAR FRIEND, — I am in a peck of troubles. My
"Epistle" is universally found fault with for its crude-

21

ness and obscurity. Twiss says he shall try to read it
again, not having Goldsmith to refer to. The simile of'
the floating beehives was lost upon him; and as to the
verses to Lady ——'s daughter they are, as he and Parsons agreed, perfectly unintelligible.

'What am I to do? I stand still in horror, and dare
not advance a step. Pray console your unhappy friend!

'S. R.

'P. S. — I shall expect you on Saturday at half-past
four.'

Richard Sharp's response to this appeal is not extant.
The simile of the floating beehives is in the following
lines, and it is now explained in a note to be 'an allusion
to the floating beehouse, or barge laden with beehives,
which is seen in some parts of France and Piedmont.'

> 'So, thro' the vales of Loire the beehives glide,
> The light raft dropping with the silent tide;
> So, till the laughing scenes are lost in night,
> The busy people wing their various flight,
> Culling unnumbered sweets from nameless flowers
> That scent the vineyard in its purple hours.'

The note not only makes the simile perfectly intelligible
but renders it impossible for the dullest not to see its
appropriateness and beauty. The note to the verses to
Lady Jersey's daughter Harriet makes them also intelligible by simply explaining the circumstances in which
they were addressed to her. The 'Epistle' fully justifies
in its present shape the long labor spent upon it. It consists of only two hundred and twenty-two lines, but no
reader can fail to perceive, as he reads it, that an unusual
number of the lines have a strangely familiar sound. As
I said of 'The Pleasures of Memory' so, to a larger extent, it may be said of this much shorter poem that it has
many expressions which have passed into literature and

have become, as it were, familiar forms of speech. 'The
insect tribes of human kind,' the contrast of home's
'simple comforts and domestic rites' with the season's
'annual round of glitter and perfume;' the line —

'Each fleeting charm that bids the landscape live;'

the couplet —

> 'There let her practise from herself to steal,
> And look the happiness she does not feel;'

and other lines such as —

> 'Guides in the world, companions in retreat;'

or —

> 'The cheap amusements of a mind at ease;'

are surely most felicitously expressed, and have lingered
in the recollection of readers and writers who have reproduced them without remembering their origin. 'The
clear mirror of his moral page,' and —

> 'Scorned the false lustre of licentious thought,'

are happy phrases from those concluding lines which
every reader will admit to be entirely worthy of Dr.
Warton's praise.

Like his other poems 'An Epistle to a Friend' was
well received by the critics. The 'Monthly Review'
prided itself that on the first anonymous appearance of
the writer it did justice to his talents, and that when
after a considerable interval he came before the world
again, it was again forward to pay its tribute of applause
to his taste and genius. The 'Epistle' it regarded as
'of a more masculine character, without falling below
his other compositions in elegance or in feeling. It is
at once correct and spirited, classic and original.' The
reviewer quotes with approval some original and happy

epithets : 'His *spangling* shower when frost the wizard
flings;' 'the arrowy North;' 'the *murmuring* market-
place.'

Mr. Hayward in the 'Edinburgh Review,' fifty-eight
years later, speaks of the description of winter in the
'Epistle,' as 'marked by the same delicate fancy which
is displayed in the "Rape of the Lock" on a different
class of phenomena:' —

> 'When Christmas revels in a world of snow,
>   And bids her berries blush, her carols flow:
>   His spangling shower when Frost the wizard flings;
>   Or, borne in ether blue, on viewless wings,
>   O'er the white pane his silvery foliage weaves,
>   And gems with icicles the sheltering eaves;
>   — Thy muffled friend his nectarine wall pursues.'

Mr. Hayward adds : 'There is no disputing the eye for
Nature which fixed and carried off the image of the
silvery foliage woven on the white pane. At one of his
Sunday breakfasts Rogers had quoted with decided
commendation Leigh Hunt's couplet on a fountain (in
Rimini) — also selected by Byron as one of the most poetical descriptions of a natural object he was acquainted
with : —

> "Clear and compact, till at its height o'errun
>   It shakes its loosening silver in the sun."

" I give my vote," said one of the guests, "for —

> 'O'er the white pane his silvery foliage weaves;' "

and Rogers looked for a moment as if he were about to
re-enact Parr's reception of the flattering visitor from
Birmingham.'

In the admirable and appreciative article from which
this criticism and its illustrative story are taken, Mr.
Hayward speaks of the poem, as a whole, 'as conveying

after the manner of Horace and (in parts) of Pope the
writer's notions of social comfort and happiness, as dependent upon, or influenced by, the choice of residence,
furniture, books, pictures, and companions,— subjects on
all of which he was admirably qualified to speak.' But Mr.
Hayward and those to whom, like Mrs. Norton and Lady
Dufferin, he applied for information, were in absolute
ignorance of the circumstances out of which the poem
had sprung, and of the training which had so admirably
qualified the poet to speak on the topics he introduces.
He interprets Rogers's feelings in those early days, not
by the struggle which called them forth, of which he
knew nothing and suspected nothing, but by the altered
circumstances of Rogers's later life.   Knowing him for
many years as the centre of the most brilliant society of
the time, Mr. Hayward could not imagine him as he was
when the poem was written, standing with the open door
before him, considering for a moment whether it was best
to enter and mingle with the crowd, or whether he should
say to his soul, —

> ' Be thine to meditate a humbler flight,
> When morning fills the fields with rosy light :
> Be thine to blend — nor thine a vulgar aim —
> Repose with dignity ; with Quiet fame.' .

His actual mental attitude was probably that of one
who was conscious that he should go forward, yet who
cherished an unaffected admiration for much that he
should leave behind, and who puts on permanent record
his resolution — amid

> ' the joyous glare, the maddening strife
> And all the dull impertinence of life ' —

to keep his early faith in ' simple comforts and domestic
rites.'   Mr. Hayward, however, speaks of his praise of
modesty, simplicity, and retirement as being made ' with

about the same amount of practical earnestness as Grattan when he declared he could be content in a small neat house with cold meat, bread, and beer and plenty of claret.' Grattau never made any such declaration. The story is one of Rogers's own, and is told in the 'Recollections:'[1] 'What a slavery is office!' said Grattan in one of his talks with Rogers, at Fredley Farm, at Tunbridge Wells, or at St. James's Place; 'to be subject to the whims of those above you, and the persecutions of those beneath you; to dance attendance on the great; to be no longer your own master. No, give me a cottage and a crust — plain fare and quiet, and small beer and — ' he added, lowering his voice and smiling with his usual archness — 'claret!' The contrast between these two versions of Grattan's words is a fair illustration of the difference between Rogers's stories as he told them himself, and the same stories as they were afterwards recounted from the imperfect memories of his auditors. To compare this expression of Grattan's with the tone of Rogers's poem is absurd. The one was half a joke, — the other was the expression of serious thoughts. Rogers had not dreamed, as yet, of the exquisite home in St. James's Place where for fifty years his friends saw him, like a picture in its appropriate frame and placed in fit surroundings, and regarded him as the impersonated spirit of the scene. 'He cultivated art as yet' — says his nephew — 'only as a student and with economy. He had not begun to form his own valuable collection; and the works of art therein recommended to our purchase are not pictures and marbles, but copies from the antique in plaster and sulphur, and engravings after Italian painters.' He was, in fact, just setting out on his career of art patronage and social success. He had two homes, — one at Stoke Newington, the other in chambers in Paper Buildings, and he was gradually deciding between

[1] Page 104, second edition.

them.   The last lines of the 'Epistle' are a record of his experience in the five years before it was published : —

> ' One fair asylum from the world he knew,
> Who boasts of more (believe the serious strain)
> Sighs for a home, and sighs, alas! in vain.
> Through each he roves, the tenant of a day,
> And, with the swallow, wings the year away.'

About this period he wrote in his Commonplace Book the sentence which was incorporated in his last note to the poem : 'The master of many houses has no home.'

The decision was probably taken during or after his autumn visit to Brighton and the formation of his friendship with Lady Jersey in 1797. In the following June, after the 'Epistle' had been published in the spring, he finally gave up the home on Newington Green, and lived in his chambers, alone. His brother Henry had already taken a house at Highbury Terrace, with his sister Sarah ; and his sister Maria Sharpe, who had taken her children there for a summer holiday in 1798, speaks of Highbury Terrace at that time as 'quite a gay place, more like the seaside than anything else.' The old house at Newington Green was put into the hands of an auctioneer for sale, and Rogers's fastidious taste was greatly annoyed by the advertised description of the place. 'I should never have known it,' writes Maria Sharpe to her sister Sarah, 'if the place had not been mentioned. I read it to Mr. Sharpe and Catharine without their at all making it out. I am sorry they have dressed an old friend in borrowed ornaments.' In these letters there are frequent glimpses of Sam, as he is always called. 'His room is much improved since you saw it,' she tells her sister in May, 1797. He is often at Sutton Sharpe's ; and Flaxman and Opie and Stothard are spoken of with Richard Sharp and the Barbaulds, the Boddingtons, and the families of the Towgoods and Mallets. One day there is a

party at Richmond to which Sam has invited them.   He
and R. Sharp, who is present, are very fond of Richmond,
but R. Sharp monopolizes the poet, and Maria complains
that he deserted them.   Another time she remarks to her
sister Sarah : 'What very pretty presents he makes to
you !   Is it not well to be the single sister ? '   The question is asked in 1800, and for fifty years after it Miss
Rogers had every reason to answer yes.

It was Rogers's custom in these years to get his friends
together pretty frequently to dinner and evening parties
in his chambers, and the meal or refreshments were sent
in from the 'Mitre,' — still a well-known tavern in a court
out of Fleet Street.   Among the stories he told in later
years Mr. Hayward has preserved one which relates to
one of these dinners.   Rogers had invited Fox, Sheridan,
Erskine, Perry (of the 'Morning Chronicle '), and other
Whig notables to dinner, and as usual had ordered it at
the 'Mitre.'   These dinners usually came in by instal-
ments, — as Sydney Smith reminds us, when, arriving
just as some portion of the repast was being delivered,
he exclaimed : 'I knew I was in time, for though the
turtle had the start of me I fairly headed the turbot.'
The guests on this occasion, however, had the start of
the turtle.   The dinner-hour came, the guests were in the
drawing-room, but there was no dinner.   'I quietly stole
out,' said Rogers, 'and hurried to the "Mitre."   "What
has become of my dinner ? " I asked.   "Your dinner, sir ?
Your dinner is for to-morrow!"   I stood aghast, and for
a moment plans of suicidal desperation crossed my brain,
when the tavern-keeper relieved me from my perplexity
by saying that he had so many dinners on hand that mine,
if ever ordered, had escaped his recollection altogether.
"Many dinners on hand, have you?   Then if you will
send me the best dish from each of them I will pay you
double; and if you won't you shall never see my face
again."   As I was a good customer he chose the more

prudent and profitable alternative, and after an hour's waiting my guests were seated and served.' 'And how did the dinner go off?' 'Oh, very well! They got a bad dinner, but they got a good story to tell against me.'

He had already begun to make those notes of his conversations with eminent and celebrated men which gave so much pleasure to his guests in later years. In the charming volume of 'Recollections,' edited in 1859 by his nephew Mr. William Sharpe, the first conversation with Fox which is recorded took place on the 19th of March, 1796. He had met Fox before, but this time he seems to have engaged in conversation with the great statesman. The first occasion illustrated the 'playfulness' which Rogers in his prefatory note attributes to Fox. The latter exhibits — to quote Rogers's words — 'his love of letters and his good nature in unbending himself to a young man.' The conversation took place at the dinner table of William Smith, the well-known Unitarian member for Norwich, and the champion in the House of Commons of the rights of Dissenters in the days when the Test and Corporation Acts and other oppressive measures remained unrepealed. There were present, besides Fox and Rogers, Dr. Parr, George Tierney, John Courtenay, Sir Francis Baring, Dr. Aikin (the eminent brother of Mrs. Barbauld), Mackintosh, and Sir Philip Francis. Sheridan sent an excuse. Rogers dined with Fox again at Serjeant Heywood's on the 10th of December, 1796, when Lord Derby, Lord Stanley, Lord Lauderdale, Lambton (the member for Durham), and Brogden constituted the party. On another day he puts on record his meeting Fox in June, 1798, at the Park Gate at Penshurst. He was mounted on a pony, and dressed in a fustian shooting-jacket and a white hat. Mrs. Armstead was in a whisky. This was a kind of light carriage, so called because it was built for rapid motion, and whisked along. Its familiar name was a tim-whisky. The con-

versation on these occasions is made by the 'Recollections' familiar to every reader. There is a glimpse of
Fox in a letter from Thomas Erskine, afterwards Lord
Erskine, to Rogers, published in the Notes to the 'Recollections' (page 11). It is dated the 17th of July, 1798:
'I called yesterday on Fox at St. Anne's, and found him
drawing a pond to please an Eton boy, a son of the
Bishop of Down. I told him he was committing a double
crime, killing the poor fish and ruining Coss, — for Coss
has a perpetual holiday there. He left off, and we had
some talk on the times. He has no hope.' There is
another short letter from Erskine without date, but
written on paper bearing the water-mark 1799, and addressed to Rogers at Paper Buildings. It shows that at
this period Rogers and Erskine had not yet established
the close intimacy which marked their later years.

Thomas Erskine to Samuel Rogers.

'DEAR SIR, — The little, foolish, and too ill-natured
epigram which I gave you was incorrect; it should have
been as below : —

> " Some newspapers to blot the fame
> That waits on Fox's patriot name,
>   By misreporting damn his praise.
> But then in far more bitter spite
> Against a hapless courtly wight
>   They truly print what M—d says ! "

'Yours ever,

'T. E.'

There is no difficulty in identifying the name of the
'courtly wight.' He was Sir John Mitford, Attorney-
General in 1799, Speaker of the House of Commons
in 1801, and afterwards Lord Redesdale. The epigram
brings out one of the methods of political warfare which

were adopted in those early days of the press, but which have been happily altogether outgrown. One of the happiest features of political controversy in these days is the fulness and fairness with which the chief newspapers of all shades of politics report the political speeches of their leading opponents. In these dark closing years of the eighteenth century political passion ran high in this country, stirred by the violent movement in France. It was quite common to accuse prominent politicians of being in communication with the enemy, and the usual explanation given by the supporters of the Government for Fox's opposition to the war, was, that he was in the pay of France. Walpole in one of his letters had made the accusation against Wilkes, and it seems to have become a common weapon of political warfare. Walpole said that he was as sure that Wilkes was in the pay of France as of any fact he knew; and there were a thousand lesser Walpoles in the last decade of the eighteenth century who were not only sure of it with respect to Fox, but who professed to know the exact amount he received, the time it was paid, and the persons who conducted the transaction. Writing to Lord Webb Seymour so late as the 26th of December, 1805, Francis Horner says : 'I could name to you gentlemen with good coats on, and good sense in their own affairs, who believe that Fox *did* actually send information to the enemy in America, and *is* actually in the pay of France.'[1] In the days of the 'Anti-Jacobin'[2] this charge was constantly urged against the journals and the statesmen that opposed the Government. The 'Anti-Jacobin' insinuates it against the 'Morning Chronicle,' which, with the 'Morning Post,' were the leading journals of 'Jacobinism.' The spirit of the time when Erskine wrote to

---

[1] Horner's 'Memoirs and Correspondence,' vol. i. p. 323.

[2] The 'Anti-Jacobin' issued its first number on the 20th November, 1797, and the last — the 36th — on July 9th, 1798.

Rogers that Fox had no hope, is forcibly illustrated by an event in which many of Rogers's personal friends, and in all probability Rogers himself, took part; and which may have tended to produce the despondency Fox felt in that gloomy year. There was a great gathering at the 'Crown and Anchor' on Fox's birthday, the 24th of January, 1798. Two thousand people were present, among them the Duke of Bedford, Lord Lauderdale, Lord Oxford, Sheridan, Tierney, Erskine, and Horne Tooke. Lord John Russell[1] was one of the stewards, and presided in one of the rooms. After the health of Fox had been drunk, the Duke of Norfolk, as chairman, gave several other toasts. These were: 'The Rights of the People;' 'Constitutional Redress of the Wrongs of the People;' 'A speedy and effectual Reform of the Representation of the People in Parliament;' 'The Genuine Principles of the British Constitution;' 'The People of Ireland: may they be speedily restored to the Blessings of Law and Liberty!' 'The Cause of Liberty all over the World;' and 'The Freedom of the Press, and Trial by Jury.' A chronicler of the time says that the seditious and daring tendency of these toasts had not passed unnoticed. The 'Anti-Jacobin' which published a caricature report of the proceedings, reminded the Duke that, under another Sovereign than the Sovereign people, 'he now holds the lieutenancy of the West Riding of the County of York and the command of a regiment of militia.' From both these offices the Duke was immediately dismissed.

The dangers of the times, however, came more immediately home to Rogers and his friends by the prosecution of the Rev. Gilbert Wakefield for a pamphlet on the Income Tax, in reply to the Bishop of Llandaff. Wakefield had been a friend of Rogers's father, who speaks of

---

[1] Afterwards the sixth Duke of Bedford; father of the Lord John Russell of the Reform Bill era.

him in a letter in a preceding chapter. He had come
to London from Nottingham in 1790 to undertake the
duties of the classical professorship in the college then
just established at Hackney, of which Thomas Rogers was
chairman. He failed to agree with his colleagues, and
left the college in 1791. He continued, however, to be
one of the friends of the Rogers family, and was regarded
by Samuel Rogers as one of those —

> ' Guides of my life, Instructors of my youth,
> Who first unveiled the hallowed form of truth ; '

whom he apostrophizes in the first part of ' The Pleasures of Memory.' Gilbert Wakefield's pamphlet was as
mild as the toasts at the Fox dinner, but it seems to
have been thought that the time had come for the prosecution of some person whose position would make his
condemnation strike terror into others ; or, as Dr. Aikin
says : ' A victim to the liberty of the press, of name and
character to inspire a wide alarm, was really desired.'
Gilbert Wakefield was therefore selected for the sacrifice,
and no pains was spared to secure his conviction. He
was not attacked at once. Johnson and Jordan, the
booksellers who sold the pamphlet, were first tried, and
sentenced, — the former to a fine of fifty pounds and six
months' imprisonment; the latter to a year's confinement. Mr. Cuthell, the publisher, was also punished;
and then the blow fell on the gentle scholar and divine.
He was tried, found guilty, and sentenced to two years'
imprisonment in Dorchester jail. This fierce blow at
freedom of discussion created almost a panic. Gilbert
Wakefield's friends did all that could be done to modify
the rigor of his confinement, and Fox kept up with him
that learned correspondence which had been begun in
happier circumstances, and which was afterwards published. Many of the Whigs made Wakefield's prison
cell the object of a pious pilgrimage ; and Rogers and

his sister Sarah were among them. The utmost consideration was shown to Wakefield by his jailers, but the
imprisonment shortened his life, and he died less than
four months after his liberation in 1801.   To the end of
his life Rogers never failed to speak of him with affection and regard, and of his prosecution and sentence as
infamous.   It brought home in the strongest way to him
and to his friends the full nature of the oppression
which they held to justify the Whigs for seceding for
a time from a House of Commons which kept such a
Government in power.

In his 'Recollections' of Fox, Rogers tells the story, as
repeated by Fox in 1805, of an apparently discourteous
reply of Dr. Parr to Mackintosh.   The same story is also
told in Mr. Dyce's book.   Mr. Dyce reports Rogers as
saying that when he read to Parr the account of
O'Quigley's death — who had been hanged on Penenden
Heath for a traitorous correspondence with France —
the tears rolled down his cheeks.   His reply to Mackintosh arose out of a conversation on the subject at a
party at which many Whigs were present.   Parr said
O'Quigley was no impostor, that he died in the conviction
that the cause in which he intrigued and suffered was
a good one.   'I am hurt,' rejoined Mackintosh, 'to hear
Dr. Parr employing his great talents in defence of such
a wretch as O'Quigley, who was as bad a man as could
possibly be.'   'No, no, Jamie,' responded Dr. Parr; 'not
so bad a man as could possibly be: for recollect O'Quigley
was a priest, — he might have been a lawyer; he was an
Irishman, — he might have been a Scotchman; he was
consistent, Jamie, — he might have been an apostate.'   I
tell the story as it is given by the Rev. C. Colton in the
notes to his satire, 'Hypocrisy.'   It has no meaning,
however, apart from the explanation Colton gives and
Rogers omits, that Parr and many of Mackintosh's
friends were greatly pained at what some of them re-

garded as Mackintosh's political apostasy. Rogers has himself recorded that Mackintosh had confessed to Burke some change of view; and at a later period he tells us that Fox resented Mackintosh's acceptance of the recordership of Bombay from the then existing Government.

The slight indications all these circumstances give of Rogers's political position in the closing years of the century combine together to prove that he and his circle of intimate friends held firmly to their Whig principles, and that though he took little part in public movements, he heartily concurred with them in holding aloof from all contact or sympathy with a Government which was, as they held, betraying constitutional freedom in the house of its friends.

CHAPTER XII.

THE contrast presented by the beginning and the end of the last chapter, which opened with poetry and the praise of country life, and closed with political persecution and danger, aptly illustrates Rogers's life during these gloomy years. How completely he was able to live in his poetry, is shown by the entire absence from it of any allusion to the outer world of politics. The chief literary excitement of this period was caused by the publication of the satirical poem, 'The Pursuits of Literature,' which appeared in parts, the first in 1794, the second and third in 1796, and the fourth in 1797. There was nothing in the poem itself to call attention to it. It is a feeble imitation of Gifford. But it was made the vehicle of an immense bundle of Notes, full of personal attacks on all the chief Liberals of the time. The first part of the poem has only two hundred and fifty lines ; but there are many pages which contain but one line or two, and all the rest of the page is 'notes.' In this way the first part swelled to a volume of more than a hundred pages. The authorship of the poem was at first a mystery, and the magazines were full of speculations about it. It was at last discovered to be by T. J. Mathias. He was a friend of Rogers, though of different politics, and Rogers had a good deal of intercourse with him in succeeding years. It is a testimony

to Rogers's literary position that the political satirists
of the period usually let him alone. One of the persons
attacked in the notes was Dr. Joseph Warton, whose
'Life of Pope' was described as 'A Commonplace Book
upon Pope.' He was himself spoken of as 'drivelling
on the page of Pope;' and a dozen pages of notes were
devoted, with all the capitals and italics by which feeble
writers attempt to make their sentences emphatic; to
what was intended to be a very severe assault upon him
as a poet, a critic, and a biographer. Warton wrote to
Rogers about it, speaking of Mathias as his 'pious critic,'
but Rogers agreed with some of the criticism, as Warton
had printed some things — such as the 'Imitation of the
Second Satire of the First Book of Horace' — which Pope
had never publicly acknowledged as his own. Nothing in
later times has created quite such an excitement and hub-
bub among literary men as this book. It was an early
product of the reaction the French Revolution had produced. Scarcely a single writer who was on the Liberal
side escaped, and gross personalities were used in an
attempt to throw discredit on them. Rogers, who knew
Steevens, used to say that Steevens had said to Mathias:
'Well, since you deny the authorship of "The Pursuits of
Literature," I need have no hesitation in telling you that
the person who wrote it is a liar and a blackguard!'
Rogers one day asked Mathias whether he had written
it, and Mathias replied: 'Can you suppose that I am the
author of the poem when you are not mentioned in it?'
But some time after this Lord Bessborough, who was
getting up an illustrated edition with portraits, asked
Rogers for his portrait for the purpose. Rogers said:
'Why — there is no mention in it of me!' Lord Bessborough, however, turned to the note in which the observation is made that, 'Time was when bankers were
as stupid as their guineas could make them;' but now
Mr. Dent is a speaker, 'Sir Robert has his pencil and

22

his canvas, and Mr. Rogers dreams on Parnassus, and if I am rightly informed there is a great demand among his brethren for "The Pleasures of Memory." '

After the publication of 'An Epistle to a Friend' Rogers seems to have devoted himself to a general course of reading and to the careful study of the principles of art as applied to household furnishing. He was thinking in these years of the 'one fair asylum from the world,' the 'one chosen seat that charms with various view ;' of

> 'this calm recess, so richly fraught
> With mental light and luxury of thought;'

in which the life of the hero of the 'Epistle ' 'steals on ;' of the humble walls which, thanks to 'the faithful graver,' 'thy gallery Florence gilds,' and the low roof which 'the Vatican recalls.' His first step, however, was the taking of a course of classical literature. His health at this time was very precarious, and he seems to have suffered a good deal mentally from the gloomy aspect of the times. In London he must necessarily live among men who were absorbed in the great struggle which the Whigs were carrying on against the war and the Government. But away from London, whether he was at Margate, or at Brighton, or travelling, he put all these anxieties aside and, as his letters show, plunged into the social gayeties of the place and of the season. This, however, was not the case in the winter of 1799. In the autumn of that year his health was so delicate that Dr. Moore insisted that he should spend the winter in Devonshire. There was no obstacle to his doing so. The business in Freeman's Court was falling more and more under the management of his brother Henry, whose ability Samuel Rogers was able to trust implicitly. Henry Rogers was now five-and-twenty, and with the other partners had relieved his brother of all concern for the bank when it was needful for him to go away.

He therefore took Dr. Moore's advice, and went to winter
at Exmouth in 1799–1800.

He made this enforced stay on the Devonshire coast
a kind of studious exile. He had left school comparatively early, and had not done much classical reading.
He knew a good deal of Latin, and something of Greek,
but he had formed the desire to make himself acquainted
with the great writers of antiquity. He could not now
rub up his classics sufficiently to enable him to read
them in the original, and he consequently furnished
himself with the best English and French translations.
These translations he read with the utmost care, making
elaborate notes and criticisms upon them as he went
along. There are two volumes of a diary of his readings
which show that almost every day had its task, and that
the task was well and patiently done. Three or four
months thus spent were felt to be well spent. They
made a great addition to his knowledge, and the vantage-
ground thus gained he never permitted himself to lose.
There is no need to reproduce these diaries. One of his
notes, however, I may extract as illustrating his views.
Recording the completion of his reading of Herodotus,
Rogers writes : —

'It is with regret that I take leave of this pleasant
old man. Of his accuracy as a naturalist Boerhaave has
remarked that daily observation has confirmed almost
all he has said, and every page shows his diligence in
collecting materials. Less severe than Thucydides, he
delights in little circumstances not closely connected
with his subject, and is fond of expressing on all occasions his own thoughts and feelings. Less frequent and
prolix in his speeches, he sometimes rises into grandeur,
and particularly in the discourse of Xerxes at the Hel-
lespont. In one respect he has greatly the advantage.
Thucydides has followed the order of times, Herodotus

that of things. Perhaps his history is too much scattered, but it is written with a charming simplicity. His was the vast design of a universal history, and the Greek and the Barbarian have equal favor in his eyes. He has given us nothing, perhaps, like the oration of Pericles, or the closing scene at the siege of Syracuse; but the invasion of Scythia by Darius is incomparably simple and sublime, and perhaps no passage in any historian is so interesting as his account of the defence at Thermopylæ. The slow approach of the Persian army and that stillness of despair with which the Greeks await its arrival, make an impression on the mind which must last for life.'

Another aspect of this Exmouth life is given in the following letters : —

Samuel Rogers to Henry Rogers.

EXMOUTH, 23 Novr. '99.

'MY DEAR HENRY, — I answered your letter by return of post, and hope you received mine. I presume the business is in train, and that everything goes on to your satisfaction. If I am in the least wanted let me know, and I shall think little of the journey, — not that I am yet tired of being here, though my friend Maltby says I shall soon be. I have never, indeed, in my life spent so many solitary hours, yet perhaps have never been so busy, and can truly say I have been less alone than I have often been in the midst of society. I have read Xenophon's " Memorabilia " and history, and am now half-way on my journey through Larcher's Herodotus; and have, indeed, a course of reading for six months before me, even in my present state of life. As to my health, I think it certainly as good as at Tunbridge, though my breast at times is very painful; but I eat and sleep and enjoy myself.

My breath is rather shorter than it was, and I am a little out of humor with the roads of this country, which are very stony and admit of no pace safely but a jog-trot, which jars me. I have, however, a little bit of sandy common between me and the river, under the bank on which I live, and on that I exercise in still weather. The walk along the sands is very delightful, and continues at low water for miles under very romantic rocks. The shore is strewed with weeds and pebbles, which afford much more amusement, particularly the last, than I had apprehended. Lord Rolle's hounds are within three miles of me; I met them this morning on the Sidmouth Road, but the distance is too great for me to derive any amusement even in my way from them.

' I am much obliged to you for the newspapers, which come regularly. Indeed, I am very luxurious in that article of news, being furnished with the three evening papers regularly after sunset from the libraries. What a strange world we live in! These consuls (how they must laugh in their sleeves!) will not immediately develop their plan, whatever it may be; but it will be amusing to see what two such men, such a head and such a hand, will do if left to themselves in Europe. Before I left town I sent Maria the receipt for bread sauce. I hope Sarah has it. I have put up a few Piranesis in my room, and they please me every hour. It is odd enough that I should find two drawings hung up there of Stothard's. Upon examining them I find they are copies of two of mine by a young lady. They look very well, and I am glad to find they make such good furniture. If John should apply to you again, may I trouble you to say, as from me, to anybody, that I believe him to be sober and diligent, and in every respect qualified to make a good servant? My present man pleases me very much; he is cheerful and obliging, and much more attentive

than John. I am glad to find that Dan has settled some-
where, though I wish it had been nearer town. I hope
it will improve upon him. I suppose Bretell has acknowledged the receipt of the writings I sent him. Mr.
Jackson speaks with great respect of Mr. Towgood's
grandfather, and inquired much after his father. He
says the picture is the best Opie ever painted. I have
not yet called upon Mrs. Towgood, but certainly shall
very soon. The Exeter Theatre opened last Monday
with Reicher, the rope-dancer from Sadler's Wells. Everybody goes to see him. How long I shall stay here
I don't know. I have taken my lodgings for a month.
It is not, I think, impossible that I may fidget for a
short time a little farther westward. . . . Adieu, my
dear Henry.

'Believe me, ever yours,

'SAML. ROGERS.'

The interval between this letter and the next was one
of studious industry. The diary of his reading for these
two months fills a considerable volume. There is no
reference in it to himself nor to the society he found at
Exmouth; nothing but a careful analysis of his reading
in Xenophon, Herodotus, and Euripides, with a plunge
into Æschylus, of whom, however, he remarks: 'To me
not half so rich or forcible as Euripides. I return to him
with great pleasure.'

The new year found him still in exile, and he writes to
his sister Sarah on the 3d of January, 1800 : —

'You fear Exmouth is dull. It is very quiet, and I
can almost persuade myself I like quiet. You, perhaps,
may like to see the *dramatis personæ.* Here are Mr.
and Mrs. Stoughton from the Vale of Usk, — neighbors
of the Waddingtons, very good sort of people, with whom
I have dined more than once. If you were to ask how

we became acquainted, we none of us know. On the
first day we stared at one another, on the second we
looked sociably, on the third ditto, on the fourth ditto,
on the fifth we bowed, on the sixth spoke. This is the
history of an Exmouth acquaintance, and indeed, what
else can we do? We meet from the four quarters, and,
as our object is the same, a general sympathy leads to a
general acquaintance. Last week, on the underwalk, a
very stately old lady, with a nod and a simper, asked me
how I did, and we are now very thick: a Mrs. Chantrey,
the very Plutarch of family biography, well versed in
Leicestershire anecdotes, and very full of Jack Simpson's
wedding, which takes place this week. Some time before, on the sands, a gentleman introduced himself to
me as having seen me in town. I have no recollection of
him, but he is a great acquisition, — has travelled much,
and lived many years in Italy. His wife, Lady Charlotte Carr, is a very pleasing, sensible young woman, —
one of the Errolls. By the means of a sedan chair I
have ventured out in an evening to them. With the
Barings, a mile off, I have often dined, but my great comfort is within a door of me, by Mrs. Labouchère's fire-
side, where I generally find myself when my eyes ache
in an evening. Her cousin, Miss Stone (whose father
Mr. Raper knows as a brother director), is a very pretty
girl, and has accompanied Dolly, in the heroism of
friendship, to pass her winter in this retreat. They
decline all acquaintance, and I believe I am the only
person they see here, though they frequently visit among
the Barings. I was invited to revel out my Christmas
week at Cowley with the whole clan, but I did not venture, and rather chose (a symptom of age and dulness,
you will say) to take my flight in the sunshine of an
October morning to Plymouth, where I expected to see
some fine scenery, and, indeed, I now pronounce it the
finest thing I have seen in Devonshire. There is a walk

under a stone quarry over against Mount Edgecumbe and winding along the sea-shore towards Lord Boringdon's which is divine.'

The next letter relates to another crisis in the history of his closest friend.

S. Rogers to Richard Sharp.

'EXMOUTH, Jan. 26, 1800.

'What you sent me, my dear friend, I cannot tell; but it has done more than all your prescriptions. A few repetitions will complete the cure, and Darwin shall make a case of it.

'Your news had been, in some degree, anticipated. I had not forgot you, and I knew that the bank, by their decision, had, at all events, most effectually stepped in between you and calamity. But forgive me if I had from the first no very great faith in your predictions. I know when your courage leaves you. "Man but a rush against Othello's breast," etc. The fury of the tempest has gone over you, but it has not left you as it found you. Your consequence as a house is now more than ever established in the world; and your own individual importance is felt and acknowledged where it should be. B. admired you before, — he will now cling to you as the man who may be truly said to have given him all he possesses; and your sensations, even on that account, must be very enviable.

'A thousand thanks for your kind inquiries. I think myself much better, and mean to return among you the Stentor of clubs and the terror of all quiet people.

'Yours most affectionately,

'SAML. ROGERS.

'P. S. So the outlaw is at last dead in his den! How has he left his books?'

This reference in the postscript is to George Steevens, the editor of Shakspeare, who had died at his house at Hampstead on the 22d of January. He had been living for some years a very eccentric life, as his biographer in the 'Gentleman's Magazine' said — 'in unvisitable retirement, and seldom mixed with society, but in booksellers' shops, or the Shakspeare Gallery, or the morning *conversazione* of Sir Joseph Banks.' Rogers and Sharp, however, met him occasionally there or elsewhere, and profited by his amusing conversation. He was one of those veterans of the literary profession to whom younger aspirants for fame look up, and whose talk of the great men among whom they lived has the most lively interest to the men who are following them along the toilsome way. One of Steevens's eccentricities was to go down to his printers at one in the morning and in the chambers of Isaac Reed, which were kept open for him, to read his proofs and get all his corrections ready while the compositors were asleep. He left his books, with one or two special exceptions, to his niece, Miss Steevens.

Richard Sharp's reply to this letter is lost. The next is from Rogers.

Samuel Rogers to Richard Sharp.

'EXMOUTH, 18 Feby. [1800].

'MY DEAR FRIEND, — Your last letter gave me great pleasure. It was not, indeed, emblazoned like Bonaparte's, nor like Lady J.'s scented with odor of roses, but it whispered of health and leisure and peace of mind. With a permit from his Maj^ys Comm^n I would send you a few bottles of our Exmouth *Elixir*, — for an idea of its effects consult Saint Leon, an authentic narrative far better conceived than executed. Moore's novel has not yet arrived here, though hourly expected. It travels, I fear, with the rapidity of a flying wagon.

'Our sun is not much obliged to you for your sus-
picions. He descends, I can assure you, every evening
into the groves of Mamhead.

'Exmouth, I fancy, is no longer the Exmouth you
saw. The walk on Chapel Hill is still the same. The
other to the bench round a tree has walked *itself* off. I
am sorry to hear you have had no vigor to write. Have
you imbibed Gray's notion of that faculty?[1] I fear he
was right. A sight of your old papers, however, will
surely awake it. As to myself, I expect soon to be
exhibited as a most extraordinary vegetable. I have
once or twice attempted to flower. You never have.
For an account of my last effort and of *yours*, see the
"Anti-Jacobin Review" for January, under the article
of "Reviewers Reviewed." Mr. Polwhele is the writer.
I have also much to say of Larcher: Homer I defer
till I can procure a French translation of which I have
a high idea. The three tragedians I have just done, —
and done well; as for Euripides, he has turned my head.
I wonder whether anybody ever read him before. I
fancy not. .

'Mr. Jackson is gone to Bath. He desired to be mentioned particularly to you before he went. He is so
altered that my servant was shocked when he saw him
last week. The last lines he wrote me are very characteristic. Will they be the last? He says so, but I will
not look that way.

'My verse is neither *idle* nor *active*. Jackson threw
a slur upon it some weeks ago, and it roused me to in-

[1] Rogers probably refers to what Gray says in a letter to Dr. Whar-
ton : 'I by no means pretend to inspiration, but yet I affirm that the
faculty in question is by no means voluntary. It is the result (I
suppose) of a certain disposition of mind, which does not depend on
one's self, and which I have not felt this long time. You that are a
witness how seldom this spirit has moved me in my life may easily
give credit to what I say.'

credible exertions for four-and-twenty hours; but the fit went off and left me languid and listless. In solitude I can conceive, but I cannot execute, I cannot finish.

'The life I have led among *those old Fograms* — the Grecians — has thrown me into a singular state of mind, not altogether unpleasing but very ill-suited to that gallipot style of painting which I have been accustomed to, and which I fear the public require.

'When you see G. P. — you are now, I suppose, properly purified and are not to be burned by Act of Parliament like the ships from Mogador[1] — pray thank him in my name for an act of friendship he has lately done me. I think myself particularly obliged to him, not so much for the thing itself, though that was something, as for the *manner* in which he did it, — a circumstance which I am persuaded is always the case with him.

'By the way, of Manchester, Mr. Baring, who called upon me yesterday, says Jackson talks of going on to Manchester to consult Ferriar,[2] if the Bath waters should not relieve him.

'I have not seen one of the Exeter wits, though I have received an indirect application to become an honorary member of their club, — a thing which I rather like, and have consented to. Polwhele has been expelled from it. Adieu, my dear friend.

'In return for these salt-water effusions I shall expect

---

[1] The ships — the 'Aurora,' the 'Mentor' and the 'Lark' — were not burned by Act of Parliament, but by an Order in Council. The goods on board were regarded as likely to communicate infection, and the vessels and cargoes were destroyed. This proceeding was the subject of a royal message to the House of Commons in February, 1800, which was referred to a Select Committee, and £41,400 was voted, on the Report of that committee, as compensation.

[2] John Ferriar, M.D., was an eminent physician in Manchester, who wrote several medical books, besides 'Illustrations of Sterne,' and 'An Essay towards a Theory of Apparitions.' He died in 1815, at the age of fifty-one.

a long and succinct narrative of all your whereabouts from his Majesty the King of Clubs,[1] to the dirty drap in Covent Garden. I am inclined to think very favorably of myself just now, though I dare not yet think of returning to you.

'Ever yours,

'S. R.

'P. S. The door opens, and "Mordaunt" enters. Moore has written me a long letter to prove that "Pizarro" is Sherry's *chef-d'œuvre*. I shall draw my pen against him in a day or two.'

It would be interesting to have Rogers's reply to Dr. Moore's absurd contention that 'Pizarro' — a mere translation and adaptation from Kotzebue — was Sheridan's *chef-d'œuvre*. It was produced at Drury Lane in 1799, and had considerable success. Dr. Moore himself was falling into the feebleness of age. 'Mordaunt,' which arrived in Rogers's room as he was penning his postscript, was the old novelist's last work. Mrs. Barbauld describes it as a very languid production. Moore asked Rogers for criticism, and Rogers had difficulty in evading the necessity of giving it. Meanwhile he writes again to Richard Sharp : —

S. Rogers to Richard Sharp.

'EXMOUTH, Feb. 5, 1800.

'MY DEAR FRIEND, — Your kind and entertaining letter was dropped by some sylph or sylphid upon my pillow this morning. You and they have my best thanks. Your account of yourself I don't like, but hope you are by this time able to visit the den at Hampstead. Pray let me know if it is yet unbarred, as I shall certainly

---

[1] The celebrated Club bearing this name was founded at the house of Mackintosh in 1801. See next chapter.

set off if it is. Now its tenant is dead we may see it in
safety. The nondescript in his *nest*, hard by, drew his
visage, I believe. Moore is, indeed, very severe upon me.
I should like to give him a *taste* of my banishment. I
hope you have spent your winter pleasantly. As for me,
I leave my time to spend itself, and often for the hour
together watch the ferry-boat under my windows, thinking of nothing less than the oxen and sheep and farmer's
wives that are in it. For the first six weeks the east
wind was here, and I can assure you tolerably venomous,
though I flatter myself less mortal in his bite than with
you. I was literally in a state of siege, the air was so
full of blue devils I could distinguish nothing, and my
world was contracted to the size of the carpet. At that
time, I fear, my health greatly suffered. I read for once
in my life, and though I felt no great inconvenience
at the time I have declined almost ever since. I am
now, however, rallying a little. The sun shines, and the
sky and sea contend which is the bluest. This morning
the wind serves, and our little fleet of coasting vessels is
dropping out to sea. The air is warm as summer, and
yet that Inquisitor in the Welsh wig sits coolly down in
the bustle of Bond Street and condemns me to linger on
till May. The very thought is frightful. I *did* hope to
return by the Ides of March.

'Jackson is, I fear, in a bad way. For the first two
months I spent half my time with him, and his kindness
has affected me not a little. Among other proofs of his
regard he has requested me to take charge of his papers,
and I shall not soon forget the manner in which he put
out his hand on the occasion. Ever since I came into
this country he has faded very visibly. In a letter which
I have this instant received from him he says : "I cannot walk a hundred yards, nor speak half as many words
without fatigue. Sleep and I are upon such bad terms
that three successive nights I have passed without clos-

ing my eyes for a single moment. This state of affairs cannot last long, and I wish for a speedy change one way or other." I do, indeed, fear that my trust will soon devolve to me, — a trust which he had the kindness to say he had long wished to leave to me. You can easily conceive how interesting he is at this moment. His faculties are unimpaired, but his countenance has lost its youthful character. Adieu! The annals of Exmouth I must reserve for my next.

'Ever yours,

'S. R.

'Shall I send you this bunch of primroses? I gathered them out of the hedge just now. How sweet they are! My best regards to B. My imagination already feasts on the splendors of the Villa Boddingtonini.'

The Jackson spoken of in the above letters was the eminent composer of Church music. One of the memorable events of this long winter exile at Exmouth was that Rogers made the acquaintance of this interesting and remarkable musician. He probably carried with him an introduction to Jackson from Sheridan or his wife. Jackson was then seventy years of age, and was in ill-health. He was fond of talking about his early days, and Rogers has made in his Commonplace Book a sketch of Jackson's life with extracts from his diary. Jackson was the son of an Exeter tradesman. At seventeen he went to London, riding on horseback as far as to Winchester, and from thence in the Winchester stage, in which he was robbed. Arrived at the Belle Sauvage in the dark, he followed the porter through Ludgate to the Saracen's Head in Friday Street — a Devonshire house — where he had a wet bed in the attic. In the morning he called on a tradesman in Watling Street with a letter of credit from his father. The tradesman was

collecting orders in the country, and was not expected
home for three months; but Jackson was accommodated
with two guineas by another person, to whom he was
afterwards able to show his gratitude. He studied
music under Dr. Travers, of the Chapel Royal. One of
his recollections was of seeing the rebel lads executed
on Tower Hill. He returned to Exeter to teach music,
and was engaged as organist at the Cathedral. His
compositions were popular, and he became famous. He
composed his music, as he told Rogers, in the organ loft
'during the intervals of the music,' as he characteris-
tically called all the other parts of the service. In these
'intervals of the music,' when less musical mortals were
praying, or listening to the lessons or the sermon, Jackson occupied himself in writing original music with a
pencil. He also composed at home for an hour after
his family were in bed at night. He told Rogers some
curious stories which give further musical views of the
relation of music to the service. A man came on foot
from Honiton to request him to play 'They that in
Ships,' having heard it in the church there. Unable to
refuse him, and ashamed to play it himself, as he had
played it so often, Jackson left the church and got
another to play it. The man came again and again;
Jackson did not know him, but he always played 'They
that in Ships' whenever this auditor was there. 'It is
for those people,' said he, 'that we compose and play,
and they must have their way.' He was once struck
with the fixed attitude of a wagoner's boy at church.
One day an unknown person grasped his arm at the
entrance of Willis's concert room and whispered 'But
a leaf in a whirlwind.' Jackson was a great admirer of
Defoe, and Rogers thought his imitation of him, 'The
Royalist,' full of invention and written with a charming
simplicity. Jackson was an intimate friend of the
Sheridans. He had known Mrs. Sheridan before her

marriage. He spoke of Mrs. Sheridan's countenance when singing as like nothing earthly. When he called on her in town after her marriage she entreated him to sing and play with her, and he did so for three hours. It was so unlike anything she had known for so long a time that she was exceedingly grateful. Sheridan had no ear or soul for music. His son Tom flourishing over a quire of paper before breakfast, and burning it sheet by sheet, drinking the cream and throwing wet wafers against the wall, was the picture, Jackson said, of a spoiled child. Jackson wished Rogers to remember that he looked forward with great composure to his end, though he could have wished for eleven years more, which would about suffice for finishing what he had in hand. 'Sitting with him one day on the castle walls he drew a fresh elm-leaf from his purse and said he had every year renewed it from a tree near Bristol,' which had for him some tender associations. Jackson died in July, 1803, and, as a token of his regard for Rogers, left to him his copies of the first edition of 'Paradise Lost,' and of the 'Faerie Queen.'

The further story of this visit to Exmouth with pleasant sketches of society at the close of the last century is contained in letters to Richard Sharp, the first of which bears witness to the revived buoyancy of Rogers's spirits in prospect of spring.

Samuel Rogers to Richard Sharp.

'EXMOUTH, March 2 [1800].

'MY DEAR FRIEND, — Your gossiping letter possessed in my eyes the elegance of a Pliny and the grace of a Sévigné. I do not so much wish you "to turn a period as to tell the news." But what have I in return to give you ? Alas, the annals of Exmouth are scanty indeed ! Never has it known so dull a winter. But something

must be done for its credit, and shall I describe the
evening parties where scandal and egg-wine circulate
hissing hot, or shall I provoke your envy by describing
myself "on the yellow sands," with a girl under each
arm, a blonde and a brunette, the last lively and pretty,
a daughter of your banker Stone, the first pronounced
and very truly by Lavater an angel on earth, a daughter
of Charles Baring, unseen by your profane eyes? No,
I will shift the scene, and describe the men who assemble almost every day. Mr. Acland, the uncle of Lady
Harriet, the heroine in Burgoyne's expedition, an old
man with very amiable and elegant manners, who enter-
tains us continually in his own beautiful little cottage covered with myrtles, the lion of Exmouth. Mr. Ducarell,
the oracle and friend of Francis in the east, a most
entertaining fellow, the Lucullus of the village. His
chauffoir and silver dishes eclipse us all. Mr. Anderson, the friend and fellow-traveller of George Matthew,
a very accomplished man, of whom I had heard much.
He is generally in my house every day. These with an
old General and Admiral who have both seen service,
and a Colonel Oakes, an invalid from India whom Anderson calls "The Impregnable," having never, he says,
laughed but once in his life, at some joke of mine, —
these make up our little party. Who should be my next-
door neighbor but an old flame of mine, a daughter of
Sir Fras. Baring's! Her husband, a partner in Hope's
house, is in the West Indies. She is here in a very
retired state with two beautiful little children, and
her friend and coz., Miss Stone, and when my eyes are
weary I generally find myself in an evening by her fire-
side. The last Bulletin from Bath is favorable, but I
have great fears. On Thursday I am to be exhibited
at the Exeter Club. My whole length over the door, as
it is market day, will, of course, attract numbers. Sir
Jno. Kennaway has written from Bath to express his

regret that he cannot be there! But it is to be a full day. You will not forget to pray for me; I fear it will bring on a relapse. As to my health, I am certainly better, and begin to build castles, — a good symptom you will say. But I fear I am condemned to a vagabond life, and if not soon re-established shall apply to the Privy Council for leave to visit Lisbon or Madeira. Under which of my titles I shall travel I cannot yet say, but I shall certainly go *incog.* In any of your evening circuits (for you are now a thoroughbred rout-man) have you met with the King and Queen? Did they look in at Will' Smith's the evening you were there? As they have begun with Lady Cardigan, I shall expect to pop upon *them and the girls* two or three times at least in the course of an evening.

'Pray write, and have no scruples on the head of expense, as we have *no taxes* to pay this year.

'Ever yours,

'S. ROGERS.'

Rogers had meanwhile written to Dr. Moore about 'Mordaunt,' and had made a rather feeble effort to escape the necessity of expressing to his choleric friend and physician his opinion of the book. Other people, ladies, had wanted to read it, and he had been obliged to let it go before he had done more than read the first volume. The doctor saw through the friendly subterfuge, and wrote angrily : —

'WOODSTOCK ST., March 3, 1800.

'If you had written to me that Lady Errol, etc., had all been applying to you for "Mordaunt" but without effect until you had finished him yourself, it would have been more flattering than that you had yielded him entirely up, and allowed those females to have their wicked will of him when you yourself had only labored through

the first volume. You do not deal so with the *works* of
Lady Jersey. When you write poetry you can praise the
author from the works, and the works from the author, —
e. g. Lady Jersey and her daughters. Well! since you
have begun without flattery, pray continue in the same
style, and let me have your *real* notion of the whole.
Don't be afraid of finding fault; as your friend Dr.
Fretful[1] says, — "I like it."

' . . . remain quietly in Devonshire till the month of
May, and then come quietly to London, where we shall be
very happy to find you in far better case than when you
left us.

'Another expedition is going forward. What interests
me more, I am sure my son will be of it. I am kept
very uneasy about that young man; they continually pick
him out for new dangers.

'The story of the Russians *not* being recalled, proves
not to be true. I am assured they are on their march
back. I have a suspicion that Bonaparte spread the
rumor of their being to act against France merely to
promote his vast requisition of men and money for the
next campaign.'

The order to remain at Exmouth till May reduced
Rogers almost to despair. In the next letter to Richard
Sharp there is a further glimpse of Jackson : —

'EXMOUTH, March 28, 1800.

'MY DEAR FRIEND, — If you had read my letter attentively (it must long ago have experienced the fate of
the Alexandrian Library) you might perhaps have seen
something which might have led you to suspect that I
did enjoy the pleasure of looking into a smiling and
open face. But your eyes were dazzled by the long and

---

[1] Richard Cumberland, the Sir Fretful Plagiary of Sheridan's
' Critic.'

splendid list of "Admirals, Generals, Colonels, Baronets, and Clubs," — a list which makes me think it was you who gave rise to the report of poor Horatia Clifford's hunting with *men*. It may relieve you in some degree to learn — that the Club I have never attended, the Baronet I have never seen, the Colonel is sick, the General gone, and the Admiral dead.   .

'Jackson came home last week to die. His legs are swelled to a dreadful size, and his dearest friends are denied access to him. I rode over to Exeter. the other day, and near the Cathedral met a chair curtained close, followed by a lady in a veil. On my way back (I had spent five melancholy minutes with his poor wife) I looked up and saw his tall and ghastly figure on the lawn before Mount Radford, whither he had been carried once more to look on sunshine and verdure.

'I pushed my horse on, and rode home to pass my solitary evening as gayly as I could. Indeed, I do not deserve your envy, and could you have seen me under all my infirmities of mind and body, you would not have written the letter you did. I pass days and days with no human intercourse. But I need not describe my life — you cannot, I hope, conceive it — you have never sat over your melancholy embers as a winter's evening drew on, and heard the gun of distress fired in the offing, and reverberated among the dismal moors and hills which abound in this country.

'One gleam of pleasure, however, I did experience last week. I owed it to the circuit, nor will I ever forget my obligation to him who paid me the visit, even tho' he should become a Secretary of State.

'I am much obliged to you for your verses; but if they had been better, I think I should have preferred a . little more of your own prose.

'I rejoice to hear of Combe's escape from his cell. He will now see more of his friends. If you should visit

him again, pray remember me very particularly to him.
His name stands very high in this country.[1]

'Adieu, my dear friend! In a few weeks when *I*
also proem my enlargement, I shall certainly visit you
in your *Apollo*, and criticise your viands and liquors.
In the mean time believe me to be,

'Yours most affect'y.,

'S. R.

' "The Ghost-seer" has greatly disappointed me. We
had already read the best part of it.'

A day or two after this another letter from Dr. Moore
brought his long correspondence with one of his oldest
and earliest literary friends to its close.

'WOODSTOCK ST., April 2, 1800.

'I dined a few days since at your friend Boddington's; Sharp was there, and Tuffin, and Johnson the
banker, — all men who mingle knowledge of business
and of the world with extensive reading. Men who

---

[1] William Combe, the author of the 'Diaboliad' and afterwards of
'The Tour of Dr. Syntax in Search of the Picturesque, was frequently
in prison for debt. In his earlier days he moved in good society, and
was recognized as a literary man of brilliant powers and promise. He
was one day visiting Uvedale Price at Foxley, when Mr. St. John
(author of a play called 'Mary Queen of Scots' in which Mrs. Siddons
used to act), who was also staying in the house, missed some money.
Uvedale Price suspected Combe of taking it and gave him a hint to
cut short his visit. Combe took the hint, and asked whether they
were thenceforth to be friends or acquaintances. 'Acquaintances,'
said Price, and Combe went away. Long afterwards he met Price and
Rogers together in Leicester Square. They both spoke to Combe, but
from that time he avoided Rogers. He wrote the 'Letters of the late
Lord Lyttelton,' which were published after Lord Lyttelton's death;
and the 'Letters supposed to have passed between Sterne and Eliza'
were by him. He told Rogers that it was with him, and not with
Sterne, that Eliza was in love, and that he once had an intrigue with
her at Brighton. He died in 1823.

derive their knowledge from books alone are more apt
to speak pedantically, and argue arrogantly, and often
absurdly.   I never before was in company with Bryan
Edwards.[1] I thought him a very sensible and entertaining man ; but there is an acumen in Sharp's observations
which pierces every topic he handles.   He showed me a
letter from you; it was a little on the plaintive : to remove the impression this made on him, I assured him
that you sometimes assumed that style because you
know how to be pathetic even when in good spirits,
and that when you were in the most cheerful mood, I
was certain you could write a delightful poem on the
pleasures of melancholy.[2]

'Your having lost no ground during a winter so prevalent in east winds, forms a strong presumption in my
mind, that on the whole you are better, and that this
will be apparent to all your friends and even to yourself,
who are not always your own friend, in the course of
this summer. . . .

'A rumor prevails that the French and Spanish fleet
with a considerable number of troops are ready to sail
from Brest, — perhaps this may be done merely to retard
our expedition; it seems already to have had the effect.
But if the enemy's fleet actually escape from Brest, the
troops we had destined for the Mediterranean will prob-

---

[1] Bryan Edwards, M. P.   He died in July, 1800.

[2] Is this the origin of the lines which have been sometimes attributed to Byron, and which appear in Rogers's poems under the heading
'To ——— '?

> 'Go, — you may call it madness, folly;
>   You shall not chase my gloom away.
> There's such a charm in melancholy
>   I would not, if I could, be gay.

> 'Oh, if you knew the pensive pleasure
>   That fills my bosom when I sigh,
> You would not rob me of a treasure
>   Monarchs are too poor to buy!'

ably be ordered to Ireland.   My son might have gone in
a most advantageous situation to the East Indies, — he
has no taste for voluptuous living, and, what is still
rarer, none for making a fortune.   When he understood
that Sir Charles Stewart had expressed a strong inclination to have him on the expedition which he is to command, he preferred that.   For my part I heartily wish
they had allowed him to remain in England during this
summer, which will be a most anxious one to Mrs.
Moore and me.   My son cannot add to his military
reputation in any subordinate command.   If ever he be
intrusted with a supreme command he may. . . .

  ' I now conclude with a truth, which I hope will afford
me pleasure to the end of my life : I am with great
esteem,

' Your affectionate friend,

' J. MOORE.'

The end of Dr. Moore's energetic life was not far off
when this letter was written.   He did not live to see his
eldest son, Sir John Moore, the hero of Corunna, intrusted with the supreme command in which, as Dr.
Moore expected, he added to his military reputation.
Dr. Moore's health was declining, and he retired to a
house at Richmond, conscious that his work was done.
He sank gradually, and died on the 21st January, 1802,
in the 73d year of his age.   This is the date given in
the memoir by Dr. Anderson prefixed to the collected
edition of Dr. Moore's works, published in 1820.   But a
letter from his son James to Rogers dated the 23d of
February announces that his father's death took place
on the previous Sunday, which would be the 21st of
February.   He left behind him two comedies, with the
direction that they should be submitted to Rogers and
Sharp, and that their opinion should be taken as to the
propriety of making them public or suppressing them.

'My father,' says Mr. James Moore, 'entertained the highest opinion of your taste, and in giving your judgment on the works, you must only consider his fame.' The comedies were never published.

Here is one of Mr. Gilpin's letters received in this spring: —

Rev. William Gilpin to S. Rogers.

'FROM MY COUCH, the 13th of April, 1800.

'I left you, my dear sir, contemplating from the shores of Devonshire the beautiful moving pictures of the Channel. What hath since become of you I know not; and am obliged to my friend Cadell to direct these my inquiries after you. Indeed, I have not thought of my friends these several months so much as I ought, having concentrated my thoughts perhaps too much within myself. Some months ago I hurt one of my legs, which hath given me a good deal of trouble. Both my legs are very old; but one, I think, is more crazy than the other, and this was the leg to which I gave offence by neglecting a small scratch which it received just in the part where the great Achilles was wounded. This example, together with that of my friend Mason, might have instructed me better, but I was stout, and continued walking about till the pain became more than I could well bear. I was then obliged to call in a surgeon, who threw me immediately on my couch, and told me if I had walked about much longer he could not have answered for the consequence. He then crammed me with bark and drenched me with wine, and by the help of poultices, bandages, and other surgical means, he hath at length (by the goodness of God) set me upon my legs — but without the permission to use them. In a few days, however, he promises me the use of them. In the mean time I would have you to know that — altho'

I was never imprisoned in like manner before, so far as I remember, in my whole life — I have behaved, I hope, very well under my confinement. I have always spoken kindly to my wife and pleasantly to my servants; and hope, indeed, upon the whole, I have gotten some credit in my family for my behavior.

'Now I know you have been criticising all this egotistical narrative, but I beg you to consider how unjustly. When you go to a shop, and inquire for a piece of homespun, and they ask you for it the price of the finest broadcloth, you have reason to complain; but when you are charged only the price of homespun you ought to be content. Now I ask you as the price of my egotistical narrative only another egotistical narrative in return. What have you then to complain of? Go to, then, and pay me honestly the price I set on my goods. Let me know where you have been, what you have been about, and how you do since I left you on the coast of Devonshire. I had, however, one more reason for my egotistical narrative, but I throw it into the bargain, as I conceive you will not purchase it, but with the levity of other young men will throw it behind you. It is to conjure you, when you come to the age of 76, to pay great attention to any hurt, however slight, you may receive upon your legs. Whether it be scratch, titter, pimple, itching, gnat-bite, pin-prick, cut, bruise, or whatever it is, never lose sight of it till it is fairly gone. Now this piece of experience, which has cost me several pounds, I give you for nothing; and yet I fear you will hardly even return me thanks for it. Tell me whether you have anything on the anvil. *You* can never put me into such a distressful circumstance as I was lately placed in. A friend sent me some of his verses to look over. I did not like his verses so well as I liked himself, but as I know poets are an irritable race I durst not tell him so. I gently told him he had put them into very

unfortunate hands, for the Muses and I had not been on
visiting terms these many years. I have not yet vented
my wrath at not finding any remarks of yours among my
papers; but I apprehend, if I pressed the matter, you
would give me some such answer as I gave my friend.
Mrs. Gilpin joins with me in our best respects; and to
your sister, if she is with you.

> 'Your very affectionate
> 'WILL. GILPIN.'

Rogers came back to London after his stay at Exmouth
greatly improved in health and spirits. He had added
something to his store of knowledge as well as to his
fund of health and energy. The two short pieces entitled 'From Euripides,' in his poems, are signs of the
mingled influences of his love of that poet and of the
exquisite country in which he read him : —

> 'There is a streamlet issuing from a rock.
> The village girls, singing wild madrigals,
> Dip their white vestments in its waters clear,
> And hang them to the sun. There first I saw her.
> Her dark and eloquent eyes, mild, full of fire,
> 'T was heaven to look upon; and her sweet voice,
> As tunable as harp of many strings,
> At once spoke joy and sadness to my soul.'

> 'Dear is that valley to the murmuring bees.
> The small birds build there; and, at summer noon,
> Oft have I heard a child, gay among flowers,
> As in the shining grass she sat concealed,
> Sing to herself.'

Richard Sharp was at this time settling in that lovely
district of Kent which is now forever associated with his
name. It is not certain when he acquired Fredley Farm,
where he so often in later days entertained statesmen
and orators, poets and dramatists, and the chief of human

kind; but in this year he was at least looking forward to the purchase. Here is a short letter from Rogers, which illustrates his mood at this period as well as the close connection between the two friends : —

S. Rogers to Richard Sharp.

‘ 8 Aug., 1800.

‘ In the hurry of pleasure, alas, my dear friend, how we speak by rote! At least I do, for I am never so inclined to be serious or melancholy as at a party of pleasure. But to the purpose : I shall be very glad once more to attend you to Mickleham, and will be at the foot of London Bridge to-morrow at one o'clock with my leathern trunk. Whether curricle or gig or chaise will be there in waiting I care not, so as you do not fail me.
‘ Ever yours,

‘S. R.’

The next letter seems to indicate that the purchase had been made.

S. Rogers to Richard Sharp.

‘BUXTON, Sepr. 11, 1800.

‘ Let me wish you joy, my dear friend. The work has been yours, but you shall not keep the reward to yourself. I will also participate in the pleasure, though but an idle spectator of another's exertions. You are indeed to be envied. In a picturesque view the grandest approach to the metropolis will now excite new sensations in your breast ; and, should you ever, like Combe, visit the chapel, the evening hymn will lose none of its sweetness by the recollection of having added a voice to the choir. As for myself, I have been wandering, like a perturbed spirit, from place to place, and in less than a fortnight shall return whence I came. You ask me if I am already fascinated. I have been, more than once, since we parted, but the ladies, alas! were preoccupied. At Matlock, where I waited in vain for the travellers from the North Pole, I passed several pleasant hours with Burgh, the friend of Mason. I am now waiting for letters at a place which, like the *caravanserai* in the desert, derives much of its beauty from the surrounding desolation. . . . I was much concerned to see in the papers the loss Mrs. S. has sustained.

'Adieu! and believe me ever yours,

'S. R.

'Pray tell Maltby that my Lord A., an old friend of his and mine, did him the honor to make many inquiries after him yesterday.'

In the autumn he was again at Brighton, but meanwhile he had written to Gilpin giving an account of himself to which his venerable friend sent a characteristic answer.

Rev. W. Gilpin to S. Rogers.

'VICAR's HILL, Jan. 23, 1801.

'And so, my dear sir, you now think you have made an honorable amends for all the trouble you have given me. I heard last of you from the coast of Devonshire; and hearing nothing of you for months afterwards, I wrote to Cadell. Cadell knew nothing of you. I desired Mrs. Oviatt to inquire of some of her correspondents in London about you. I could learn nothing: nor, in fact, had heard a syllable, till a few days ago you came dancing in, with all the festive confidence of a man who had done nothing amiss. "I have been in the North — I have been in Wales — and I am now at Brighton." And pray, why could you not have told me this, or a part of it, a year ago? I have another quarrel with you. When you write a letter in answer to one you have received a year or two before, never refer to any part of that letter unless you know the writer keeps a copy of it; but write *de novo*. For want of this caution I have been puzzled with several passages in your letter referring to things now totally forgotten. Pray, did I ever break your shins? You seem to allude to some transaction of that kind; but I remember nothing about it. If I did, it must certainly come under the head of casualties. But my wrath is now appeased. I shake hands with you; and all is well.

'Your epic, which you mention so enigmatically that I hardly know whether you are in jest or earnest, reminds me of an anecdote of Dr. Brown, author of the famous "Estimate;" though I think I have seen it in some memoirs of him *in print*. Bishop Warburton (whose practice, I have heard, it was, to write civil letters, and do civil things, to ingenious young men to 'list them into his service) put into Brown's hands an epic poem which had been *planned* by Pope. The story, I think, was the *discovery* of Britain by one of the heroes who had escaped from Troy. Brown finished three or four books. He was very intimate with my father, though but an unpleasant man to live with; and I remember he showed me his first book when I was a lad at Oxford. At the pillars of Hercules his hero makes a pause on entering the great ocean. But alas! there his muse, like yours, forsook him. So that, it seems, the Atlantic is the gulf of epic poetry. Homer prudently kept snug in the Ægean, and Virgil in the Mediterranean. If they had ventured through the Straits, they had probably been drowned, like Brown and you.

'In return for your very affecting story of the poor girl who was killed by the fall of a wall, I'll tell you one which has lately given me much pleasure. In this parish lives a man of the name of Harnett. He lives by fishing and dragging for oysters. His son, a lad under age, used to assist him. As they were fishing out at sea, about 7 or 8 years ago, a man-of-war's boat rowed briskly up to them, and carried off the lad. He was very affectionate, and, of course, disconsolate. However, finding there was no remedy, he took the press-money, and it was some comfort to him that he could send his poor parents a guinea out of it. In the mean time he bestirred himself, and became one of the best seamen in the ship; insomuch that the captain took notice of him, made him first his cockswain, and afterwards raised him to be master's mate. He had a little ambition to climb on; but, unfortunately, he had no friend to whom he could apply but the old minister of his parish. With him he had made a great interest; for he had been continually sending money out of his own little stock to his poor parents, — not less, I believe, on the whole, than £30, for a good part of it passed through my hands. I was much disposed, therefore, to serve him; and was more fortunate than I expected. I have a slight acquaintance with Sir Andrew Hammond, Controller of the Navy, to whom I wrote in favor of my friend. Sir Andrew immediately sent for him to be examined, and being pleased, I suppose, with the young man's sense, modesty, and skill in his profession, sent him back to Spithead; and almost before he got there sent him a commission to be master of the "Harpy," sloop-of-war, in which situation he tells me he is quite happy. He sent me a letter of thanks, and I sent him a letter of good advice. About a fortnight ago the "Harpy," lying at the mouth of our river, waiting to convoy a Lisbon fleet, Mr. Harnett came on shore to visit his parents. He visited me also; and instead of coming to the kitchen door with a thrum-capon, a basket of oysters on his shoulder, and a pair of shoes which were neither akin to each other nor to his feet, he was introduced into the parlor — dressed in a handsome uniform,

and with a hat cocked as bravely as the best of them.
You don't mention your health. The book I have not
heard of. Mrs. Gilpin joins in kind remembrance to
your sister and you:

　　　　'With, dear Sir,
　　　　　　'Your sincere and affect*
　　　　　　　　'WILL. GILPIN.'

A letter from Rogers to his sister gives an account
of what he was doing at Brighton in the first few weeks
of the nineteenth century.

Samuel Rogers to Sarah Rogers.

　　　　　　　　　　'BRIGHTON, 19 Jany., 1801.

'By an unfortunate mistake at the Post Office I did
not get my dear Sarah's letter till this morning. After
dining with Mrs. Mostyn (my old friend Cecilia Thrale)
I have resisted the temptation of an assembly at Lord
Tankerville's, and have come home to converse a few
minutes with her who, I may almost say, is to me more
out of sight and less out of mind than anybody I know
in this world. I am now, however, happy to think that
I shall very soon see her and hear her, and can even
number the days of my absence from her. Brighton is,
as you imagine, my dear Sarah, still very gay, and you
will believe it when I tell you that I have for this very
day four dinner and three evening invitations. Indeed,
I am in great danger of being spoiled; and by nobody
so much as yourself, in which you would be particularly
blamable, if you had not yourself basked in that kind
of sunshine without injuring your complexion by it, the
complexion of your mind, I mean. Yesterday I spent the
day very pleasantly with a large family of the Casama-
jors, who form a concert by themselves, — the girls and
their brothers ranging round the harpsichord and singing
glees and anthems with a decorum and a harmony which

would delight you.   The eldest son officiated at Peters-
burg for Lord Whitworth with great credit to himself.
As to Mrs. Pigou, who is my great patroness here, she is
delightful.   I must introduce her to you.   Not less so
are two of Lady Tankerville's daughters, tho' almost
children, whose ambition it is to retire into some cottage
and enjoy each other's society for life, — *à la mode de
Llangollen*.   Here is also one of Mrs. Maltby's sisters
who was always a great favorite of mine.   She is now,
alas! married to a man of large fortune, but who is well
worthy of her.   The ladies here are in general above par,
but the men as much below it.   The Ellises are here,[1]
but live very privately.   I am their only guest.   Here
are also the Miss Thrales, Mrs. Piozzi's daughters.   From
some accident I have never been acquainted with them,
though they accuse me of having shunned them.   They
are very elegant, sensible women, and are a great addition to the society here.   Mrs. Pigou, the Thrales,
the Tankervilles, and two or three others meet at one
another's houses every day — I should say every evening
— and the harp and piano generally mingle their voices

---

[1] George Ellis, F. R. S., F. S. A.; died 10 April, 1815, aged seventy;
wrote in 'The Rolliad' the invective against Pitt: —

> 'Pert without fire, without experience sage.'

In 1790 published 'Specimens of Early English Poetry.'   Wrote on the
formation and progress of the English language.   Went to Lille with
Lord Malmesbury in 1797; changed his politics and joined the 'Anti-
Jacobin.   He was much beloved by his friends.   Scott addresses him
in the introduction to the fifth canto of Marmion: —

> ' Thou who canst give to lightest lay
> An unpedantic moral gay,
> Nor less the dullest theme bid flit
> On wings of unexpected wit;
> In letters as in life approved,
> Example honored and beloved,
> Dear Ellis! to the bard impart
> A lesson of thy magic art.'

with ours in the conversation, and make it very pleasant. I should not omit General Forbes, the General of this district, a very amiable, pleasant old man who has seen a great deal of service in both hemispheres. He goes up to town this week to kiss hands on his promotion, and I believe I shall accompany him on Wednesday. Adieu, my dear Sarah! Give my love to all, and believe me,

'Ever yours,

'S. R.

'Among the persons of the drama I must not omit my old friend Nicholls [1] (the M. P.), who is here with his family. They have retired into the country, and two months here are given them in lieu of a journey to London!!! With regard to the christening, I do believe I should have been present if it had come to me in time. You will shake your head and say I am much obliged to the Post Office for saving me from a dilemma. I wrote to Mr. Gilpin last week, and mentioned you particularly in it. Indeed, I could not do otherwise in answer to your inquiries. Pray tell Maria that I deserved more than an intention to write a postscript from her. I am glad Mr. Raper has dismissed his doctors. With regard to the tragedy I can only tell you it rests on newspaper authority. I must have written it in my sleep; and what has become of it I cannot tell. If it should be found under the pillow, you shall have the first sight of it, a perusal I am sure you would not endure. I am sorry to hear such tidings of Quarry Bank. I am sure I should soon die there of a nervous fever.'

[1] Mr. Nicholls was member for Tregony.

24

CHAPTER XIII.

'The King of Clubs.' — 'The Bachelor.' — Rogers Building. —Paris in 1802. — Letters to Henry Rogers, Maria Sharpe, Mrs. Greg. — Fox and Rogers in Paris. — Fox and Mackintosh. —Rogers's new House. —His final Settlement in St. James's Place.

'THE King of Clubs' referred to in the letter to Richard Sharp was not actually established till the first year of the nineteenth century. It was founded by a group of friends who were in the habit of meeting at Mackintosh's house: Rogers, Richard Sharp, Scarlett, Robert Smith, and John Allen. Scarlett, afterwards Lord Abinger, tells us that the chief figures in its social intercourse were, in addition to those already mentioned, Romilly, Dumont, Tennant, and the Rev. Sydney Smith. To these were added Lord Lansdowne, Lord Holland, Brougham, Lord Cowper, Lord King, Porson, Payne Knight, Horner, Bryan Edwards, Jeffrey, Smithson, Whishaw, Alexander Baring, Luttrell, Blake, Hallam, Ricardo, and Hoppner. Francis Horner speaking of visits made to the club in the spring of 1802 mentions that he met there Abercromby, Tom Wedgwood, and Maltby, and that the conversation consisted of literary reminiscences, anecdotes of authors, and criticisms of books. The Club met monthly at dinner at the old 'Crown and Anchor' in the Strand, where the Whig Club met for somè years on Tuesday evenings. 'The King of Clubs' was one of those conversation clubs which had superseded the coffee-houses and the taverns in which Addison and Johnson had spent so much of every day in pleasant talk. In those times men prepared their observations beforehand,

and so led the talk as to bring them in. There is a story
of Richard Sharp having one day seen on the desk the
notes of the conversation in which his partner Boddington was to join in the evening. Sharp was to be of the
party, and he committed to memory the prepared im-
promptus of his friend, assisted him to lead the conversation in the right direction, and then forestalled him
with his stories and clever things. There was nothing
unusual in Boddington's preparations. Men read books,
recorded good stories, and reserved criticisms on men
and things for the evening talk. The two most brilliant
talkers in 'The King of Clubs' were Mackintosh and Sydney Smith. Sydney Smith said of Mackintosh that his
conversation was more brilliant and instructive than that
of any human being he ever had the good fortune to
be acquainted with. But Rogers, a still more intimate
friend of Mackintosh, said that he sacrificed himself to
conversation, read for it, thought for it, and gave up
future fame for it ;[1] and Mackintosh is not the only man
in this brilliant group of whom the observation may be
made.

There was at one time a prospect that much of the
wit and learning poured into these conversations would
take permanent form. Rogers and his friends proposed
to establish a literary paper, to be called 'The Bachelor,'
and published twice a week. Mackintosh tells us that
this paper would probably have imitated the aim, even
if it had not equalled the execution, of the essayists of
the reign of Queen Anne. The men to be associated in
the enterprise were : Rogers, Mackintosh, Robert Smith,
Scarlett, and Richard Sharp. The execution of the pro-
ject was frustrated at the moment, and never resumed.
Rogers has left in his Commonplace Book an outline
of the kind of contributions the paper was intended to
contain. This sketch is amusing. It is clearly Rogers's

[1] Moore's 'Diary,' vol. vi. p. 292.

own, particularly the motto from Gray, and the outline
of the 'History of a Voice.'

Periodical Paper — The Bachelor.

Poor Moralist, and what art thou ? — *Gray.*

First — His history : his attachments and adventures.
Last — His marriage concludes the paper.

1. On War. 2. On Courtship. 3. History of an old house.
4. History of a voice, a musical cry in his cradle, cries wild
    lavender and matches, frightens the birds from the corn ;
    a ballad-singer, sings with the miners in Castleton Cave,
    with the singers at the parish church, catches cold, a
    deputy crier, a chorister in a cathedral, sings at concerts,
    marries a rich deaf dowager, and sells his voice in
    Parliament.
5. Letters. Cairo flea. An antiquarian's conjecture in the
    next century, 1895, on a board lately dug up inscribed
    'Man Traps.' Lord Stanhope's Reasoning Machine.
    A Christmas in the country. A husband's threat to a
    wife : 'I 'll wear a wig.' History of a Talker and Listener.
    Éloge upon Snuff.

Rogers, however, had at this period another occupation for his leisure. He was designing the dwelling
which for more than half a century was to be the admiration and the envy of his contemporaries. We may
take it for granted that he had by this time given up
all thought of marrying, and settled down to the life
of a bachelor. His house, if not actually planned as a
bachelor dwelling, scarcely contemplated family uses.
He and Sir John Lubbock bought a house of the Duke
of St. Albans, in St. James's Place, and made two houses
of it. The reconstruction thus rendered needful gave
Rogers an opportunity of making for himself a home in
accordance with his tastes, and he devoted himself to
the agreeable task with the most striking success.

The summer and autumn of 1802 offered him an unusual opportunity for the study of art, and he went into
it as systematically as he had gone into classical reading
during his Devonshire exile.

The Peace of Amiens opened Paris to Englishmen, and
there was an immense outflow of visitors from this country to the republican capital. It had been practically
sealed from about the time of Rogers's visit in 1791; for
the horrors of the Terror had closed it as much as war.
In 1802, therefore, there was the greatest curiosity to see
the city over which the revolutionary storm had swept,
and which had since been enriched with the spoils of
Europe. The Louvre contained at that time the most
splendid collection of pictures and statues that had ever
been brought together, and artists and men of taste took
occasion of the brief gleam of peace to rush over and
feast their eyes on the unexampled sight. Rogers's
brother-in-law, Sutton Sharpe, had gone over early in
September, and found himself in a crowd of artist
friends: Flaxman and his wife, Mr. and Mrs. Opie,
Fuseli, then at the height of his fame, and Farrington,
R. A., who was his companion in the journey; Benjamin
West, president of the Royal Academy, and his son
Raphael West, then expected to attain an eminence he
never reached; Shee, afterwards Sir Martin Shee, and
President of the Royal Academy; Hoppner and his wife,
and others less known to fame. Erskine and his son,
and Travers the surgeon, also occupy a prominent place
in Sutton Sharpe's letters. In a visit which Boddington,
the two Erskines, Rogers, and Sutton Sharpe made together to Versailles, Sutton Sharpe says: 'Erskine was
in the most prodigious spirits. Half-mad with joy he
walked about the gardens, exclaiming: "What a delightful place, — but it won't keep people's heads on their
shoulders!" Erskine was introduced to the First Consul
as an "avocat," but Bonaparte did not understand his

rank and eminence, and took no notice of him.' Mill-
ingen the antiquary, Townley, and Champernowne, the
well-known collectors of objects of art, with Dr. Carrick
Moore, brother of Sir John Moore, were also in Paris at
this period, and formed part of the wide circle of friends
and acquaintances in which Rogers found himself as soon
as he joined his brother-in-law. His old friend Gilpin,
in a characteristic letter, which, like all Gilpin's letters,
is worth reproducing for its own sake, gave him a commission based on doubts which were widely prevalent at
the time.

Rev. Wm. Gilpin to S. Rogers.

'My dear Sir, — I write immediately, not to answer
your letter, but, as you are going to France, to give you
a commission to the Belvidere Apollo. With my compliments beg to know whether he is the real Apollo, or
a fictitious one ?

'About a month ago a gentleman, the Dean of Ely,
called upon me and informed me that Mr. Wyatt (whom
also — as you are now so united by brick and mortar — you
may have an opportunity of consulting) told him that the
king had sent him to Paris, to inquire about the Italian
statues ; that he had formerly been intimately acquainted
with the Apollo in Italy, and that he was certain the
Apollo at Paris was fictitious. Now I do not assert that
Mr. Wyatt *told this to the Dean*, but that the Dean had
been well informed, at least, that Mr. Wyatt had said
this. I shall wait, with great impatience, to hear from
you on your return, — not only to satisfy me on the point
in question, but to hear you relate all the wonders you
have seen ; and to tell me whether you think the *crying*
or the *laughing* philosopher would meet with more game ?
For myself, though I do not exclude Paris and France
from the last circling rim of my benevolence, yet, con-

sidering the world as one great State, the French are certainly placed by Providence in one of the most ignominious offices in it, that of presiding over gibbets and whipping-posts.

After all, I think it more than probable you may not go to France at all, but may conclude your journey there as you did that to America. If you go, may heaven defend you, and preserve you safe out of the den of the European Cacus!

'Yours, truly sincere,

'W. G.

'V. H., Sep'. 8, 1802.'

Rogers's letters to Gilpin have not been preserved. The following letters, addressed to members of his family, tell the story of this visit to Republican Paris.

Samuel Rogers to Maria Sharpe.

'CALAIS, Wednesday.

[Postmark 16 Sepr. 1802.]

'MY DEAR MARIA, — After a passage of three hours I sit down to fill up the interval before dinner. We had above forty people of both sexes on board, among whom were Mr. and Mrs. Howard. The lady sat in the body of her chaise on deck. Everybody was ill except myself, who made use of the recipe you recommended to me — a diachylon plaster — with great success, and I now write particularly to thank you for it. My fellow-traveller is delighted with the novelty of the scene, but anxious to proceed. We are, however, detained for the passport, and must console ourselves with the Comédie, which begins at half-past five. I need not describe Calais to you. The people are just as we saw them; the military cocked hats are enormous; the women's heads are as large as ever; and six little children, not bigger

than Sutton,[1] or very little bigger, were dancing together
a *cotillon* in the street just now, the boys *with long tails*,
to a passing tambourine. We had a delightful journey
yesterday. Lord Whitworth did not make his appearance, but we met on the road innumerable parties of
gypsies, bag and baggage.

'After a grand entertainment of soup, cutlets, fish,
fowl, partridges, etc., we went to the Comédie. The
Municipalité sat under a very handsome canopy in a kind
of state box. The drop-scene between the acts was inscribed with the names of Eustache, St. Pierre, etc., the
six heroes of Calais when besieged by Edward III.; and
the orchestra consisted of above twenty performers, as
close as they could sit, who, together with the actors,
made as much noise as they could. The acting was far
from bad. There again we saw your neighbors, Mr.
Howard and his wife. In a very handsome retiring-
room they served you with raspberry vinegar and other
refreshments. Adieu, my dear Maria! Give my love
to Henry when you see him, and also Sarah and Mrs.
M——, not forgetting the children all.

'Ever yours,
'S. R.

'We have engaged a very old chaise to Paris *à la
Yorick*. We pay 6/ 6/ 0!!! To-morrow hope to sleep at
Abbéville.'

Samuel Rogers to Henry Rogers.

'Hôtel Marigny, 13 Octr. 1802.

'My dear Henry, — By two kind letters from Maria
and Sarah I rejoice to think you are all assembled, first
on your own account and next on my own, as I hope
soon to rejoin you, though perhaps at this moment you

---

[1] Sutton Sharpe, his eldest nephew, afterwards the eminent Queen's
Counsel, whose premature death in 1843 disappointed many hopes.

may be scattered over the world again. As for me, my
life is a little better regulated and my mind more collected, though every day is a scene of dissipation. At
first I was worn out before it was half spent; but my
spirits are now less hurried, and the impressions I receive less violent and frequent: in short, I begin to be
in my sober senses. Mr. Sharpe must have described a
fête when the garden front of the Tuileries was illuminated, and when, with other consuls, B. sat uncovered
for above twenty minutes in a balcony in the centre,
while an orchestra of above a hundred persons was
playing a concert below in the open air. On Thursday
last I was present at a very different spectacle, — the
monthly review of the troops which were drawn up,
horse and foot, before the Tuileries to the amount of
about 6,000. At eleven an old-looking plain yellow
coach, drawn by six blood bay horses, the coachman and
postilion in large cocked hats, attended by many guards,
brought up Bonaparte at a great rate to the door of the
palace from St. Cloud; and a few minutes afterwards,
an English post-chaise and four of the same color, the
boys with silver-laced caps, brought Madame Bonaparte.
At twelve, in a plain blue coat with gold epaulets, he
mounted his white horse (given to him by the Emperor)
most richly caparisoned with crimson and black and
gold, and attended by generals and mamelouks, whose
rich and grotesque habits heightened the splendor, rode
in a kind of managed pace up and down the several files
of foot and horse, which were so long and numerous that
he must have ridden about a mile. He then returned
to the centre within a few yards of me (for I was at the
palace window next the door) and the troops marched
by in succession before him. It was no sooner over
than six or seven well-dressed women (as indeed had
been the case whenever he had stopped before) pressed
round him with petitions in their hands, which he re-

ceived, saying something to most of them. He then
alighted, and on the staircase stopped several times to
speak to the officers. I was there alone among the sen-
tinels. His profile is very strong, and his face one dead
tint of yellow, but not disagreeable. His eyes are of
light gray, and his eyebrows scarcely distinguishable.
His head has been said by a celebrated portrait-painter
here to be *une tête morte*, but his countenance has a
cheerful easy character, and exhibited, when I saw him,
no very remarkable degree of thought or animation,
though very capable of expressing both. His manners
are very simple and unaffected, and he took snuff and
scratched his head all day. It was a very noisy and
splendid scene, and the windows and roofs of houses
were crowded with spectators. Fox and Erskine dined
afterwards at a public dinner with him, and he had a
long conversation with both. The troops were very fine
men, and the dresses of the different corps were more
varied and picturesque than among us. The music was
very loud and unaffecting.

Last Sunday I paid a visit to Mad° le Brun, the
painter, and admired the floor inlaid with precious
woods. In the evening I went with Boddington to
Mad° Cabarus, who lives in a most superb house, and
who received us in a bedchamber, not less elegant,
tho' less rich, than Madame Récamier's. Her beauty
extinguished Lady Oxford who was there, and she gave
me an invitation to dinner every day with her while I
stayed at Paris. I was introduced, I suspect, as a friend
of Lady Jersey, and the similarity of her life and history to that of her ladyship may have rendered her
civil to her friends. Last night we were again at the
Opera, and Vestris outdid himself. Surely the troop of
French dancers are more like gay creatures of the
element than mortals like ourselves. Mr. Salmon and
Mr. Mallet are very busy and very happy everywhere.

On Tuesday we dined with Tallien, who was the first man in Paris for many months. I afterwards saw Mdlle. Duchesnois in Andromaque, and it was the only thing like acting I have seen in Paris. Adieu, my dear Henry! In a day or two I shall write to Maria. Give my love to Mrs. M. and also to M. and S., and thank them for their kind letters. I am sorry you think you are disturbing my imagination full of pictures, when you write to me.

'Ever yours,

'S. R.

'Boddington talks of leaving here on Saturday. Parsons, who is sitting by me and who is come to Paris, desires to be remembered to you. Remember me to Sharpe.'

S. Rogers to Maria Sharpe.

'Nov. 2, 1802.

'MY DEAR MARIA, — I am happy to learn from yourself that you are all assembled on the sea-shore. Pray stay if you can till I arrive, which will now, I hope, be in three weeks at farthest. Thank Sarah for her kind letter. In writing to one, I write to the other, for in my mind you are inseparable; and distance produces only one effect upon me, to attach me still more strongly to those I love. I know there are different opinions upon that subject, and I have sometimes fancied them just with regard to those who maintain them; certainly not so with regard to myself. I could say a great deal on this subject, but I know you will expect other things from me. I forget where I left off last. Mr. Farrington gave you a full account of our good fortune, — how we stood on the same stone step with him, Bonaparte; how he looked at us face to face; and of the various events of that eventful day. Henry is also in possession of a despatch on that subject. On the next, 8th, I went to the Abbé Sicard's lecture, and was very agreeably disappointed; the ingenious and expressive countenances of the boys would have interested me for a whole day together. In the evening saw Tamerlane; the old Greek practice of dancing to a chorus is very delightful and affecting to me. I had proceeded so far when I was told that Mr. Fox's carriage was waiting for me; so away I went with him and Fitzpatrick and Mrs. Fox, etc., to the Luxembourg, which Fox had a great desire to see. The next day we saw the Gobelins, the garden of plants, and I afterwards dined with them, where I met my old acquaintance Lafayette, — once a sprightly, *petit maîtrish* Frenchman, now mellowed into a most amiable man, still very handsome, but silent, thoughtful, and melancholy. Mr. Fox has finished his historical researches, and is now seeing the sights. This morning, the Consul being on a progress, I saw St. Cloud, a most princely residence on the Seine, here a noble river. The rooms are very numerous and furnished in the most costly manner with silk and velvet, porphyry, bronze, and gold, but they were more gaudy than rich, a style affected in their country houses. There, behind a door, and among some bad pictures, hangs the Madonna della Sedia, — in very fine preservation and surpassing, indeed, all prints and copies of it. It was *not* brilliant, but very sweet, and the little elbows and shoulders of the children were painted in a way I had no conception of before. The mother's countenance rather fell short of my hopes, which had been raised extravagantly; but I was hurried along with many others who had never heard of such a picture, and I hope to see it again. Mr. Lambert is arrived here, and *not alone*. He is on his way to Italy. Mr. Nicholls and his two daughters have also spent a week here on their way to the South of France. They had lived in my hôtel four days before I found them out. The Concannons are here, and give grand parties every week, to which I have been invited, but I have not been. They have Morgan the stock-jobber's daughters with them! Mad° Cabarus also opens her house to-night in great splendor, but I rather preferred Vestris and the Opera. Here also has arrived, on his way from Rome, Mr. Champernowne, son of Mrs. Harrington of Clent, and as he proposes to set off in ten days I have partly agreed to accompany him. Mr. Boddington left me last Wednesday in company with Mr. and Mrs. Mackintosh, with whom I was to have returned. I have heard from them twice on the road, as at every stage they all remembered something undone. I have now the whole apartment to myself, and his servant Gerard has fallen to me by inheritance.

'The galleries are still inexhaustible, but the painters are a great loss, for no human being enters into one's feelings now. Parsons has been there twice since he left England, and Fox only three times! I am generally a kind of *cicerone* to the new-comers, being almost always there. At first sight it seems delightful to introduce others for the first time to such things, but you would be soon sick of it. The Miss Morgans mistook the Transfiguration for some new picture, and their remarks eclipsed those in " Evelina " on the pictures at Vauxhall. I have spent an evening with Canova, who is come to take a likeness of Bonaparte for a colossal statue to be placed in the grand square of Milan. I was much pleased with him ; David and Kosciusko were also there, as was also Le Grand, the architect who built the Cornhall, — since burned ! He fondled a little pug whelp in his breast the whole time, and seemed a great coxcomb. In my walk one evening I was attacked by a sharper who led me about to see a billiard match between Clotilde the opera dancer in men's clothes and an Englishman. He wearied my poor legs while he was extolling the symmetry of her form ; but at last we met a man on the staircase who said it was put off till the morning. His intention was, it seems, to draw me to the gaming-table, — for he has since attacked Parsons and Fitzpatrick : the last the coolest gamester in Europe, and the first not likely to risk his money. Surely he must be *very green* to attack such men ! I have twice seen the English taken off on the stage, and I was sorry to hear the actor talk very much like ourselves. Boddington, who could not deny it, said the actor was a bad mimic and *could not* talk ill; but the immoderate laughter of the audience convinced him of the contrary. I have seen " Puss in Boots," and am told " Cinderella " had a great run last year.

'Adieu, my dear Maria! Pray give my love to all, and a kiss sent across the ocean to four. Give my kind love to Patty and hers.

'To prevent a mistake I shall direct to you in town.

'Ever, ever yours,

'S. R.

'Mr. De Grave desires to be remembered to you all. Lusignan lives in very elegant apartments near the Palais Royal, and is a very gay man; I have not yet seen him. The English here are still innumerable, Paris being now thin of fashion; at the theatres every word you overhear is English.'

Samuel Rogers to Henry Rogers.

'PARIS, Dec. 4, 1802.

'MY DEAR HENRY, — . . . I have now fixed my day of departure. On Friday next, the 11th Dec^r., I shall turn my back on the gayeties of Paris, — with some regret, but with more pleasure. In the galleries I shall often wander in imagination, but the days are now so dark and sad, with such little intermission, that I have lately found but little enjoyment there. I have paid a

morning visit to Mad^e du Port. I was introduced by
De Grave, and received with great civility as her husband's friend, under which name I was introduced by
her to her daughter, a very pretty girl of 16. I was
afterwards told that to see the daughter is considered
a very great compliment, and indeed so she thought by
the very marked manner in which she promised me
that pleasure when she stepped out for her. After a
few minutes she told her " she might retire." Mad^e du
Port is certainly the most elegant and pleasing woman
I have seen in France, but then I have literally seen
nobody. She is about 35, and still very handsome. I
understand that where she lives (near the Bastille, about
a league from me) there are above 150 families in obscurity
of the most accomplished and best bred people in France,
strict in their manners and life, even beyond our English notions of regularity. I have since paid a *different*
visit to M. de Lille — no longer *Abbé* — now a married
man. He received me in a large room in an hôtel once
belonging to the Duke of Richelieu. There were two
or three gentlemen with him. In a recess were two
beds side by side. The curtains of the nearest were
drawn, and a young lady was frequently called to it by
whispers, for there in high health, at two o'clock, lay
Mad^e de Lille! I have since dined with them, and was
overwhelmed with her civilities. The dinner was very
ill-served, and lasted near two hours. Among other
dishes was a roast hare, which, as she told her French
friends, was given in compliment to me, it being a very
great rarity in England, and never but at great tables.
After dinner she threw about her some ugly and dirty
English doylies, which she also explained as the English
fashion, and of which I felt quite ashamed. She concluded by making me swallow a dish of strong green tea,
to remind me of old England. I feel no desire to repeat
my visit, tho' I could now enjoy his conversation, which

I had never done before. I have seen little of the Wm. Smiths for the last fortnight. Their feelings are indeed so little in unison with my own that I keep out of their way. The same may be said of the Edgeworths, tho' they are abundant in their civilities. I have lately looked into several of the *bals bourgeois*, and with great pleasure. The decorum and enjoyment I have seen there have often sent me home to bed with very pleasant feelings. Tom Boddington is returned to Paris, and enjoys himself as much as so fastidious a gentleman will allow himself. Last Monday I was led by fatal curiosity to hear High Mass in honor of Ste. Cecilia, in the church of St. Eustache. I departed before it was half over, but have been confined, with intermissions, ever since. Mr. Champernowne has gone directly by Havre and Southampton to Devonshire, and I shall now return home with Mr. ——, a very friendly pleasant man, whom I have known slightly for some years. Happy is the man who leaves Paris first! Mr. Boddington and Mr. Mackintosh sent me commissions twice on the road, and Mr. Champernowne has left me twenty legacies, to my utter horror and dismay. Mr. Fox has also written from St. Anne's, to desire me, among other things, to bring Mrs. F. a grate, shovel, and tongs! I have just heard an unexpected piece of news, — Mr. Thomas Hope's death. It comes in a letter from his brother Henry, who says a merchant has written him word of it from Marseilles. Adieu, my dear Henry! Give my best love to all, and believe me

'Ever yours,

'S. R.

'By way of P. S., I shall add a few lines to another person. N. B. — It is here for the first time committed to paper, and I don't half like it, now it is written, so forgive faults.

' *To the Fragment of a Statue of Hercules called the Torso of the Belvidere.*

' And dost thou still, thou mass of breathing stone
(Thy giant limbs to night and chaos hurl'd),
Still sit as on the fragment of a world,
Surviving all, majestic and alone?
What though the Spirits of the North, that swept
Rome from the earth, when in her pomp she slept,
Smote thee with fury, and thy headless trunk
Deep in the dust, 'mid tower and temple, sunk;
Soon to subdue mankind 't was thine to rise,
Still, still unquench'd thy nobler energies!
Exalted minds, with thee conversing, caught
Bright revelations of the Good they sought;
By thee that long-lost spell in secret given,
To draw down Gods, and lift the soul to Heaven.'

These lines are dated 1808 in their published form. The only change made in them in the interval was the substitution of 'unquelled thy glorious energies' for 'unquench'd thy nobler energies,' and 'aspiring minds' for 'exalted minds.' The request from Fox to which he alludes, was conveyed in the following letter: —

C. J. Fox to S. Rogers.

MY DEAR SIR, — Mrs. Fox says you would willingly do any commission for her, and she has no scruple in troubling you, 1st, to go to Fonciez's, the jeweller, Rue St. Honoré, and to buy for her two little carnelian hearts, with little rings and chains to fasten them to chains round the neck. Mme. Fonciez will recollect that my wife looked at them and asked the price, it must not be more than three louis 9½ each. 2dly, to go to the Palais Royal, the first or second shop on the right (I think) as you go in, to buy a pair of *fire-dogs, tongs, and shovel,* the price all together two louis. I meant to buy them, but said I would call again, and forgot it. If you can bring these things yourself we shall be much obliged to you; if not, pray send the *doys*, etc., to me at Quiliac at Calais. The smaller things you will of course bring yourself, or send by some friend.

'If you will be so good as to pay for them I will settle with you on your return or send an order to Perrégaux; and for the interest of your money I know no way to pay you but by insisting again on your reading "Isacco," which, when you have done attentively, I trust you will not think of comparing "Douglas" with it.

'I am, with great regard, dear Sir,

'Yours ever,

'C. J. Fox.

'St. Anne's Hill,
    '18 Nov., 1802.'

There is a further account of Republican Paris in a letter to Mrs. Greg, wife of Mr. Samuel Greg of Manchester, mother of the late Mr. Samuel Greg of Bollington, and of Mr. William Rathbone Greg, author of 'The Creed of Christendom,' and grandmother of Mr. William Rathbone, now M. P. for the northern division of Carnarvonshire.

S. Rogers to Mrs. Greg.

'Paris, 5 Dec., 1802.

'My dear Mrs. Greg, — You may be surprised to receive a letter from Paris, and yet from *me* perhaps it will excite no wonder. Alas — I have no ties to fix me anywhere! Many ages ago, I forget in what Olympiad, I received from Manchester what demands my best thanks. Of the letter I will say nothing, for it deserves everything. The present was most acceptable also — for Gesner was a favorite with me in early life — nor has he even yet lost his charm. The translation does honor

to the writer, and the preface is worthy of the great
name you hint at. The embellishments are very elegant,
and you will think me sincere when I say so, for I have
long had some of the original drawings in my possession.

On the 13th of Sepr I set my foot in France. At least
so says my almanac, but my memory assures me it was
two thousand years ago, so busy have I been, though to
little purpose, since I came here. Not but that I was
disappointed at the little novelty I met with on the road.
The pedler on his ass and the wagoner with his team
wore the same huge cocked hat, and the postilion had
his ear-rings, his jack-boots, his tobacco-pipe, his long
queue, his harness of ropes, and a whip that smacked
through every note of the gamut. At Chantilly I wandered alone till dusk along half-dismantled terraces and
among urns and lions fast covering with verdure. The
old *château* is no more, and the stables were occupied by
a regiment of horse. The cathedral at Amiens had lost
little of its splendor, and many people were saying their
masses in various parts of it; but the abbey of St. Denis
was filled, when I saw it, with casks of American corn.
The royal monuments are removed to Paris. They are
ranged chronologically with a thousand others from different parts of France, in the convent of the little Augustines; and there in the garden among cypresses is the
tomb of Abelard and Eloisa. It was noon when I arrived
in Paris; and wandering about in search of lodgings, I
found myself at the door of the Louvre. Who could
resist? I entered with other people, and in an instant
stood mute in the presence of the Marbles of the Capi-
tol, the Laocoön, the Torso, and the Apollo Belvidere. I
need not describe to *you* what I felt at the sight of what
I had heard and dreamed of so long. I walked about —
neither asleep nor awake — and at last ascended a staircase, where a gallery without end opened itself before
me. It was, indeed, "the pomp and prodigality of

Heaven." First came the pictures of France, then those
of Flanders and Holland, then those of Italy. Altar-
pieces, which singly gave celebrity to cathedrals and
little cities, now hang side by side, and in the multitude
are passed almost without a glance. I spend hours every
day there. Things of such excellence must be approached
by degrees; and I can truly say that the more I look
the more I admire. Our artists, who certainly came with
no favorable prepossessions, were very agreeably surprised at the excellent condition of the pictures; and
particularly of the Transfiguration and the St. Pietro
Martire of Titian. This morning I saw Raphael's St.
Cecilia laid on its face, and about to receive a new
canvas. The worm-eaten board on which it was painted
has been cut away with the knife (what excellent nerves
there are in France!) and what I looked upon was actually the back of the thin coat of paint. It is a delightful
reflection that the colors of such a pencil can survive the
solid mass on which they were laid, and may be transferred from surface to surface while the world endures!
The gallery is open to the public twice a week, — to
strangers every day, — and so also is the library, where
hundreds are sitting and reading constantly, at the tables
in the long suite of rooms, with the greatest silence and
decorum. When you enter you are struck with surprise at the number, for from the stillness you expect
nobody. The bronze horses from Venice are placed over
the gates of the Tuileries. Bonaparte has twice exhibited himself to the people since I came here. Once at
his monthly review in the Place du Carrousel, when, on
his white charger superbly caparisoned and surrounded
by mamelouks and general officers, he rode up and down
the ranks of six thousand, horse and foot. At every
turn he received petitions, which were delivered into his
hand by many well-dressed people, some of whom he
questioned as he ran his eyes over the papers. And once

again, on the evening of a festival, when the garden
front of the Tuileries was illuminated, and when, between
the two other consuls, he sat uncovered in a balcony in
the centre for above half an hour, taking snuff continually, while an orchestra of a hundred and fifty performers played and sang in the open air immediately under
him. At his *levées* he is more inclined to talk than to
listen, which is the case you will say with some other
great people ; but his manners are very simple and pleasing. His profile is very striking and elegant, but his
eyes are of a light gray, and his eyebrows scarcely distinguishable ; and his face is overspread with one dead
yellow tint.   His head, to use the expression of a celebrated painter here, is *une tête de mort*, — but it is the
head of a giant. He measures in height but five-feet-
five ; but his hat, when he has left it on the table, as I
have been assured by those about him, has moved round
the head of the tallest and most robust general in his
army. He lives entirely at St. Cloud, which overhangs
the Seine, and is fitted up most sumptuously with gold
and porphyry and bronze. He travels very fast, attended
by guards, in a plain old-fashioned yellow coach and six
blood horses, his servants wearing cocked hats ; but M⁰
B.'s carriage is a light chaise and four *à la mode Angloise.*
It is singular to see a postilion on a blood horse *under*
an immense cocked hat. I wish I could give you a
tableau de Paris.   But where shall we begin ? with the
narrow streets, where the approach of a voiture, or of a
cabriolet with its tinkling bell, and its cry of "Garde !
Garde !" produces a flight and a rout ; or with the
squares and bridges, where an array of shoe-blacks, formidable in number and outcry, salute you with "*Ici on
tond des chiens et coupe les oreilles aux chiens et chats ;*" or
shall we walk in the Tuileries Gardens, where there are
more statues than trees ; or shall we look into the *bals
bourgeois,* where a hundred couples waltz nightly ; or are

you inclined for a spectacle? Will you see "Puss in Boots" wash her whiskers with her paws, as she does every evening on the Boulevards, to the delight of all the grown children; or shall I introduce you to Mdlle. Duchesnois, who was crowned last night in Phêdre amidst tears and acclamations? No, rather come with me and admire "those gay creatures of the element," the *corps de ballet*, who will enchant you with their delicate movements, and with their beautiful groups in groves and caverns and among the "plighted clouds." Vestris is still himself, though his mistress, a celebrated dancer, died last week — and was refused burial by the *curé ;* who, however, was suspended for it by the Archbishop of Paris. Perhaps, most of all, I have wished for you in the Abbé Sicard's "Academy of Deaf and Dumb." What ingenuous and speaking countenances, and what triumph in their eyes, when they catch and write on the wall the ideas communicated to them! The furniture here is very elegant, and your old friend Mad° Récamier outshines the Consul himself. Her bath and bedchamber are hung with silks of many colors, and lighted with aromatic lamps and alabaster vases. Her bed is an Etruscan couch, and every table is supported by caryatides in bronze and gold. But you must now wish to return to England. What a sad variety of smells there is in Paris! Surely snuff-taking is an act of self-defence here; and what effluvia from the kitchens, morning, noon, and night! Who would refuse his assent here to the definition that "man is a cooking animal"? The painters and lawyers are returned to London, and are succeeded by a flight of fashionables from Spa. The Wm. Smiths are here; and also the Edgeworths; but I fear I am growing unfit for society, for I can find none whose feelings are in unison with my own, and a solitary walk along the Boulevards, and a *tête-à-tête* with the Apollo or the Transfiguration, are my greatest consolations. Pray

remember me particularly to Mr. G., who will elucidate
any obscurities in this long letter; and to each and to all
of your little society, not forgetting my dearest friend
Betsy. Tell her I have played the same part in Paris
which she played in London last spring, but with much
less *éclat*. In less than a fortnight I shall return to London with much regret, but with more pleasure. The
French are a lively and clever people. Of their morals I
shall say nothing, though there are many noble exceptions. In the comforts of life they are many centuries
behind us, but in its elegancies they have no rivals; and
in their liberality to strangers they are models for the
rest of the world. I have taken much pleasure in the environs of Paris; the little hills covered with vineyards
wear still the last red tint of autumn, and the sight of a
great city with no smoke over it is to an Englishman a
phenomenon. It is singular, too, that I recollect no wind
through the equinox here, — a turbulent visitor I could
well dispense with in our island. In the Palais Royal
the gaming yields immense sums to the revenue. There
are many tables open from 12 at noon till 8 in the morning, surrounded by young and old of both sexes. I hate
the sight of their illuminated windows as I return home
in an evening. In many of the coffee-houses there are
orchestras of music which continue playing and singing
with terrible fury from dusk till midnight. In the "Café
des Aveugles" there is a band of blind men and women,
a melancholy spectacle, and in some of the *caveaux*, or
cellars, little dramas are acted to allure company. In
the theatres all now *sit* in the *parterre*, a change effected
by the Revolution; nor could Yorick now address them
with "In England we sit more at our ease." Every
woman here carries her pocket-handkerchief on her arm
in a kind of work-bag; and I have seen dirty nursery
girls with a tottering infant in one hand and their *ridicule* in the other. The houses have no *verandas*, and

the window curtains are of two different colors, crossing each other, which have a very rich and lively effect. But I have now exhausted my paper and your patience. Adieu, once more! You see I have not forgotten you, though a sea lies between us, and many a province and many a field of battle.

'Your ever affectionate friend,

'SAMUEL ROGERS.

'Mr. Fox has left us, to my great regret. He was delighted beyond *measure*.'

Rogers was much with Fox during this visit to Paris, when some of the conversations recorded in the 'Recollections'[1] took place. Walking in the Louvre they one day met Mackintosh, whom Fox passed with a nod and the briefest of salutations, telling Rogers he was angry with Mackintosh for accepting the place in India offered him by a Tory Government. But General Richard Fitzpatrick, whom Rogers met at Fox's dinner-table, as well as at the Luxembourg and the Gobelins, told Rogers that their wives were at the bottom of the coolness. Fox had lately publicly acknowledged Mrs. Armstead, to whom he had been married privately in 1795, as his wife, and Mrs. Mackintosh had not paid her a formal call. A fortnight before Rogers arrived in Paris Fox had dined with Bonaparte, when the First Consul had told him that some persons thought Windham had assisted in the plot to blow him up by an infernal machine. Fox told Rogers that he had energetically protested that the suspicion was a libel on Windham, and that no Englishman would mix himself up in such a business. Rogers afterwards told Windham what Fox had said in his vindication, and Windham replied that he would have done the same for Fox.

[1] Recollections, pp. 20-28, 35.

The next conversation with Fox recorded in the 'Recollections' is dated January, 1803, and took place during a visit of Rogers to Fox at St. Anne's, 'a small low white house on the brow of a hill commanding a semicircular sweep, rich and woody.' Rogers was then busily occupied in preparing his new home, and he puts on record Fox's remarks that a distance is essential to a house, and that the Green Park is the best situation in London.

The bow windows of Rogers's new house looked over the Green Park. He was fitting it up with great care. He had made notes of household arrangements he had seen in houses in which he had visited; had given much study to questions of decoration and ornament; and had designed the furniture himself, with the assistance of Hope's work on the subject. The mantel-piece in the drawing-room was executed by Flaxman, who superintended the general decoration of the walls and the ceiling. Stothard designed a cabinet for antiquities, ornamenting it with paintings by his own hand. By an accident it happened that some of the wood-carving in the dining-room was executed by Chantrey. Rogers only knew this five-and-twenty years afterwards, when Chantrey had become famous. Much of the work was done under Rogers's personal supervision; and with drawing in hand he one day received a journeyman sent by a wood-carver to execute some ornamentation on a sideboard in the dining-room. At dinner, long afterwards, in the same room, Chantrey, pointing to the sideboard, asked Rogers whether he remembered the circumstance, and Rogers, who never forgot anything, recollected it clearly. 'Well,' said Chantrey, 'I was that journeyman.' The furniture and decoration followed the Greek models, and one of the striking features of the house was its large and beautiful collection of Greek vases. 'Round the staircase,' says his nephew, 'was added a frieze, taken from the Panathenaic procession among the Elgin marbles.' Rogers's long studies in the Louvre in the previous autumn had done much to complete the formation of that perfect taste which found expression in the furniture and decoration of his house.

A contemporary account of Rogers, of his house, and of the company he gathered in it, is given by Dr. Burney in his diary under the date of the 1st of May, 1804. Dr. Burney says of Rogers that 'he is a good poet, has a refined taste in all the arts, has a select library of the best editions of the best authors in all languages, has very fine pictures, very fine drawings, and the finest collection of Etruscan vases I ever saw; and moreover, he gives the best dinners to the best company of men of talents and genius I know; the best served, and with the best wines, liqueurs, etc. . . . His books of prints of the greatest engravers from the greatest masters in history, architecture, and antiquities, are of the first class. His house in St. James's Place, looking into the Green Park, is deliciously situated, and furnished with great taste.'

This account of Rogers's house and parties in 1804 may be compared with a description written by Charles Sumner, the American Senator, in a .letter to G. S. Hillard, thirty-five years later, in January, 1839: 'You have often heard of Rogers's house. It is not large, but the few rooms — two drawing-rooms and a dining-room only — are filled with the most costly paintings, all from some of the great galleries of Italy or elsewhere, most of which cost five or ten thousand dollars apiece. I should think there were about thirty in all; perhaps you will not see in the world another such collection in so small a space. There was a little painting by Raphael, about a foot square, of the Saviour praying in the Garden, brimful of thought and expression, which the old man said he should like to have in his chamber when dying. There were masterpieces by Titian, Correggio, Caracci, Guido, Paul Veronese, Rubens, Barocchio, Giotto, and Reynolds. He pointed out the picture of an armed knight, which Walter Scott always admired. His portfolios were full of the most valuable original drawings. There were all Flaxman's illustrations of Homer and the Tragedians, as they left the pencil of the great artist. Indeed, he said that he could occupy me for a month, and invited me to come and breakfast with him any morning that I chose, sending him word the night before.'

Rogers had now cut himself entirely free from business. His youngest brother Henry had become the active partner and working head of the banking firm, and there was no occasion for the chief partner to trouble himself with its concerns. His income, though not large, was sufficient for one who had only a bachelor's establishment to maintain, and who led 'the life of satisfied desires.' He had no expensive habits beyond those which sprang from a determination to make his house the ideal abode of the man of taste and the man of letters. He had not even the ambition to become the patron of poor authors, though circumstances were continually forcing that duty on him. His wish was to surround himself with what was best, and he chose his friends as he chose his pictures and his furniture, — for their quality in this noblest sense. It soon became known that the charming house in St. James's Place, about which society was talking, was open to all who had a claim to be regarded as men of letters, or artists, or wits, or statesmen: though of the latter, it was chiefly the Whigs who found themselves at home.

INDEX.

University Press: John Wilson and Son, Cambridge.